ELECTRONIC VILLAIN

"Someone is tampering with BANKNET, Mr. Harrington."

"Someone . . . ?" The banker was instantly attentive.

"I know it sounds crazy but it rather seems to be Alloway." Embarrassed, Webb averted his eyes. "It's all very strange."

"What did you say?"

"Alloway," Webb said. "That's the only person it could be . . ."

"Do I have to remind you, the man is dead," Harrington interrupted brusquely.

"But his program isn't, that's what I'm saying. It's still busily working. HE MAY BE DEAD, MR. HARRINGTON, BUT HE'S ROBBING YOU ALL THE SAME."

THE

CONSULTANT

A NOVEL OF COMPUTER CRIME

John McNeil

BALLANTINE BOOKS • NEW YORK

Library of Congress Catalog Card Number: 77-27034

ISBN 0-345-28108-X

This edition published by arrangement with Coward, McCann & Geoghegan, Inc.

Printed in Canada

First Ballantine Books Edition: April 1979

One educated guess is that upwards of half the computer users in the world are discontented—but that three-quarters of those have only themselves to blame.

—The Economist

PROLOGUE

"When this is over I shall sleep for a week," Mike Harvey said, pausing to light a cigarette. "No kidding." He rubbed an unshaven chin.

Christopher Webb smiled and followed him down the bare, ill-lit corridor. Their footsteps echoed. It was an old building, marble-floored and with Gothic niches that had once presumably held statues. The lights, at intervals along the stone walls, were in the form of bronze hands grasping torches. Webb thought how perfectly the place suited the London Alliance Assurance Group.

"Damn!" Harvey said, as they turned a corner and encountered a No Smoking sign. He hesitated for a moment before giving in and tossing his cigarette away. It twisted a thread of smoke across the passage, then fell among the others that lay crumpled in a tub of sand.

They pushed through big double doors sheathed in white melamine. Webb felt the air suddenly sharp on his face, like an early morning breeze. It was chilled and cleaned, completely without taste. Static pricked at his fingers as he reached for the next set of doors. Then he pushed and they came into the computer room.

A rough mat snatched the final traces of city dust. A short ramp led up and they were on a raised deck, a foot above the concrete floor and the hidden coils of thick cable that tangled across it. Before them stretched long, regular rows of metal cabinets severe in red and black. A bank of disc drives whined with the effort of sustained high speed. Behind, tape units added their quieter tones of motors and rushing air. The lights gave a hard, even brilliance that cast no shadows.

"It must have been a hell of a job getting the system down here," Harvey remarked. He pointed up at the ceiling. "One of the operators told me they had to cut great holes in the pavement. Lombard Street was closed for a whole weekend."

1

"It's certainly a heap of equipment," Webb said without enthusiasm. It was late in the evening, and computers had long ago started to look the same—as if he had seen too few, not too many. Enthusiasm he left to younger men. Programmers like Harvey. They took a shortcut past a busy line printer.

"Welcome to Operational HQ," Harvey said cheerfully, opening a side door and waving Webb through into a storeroom. Lines of metal racks reached to the ceiling, filled with spools of magnetic tape, and the glare from bare fluorescent tubes was almost uncomfortable. In a far corner there was a teletype and a chair with a denim jacket draped carelessly over the back.

"Whose idea was this?" Webb asked. "Putting you down here?"

"Mine actually."

"It's hardly the best place for a client meeting, is it," Webb said with disapproval. There was a pronounced hiss of air-conditioning and other sounds that squeezed their way in from the computer room outside.

"It couldn't be helped, Chris. This is the only suitable teletype in the building. The only concealed one, if you follow?"

"And what if this is the one our man usually uses?"

"Then he'll get a shock when he turns up, won't he." Harvey gave an exaggerated wink.

"Who knows you're here?"

"The security man, Chambers."

"Who else?"

"One or two of the operators will have seen me coming in and out. But I don't think they take much notice."

Slowly, Webb studied the room. There was no glass panel in the single door. There were no outside windows—there couldn't be, two levels below the street. Harvey had chosen well, he decided. It was a good place to be.

"This had better bloody work," he said.

The programmer looked hurt. "I've been at it nonstop for nearly forty-eight hours, Chris. A program that really needed a week to write and test properly." But then he gave a weary smile intended to reassure.

2

"It'll work, I promise." He sat at the teletype and switched it on.

Webb pulled nervously at a lip as he surveyed the room once more. He noticed Harvey's plastic document case lying on the floor and, frowning, picked it up to place it neatly on a shelf.

"Chambers is due here at any minute," he said meaningfully. "Our client, remember?"

Harvey shrugged. "I know."

"He's Head of the Investigations Section here, Mike. He's not a computer man, you do realise that?"

Harvey gave a slow, questioning nod.

"Chambers is a hybrid. He's part policeman, part insurance man. That's what his job demands. He knows buggerall about computers and doesn't pretend to. And he doesn't begin to understand programmers and their untidy ways."

"Is that remark aimed at me?" Harvey demanded indignantly.

"Square between the eyes. Put that jacket on, smarten up a bit. You're costing London Alliance ninety quid a day. Look as if you're worth it."

Almost sulkily, Harvey pulled on the jacket, staying seated despite the extra effort it obviously involved. Webb then produced a comb and handed it over, smiling as the younger man dragged it through tousled hair.

"You'd make a good Jewish mother," Harvey muttered as he gave the comb back. Then he turned to the teletype to hold a brief dialogue with the computer, sitting back satisfied when it acknowledged tersely that he was there:

    //HARVEY 25/8
    //PROGRAM NAME: = SLEUTH
        BEGINS

Webb waited, but the terminal fell silent again.

"Is that all?" he asked.

"It's running in background mode," Harvey explained. "There won't be any more until something happens in the computer that's relevant to us."

"Of course." Webb was pouncing on some discarded

3

computer output, strewn on the floor. He folded it with care and dropped it into a wastebin.

"I wonder whether it will be fraud or embezzlement?" he said thoughtfully.

"Is there a difference?"

"So I'm told. One means jail. The other usually doesn't."

Douglas Chambers wanted sound reason for being summoned back to the office at nearly midnight. His brusque entry made that clear. The door was bounced hard against hydraulic dampers. Outside, a tape drive sighed a breeze from fast-spinning plastic.

"I'm sorry to drag you in at this time of night," Webb said. "It couldn't be helped."

The big man gave a gesture designed to show irritability. "I had to cut short an engagement, know that? Some very old friends." And yet something in his manner suggested he was used to late night calls, or had been once. Webb wondered whether he had ever been in the police force. His stomach protruded, pushing a bulge of blue over his trousers. Perhaps he could not break the habit of wearing blue shirts.

"I originally thought of going ahead without you," Webb said, "and giving you a report in the morning. But then I decided you'd probably prefer to see it happen at first hand."

"See what, Webb?" Chambers moved closer, bent slightly forward as if on a scent.

Webb measured his words for best effect. "That computer system out there is under attack. Or rather, we expect it to be, shortly after eleven-thirty."

"Are you sure?"

"Absolutely."

Chambers raised heavy eyebrows. He looked around and, finding nowhere to sit, leaned back against a tape rack. The spools rattled.

"Well, well," he breathed, expelling air that smelled unmistakably of beer.

"You seem surprised," Webb said.

"I am."

"And yet you hired us to look over the computer system. To see if anything was wrong."

4

"To see if everything was all right," Chambers corrected. "I had a hunch, yes. No more than a gut feeling. But I hoped I was wrong. To tell you the truth, I expected you to give the system your seal of approval."

"No way," Webb said, shaking his head. "This time last week Harvey discovered something rather interesting."

"I came across two Zombies," Harvey grinned. "How about that?"

"You bloody *what?*"

"What he means," Webb said, "is that some of the people your company insures and who should be dead are not."

"Not dead inside the computer, that is," Harvey added.

"I see." The big man's expression belied the words. He subjected Webb to a long, searching gaze. The computer consultant was tall, in his thirties. He had an air of confidence bordering on the arrogant that Chambers found himself admiring, just a little, although not actually liking. Without having to say a great deal, without seeming to do very much, Webb somehow gave the impression that he knew his job thoroughly. Perhaps, Chambers considered, it was something consultants practiced, a trick of the trade. A certain look and a computerside manner. The clothes were expensive, if a bit on the sharp side. The briefcase, placed beside the teletype, had the appearance of black crocodile and after a moment's guarded scrutiny he came to the conclusion it was the real thing.

"Look," he suggested at length, "why don't you tell me all about it up in my office. We'd be more comfortable up there."

"Sorry," Webb said. "But we need this terminal to keep the computer under surveillance."

Chambers narrowed his eyes. "Surveillance?"

Webb smiled. "That's what I said."

"Pity, that. I've got some booze up there. And I could have a smoke. Down here . . ." Chambers gave a disdainful gesture. "Bloody rules!"

"It's the disc units," Harvey said, indicating the

5

computer beyond the door. "Smoking endangers their health."

Chambers cast around and discovered a large sealed carton of magnetic tapes. Grunting, he dragged it over and settled on it.

"Surveillance, eh?" he said with a wry grin. "Well, I'll be damned."

Webb moved beside the terminal, standing almost stiffly as if to present a lecture.

"It's a very simple story," he began. He checked his watch. "Nothing will be happening for fifteen minutes or so. We can easily cover the ground in that time." He glanced nervously down at the teletype. The motor could just be heard churning quietly inside the casing. But otherwise the terminal was inactive and almost silent.

"At any instant there are thousands of retired or disabled people receiving pensions from London Alliance. Some have payment made direct to their banks, others are sent a monthly GIRO cheque. The routine continues month in, month out, until a pensioner dies. When he does, you require that some appropriate person lets you know—a surviving relative, an executor, someone like that. And then the company can stop making payments."

"This is all basic stuff," Chambers protested mildly.

"Bear with me. Suppose someone chooses to conceal a death from you? Suppose, further, that they inform you of a change in address instead. To their own, of course."

"Or an accommodation address," Harvey suggested. "A money drop."

" . . . Then they stand to collect a monthly gift from you for many years."

"I've known it to happen," Chambers remarked, unconcerned. "And long before the computer came along. That's why we do spot-checks on policy holders. It's not a trick someone could get away with for long."

"Oh, no?" Webb said. "A man dies, right? You complete the formalities. The paperwork is finalised and his file is closed. That dies, too, and is buried in your archives. The man is gone and your investigators have

6

no reason to consider him further. He is no longer a charge on the company, is he? Or so you think."

He paused, shivering slightly in the chilled air. In the computer room a program run ended and an entire bank of tape drives rewound at full speed. The sound reached them as a long, distant howl, shrinking slowly to silence.

"But if he's dead?" Chambers said pensively. "I mean, really dead . . . ?"

"Look, the normal office procedures have been completed," Webb explained. "Now the request comes here to the computer centre to kill off his records. But what if that request is never obeyed? Instead, the files held on the machine are merely altered to indicate a change of address. The relatives will never know, and you'll go on paying *ad infinitum*."

Chambers took only a moment to consider the idea before giving a slow series of nods.

"Who is it?" he asked quietly.

"One of the computer staff," Webb said. "It has to be."

"But who?"

"That's why we're here." Webb broke into a broad smile. "We haven't the faintest idea."

"Not quite true," Harvey said, referring to a scribbled note. "Whoever it is answers to the name AA3795."

"AA, for short," Webb said.

After some minutes the terminal stirred into life, beating out a staccato message:

//SLEUTH SYSTEM REPORT—
PENSION UPDATE STARTED

Harvey looked at his watch. "Bang on schedule."

"You haven't explained the significance of the terminal," Chambers pointed out. "Not really."

"Your thief uses one just like this," Webb replied. "It's how he breaks into the system."

"How he resurrects the dead," Harvey said brightly.

"Ah." Chambers looked blank.

Harvey felt that he ought to elaborate. "It's like this. Last week you had twenty policyholders reported dead.

7

But I found some survivors. Twenty special data cards were read by the computer, yet only eighteen people died in there. Eighteen dead and two new Zombies, that's what I found. And it's all done from a teletype."

Right on cue, the terminal rattled another message,

***NUMBER OF T/TYPES ONLINE = 2 LOCAL
= 0 REMOTE

"Great!" Harvey exclaimed. "That makes it so much easier." He turned to smile at Chambers. "The terminals are all in this building, see? We're in for a real chase, just as I hoped."

The big man rose to read the listing, then shook his head.

"Now, hold on a minute . . ." he said with a helpless gesture.

"It's all to do with the pensions programs," Webb explained patiently. "One of them is designed specifically to deal with newly reported deaths."

"I'll take your word for it."

"Well, our friend AA has inserted a patch. So the moment that program is loaded tonight the fun will begin. The computer will check whether the number AA3795 has been logged in recently at any of the teletypes. If so, it knows that AA is there and waiting for action. And it will permit him to nominate the pensioners he wants resurrected as Zombies. It's as easy as that."

"How many teletypes are there?" Chambers asked. "Do you know?"

"Twenty in this building. Mike's program tells us that only two are in use at the moment. But there is a problem. The computer allows remote dial-up over telephone lines, to service the branch offices. And using a remote terminal, our man could be miles away. Anywhere."

Chambers pulled a crumpled packet of cigarettes from a pocket, looked accusingly around the room at the rows of magnetic tape, then slowly put it away again. "What in hell's name is a patch?" He spoke with the gruffness he used to mask ignorance.

"A change added after the program has been

8

prepared and tested," Webb replied. "Someone else reading the program listing will see no sign that it's there."

"But doesn't that mean that anyone can simply . . ." Chambers broke off, disturbed by the discovery.

"Terrific, isn't it," Webb said. "Invisible crime."

There was another clatter from the terminal as the golfball head bounced rapidly over the paper, leaving a fresh trail of text in its wake,

```
***NUMBER OF T/TYPES ONLINE = 2 LOCAL
                            = 1 REMOTE
```

"Bugger!" Harvey shouted. "It's almost time. That has to be him! He's too smart. He's bloody outside somewhere."

"I'll still get him, though," Chambers said with a sly smile. He slashed a finger across his throat. "All I have to do is follow the trail, the addresses he so thoughtfully supplies. Isn't that right?"

Webb gave an admiring nod.

"I should have gone in for computers," the big man said. "I'd have been good at it."

```
***NUMBER OF T/TYPES ONLINE = 3 LOCAL
                            = 1 REMOTE
```

"Surprisingly busy for the time of night," Harvey observed.

"What will you do with him?" Webb asked Chambers.

"It's not up to me, is it."

"What will the company do, then?"

"Who can say. It'll be discreet, that's for sure. That's the way we do things." Chambers gave a shrug meant to convey lack of interest.

"But he *will* be fired?"

"Not necessarily. At worst, he'll be asked to resign without a fuss. More likely, he'll be moved where he can't do any harm.

"And that's all?" Webb protested.

"Look," Chambers returned, "he can't have taken that much, not from what you've told me. Petty embez-

9

zlement, that's all." He turned his attention to the teletype as it began to clatter again.

<pre>
***   SLEUTH SYSTEM REPORT—
      DEATHS UPDATE STARTED
      BODY COUNT FOR THE WEEK=16
</pre>

"You certainly have a way with words," he uttered sarcastically to Harvey.

"Not many today," the programmer said, unabashed. "It must be the mild weather."

"If I caught one of my staff with his hand in the till ..." Webb said persistently.

"Try working in this business for a few months," Chambers retorted. "Try getting out of that cosy professional consultancy of yours into the real world. You'd soon see the extent of the fiddling that goes on. Policyholders, staff, they're all on the take. Nicking paper, stamps ... anything that moves. It's a fact of life."

"If you say so," Webb remarked. "I don't know why we bothered."

"The fee, I should think," Chambers said. "Over a thousand quid a week for the pair of you! You've probably made more out of this than he has."

"Very likely." Webb had to smile.

Harvey was studying the second hand of his watch.

"Come on, come on," he muttered. "Only sixteen records to process. It should all have been over by now." He and Webb exchanged anxious glances. Above the sound of hissing air they could hear no activity from the machine outside.

"Christ, I could do with a smoke," Chambers said. "I'll tell you that for nothing."

The terminal suddenly demanded their attention again, the motor giving no prior warning. The lines spilled onto the page and then the paper was ejected rapidly upwards for them to see,

<pre>
***   SLEUTH CAPTURE************
      TERMINAL ADDRESS=   14
</pre>

"That's internal!" Harvey shouted in delight. "Bloody internal, after all." He produced a typed list from a pocket and began frantically scanning the entries.

"Third floor," he announced. "Actuaries Department, Room 327."

Chambers stared in disbelief. "But I thought you said it was one of the computer people!"

"Oh, it will be," Webb said confidently. "He's just chosen somewhere nice and private."

"Like us," Harvey noted, grinning from ear to ear.

Webb prodded the big man with a friendly finger. "If you go now, and very quickly . . . you'll catch him, won't you?"

They drove through a silent City, darkened and deserted save for the occasional cruising cab. Approaching Fleet Street, London began to come alive. Lights blazed in the newspaper offices and cars lined the kerbs. Webb quartered the back streets until he found an open basement bar. It was not the kind of place he would normally go, he told Harvey, but where else was there? They went down narrow stairs, and he gave what seemed an exorbitant sum for temporary membership.

"London Alliance will pay," he declared breezily, ordering doubles of the rarest and most expensive malt whisky they had.

"Really . . . ?"

"Well, it will go on their next bill, which is the same thing."

Harvey laughed a trifle uncertainly.

"Travel expenses," Webb said, elaborating.

"Taking paper and stamps. Scotch, even." Harvey gave a passable imitation of Chambers' burred Lancashire accent.

"He said it. They're all at it. Why not us?" Webb's smile faded, and he was suddenly serious. "They've got no real defences in that company, Mike. When they're hit, they don't hit back."

"They're stupid buggers," Harvey concurred, wriggling on his tall bar stool.

"That wasn't what I said," Webb remarked sternly.

"Same thing."

"How old are you, Mike? Twenty-three?"

11

"Twenty-four."

"I'm thirty-five."

"So?"

"So I've been around longer. The client pays the bills, never forget that. He hires us to tell him something he doesn't know, or do something he can't do himself. He's bought the right to be as stupid as he damned well likes. But don't ever let yourself *believe* he's stupid, not for a minute. That way you'll make mistakes." Webb laughed. "You're good, Mike, but you're not yet a pro. I am."

Harvey glanced away, pulling uncomfortably on the cigar Webb had forced on him. He did not really like Havanas, he concluded. Much too strong.

"Stupid buggers, for all that," he said defiantly.

"I meant it when I said you were good," Webb told him. "Cocky, but good. I didn't realise you were that capable, to be honest. I was bloody impressed."

He drew a shy smile of appreciation. "I'll pull that patch out first thing tomorrow, Chris. They won't know where to find it."

"AA was pretty good, too," Webb mused. "I feel sorry for him in a way. It was such a smart-arsed idea. Clever."

Harvey was stabbing the cigar into an ashtray, giving up the struggle.

"It didn't need much to make the plan foolproof," Webb went on. "A few small changes to obliterate the trail of addresses. A remote terminal. We'd never have caught him then." He downed the remains of his glass with evident enjoyment. "A great malt, that. I rather think Chambers will be so overwhelmingly grateful that he'll send me home with a full bottle tonight." He saw Harvey eying him somewhat uneasily and added quickly, "For the drinks cupboard, Mike. Not for now, if that's what's going through that suspicious mind of yours."

Harvey chose to look away again. "I'll do it first thing, though," he promised. He felt a need to say it once more.

"Lightning never strikes twice," Webb said with a strange smile. He caught the younger man's arm. Harvey thought the grip was slightly unsteady. Maybe not.

12

Maybe it was his imagination. He suddenly felt dog-tired.

"I just don't see them thinking to do it if I don't," he continued after a protracted yawn.

"Leave it!" Webb snapped. He beckoned the barman, pushing the two empty glasses towards him.

"Leave it?"

"The bloody patch! Leave it there!" Webb leaned closer. His eyes were perfectly round, inches from Harvey's, the pupils small dark spots that fixed him with an unblinking stare.

"I have an idea . . ."

Part One

CONTRACT

"All materials and information furnished to staff are provided solely for use in the discharge of authorized work functions on behalf of the bank. On the termination of employment, the employee is obligated to return to the company any materials then in his possession, and thereafter to continue to hold in confidence all information gained while working for the bank."
—Staff contract,
Security Central Bank of Ohio

Chapter One

Sitting, looking straight ahead, Alexander Harrington might have been in a glass case in the sky. He rested on the softest of leather chairs, his feet floating on a drift of white wool. Huge tinted windows filtered the autumn sun and printed the clouds a delicate shade of grey. He could just see the abrupt tops of other buildings, their sheer walls like glazed graph paper. But not many. He was in the select company of office blocks whose great height proclaims wealth and power. To one side, the Stock Exchange Tower. Almost hidden behind it, the headquarters of National Westminster Bank in Drapers Gardens. He allowed himself the faintest of smiles as he realised that he was, just, above the summit of the rival bank.

Harrington rose and walked to a wall. He tapped the glass, sliding fingers along it as if entranced by the hard transparency, a man perhaps unused to windows. Then he rested both hands and his forehead against it, pressing with his nose like a child to look down. Now he could see the City, far below. There was the small *piazza* he had crossed minutes before. The outer skin of the building seemed to angle inwards beneath him as it dropped towards Leadenhall Street. Down there, people and cars were minute, frozen by distance. He was above the circling gulls.

His eyes, set in a thin, hawklike face, searched first for oddities hidden from those below. It was always detail that fascinated Harrington—the unexpected. Offices bared their roofs to him, irregular and cluttered. His gaze swooped to shacks and cooling plant and the windowless huts housing lift machinery. A tiny slope of glass signalled sunlight, and he found a greenhouse ringed with pots and tubs, perched precariously on a modern block near Moorgate. Untidy pyramids of bricks and masonry lay, weathered and forgotten, in the shadow of a parapet. He saw how time had etched the buildings with streaks of fuzzy grime. He rediscovered places where no man could have been since they were built.

Behind him, by the lifts, a girl chosen to complement the cool beauty of the Chairman's Suite used two slow fingers on an electric typewriter. It was the only sound. Whatever noises rose from the streets were lost outside the double glazing. Harrington put an ear to a pane and thought he could hear the wind.

He watched as a crane, nesting on the naked frame of an unfinished tower, scooped materials from the distant ground. A man in an orange helmet and heavy boots walked a slender girder just below him, higher than any circus performer and with only the banker for an audience. Harrington closed his eyes, feeling his heart beat faster. He moved quickly along the viewing gallery to escape the sight, drawing skinny fingers across the cold window. Now, he assumed, he was right under the roof-level sign, although he could not see it: WATERMAN, in great yet subtle letters, black on black. He had a profound dislike of the bank's headquarters. All that dark metal and matching glass. He liked the old, not the new. Some might find that strange in view of his job as head of the bank's computer operations. But he had never found anything particularly endearing about computers. It was a living and one did one's best. That was all.

"You should see it on a clear day."

The girl was beside him. He had not heard the typing stop. How long had she watched him, leaning against the window like that? And why hadn't he noticed the mist before? It was a thin, half-hearted ground haze that clung low to the Thames, climbing at bridges to blur their outlines. The hills to the south were smudged with a wash of brown.

"We don't seem to do anything properly in this country any more," Harrington said, attempting small talk. "Not even mist. Now, San Francisco on a day like this—that's really something." He glanced down to discover a cup of coffee in his hand. "I was thinking how drab it all is, to be honest. Down there you're too busy fighting the crowds to notice. It's so ordinary, really,

London." He took a final look as if the view must last him a long time.

"You haven't been to a board meeting before?"

He shook his head.

"They started about an hour ago," the girl told him, nodding towards a closed door. "I'll tell you when."

Harrington pulled a gold watch from his waistcoat pocket. It was nearly time and here he was staring out of windows! He returned to the group of leather chairs, this time taking one with its back to the view. Soon he would know what this was all about.

He turned through a well-handled copy of *Management Today,* knowing even before he picked it up why it was there, prominently placed on a big glass table. It fell open at the full-page photograph of Meyer Waterman and the chairman, Sir Neville Johnson. Opposite, the headline told of "Waterman's Challenge for the First Division." Harrington, like most of the senior executives of the bank, knew the article virtually word for word. He could recite every cautious warning to Lloyd's and Barclays to watch their backs, every line of praise on the bank's confident passage through the stormy property and foreign exchange crises of some years ago. Most of all, he remembered the description of BANKNET, Waterman's extensive computer and communications network, and the part it had played in the bank's recent dramatic growth. Fresh life breathed into one of the City's oldest institutions by the newest of technologies, the writer said. Waterman's spent more on computing per branch, per employee, per pound of assets, than any other clearing bank. Its profit margin was the highest. Those two factors were unavoidably connected, the magazine reasoned. Hence the photograph, on page 57, of David Clement, the director who had shaped the computer policy and guided its implementation.

Clement! Always bloody Clement, getting the credit, the public attention! Harrington tossed the magazine back onto the table. Across the room the girl continued to tap her slow, erratic text and the sound reached him over the thick white carpet. It was like a bird he had once heard in his garden, cracking a snail shell on a wall that rose from a blanket of snow.

19

"I believe," Sir Neville Johnson said, "that you already know most of the people here."

Irregular piles of paper patterned the glossy wood surface of the board room table. Behind the chairman, against a rosewood wall, a gold admiral's barge floated on an heraldic azure sea. Beneath the shield a single date pronounced the bank's pedigree: 1773.

"Why don't you sit down, Alex," Clement said.

Harrington took an empty chair, looking at the faces around the table. He did, indeed, recognise most of them. A few from regular contact in his day-to-day work. Kenneth Milbourne, MP, from his television appearances as a member of the Conservative Shadow Cabinet. One or two who had come on "the Tour"—the visitors' guide to the Data Centre—and cared more about the sherry than the computer equipment. The rest he knew from the kind of social events that large organisations imagine will shrink them to family businesses again, but which serve only to expand the distances between levels of command.

"David Clement felt strongly that you should be here," the chairman explained. "It must have seemed somewhat discourteous that we have not forewarned you of the subject. However, I regarded that as unavoidable." He put on his glasses to read his agenda, as if he had already forgotten the item.

"We wish to discuss the security of our computer system. You are with us because you should have the opportunity to influence any views we form. Conversely, any decision the board makes today will affect you and your staff."

Harrington stared across at Clement. You should have told me, you bastard, he thought furiously. Am I supposed to improvise in front of this lot? Most of them would believe a tape recorder was a computer if you told them so.

They were looking at him. All the faces except Clement's. It was a typical Clement tactic, he realised then. Diversion. Someone else on hand to take any flak.

The chairman gave a meaningful cough.

"We have given great thought and effort to the security of the various systems," Harrington said quickly.

20

"The BANKNET procedures, the many checks and controls, our physical safeguards. Those of you who have visited our London Centre, LDC, will be aware at first hand of the stringent precautions, the enormous lengths to which we go. I will be delighted to explain to you any point of detail that you wish."

At that stage he had, he judged, precisely filled the courtesy slot offered him.

Clement leaned forward. "Well said, Alex. Couldn't have put it better myself." He gave a very public wink. "I trust you won this morning? We'll need our wits about us today, you and I."

"Won?"

"The Motorway Grand Prix," Clement said with a broad smile.

"Alex," he announced to his co-directors, "is the fastest thing on wheels this side of the Nurburgring. I sometimes suspect he's compensating for something."

There were a few forced laughs.

Harrington gave no hint of what he was thinking. He had become good at that, out of necessity. His was an impassive face but alert, looking both intelligent and reliable. He never allowed himself to seem especially worried, but neither could he quite manage the appearance of calm.

He did not look like a fighter, at least not any more. But the bruises of two stormy earlier careers were there—lining his stomach so that he had to chew secretly on white tablets of chalk and magnesium. It had taken him a long time to discover that new ideas did not really suit him. On his fortieth birthday the realisation had hit him that he was a natural conservative. It had been a shock at the time, tearing up so much of his previous life. But he had come to Waterman's not long afterwards, resolved on a change of tactics—giving up the attempts to win and settling instead for ensuring that he did not lose, not when it was likely to matter. And now he found himself, in his middle years, almost satisfied with where it had got him. If it had not been for Clement the satisfaction would have been complete, or so he fondly believed.

"The journey was quite quick," he said in studied reply. "It usually is."

21

The chairman was tapping a pencil impatiently. He turned to a short, dark man on his right.

"Ivor, you wanted this topic aired. Perhaps you would lead off?"

Ivor Susskind was chairman of the bank's Policy Steering Committee. Alone of those in the room he smoked, puffing in a leisurely way on a modest Dutch panatella.

"I have deliberately not tabled a paper because of the very high confidentiality of what I have to say," he began. "I am working on the principle that a secret spoken here will remain one, whereas one written may well not."

He looked especially to Harrington, who nodded his acceptance of the confidence.

"Last month I attended the American Bankers Association conference in San Diego. It was the usual bunfight, as I expected, but I made some useful contacts. Whilst I was in the United States I took the opportunity to visit Security Central of Ohio. Some of you will be aware that the president of that bank, Gerald Shultz, is my brother-in-law." He glanced pointedly down the table. "I didn't see why family connections should be your exclusive preserve, Meyer, and neither did my sister, Anna."

It was an old joke but one that Meyer Waterman found as amusing as ever.

"I planned simply for several pleasant days in Cleveland. As it happened, I found Gerald and his senior people in the middle of a major crisis, one of the biggest in the history of the bank. Their computer system had been rigged—very thoroughly so. It was done by one of their most senior and trusted software designers. He had resigned, apparently quite innocently, nearly a year ago. Since that time, the computer continued to work very actively on his behalf, creaming off funds into a private account."

He paused, scanning the attentive faces and stopping on Harrington with such a prolonged, searching gaze that the Head of Computer Services could almost have believed he was being held responsible for what had happened four thousand miles away.

"The amount involved is estimated to be eight million dollars," Susskind said then.

"Good grief!" Milbourne exclaimed.

There were other declarations of amazement.

"Lloyd's International would gladly have exchanged that for their Swiss fiasco," Clement muttered. Then, seeing the surprise his remark prompted he added hastily, "What I mean is that one can lose far, far more through conventional banking operations than by computer fraud. But don't get the idea I'm not shocked. Of course I am."

"Shocked?" Waterman said acidly. "I have nightmares about just this kind of situation. Nightmares, David."

"Any comments, Harrington?" the chairman asked.

"No, not yet."

"It was discovered quite by accident," Susskind continued. "By a comparatively junior analyst who was playing around with the system in a way he strictly shouldn't have been. Lucky for them! None of Security Central's audit procedures had shown any prior cause for concern. Gerald was not amused."

"Still, they did find it," Sir Neville said. "That's something."

"The basis of the fraud was what some American computer experts have come to call a tax patch. Briefly, that means the system was illicitly altered to levy a kind of unofficial tax on every transaction passing through it. There is a rather large number of transactions every day, to put it mildly."

"As with BANKNET," someone pointed out.

"Precisely. The levy varied between a fraction of a cent and a few cents . . . much too little to be noticed in any individual case. But multiply small numbers by some very large ones over a period and the total is . . . well, I've told you. None of you, I hope, will remember that exact figure on leaving this room. It is a very great embarrassment to Gerald."

"They have the man, I presume?" It was the managing director, Hugh Lindsay-Jones, who spoke.

Susskind gave him a sad smile. "Unfortunately, they *thought* they had him. They found the number of the account into which the skimmed dollars were being

23

paid. At that point, not unnaturally, their first concern was to stop the tax on the customers. So the patch was removed."

He blew a billowing stream of cigar smoke over his shoulder. It hovered for a moment, imitating the clouds moving slowly outside, as though the intervening glass did not exist.

"Their man had booby-trapped the system. I'm told that is the correct technical phrase. Removal of the patch caused the computer to deposit one hundred dollars in a second account no one had suspected was there. That seems to have been an alarm, a warning. The gentleman has not been seen since, and neither has most of the eight million."

Lindsay-Jones made as if to speak again, but Susskind held up his hand.

"At the instant the internal alarm went off, ten complete disc packs of vital customer data were wiped clean. At first Gerald assumed it must be to conceal some further evidence. His opinion now is different. He believes it was just malicious fun. That was the phrase he used."

"My God!" Harrington exclaimed. For some reason he found the senseless destruction of data far more disturbing than the actual theft.

Noting the comment with a grave nod, Susskind continued, "Security Central has automatic cash dispensers in every city and major town in the state of Ohio. The man could examine his alarm account as often as he liked, twenty-four hours a day. And nobody would suspect anything. They record cash withdrawals, of course; they don't record enquiries. Everything that bank did made theft easy. Nothing they did stopped it."

"David Clement is anxious that we install just such automatic dispensers here," Waterman remarked with feeling.

"One thing at a time, Meyer," Clement countered quietly. "The board hasn't had my formal proposal yet. I'll deal with any likely dangers, as you'll see."

Harrington noticed that he spoke with his head down, doodling and apparently unconcerned. Sly bastard!

Lindsay-Jones asked, "What are their plans now, at Security Central?"

"First, they will keep it deadly quiet!" Susskind replied. "Second, Gerald will write off eight million dollars against unforeseen cost overruns on system development."

"Blame the computer but in a way Wall Street won't mind!" Waterman noted in his most cynical voice.

"If you like," Susskind said. "It will still hurt. Third, Gerald will make damned sure it never happens again. Concise, dynamic action well after the event!"

"Stable doors," someone said.

"Now we come to the point of all this, if it isn't already obvious. With us, any action must be *before* not after trouble. As far as we are concerned at Waterman and Company, I don't ever want to see a situation like it. Not remotely like it." He was standing now, probably without realising it. "We must be *safe*, gentlemen. And I need to be totally reassured, beyond all reasonable doubt, that we are."

"We're looking at you, David," the chairman said to Clement.

"One can never be one hundred per cent sure, and Ivor knows it. Computer systems are just too complex for that. There is almost no way to prevent a clever, determined person from patching in unauthorised programs—Alex will confirm that. With BANKNET we get as near total security as is humanly possible. But we can give no unconditional guarantees. It would be irresponsible."

"If necessary," he added as an afterthought, "we could follow the example of the department stores and plan on a certain acceptable level of loss. A fraction of one per cent, say. We'd still be the most profitable clearing bank by a long chalk."

Waterman shook his head furiously.

"What do you think, Harrington?" the chairman asked.

Harrington had hoped the pressure would stay on Clement while he collected his thoughts. He realised he should have known better.

"Frankly, I detect the discovery by Mr. Susskind of original sin. We don't, I trust, need a bank in Cleve-

25

land to warn us that systems handling money are an open invitation to plunder? That was true long before electronics."

Susskind leaned forward, puzzled. "Mr. Harrington, you're disappointing me. Are you trying to suggest that the game hasn't changed!"

"I'm saying that we're not fools. We know the risks and we take the necessary precautions."

"Then BANKNET would be secure against the kind of fraud I've just described?"

"Yes, totally."

"You're quite sure?"

"It's such a familiar trick I'm amazed the Americans allowed themselves to be caught. BANKNET checks automatically and secretly on certain levels and types of money movement. We would instantly detect any account with such large numbers of small credits flowing in all the time."

"You say secretly. But someone knows, someone had to program those checks, surely? I presume you didn't?"

"All secrets are relative, Ivor," Clement interjected. "Like the one you told us earlier."

Susskind kept his eyes on Harrington. "Original sin apart . . ." He produced a fleeting smile. "Are you telling us that there is *no* fraud that could succeed with BANKNET? That you've thought of everything?" He sounded unconvinced.

Harrington, momentarily unsure, exchanged glances with Clement before opting for honesty. It was usually safer, if more uncomfortable. "No, I can't promise we are completely secure. But I can claim to have one of the most strictly controlled software teams you'll find anywhere. That's where the biggest danger lies, as your friends across the Atlantic have learned to their cost. So I watch my staff constantly, box them in."

"I wish somebody would tell me what software *is*," Milbourne said loudly. He dug an elbow into Waterman. "I can imagine, Meyer. But it's nothing to do with computers, know what I mean?"

An embarrassed silence followed his burst of laughter.

"Shall I . . . ?" Harrington asked, and received a nod of assent from the top of the table.

"Hardware is what you can touch—the actual computer, all its peripheral devices such as disc and tape drives, card readers, terminals . . ."

"I know *that*," the MP said dismissively. "It's obvious."

"Without software all that is quite useless. The software brings it to life. Software, computer programs—they're the same thing."

"You were telling us?" Sir Neville said irritably.

Harrington had to think. "Oh yes—staff. Well, as I said, my software staff are very strictly monitored. We employ only people who are very carefully screened and who we believe to be honest."

"No procedure ensures that!" Susskind retorted.

"I agree wholeheartedly. You described the man at Security Central as one of their most trusted employees, did you not? The difference here is that I trust *nobody*. It's the only way. I use the members of my software team to provide a series of close checks on one another. I'm sure they don't even realise the extent to which they are doing it. I think it works."

"What about pranks?" someone asked. "Malicious fun, I believe Ivor called it."

"I find it hard to make any promises there," Harrington said thoughtfully. "If one of my people went suddenly—crazy, shall we say—a lot of damage could be inflicted very, very quickly. An emormous amount of computer information can be destroyed in a single second, you know."

"And if so?"

"All our vital records and programs are duplicated, some are triplicated. The master copies are physically separated from the working versions. Deliberate destruction would result in . . . er, inconvenience, not catastrophe."

"I'm glad to hear it," Susskind said.

"Frankly, I fear external disaster more, things outside my control. An aircraft crashing on a Data Centre, say. Or some attention from our bomb-happy friends in Ulster. I tend to assume that we're target pillars of the Establishment."

"But such unlikely incidents apart . . . all is well,

you would say?" Susskind adopted a deliberately sceptical tone.

"I hope so."

"You hope!"

"Well . . . yes."

"Forgive me, Mr. Harrington, but I do not find a mixture of hope and complacency very reassuring."

Harrington was studying his thin fingers, pulling at them and locking them together. He did that sometimes.

"This board's policy has been to push computing in the bank very fast indeed." He took a deep breath, riding his favourite hobby horse. "Often as fast as the technology will allow. Any uncertainty I feel is because of that, and only that. Sometimes excessive haste can bring with it dangers that a more considered pace would . . ."

"Alex!" Clement wore a pained expression. "Look at the results. Look at the share price, man." His gold pencil was waved towards the window, symbolically at the City itself. "They're not fools down there."

"Nor up here, I hope," Lindsay-Jones said, raising eyebrows at Harrington.

"I wasn't questioning, just observing. It's your prerogative to create policy, of course it is. But we have to meet the challenge of making it all happen." Dropping his head a fraction, Harrington added rather lamely, "I think my people do a magnificent job."

Meyer Waterman rose from his seat and began to pace across the panorama of grey-tinted clouds drifting behind the vast glass wall. He had a fringe position on the board, nominally executive but with little real power. Yet his ancestry carried real weight, and he was strongly identified with the bank in public eyes. On a number of occasions in the past he had opposed Clement bitterly. Now all the heads followed his slow movements.

"Ivor told me about Cleveland some days ago," he said at last. "I was intrigued that Gerald Shultz had decided to cover the matter up. Of course, we should probably do the same. Anyway, I have been doing a little research. I have found that computer crime in the U.S. is known to be running at many million dollars a year. Add the cases, like Security Central, which are discovered but kept secret. Then add those which are not yet discovered . . . I think there must be quite a few, don't you? In all we might hazard a guess that computer crime over there is running at well over one hundred million dollars a year, perhaps even twice that figure. And that's leaving out exceptional cases like the Equity Funding fraud in Los Angeles which accounted for some hundreds of millions by itself. Calvert in Economic Intelligence agrees with my estimates, by the way. I put him onto the problem."

"You didn't mention Gerald's problem?" Susskind looked worried.

Waterman shook his head. "Of course not. Actually, one of Calvert's research assistants dug up some fascinating case studies. I can circulate them if you feel like some horror stories at bedtime."

He fixed Clement with a determined gaze. "What most disturbed me, David, was that the majority of the known instances were found completely by chance. I can give you a typical example. The president of a New York based insurance company checked into a Miami hotel and came across one of his middle-level software designers staying in the best suite. A *very* expensive best suite. Tick, tick, tick, he went. You know the kind of thing."

"This is not America, Meyer," Clement pointed out with a smile.

"The technology is the same, as you well know," Waterman snapped back. "And this bank happens to be rather bigger than Security Central. The population of Ohio is about eleven million. Our British market is five times that. Add our markets in mainland Europe . . . you'll get my drift, I think." He moved round the table to stand immediately behind Clement. "I believe I am right in stating that neither David Clement nor our guest can guarantee total immunity to illicit attempts against our computer system. Correct?"

Both men nodded reluctantly.

"And it is also correct to say that this bank is now completely and irrevocably dependent on that system?" He shook a finger at Clement, who had turned to face him. "I know what you're going to say, David! That the new Waterman's *is* its computers, and that's how it must be these days. Well, perhaps. I won't dredge up old history."

"I'll drink to that," Clement said lightly.

"It's not the risk to money that concerns me," Waterman went on. "It's the question of our *reputation*. I don't want this bank to look foolish. And I don't want to see my family name associated with avoidable fraud. That is what this is really all about." Without warning he slapped his hand down on the table. It was a gentle, almost silent gesture, yet he made it dramatic and arresting. "It won't do," he proclaimed loudly. "I insist on one hundred per cent security. Nothing less can be acceptable to this board or to our customers."

He resumed his seat amid a murmur of assent.

"That will be a trifle difficult, Meyer," Clement said evenly. "One must be realistic. Don't you agree, Alex?"

"You don't have total security of cash at the branches," Harrington protested, caught off guard.

"Perfectly true and quite irrelevant," Waterman replied in a cold voice. "If money is snatched in the streets Securicor looks foolish, not us. For it to happen actually inside a branch requires violence. And that makes the public sorry for our counter staff and hence for the bank as a whole. But in our computers, misled by one of our own employees . . . ? I repeat, I do not wish to be made a fool."

"Can I ask what Meyer has in mind?" Clement said. "I suspect there must be something. He and Ivor often hunt in pairs."

"Yes, we should have an action," the chairman agreed. "This is a board, not a debating society."

"I have a firm proposal," Waterman said. "An audit. I want a systems audit."

"That's looking, not bloody doing!" Harrington spoke from the heart, he couldn't help himself. His immediate reaction was that he had an operation to run. He was appalled by the prospect of diverting staff to take measurements, monitor procedures, write reports to be read once, then gather dust.

"I'm . . . sorry," he added. His hand, concealing a tablet, brushed his mouth.

"I'm just an old-fashioned banker," Waterman said with mock modesty. "If I think I'm ill I consult my doctor. I don't wait till rigor mortis sets in. Nor do I try to examine myself—one uses an expert for that, an outsider. I want an audit done here, a diagnosis of possible ills. And I want it done by the best available doctor, in other words a specialist consultant. Any other way—and please don't misunderstand me, David— would be suspect."

Clement held up a hand submissively. "Your analogy is striking, Meyer. I'd hate you to catch something."

"Does that mean you agree with the proposal?" the chairman asked with a barely concealed smile.

"If an audit will reassure Meyer and the rest of the board, then of course it shall be done. Alex Harrington will do it gladly. Eh, Alex?"

Head down, Harrington found himself contemplating his fingers again. "It could disrupt the work at the Centre," he observed gloomily. "And consultants! I wouldn't give you twopence for some of them. Reporting back to you at the end of the job the very things you told them at the beginning."

"Then we'll just have to find one who isn't like that," Clement said in a manner Harrington recognised to mean that argument would be futile.

"I will do it, if that's what the board wants."

"Is it, gentlemen?" Sir Neville asked with an enquiring look down the table. There was a unanimous show of hands. "Good. It all rests with you, then, Harrington. Perhaps you'll agree on a budget with David before proceeding. We'll look forward to reading the report in, what . . . three months?"

"More like six, I'd say," Harrington ventured. "You'll want it done properly."

"Six, then. Formally let the minutes show the action as against David Clement."

I wonder, Harrington asked himself as he rose to go, how often that has happened?

The girl at the typewriter smiled farewell. At first the lift refused to move and Harrington stood there, self-consciously framed in a rosewood panelled box.

He jabbed at the button again. After what seemed an eternity the doors slid shut and the floor dropped beneath his feet.

His first board meeting, he was thinking, and it had to end in defeat. Well, a kind of defeat. He tried to control the almost irrational sense of dismay that swept over him. Clement was right . . . for once. It all depended on who did the audit. And how it was done.

He unbuttoned his collar and loosened his tie just a fraction, not so much that it would show. It wasn't his territory up there. He was a mole, a subterranean worker from the London Data Centre. Wind rushed past the lift. Harrington was carried swiftly downwards to where he belonged.

Chapter Two

It was not the way Webb normally went to his office. Usually he took an elaborate route, refined and tested over months. To move quickly through Central London you have to know the side streets, covering twice the distance to halve the time. What is the point of a fast car if you have to crawl, hemmed in on every side by cheaper metal? But there he was in Wigmore Street, trapped in slow-moving traffic, the morning ebbing away. Webb held down a switch on the fascia and the roof panel slid back. Sunlight flooded in, bright but with the softness of late October.

Blinking, he looked across the street to see the blue symbol of IBM beckoning from a corner building. That was why he had come that way today, of course. The building. He glanced up to the fourth floor, counting windows until he found his old office. Five years ago and it seemed like yesterday.

He had been a computer salesman then, younger in every way, sharp and eager. Working long hours more because he had the energy to spare than anything, or so it must have been, thinking back. He had soon developed his own impressive list of contacts—people who relied on him and respected him but somehow, he sensed, never quite trusted him. Nobody trusted IBM salesmen. Once Webb realised that, he hated every minute.

Meeting Andrew Shulton had been inevitable, really. Andrew's room was just along the corridor. He was the same age, equally ambitious, moving equally fast. Everyone had said how alike they were—like brothers. Besides, Shulton's office was a baited trap, as Webb told him later. An open door and a stunning secretary parked right where you looked as you came out of the lift. Alison Osborne she was then, Alison Webb now. What, he wondered, would she be called next? Not Alison Shulton, for sure, although it wouldn't be for want of trying, on both sides. Webb could not care less. Or so he constantly tried to convince himself.

Golden leaves patterned the road and pavements at Cavendish Square. One drifted with seesaw motion onto his windscreen. He flicked the wipers but it was just out of range, gummed to the glass. When he stopped at the next set of lights he got out quickly to remove it. So untidy. It crunched and disintegrated in his hand.

Ahead, a Rolls-Royce Corniche turned the corner, glinting fresh polish. Webb moved behind it into Mortimer Street. Lavender paintwork, white upholstery, white soft top—it would have to be a gown manufacturer, he thought. Around there the Rolls-Royces and Ferraris were always ragtrade, always in violent colours, with boots and back seats full of skirts packed in polythene. Fashion showrooms lined the road on both sides. A stranger to the area would notice those, passing through. The computer consultancies were less obtrusive—just small nameplates by the doors and lights that burned into the night as the programmers chased their bugs.

Men start new, small companies for many reasons. For Webb the motivation had been money and he had never pretended otherwise. For Shulton it had been an escape, a way out of IBM before he was trapped by position and pension and the inertia of advancing age. Systems Technology Limited had been his idea, or so he claimed now. Webb could honestly not remember. The money to get it going had certainly been Shulton's.

Family money. As a result, he owned most of the company. That was, as he often said, only fair, and at the time there had seemed nothing wrong with the arrangement. Later, Webb had come to believe that owning a small part of the company you work for was far worse than owning none of it. But that was much later. It had been good for the first year or so. Exhilarating.

Just ahead, an old woman was pulling remnants from a dustbin, stuffing dark pieces of cloth into a carrier bag and scattering unwanted cuts in yellow and bright green all around her. The Corniche parked right alongside and Webb had to wait, his way blocked by a broad open door, as the driver struggled out, lost under cardboard boxes and coathangers.

The first SysTech office had been up a back street, just to the left. Webb could see the corner in his mirror. He would have passed it without a thought if it had not been for the Rolls. Well, maybe not.

Three crowded rooms in a dingy old building. Fresh white paint inside and new white furniture edged in chrome. Draughts in winter and insidious cracks in the walls that no amount of attention could conceal. Surprisingly, the clients had not minded at all. The office was quaint, many thought. Cheap, too, keeping down the overheads and hence the fees. And they were where everyone expected them to be—in the "Computer Belt," as those in the know called it. All around, other small software companies, their names confusingly similar, vied for the lucrative gaps that were opening up in the blooming computer market.

He and Andrew had shared a tiny front office, living, as Shulton once described it, in one another's wastepaper, on either side of a common desk. Across the narrow street they looked straight into a sweatshop. Bare bulbs blazed, and by the window a Cypriot worked endlessly at a steam iron. He was there pressing shirts when they arrived in the morning, and often they left at night before he did. Success had eventually driven SysTech out of its first address. But so in a way had the Cypriot. He had exhausted them.

Two years ago they had moved the company to one of the old houses on the north side of Fitzroy Square. Now they were just beyond the main concentration of their rivals in the computer belt. That pleased Webb, who had never liked the place. Shulton was happy, too. They were still near enough to be in touch with what was going on, just far enough away to be seen as different. Their building was not in the most attractive and unspoiled row—that lay to the east of the square. But the large old house confirmed to their clients that SysTech had come of age. More than that, it demonstrated the seriousness of their profession. They were, as Shulton never tired of pointing out, aspirants still, chasing the social rank of solicitors and architects. And they did, after all, charge rather more for their services.

Webb turned out of Mortimer Street, weaving through tight streets, then plunging down into the bleak darkness of an underground car park. He left the silver Porsche, turning as he often did to look back at it as he walked away. He had not, to be honest, done too badly out of SysTech. It was just that he had not done well enough, as well as Shulton. A minute later he was in Fitzroy Square.

He sat by his tall window, overlooking the trees. Susan Faulkner brought him hot coffee and the mail, peeling a letter from the top to hand it over.

"I think you'll want to see this first, Chris."

Webb read it several times, a smile appearing, feeling properly awake for the first time that day.

"Get Harvey, would you," he told her.

"He's not in today," Susan said. "With a client in Bristol, I believe."

Webb swore. "Then get Shulton down here."

She went back to her desk just across the room and dialled, watching him closely. When Webb did not expect problems with Andrew he went up a floor to see him. When he thought there might be trouble he summoned him down. Susan knew that, he could tell. Never screw your secretary, he was thinking, not even once. For ever after they watch your every move and try to read meaning into it. The feeling could be most uncomfortable.

"Good luck with him." she said over the intercom.

Quietly, Webb swore again.

"This is an Invitation To Tender," Shulton declared with a calculated show of indifference.

"Very good!"

"Contracts, I get excited about. Not ITTs."

"One of the little frustrations of life," Webb said. "First we have to bid it, *then* we get the contract. Remember?"

Shulton shook his head. "No chance. A pity, but we're too small. Too small and too unknown."

"It's a one-man job, Andrew!"

"Yes, plus another two hundred back at home base. A big old bank like this, they'll want to deal with a big old outfit. There are maybe six companies who can land this job, and you know it. Write a nice thank-you, huh, and can we please come back in five years' time."

"I assume Waterman's think we have a chance. Otherwise, why bother to ask us?"

"Us and how many others!" Shulton stabbed a finger at the letter. "It's a Carbon, Chris, or hadn't you noticed? Half the computer consultancies in London will have one. Most of them like us—flattered and without a hope."

"I don't think so, somehow."

"Really . . ."

"Yes, really. Your first guess agrees with mine—six others at the most. More than that would be too much trouble for the bank."

"People like Marriott and DSL?"

"Very likely."

"They'll walk all over us."

"Six to one," Webb insisted. "I've known far worse odds."

"At the tables in Mayfair? I bet you have."

The barbed remark was too near the truth for Webb's liking. He leaned forward angrily. "I'm going to bid it, Andrew, whatever you say."

"I see."

"I'm being polite . . . telling you first."

Frowning, Shulton picked up the letter again and reread it very slowly.

"Who do we know at Waterman's?"

"No one. I've never even met them."

"You've sent them sales literature, then? A letter?"

"No, nothing."

Shulton eased back in his chair. "Short letter, isn't it?" he remarked meaningfully.

"You might say that."

"It bloody stinks! A put-up job. They've already decided who they want and someone in Contracts is making it look competitive. Making it seem fair."

"Waterman's? I hardly think so."

Shulton showed mock disapproval. "On Monday I had a lousy time at our bank renegotiating the terms for the company loan. Try it sometime, Chris! We were done, screwed. I don't share your faith in the ethics of banking."

He placed the letter carefully in front of Webb. There was an embossed shield at the top, dead centre. The sun, filtering through the trees and not yet eclipsed by the Post Office Tower, turned the tiny barge to shining gold.

"Surprise me," Shulton said. "Tell me the consultant you were planning to offer these fine City gentlemen."

"I had in mind Christopher Webb, actually. No one else in SysTech could touch a job like this."

"Mmm." Shulton gave a wry smile. "I hope they're as impressed with your experience as you are."

"What about London Alliance?"

"What about it? A bit over a thousand, that was all the guy got. Big deal."

"Kestrel Records, then? Four people caught with their greedy hands in the computer. Two staff, two outsiders. Embezzlement, fraud and conspiracy to defraud." Webb looked pleased with himself. "Not exactly an everyday occurrence in this business."

"It was crummy. Those guys never stood an ice cream's chance in Hell."

"Who cares. I'll see that the bank gets to hear about that little episode."

"A bit uncouth for City tastes, surely," Shulton suggested. "I mean, a small pop record company, a squalid bit of stealing."

"That's why I'm hedging my bets, Andrew." Webb turned the letter round and pointed. "They specifically ask for a brief response. If I was going to do that my reply would already be in the post."

"Meaning what, exactly?"

"That I'm going to work full-time on this bid. That's the catch. Four weeks of my time plus a fair amount of one more man. You know, to do background research on Waterman's. Legwork."

Shulton gave a low whistle of surprise.

"At a guess," Webb offered in justification, "the job will run for six man-months. Say twelve thousand pounds in fees."

"Twelve K . . ." Shulton was suddenly interested.

"That's what I said. Twists the arm just a fraction, doesn't it, Andrew?"

Shulton picked up the letter for the third time. He could see no information on which Webb might have estimated the value of the contract.

"You plus one," he said in a resigned voice. "What kind of man were you thinking of?"

"Not kind of man. A man. Mike Harvey."

"I had a feeling you'd say that."

"He's the best we've got."

"You apart, of course," Shulton declared sourly. "No go. He's already sold."

"Hell, Andrew. He worked with me on London Alliance and Kestrel. He knows the ropes."

"He's with a client in Bristol. Two months at least. Didn't you know?"

"Damn!" Webb moved to the window and gazed across the square. The Post Office Tower was now well into its daily performance as a giant sundial. He looked up at the bare midriff. It was noon. He could tell that from the bright halo where the antennae hung.

Waterman's was a money machine, he was thinking. That was all a bank was when you came down to it. A great, ripe money machine. It *had* to be Harvey.

"Tell you what," Shulton said helpfully. "You can have Kennedy. For one week, starting now. All right?"

"Kennedy!" Webb swung back, astonished. "What the hell does he know about banking or high-security systems! I need a man who's done it, not some junior programmer wet behind the ears."

"Kennedy," Shulton insisted. "Everyone else is sold, see. I'm sure that Jake will do some useful legwork

. . ." He paused, choosing his words with care, ". . . given the right direction."

Webb presented his back. He could feel, not see, Shulton stopping midway to the door, raising his voice to be sure Susan could hear.

"Four bloody weeks! When you fail I shall shit on you from a very great height."

"You'll enjoy that, given the chance."

"I rather think I will."

Webb heard the door close. He saw his faint reflection in the glass and patted a springing curl of brown hair back behind an ear. It was dusted in places with the first traces of grey. Computing was a young man's game, he thought. At thirty you were already too old, the pace of endless change was beginning to tell. And at thirty-five . . .

He was sure he would get the contract. Well, fairly sure. What he would do then, stuck at Waterman's with that huge, sophisticated system, he had no idea. Why the hell had Harvey allowed himself to be sent off to bloody Bristol?

Jake Kennedy passed the letter back to Webb.

"There isn't much there," he said.

"You're trying to impress me with your grasp of the situation," Webb remarked cynically.

"Andrew Shulton doesn't seem to think we . . ."

"Stand a chance. I know. Coffee?"

"Please."

"One or two?"

"One lump, no milk."

"I meant cups, Jake. I always have two. Susan there calls me an addict, a doubles man."

"I'll stick with the one, all the same."

Susan was already leaving the room.

"Open plan," Webb said ruefully, with a nod in her direction. "It's like being at the wrong end of a microscope."

Kennedy glanced around. They were in Webb's territory. At least that was what the staff called it for want of a better name. Most of the building had been opened up, with doors and parts of walls removed and a long, rather plain extension added at the rear. Few

39

small rooms—proper rooms, that is—were left. Webb and Shulton occupied what they called offices, but they were really only personal zones within larger communal areas, the boundaries low walls of bookcases. Webb had a desk and two chairs, a few shelves sparsely occupied by books and journals. He had an expanse of brown carpet noticeably smaller than Shulton's on the floor above. But a larger expanse than any other but Shulton's.

"Th eother bidders will do exactly as Waterman's ask," Webb said. "Their hope will be that it's their man whose career résumé looks best or whose manner seems the most dependable. Maybe the Sales Director comes in on the same train as someone from Waterman's. Who knows. Maybe they've oak panelling in their client meeting rooms."

"We're not exactly establishment," Kennedy agreed.

"The odds are against us, Jake, and I'm going to lengthen them further. I'm going to send Waterman's a great fat dossier on Waterman's. What they do, how they do it, what they're afraid of."

"Sounds great."

"It's not what they've asked for! In fact they've as good as told us not to. If they play this by the book we'll be disqualified the moment they see it. But if not . . ."

Webb smiled, rubbing hands.

"How will you do all that, Chris?"

"We, Jake, we. I don't know yet. That is one of the problems you and I must put our minds to."

"I shan't be much use to you, I'm afraid," Kennedy muttered.

He was as casual in appearance as Harvey, Webb noticed. But otherwise they could not have been more different. He was much shyer than Harvey, with less sign of drive.

"Frankly, you weren't my first choice," Webb confessed. "But you'll do. You'll help just by being around to be talked at. And you'll do my research. Look, I don't even know the first thing about Waterman's. Are they the sixth-largest bank in the country? Tenth? Do you know?"

"No idea."

40

"You can find that out, for a start."

"You mean research the banking side of banking?" Kennedy sounded worried.

"That's right."

"Bloody hell, Chris." Kennedy was out of his depth several days earlier than he had expected. "You must be aware of what I've done before? Or what I haven't, more to the point. You know my background."

"Perfectly."

"But I'm a programmer, just that. I'm not a merchant banker, and I've no desire to be."

"Clearing banker," Webb said tartly. "Waterman's is a clearing bank. We do at least know that."

"See what I mean?"

"You're all I've got," Webb said. "I hope you're not going to let me down."

Kennedy picked up the letter again. Not to read but as something to cling to, buoyancy. Drowning in front of a director was not a pleasant experience.

"They don't say much about the computers," he said suddenly. "I really ought to find out about them. It's more my line."

"They're not in the least concerned about the computers, Jake. Some companies would be, but not people like this. They're sophisticated users, you see. They know the dangers."

Kennedy seemed not to understand.

"It's their *staff* they're worried about. Computers don't nick money. People can and for all I know probably do at Waterman's. They will be very anxious that their staff don't get to know this audit is taking place. Want to take a bet on that?"

"In which case why bring in outsiders? We know now and others know."

"They have no alternative," Webb retorted. "And we are going to keep our mouths shut, understand? You will say nothing, Jake, inside this building or out. And I can promise you the competition will do the same."

Susan reappeared, to place two cups in front of Webb and one beside Kennedy.

"We don't have their Annual Report," she said. "I

41

checked. NatWest and Barclays, yes. Even Coutts. But not Waterman's."

"Order one for Jake, would you," Webb said.

"Will do."

"Tell them he'll collect it, if it will save time."

She gave Kennedy a sympathetic smile and went back to her desk.

"It's an intriguing problem," Webb said. "How to persuade a company that doesn't trust its own staff—to the extent of twelve K's worth of secret audit—to trust me. Have you thought of it that way? I mean, what do I do? Buy hornrimmed glasses and dye my hair more grey than it already is?"

"You haven't said yet what *I'm* supposed to do."

"I want everything you can find out about Waterman's. General background, range of banking services, financial performance."

"And how am I supposed to do all that?"

Webb sighed. "In the library downstairs you'll find a row of glossy magazines called *The Banker*. I don't read it and neither does Shulton, but we buy it each month all the same. Education of the staff in the nastier facts of life, that was the idea. It's time they were dusted off. There are also yearbooks, reference books, that Annual Report when it comes. Use the financial information services if you have to. Use your head, Jake, and do it. Got that?"

"I think so," Kennedy said dubiously. "You'll want a briefing at the end, I suppose?"

"Yes, literally. Get as much data as possible, then boil it all down to as little as possible. Not some clever report full of bullshit, but the relevant facts. Relevant gossip, too, if you should chance across any."

"I know a merchant banker, actually," Kennedy said, perking up. "The kind of guy who would know all the inside stories. He works at L.N. Levene."

"Fine."

"We were at Cambridge together."

Webb stared, then shook his head. "Forget it," he ordered brusquely. "Just spare me twenty-two-year-old bankers! You've got a week, don't waste it. I want that report on my desk first thing next Tuesday. I'd

42

prefer it before I meet their man Harrington this Friday, but . . ." He shrugged.

"I could try, I suppose."

"You'll need the weekend," Webb promised. "Every hour of it. You'll see."

Kennedy gave a resigned half-smile. He gulped down his coffee and got up to return to his own small work area up two floors and rather farther from the window than Webb's. Knock down the walls and new barriers arise, new totems of hierarchy. At SysTech they were windows. Kennedy had a theory that salaries were inversely proportional to the distance of desks from windows.

"Will I meet him with you?" he asked hopefully.

"Can you think of any questions?"

"Not really."

"Then I think it ought to be just me."

When Kennedy had gone Susan came over.

"You were a bit tough on him."

"People were a bloody sight tougher than that with me when I was young," Webb stated. "It never did me any harm."

The day moved on. Webb sat at his desk, reading and rereading his letter, refusing phone calls and interruptions. The more he read the more baffled he became. It was quite the most concise, the least helpful Invitation To Tender he had ever seen.

"STRICTLY CONFIDENTIAL
Gentlemen,

Waterman and Company, Bankers, invite the submission of proposals for an audit of the security of the Bank's computer systems and their installations. The intention is to establish the effectiveness of the existing protection against deliberate or accidental system corruption.

The BANKNET system is based on IBM 370 computers and substantial experience of these machines is essential.

Due to the sensitive and private nature of its computer operations the Bank is prepared to provide only very limited information at this stage. It is

43

recognised that this will inevitably restrict the scope of the responses possible from bidding companies.

BRIEF written proposals (four copies) shall be submitted no later than 10:00 a.m. on 21 November. A verbal presentation to senior Bank staff will be arranged shortly after that date. Proposals shall include career résumés of the staff offered for the work, together with details of daily fee rates. It is preferred that the audit be carried out by one senior consultant. Alternatively, a team size of two is considered the maximum that will permit the work of the Data Centres to continue without undue disturbance.

Questions should be directed to Mr. A. Harrington, Head of Computer Services, who will be pleased to meet company representatives.

It is requested that the intention to institute this audit, and all information given to bidders, be kept in the strictest commercial confidence."

"It's not enough," Webb complained to Susan when she brought him a sandwich lunch. "It's not nearly enough."

She thought it best to make no comment, and left him to it. It was a long time since she had seen him so engrossed in his work.

The sky darkened, with the sharp greyness of evening beginning to drive out the pale blue. Lights were coming on across the square and the Tower was a tall, glowing column pointing to the early stars.

"That's it!" Webb exclaimed suddenly, reaching for the telephone.

"Sue, see if Adrian Ross is still in his office."

Looking over, he could tell that she had not understood.

"Adrian Ross and Partners," he explained. "The recruitment consultants." This time he saw her opening her card file.

Ross began with a cheery greeting. He hoped that SysTech was booming, that Webb, Mrs. Webb and the boy—it was a boy, wasn't it?—were positively booming, too. He always sounded that enthusiastic when he smelled business.

"I was thinking of recruiting someone," Webb said, amused to see Susan's face.

"I assumed so," came the reply.

"A really top-level banking man. He must know IBM 370's, and the more senior he is the better. Not a desk type, Adrian. A man who really understands the business."

"Salary?"

"No problem. Eight K, maybe even ten K or above. I don't mind as long as it's the right man."

"I'll check my lists and call you back. Morning okay?"

"I had a very specific type in mind, actually," Webb said slowly. "Someone from a bank like Waterman's, if you follow?"

There was a pause before Ross gave his considered reply.

"How much like Waterman's, Christopher?"

"You know what I mean."

"My fee for headhunting is higher, you realise that?"

"I can imagine."

"Thirty per cent of first year's salary."

"I take it back," Webb breathed. "I would never have imagined."

"It's a lot of work, old chap. Lots of hassle and expense. You'd be surprised."

"Payable when he joins, though?"

"Of course. No deal, no fee."

"Okay," Webb said. "But not the boss man. Not Harrington."

"I do understand," Ross said reassuringly. "He won't get a sniff of it, you have my word. But it won't be easy. They're very stable people, Waterman's— good perks, excellent conditions, squash courts and high pensions and lots of motherly love. Hold on . . ." He was back after a moment. "They have a very low staff turnover, according to my records. Could be tricky."

"Then be tricky!"

"Naughty," Ross said, feigning shock. "I'll call you, though."

"Do it soon, Adrian. I'm in a hurry."

"Yesterday, Christopher. I'll do it yesterday."

Chapter Three

"So many churches!" Harrington said. "You'd imagine that people in this square mile pray as much as they think of money."

"Perhaps they did, once," Webb observed philosophically.

Through the windows of the Waterman Building the great bulk of St. Paul's sat astride Ludgate Hill, looking not quite right when seen from that height—too big and with the dome curiously like a policeman's helmet. The spires of other Wren churches speared the tight spaces between new office blocks.

"I'm not really used to views," Harrington said as an aside. "I'm a mole, you see. You will be as well if you win this job."

Mole? Webb thought. Yes, he could almost be with that brown face and the slow manner punctuated by slight twitches. Rather thin and severe, though, and hardly what one would call furry.

Harrington took a seat, indicating that Webb should do the same. He had been anxious at first to explain that the room was not his personal office. Webb wondered why that mattered so much. Certainly, the room expressed no real character. There were no silver-framed family photographs, no private objects littering the desk. Yet because of that the man fitted the office perfectly, just as if he had planned every detail—the absence of nonessentials being as revealing as what was there.

"There's only one of you, then," the banker remarked. "Most of the other consultants I've seen came in a flock of three or four. I'm either impressed or disappointed. I'll know which later, I expect."

"Systems Technology is a small company," Webb said firmly. "If we get the contract the team you'll see will consist of me. Why pretend otherwise?"

"And what will that small team cost us?" Harrington asked with the hint of a smile.

"My fee will be a hundred and fifty pounds a day. That's almost certainly lower than the other rates you'll be quoted."

"Not exactly bargain basement!"

"The only reason is that we're small and so is our overhead," Webb said, ignoring the remark. "You won't be asked to pay for the upkeep of the big office I don't have and can't be in anyway while I'm working on your project."

"It is a little lower," Harrington admitted. "I must say, I hadn't realised until we began this exercise what levels of fee are charged in your business, Mr. Webb. Waterman's is obviously in the wrong field."

"I'm sure you get by."

Harrington was looking down, rubbing the knuckles at the back of one hand with the fingers of the other.

"I'll tell you what I've told all the others. My opening speech, if you like, after our initial fencing. First, no lunches—expensive or otherwise—so don't bother to offer. If it is ever appropriate we'll buy you one. Second, miss that tender deadline by one minute and your submission will not be considered. We mean that, it's how we do things in this bank. Next, perhaps you'd note that your presentation to us will be on December sixth at ten sharp. The format and the attendance from your side will be up to you. I would venture the opinion, though, that one person, whether that is the complete team or not, would be a little outnumbered."

"Two, then," Webb proposed. Perhaps he could get hold of Harvey, just for the day. He did not want Shulton there.

Harrington looked disappointed. "Let's make it three, shall we? Some of my colleagues may take some convincing that your company exists. A partial show of the troops is in order, I feel." He was trying to be helpful.

"We can manage that." Webb did not much like the banker. He was not a man you could feel comfortable with.

"Next, since you are bound to ask—no, we will not say which other consultancies we have invited. But you are in select company. The number is small. If you guess five in total you would be wrong, but not by much."

47

"How about that!" Webb said under his breath.

"Finally, I am prepared to tell you very little more than the minute amount of information you already have. If that makes this appear more like an initiative test than normal competitive bid . . . well, perhaps it is."

He sat back, studying Webb closely, giving the distinct impression that he was there not to provide answers but to hear what questions were asked.

"Why do you want this audit?" Webb began.

"I would have thought that was obvious."

"Not necessarily."

"We have persuaded ourselves over a period of years that our BANKNET system is immune to interference. It seems time to learn whether other. . . outside experts endorse that view."

"Then you don't suspect any fraud at this moment?"

"I'm ruling that question out of order, Mr. Webb. If I did suspect fraud, as you put it, I'd be a fool to tell you. You might not win the contract, after all."

"But if I do, will you tell me then?"

Harrington found the question funny. "That reminds me of the problem involving the tribe that always lies and the one that always tells the truth! You must see, surely, that I can't give you an answer? Your primary assumption has to be that we suspect nothing. A good audit will reveal any irregularities, anyway, will it not?"

The hands continued to roam over each other, Harrington's eyes alternately on them and on Webb, direct and unblinking. When he glanced away he gave Webb the impression that it was not due to any embarrassment, just the discovery of something temporarily more interesting. He gave away nothing. You wrote that letter, Webb decided. There can't be two like you at Waterman's.

"Your letter implied that you have a number of Data Centres," he said.

"Two."

"I presume one is in London."

"That will be fairly obvious."

"And the other . . . ?"

"I'm not prepared to say."

"That isn't very helpful."

48

"First-line security. I would expect someone in your business to appreciate that."

"Are you prepared to say who will read our proposal?" Webb tried to sound patient.

"It's not exactly a proposal, is it? A letter of offer will suffice. Please don't inundate me, Mr. Webb. I can't abide bullshit."

"You asked for four copies . . ." Webb said, persisting.

"One each for the three directors making up the Policy Steering Committee of the bank. And one for me, of course."

"Who will attend the presentation from your side?"

"The same four."

"And what would you say is their level of understanding of computers? Low?"

The older man gave a thin smile. "Perceptive fellow. You may assume *I* know a fair amount. You may also take it that I am a modest person, somewhat given to understatement. As for the others, I believe one of them might just recognise a computer if he were to be pointed at one."

It was Webb's turn to look amused. "Am I to understand that my presentation should be . . ." He was searching for the right word. He settled for "simple."

"We are looking for a consultant who thinks deep and talks shallow," the banker confirmed, nodding. "Jargon will make you a very unwanted person."

"December the sixth," Webb said. "Where does that come in the batting order?"

"I'm not sure that I see the relevance of your question."

"It's just that I called you within two hours of your letter hitting my desk. I still seem to have landed at the back of the queue for this meeting, this round." Webb had the sudden germ of an idea. It was crazy, probably. Shulton would certainly think so.

Harrington was watching him with interest but he gave no reply.

"I'm only curious. It's not giving much away surely?"

"You'll be last," Harrington stated with a trace of discomfort. "At the back of the queue, as you call it.

49

An advantage or a disadvantage, depending on how you choose to view it."

"What one might term the outside position," Webb suggested.

"An arbitrary arrangement, nothing more." Harrington was not convincing.

"We can do this job," Webb declared. "Better than anyone."

"You would not be here if there wasn't some possibility of that."

"But we're not the obvious choice, I know that. I was wondering, what made you think of us?"

"It's interesting you should ask that. You see, I had one more question for you." The banker sat back, taking his time.

"I'm a careful man, Mr. Webb. When we decided on this course of action I did my research first. I read a bit, talked to a few people. There aren't many cases of computer fraud that reach the courts, make the headlines."

"Ah . . ."

"I've had a word with Alan Spencer."

"The Computer Manager at Kestrel Records."

"That's right. Tell me about it, would you? What you did?"

"Hasn't Spencer done that?"

"I want your version."

"They have an on-line ordering system," Webb explained. "Just a small computer, nothing elaborate. It allows the salesmen to enter their orders direct from a number of regional offices. The trick was simple. Dial in an order for records, then dial again later to cancel, giving a special code. The records were delivered just as originally requested, but no bill was ever issued. It was never a big deal, just spending money, really. A tax-fee nibble."

Harrington fixed Webb with a very direct stare. "You've described the fraud, Mr. Webb. I asked what *you* did."

"That could take some time."

"Not the technical details, just your approach to the problem."

"My philosophy, you mean?"

"If you must call it that, yes."

"Well, I studied the system and decided what the weaknesses might be. Then I turned my attention to the staff, to see who seemed to be in the best position to . . . exploit weakness. To fiddle, if you like. Put the two together and . . ." Webb gestured how easy it had been then.

"That's precisely what Spencer said." Harrington got up abruptly, leaving Webb still sitting, puzzled.

"It got a bit rough, I hear," Harrington said. "Spencer had his eye blacked in the scrum, he told me."

"The techinical phrase is 'resisting arrest.' " Webb smiled and rose, taking his briefcase.

"We're more civilised here. At least, one would like to think so." Harrington stood hesitantly, his hand on the door handle. "Spencer also said . . . I really don't know what you'll think. But his opinion was. . ." He broke off, his eyes on Webb.

"If I'm going to work for you, Mr. Harrington . . . ?"

"He ventured the opinion that you were successful there because you outsmarted the thieves."

"How else!"

"What I mean is, you thought exactly as they did. You were capable of thinking dishonestly, that's what he said to me."

"Did he, though!"

Harrington had not intended to anger Webb. It was quite clear that he had.

"Don't let it worry you, Mr. Webb," he said soothingly, opening the door. "It's not exactly a failing, is it? Not when one is in the business of chasing fraud, eh?"

Silently, Webb shook hands. The banker's was taut and bony, very cold.

"It's a gift," Harrington suggested. "Used properly."

Without further comment, Webb strode away down the broad, carpeted corridor. Hell, did he though!, he said to himself. He waited for a lift, remembering a comment he had made to Kennedy only a day or so previously. "How do I get their man Harrington to trust me?" he had said. And it turned out not to be like that at all! It had never occurred to Webb that a com-

51

pany wanting an audit might be searching not for a consultant they trusted but for one they did not. It was almost funny.

The lift doors slid open, then closed behind him. Thinking dishonestly . . . was that really what Spencer had said? What he believed? It disturbed Webb greatly, and he was not thinking of the Waterman's contract.

"He didn't even offer me coffee," Webb realised as he stood outside on the *piazza*. He turned up his coat collar against a chill breeze. Immediately across the street he saw a small sandwich bar and he went there, taking a stool in the window. Opposite, the Waterman Building soared in dark grey metal and matching tinted solar glass, wearing its outer skin like a sober City suit. He ordered coffee and it came instantly, tasting instant, but it was hot and that was what he wanted. He wondered whether any of the others had been given coffee? A little thing like that could matter, could be very revealing.

A taxi drew up on the other side of the street and a girl got out, standing for an instant as if unsure where to go. Then she was walking across the marble paving, past the fountains towards the great glass doors with their engraved admiral's barges. Webb watched her thoughtfully.

"So I'm last in the queue, am I?" he murmured. "How very interesting."

He raised cupped hands over his eyes and tracked her, like a hunter stalking prey. It cheered him up considerably.

Half an hour later he was back at Fitzroy Square. He went straight down to the basement, to the small computer terminal room. It was one of the few places in the building where he could be alone and unobserved. He locked the door and switched on the teletype, then dialled a number on the telephone. A distant computer answered with a familiar howl in his ear and he hit the DATA button on the receiver.

"KESTREL RECORDS," the terminal said, "CODE PLEASE."

Webb replied by keying in a series of digits.

"VALID," the terminal confirmed, "WHAT FUNCTION?"

Webb asked for "SNATCH." The program name had been Harvey's idea. Sometimes Webb found himself thinking what an odd sense of humour the man had. Not now.

"ACTION?" the teletype asked.

Webb hesitated. "This hurts me more than it does you," he said grimly, then forced himself to type, "ERASE."

It was an order for suicide. The SNATCH program obeyed by wiping itself out immediately.

"WHAT FUNCTION?" the terminal printed again, and Webb knew for certain that all trace of their illicit program had gone. He began to breathe more easily.

"END," he told the computer.

"BYE," it said, signing off.

What a pity, Webb thought. It had been nice while it lasted. They hadn't made a great deal, and it had been more trouble than London Alliance. Disposing of the records had been tedious. But it had been a profitable nibble, all the same. He had better call Harvey soon to tell him what he had done.

Chapter Four

Jake Kennedy walked past the Bank of England, a battered briefcase in one hand and an A-to-Z Guide To London in the other. He found the Yard he wanted hiding behind an unobtrusive arched entrance off Lothbury. The offices of L.N. Levene spanned the far end of the short street. The modern building looked out of place, with its marble cladding and huge windows sandwiched between old, cramped offices that had presumably once been private houses, built for prosperous merchants. Kennedy could not imagine why anyone had ever chosen to live there. He disliked the City, regarding it as too full of the wrong sort of people by day, too dead at night.

The Levene Building appeared quite small from the

outside, but when he entered he found it surprisingly spacious. Marble and leather were everywhere. There was an aura of money about the place, comforting but not comfortable. He remembered how the acrid tang of the factory drifted across the car park to his father's office. In a merchant bank the smell of their trade hit you just as surely, unmistakable as you came through the doors.

A uniformed porter sat, bored, at a slab cantilevered from a thick column. Kennedy asked for Paul Issacs and was motioned to a chair of hide and stainless steel. His clothes drew disapproving glances as he waited. He was used to it. He was in the tight blue jeans and leather jacket he wore always, wherever he went. It was rumoured by his close friends that he owned a single tie, a museum piece kept in some forgotten drawer. If so, only he had ever seen it. Whatever the weather, his shirt collar was open, with a gold token hanging just where there began the hint of tough blond curls.

Isaacs arrived, shaking hands solemnly before leading the way up the stairs.

"You don't change, Jake," he said. "It'll set my career back two years just to be seen with you." He gave the impression he was only partly joking. "You should jazz yourself up. My studies show a return of at least ten extra quid in salary for every one spent on clothes."

Obviously he kept his own counsel. Kennedy had never seen him so immaculate, dressed like a successful banker but with a face and figure that gave the game away.

"It's a good yield," he added persistently.

"I'm happy as I am, thanks."

"There's no such thing as an old programmer, so I hear," his friend proclaimed, shaking his head sorrowfully.

"When it's time. Not before."

On an upper floor they came to a big room, more like a palatial sitting room than an office, and Isaacs settled into a great leather chair.

"Jesus!" Kennedy said in awe.

"Not in this building, if you don't mind," Isaacs said

54

with a grin. "Try Holy Moses." He peered from the chair like an owl in an oversized egg.

Kennedy perched deferentially on the edge of a long and deep settee. On the facing wall there was a large canvas, expensively free of color or texture or content.

"Amazing," he declared, his head swivelling as he took it all in.

"Much as I'd like you to believe otherwise this isn't my office." Isaac's voice was tinged with regret. "Louis Levene calls this the Parlour. It's our meeting room for top clients."

"Still," Kennedy said, "if you judge people by the rooms they're let loose in . . ."

"I have a quarter of a tiny office upstairs and I'm worked mercilessly, learning how to assess what we call situations." Isaacs helped himself to a cigar from a sliver box. "Don't ever believe that we're idle in this part of the world."

Kennedy declined the cigar proffered as an afterthought.

"On the other hand," Isaacs could not resist adding, "I get twice what Shell used to pay me as a trainee economist. Can't be bad."

"Lucky man!"

Isaacs laughed. "It's never luck. I knew very well what I was doing when I married my father-in-law. He's a close buddy of Louis Levene."

It was an edgy laugh. Kennedy could see now, of course, that he did not fit the room. Observed closely, he was far from at ease, almost nervous, in fact. He sat in the chair, touched it, with all the unfamiliarity of a customer in a furniture shop.

Isaacs handed over a beautifully bound report, his manner changing, becoming more formal. "This is for you, Jake, what you told me you wanted. It would be great to chat but I can't stay long. We've got a bit of a flap on."

Kennedy was flicking through the report, scanning the chapter headings and the many charts and tables in disbelief.

"A lot of work has gone into that," Isaacs told him, happy with the reaction. "There's all you could possibly want to know about Waterman's. Nothing really secret but some stuff I don't think you'd be likely to pick up anywhere else. We use our patent ETG method."

"Your what?"

"Ear to the Ground."

"*You* did all this, Paul?" Kennedy asked incredulously.

"I . . . wouldn't say all," Isaacs replied evasively. He sneaked a look at his watch, then glanced expectantly towards the door.

"I just don't know what to say." Kennedy sank deep into the settee, scratching thick, curled hair. "I expected a talk, nothing more. Nothing like this."

Isaacs gestured dismissively. "Just tell me why you're so interested in Waterman's. That's all I want in return."

"I can't, really."

"Quid pro quo, Jake. It's only fair. The work that went into that document . . ."

"I'm sorry." Kennedy's expression was agonised.

"So am I. No trade, no deal." His friend reached over and retrieved the report.

"You wouldn't be interested," Kennedy said hurriedly. "It's just some computer job, that's all."

"Pull the other one!"

"There's no high finance or anything like that, honestly," Kennedy said in a last-ditch defence.

Isaac's gave a triumphant smile. "Which is why you phone me up all hot for full financial details and the latest City gossip, I suppose?"

Kennedy could think of no reply. He sighed, then fell silent for a full minute. Isaacs sat opposite, drawing on his cigar, his fingers drumming pointedly on the report, his eyes straying at times to the door.

"All right, then," Kennedy conceded, and he explained about the audit and what Webb had asked him to do. "It's not my scene, Paul. That's why I called."

Isaacs was trying to comprehend. "I know what an ordinary financial audit is, but what the hell is a computer audit?"

"Just an investigation, really."

"Why, Jake? What's wrong?" Eagerly, the young

56

banker sat forward. "Is something wrong with BANK-NET?"

"We don't know. Perhaps nothing, perhaps fraud. That's the whole idea of the audit, presumably. To find out."

"Fraud would be absolutely sensational!" Isaacs was thrilled at the thought. "Imagine, a computer rip-off at Waterman's, of all places!"

"Do keep it to yourself," Kennedy pleaded anxiously. "Please."

"But of course, Jake. Trust me."

"Just bloody do. Quid pro quo."

"Sure, my word is my bond and all that." Isaacs flipped the report back, to land on the settee.

Kennedy had scarcely opened it for a second examination when the door opened. A man in his early thirties entered, even more impeccably dressed than Isaacs. His height added emphasis to the elegant appearance; he was well over six feet tall. He stood for a moment in the doorway, assessing Kennedy through heavy-framed glasses.

Isaacs jumped up to make the introductions. "Jake Kennedy, Clive Greengross."

"Clive," he explained, "is our resident expert on Waterman's. That report is mainly his doing." He took a corner of the settee, leaving the big Italian chair free for the newcomer.

Hell, Kennedy said to himself, regretting having come, having ever telephoned. He felt suddenly shabby, almost disreputable under the steady gaze. It was an unaccustomed experience.

Greengross turned his attention to the room, ending with a questioning look at Isaacs. Then he shook Kennedy's hand with an unusually firm grip, keeping the palm extended when he finally let go, a gold bracelet peeping from under the cuff.

"Your brief from Waterman's? Have you got it with you, Mr. Kennedy?" Saying the "Mr." seemed to amuse him.

"It's only a short letter . . ."

The hand remained where it was.

"Yes, I have it," Kennedy told him reluctantly.

"I'd like to see it." It was almost an order.

Kennedy produced the letter, and Greengross read it rapidly. It obviously pleased him.

"Cautious buggers, as ever," he remarked. "Is it okay if I have a copy made? It'll be done in no time."

"That's my own copy. I suppose you can hang onto it."

"You realise what this audit means, I presume? How enormously significant it could be?"

"Not really," Kennedy confessed.

"Nor me, I'm afraid," Isaacs said.

Greengross took the big chair, choosing not to elaborate.

"I can give your friend no more than ten minutes, Paul. I'm due at a client's." He turned to Kennedy. "How much do you know about banking?"

"Zilch."

"But you do at least know that Waterman's is *the* bank of the moment? You must have read that? The papers are full of it."

"The business sections, you mean?"

"Sure."

"Never look at them."

Isaacs contemplated Kennedy sadly. "As I said, Jake, you don't change."

Greengross polished his glasses as he considered what to say. Then he began. "Let me give you two fundamentals. First, you've been approached by the Rolls-Royce of British clearing banks. Not the biggest, but widely regarded as the best in a number of important respects. Second, banking itself is at an interesting point right now, and that places Waterman's at something of a cross-roads. I see them as in a position to become much bigger, perhaps change direction in some way—offer an entirely new type of banking service, for they want to be in the future, and it won't be easy. In short, Waterman's have to decide what kind of outfit they want to be in the future, and it won't be easy. In the meantime, it's keeping us thoroughly on the edge of our seats."

"Can I stop you a minute?" Kennedy asked. "I was told to find out how big they are in relation to the other banks, and I still don't know."

"Big?" Greengross waved a hand in the air. "Comparative size is not something I normally bother about. It doesn't tell you nearly as much about a company as you might think. But if you want a simple measure, the Midland Bank has the largest number of branches, with National Westminister a close second. Both have around thirty-five hundred in the U.K. Waterman's are way behind with only twelve hundred and sixty. The profit picture is far more interesting, I think. I've given the recent figures in a table near the beginning of that report. I suggest you look at that first." He stretched out a hand. "Can I have it a second?"

Kennedy passed it over, and Greengross checked a page of numbers.

"Next year's profits are still here," he said sharply to Isaacs.

"*Next* year's . . .?" Kennedy echoed.

"I should have warned you, Jake," Isaacs said, reddening. "Play everything in there very close to your chest. Those profit projections are our confidental estimates. They're worth real money, and I bloody mean it."

But Greengross carefully folded the page and tore out the final column of figures.

"What a shame," Kennedy remarked as the slip of paper was crumpled into a pocket. "I'd love to have inside City information."

Greengross then ripped out several complete pages. "Some of my conclusions, and I'd rather you didn't see them either." He smiled at Kennedy's reaction. "Look here, all you really need to know for your purposes is this. In the last financial year Waterman's pretax profit went over the hundred Meg mark for the first time. Proportionate to the scale of their operations that's absolutely staggering."

"Meg?"

"Million pounds," Isaacs explained.

"You'll also find that back in 1974 they actually made a higher profit than Lloyd's and Lloyd's have twice as many branches as our friends in Leadenhall Street." Greengross spoke softly, with respect.

"Sounds impressive," Kennedy commented.

"Too damned right it is. Particularly since '74 was such a god-awful year for banking as a whole. That's why I have given it such extensive analysis in there. In boom times everyone does well, yes? In fact, I define the ultimate boom as a time without a single bankruptcy. But the acid test of management ability and staying power is the performance during economically rough periods. And in '74 Waterman's showed what they were made of. Most of the other banks found the going a good deal harder."

"Currency problems, wasn't it?" Isaacs said. "Jake and I were still up at Cambridge then."

"Correct. Exchange rates went wild in the backwash of the oil crisis. As you probably know, Mr. Kennedy, banks are constantly buying and selling currency forward. Get the sums wrong because the fluctuations have gone way beyond what you've forecast and you can lose a packet. In '74 plenty of banks did! In West Germany, the Herstätt Bank was completely wiped out. In Lugano, a very junior employee lost Lloyd's International thirty-three Meg in uncontrolled currency dealings."

"I understood that was fraud," Isaacs remarked.

"No, just an excess of zeal."

"I find it hard to imagine that many million quid's worth of zeal," Kennedy said.

Greengross flashed a very white smile. "Nor me. In complete contrast, Waterman's kept an iron grip on their foreign exchange departments. They were probably the first bank in Europe to fully computerise all currency handling. That guarantees, so they claim, that their junior employees are safely kept doing the donkey work. I believe them."

"Pity, really," Kennedy mused.

"Isn't it, just," Isaacs agreed. "Why should the executives have all the fun of losing money!"

Greengross displayed gold as he checked the time. "A quick word on the computers, perhaps. Then I really must push off."

"No need," Kennedy told him. "I was ordered to stay off that subject. Just the money side, I was told."

"You're joking!"

"No." Kennedy was taken aback by the other man's reaction.

"Well, in that case you were badly briefed. Shall I prove it?"

The programmer shrugged. "You're the expert."

"You see, with Waterman's it's impossible to separate what you call the money side from the computers." Greengross tossed the report back, accurately hitting Kennedy's lap. "David Clement is their director responsible for computing. Appendix One is the transcript of a speech he gave last spring. Big occasion, Mr. Kennedy. An impressive array of international bankers, the best silver out at the Guildhall, full evening dress with decorations . . . the lot."

"I have it," Kennedy said after some frantic page turning.

"I'll paraphrase, shall I? Clement claims that his computers—he always calls them *his*, by the way—go far beyond the conventional support role. They underpin the entire forward strategy of the bank. At one point he actually refers to Waterman's as the Electronic Bank. It wasn't always that way, for obvious reasons. Waterman's was established way back in the eighteenth century and that was a little premature, as Clement points out, for the computer revolution! I sense he genuinely regrets that because he remarks that the bank therefore had no alternative but to mark time as a small family concern until the invention of the punched card. Loud guffaws all round, I imagine."

"A funny man, eh?" Isaacs said.

"Good after-dinner stuff, Paul. Actually, Louis Levene tells me the jokes are all he bothers to listen to on such occasions. They're usually the secret truth managing to escape in disguise, so he says."

"It's a thought," Isaacs agreed seriously, filing it away for future use.

"Anyway, from the dawn of the computer age, Waterman's have been eager buyers, always latching on to the latest developments. As you'd expect, they make good use of all the equipment they've bought. Customer accounts, foreign exchange, the KEYNOTE credit card service . . . you name it, it's all on the computer. But you're missing the point if you think that's what BANKNET is really there for. It's actually a lever, to crank up the share price. At least, that's my personal theory. The amazing thing is, it appears to work."

"I don't follow," Kennedy confessed.

Greengross studied him for what seemed an age. His spectacle lenses were thick, making his eyes look very large.

"1974," he said. "That's why I regard it as so important, a turning point. While Lloyd's were losing all those millions in Switzerland, Waterman's were raking in more money than ever before from currency dealings. And while National Westminister were writing off over forty Meg against losses on property loans in this country, Waterman's were doing very nicely financing construction projects in France and Belgium. So they emerged from a very messy period with greatly enhanced reputation. The investment managers love them, which is why their share price is so high, relatively speaking."

He rose, carefully straightening his chalk-striped jacket.

"A lot of City people attribute a great deal of the Waterman's magic to BANKNET. Computers as a direct investment are considered lousy in this country—you probably know. But as an electronic prop in a show of financial wizardry, they're terrific. That's why I insist that BANKNET isn't really there primarily to do the accounting."

He was edging towards the door.

"The rumours," Isaac called out. "You ought to mention them."

"Rumours?" Kennedy said. He got up to show his interest.

"We get them all the time," Greengross remarked in a matter-of-fact way. "Right now there are stories in the air of a possible takeover of Waterman's by one of the big three clearing banks. At a pinch, it could almost be the other way round, with Waterman's gobbling up a bigger brother. They nearly have the share leverage to do it. And that would be cheeky, very cheeky indeed."

He was moving away with an air of finality. "I really must split." He waved the letter from the bank. "Thanks again for this. It's certainly food for thought."

"One more thing," Kennedy said, following doggedly. "You never explained why the audit is so significant."

"*Could* be, I said." Greengross shook hands, gripping even more firmly than before. He put his face close to Kennedy's, speaking confidentially. He had obviously lunched well. The programmer could smell the brandy.

"If you chaps find something wrong with BANK-NET and if word gets out, you could cause Waterman's one almighty headache. Dent the computing image a fraction and I'll give you a hundred to one you'll hit the share price pretty badly for a while. Reputation is a fragile asset at the best of times. And right now . . ." His hand crushed an imaginary egg.

"Does it matter that much?" Kennedy queried.

"It could make the difference between gobbling and being gobbled." Now the hand snapped hungrily at the air.

"Ah," Kennedy said with a wise nod.

Greengross had turned in the doorway to look askance at Isaacs.

"Is that one of Louis' Monte Cristos, by any chance?"

Isaacs examined the cigar as if he could not remember.

"Mine, actually."

"Liar," Greengross told him, then left.

"He really is bloody switched on, isn't he?" Isaacs enthused. "Absolutely shit-hot."

Kennedy endorsed the opinion.

"I must go too, Jake. I hope it's been useful?"

"Very." The report was clutched appreciatively.

Isaacs went to the door, looked both ways, then scuttled across to the top of the wide staircase. Kennedy had to smile as he realised why.

"We weren't supposed to be in there, were we?" he said, catching up.

His friend looked shamefaced. "Can you find your own way out?"

"Easily, and I'm very grateful for your help, Paul."

"Think nothing of it. Mutual benefit and all that. I'm sure Clive will be able to read between the lines and work out what your audit is likely to mean. It could do me a lot of good."

"I didn't want to say so in front of your Mr. Green-

63

gross, but you had promised to keep it to yourself!" The rebuke was made as mild as possible.

"Don't worry so, Jake. We've been watching Waterman's long before you called me. It's a live situation. Clive has been researching them for months. He expects something to break at any time and wants to be ready. Some of the big investors may well need the benefit of our expensive advice."

"Hold on!" Kennedy stood awkwardly, one foot on a lower stair, a hand frozen inches above the bannister. "You said that report was prepared specially for me!"

"I never did! And I had a devil of a job persuading Clive it would be worthwhile giving you one."

Kennedy was showing signs of anger, more at himself than at the other man. He should have seen it before. All that tearing out of pages!

"You've got a copy, why should you care how?" Isaacs said coldly.

Kennedy was speechless.

"If anything does crawl out of the woodwork at Waterman's, you will let me know? Quid pro quo and all that."

"You bastard!"

"Survival, Jake," Isaacs said. "That's what the game is, survival."

Chapter Five

Susan Faulkner placed a small leather pouch on Webb's desk and waited to see his reaction.

"Was it expensive?" he asked, weighing it in his hand and finding it surprisingly heavy. "It feels it."

"The man in the shop said no, considering what you get."

Webb was unzipping the case.

". . . But I call a hundred and ten pounds outrageously expensive, don't you?"

"Christ!" Webb was shocked. "That'll make my sales expenses look sick this month."

A pair of miniature Zeiss binoculars lay in his hand,

64

no bigger than opera glasses and with the barrels folded together to bring them down to pocket size. He felt the weight again before opening them out.

"Eight by twenty," he read. "Sounds about right. And so small, Sue, so wonderfully unobtrusive."

He trained the glasses across the square, noting the precise balance and enjoying the slight resistance of the focussing action, still tight from the factory. The image was crisp and brilliant, seemingly more three-dimensional than the real thing.

"Superb," he said in judgement, forgetting the cost. Lovingly, he folded them and returned them to the case.

"You'd better get Jake down here. He must be dying to be told how clever he's been." The leather pouch was slipped out of sight into a drawer.

"You're like a man with a new toy," Susan said, making no sign of leaving.

"A rather special toy," he agreed. "How did I ever get this far in my career without such an essential piece of equipment?" It was said in a way intended to tease.

"You still haven't told me what they're for," Susan said crossly. She leaned across the desk. "Spying or something?"

Webb made a play of being offended. "Goodness me, no." Then, beaming, he said, "The polite term is market research."

Susan had learned long ago not to ask for explanations of Webb's private jokes.

Webb closed the Waterman's report and looked long and steadily at Kennedy, giving no clue to what he thought of it.

"My tutor was one of the laziest men at Oxford," he said obliquely. "He was also one of the most successful. Would you like to hear his theory on the purpose of university education?"

Kennedy was taken aback but said, "I suppose so," in an unenthusiastic voice.

"The idea, according to him, is not to teach you how to think. It is to train you in ways of finding the existing information that saves you *having* to think."

65

"True of Cambridge, too, probably," said Kennedy, who had not always enjoyed it there.

Webb patted the report affectionately. "This tells me you got a good degree, Jake."

"A First, as a matter of fact." Kennedy began to smile as he grasped Webb's point.

"See what I mean," Webb said, allowing a laugh at last. "This is bloody brilliant. Far better than I ever dared hope."

"Twenty-two-year-old bankers do occasionally have their uses," Kennedy pointed out, modestly.

"I take it all back." Webb regarded the programmer with genuine admiration. "I want you at that presentation, Jake. No doubt about it."

"I'd like that very much."

"I'll feel so much safer with a financial expert on hand!" Webb gave another laugh.

"Are we in good shape, would you say, Chris?"

"Far from it." Webb's mood changed abruptly. "You're done your bit. Mine was to find out about the BANKNET security procedures. So far, all I've established is that they work extremely well at keeping me away! Harrington does a convincing imitation of a mute clam, and everything else I've tried has drawn a complete blank." The telephone rang and he chose to ignore it. "The presentation doesn't bother me at all. I can see how we should handle that. But we still don't have the beginnings of the proposal I wanted, and time moves on." The telephone rang again.

"I'm off the job as of today," Kennedy reminded him.

"True," Webb said with obvious regret. He finally picked up the receiver in response to frantic hand signals from Susan.

"It's Adrian Ross," she said. "Do I go on trying to persuade him you're not in the office?"

"Hell no," he snapped. "Talk of the devil," he said to Kennedy. "Stick around."

"Your girl can be hard to get past," Ross complained.

"I'd given you up, Adrian."

"Really?" The headhunter sounded disappointed at

the welcome. "And there I am beavering away on your behalf, Christopher. I've found a damned good man for you, you'll be pleased to hear."

"From Waterman's?"

"Naturally. That's what you wanted, isn't it?"

"I bet you walk on water, too," Webb said, impressed.

"I could probably learn—for a suitable fee."

"Senior, is he?"

"He's their top systems man in Manchester. The name is Stephen Elliott."

"*Where* did you say he was from?"

"The Manchester Data Centre. MDC, to the initiated."

Webb covered the mouthpiece with a hand and raised a triumphant thumb at Kennedy. "So much for first-line security, Jake."

"He's definitely got itchy feet," Ross went on. "They'll need a bit of greasing, though. Waterman's pay him seven and a half. You'll probably have to go up to nine to lure him to London."

"When can I meet him?"

"He could be in town this Friday, if that suits you."

"Friday. That was his suggestion, was it?"

"Yes . . .?"

"I see," Webb said with a sigh Ross was intended to hear. "Married, I suppose?"

"Yes. Three kids."

"And he wants a weekend away from home at my expense, Adrian?"

"That's his business, don't you think," the heathunter replied frostily. He dictated a telephone number. "He's expecting you to call and confirm. But with discretion if you don't mind, Christopher. That's his work number, the Data Centre."

"I'll do it straightaway," Webb promised. "Do I call him Stephen or Steve?"

"Stephen, I'm afraid."

"I don't much like the sound of that. Is he pompous?"

"Just a little. I was about to warn you. But nothing to worry about."

"Is there anything else you ought to tell me, Adrian?"

"No. You'll get on fine, I guarantee it."

"Well, well," Webb said happily when he put the telephone down. "We may even make it yet, Jake. That could be quite a proposal we send to Harrington and his chums. All their secrets mysteriously laid bare."

"I'm not very practiced at following half-conversations," Kennedy stated sourly. "Do I deduce that you're planning to hire a man from Waterman's?"

"Not quite, but close."

"Isn't that rather farfetched for a single contract?"

"Definitely." There was a glint in Webb's eye. "And if we poached one of their men right now, it would infuriate the bank, almost certainly sink us without trace. That's why I'm not actually hiring. Just interviewing."

"I see." Kennedy clearly did not.

"People talk very freely at interviews," Webb explained. "Prod them a bit and it's better than a psychiatrist's couch. They come straight out with all the things their employer is doing wrong and that they think they could put right, given half a chance. I mean, they have to say that to impress you, to get the job."

"But there isn't a job," Kennedy said. "It's hardly fair."

"Oh, do grow up, Jake. It's not exactly one-way exploitation. He'll probably stay overnight with a girlfriend and charge us for a hotel."

"It's still a lousy trick."

"And that, I've no doubt, is what Ross will say when I turn his man down," Webb declared with a grin.

Chapter Six

It was a chill, overcast Monday. The City, forced back to life after the quiet of the weekend, resisted, stirring reluctantly. Nothing moved quickly. The office lights took on prematurely the pale yellow normally reserved for evenings in late winter. Where Webb was there were no trees.

He went early to the sandwich bar in Leadenhall Street, drinking coffee in the window where he had sat before. The traffic inched by, lapping the kerb in slow waves that built to a flood at 9:00 and 9:30, then thinned. Across the road occasional cars and taxis dropped passengers at the Waterman Building. Webb watched with only desultory interest because it was still too soon. He was purposely well ahead of time, being cautious.

The cafe was quiet. The few customers wore identically grey raincoats from Burberry or Dunn's and ate hurriedly standing up, with eyes that said they had overslept. Webb thought it was how a Soho magazine shop must be out of view of the street. The same coats, the same furtive men lacking enjoyment, just satisfying a need. He bit on a doughnut and gave up, dropping it back onto the plate.

"What's it like to be old and unloved?" he asked it, just loud enough for the proprietor to hear. The man was behind the counter, part-shielded by a long glass case with the shelves still bare. He rolled up his sleeves and prepared to cut sandwiches, then came to the door wiping clean hands on his apron from habit, sniffing the air.

"How does it look?" Webb asked, turning.

"Cheese," the man decided. "It'll be more cheese than anything else today. It always is when it's nippy like this."

"And mustard on everything else?"

"You've got it," the man said with grudging respect.

"I'd like to stay awhile, if that's all right?"

The man looked curiously from Webb to the doughnut, then back. Webb beckoned him closer.

"My wife works over there with the bank. Some bastard's up her, I'm sure of it."

The man began to back away, his eyes narrowed, wondering.

"I want to catch them together."

"Look, Mister . . ."

"I think I can." Webb placed the binoculars on the

69

counter spanning the window, where the man could see. "Do you mind?"

A slow, knowing smile appeared.

"If it's her boss . . ." Webb said with restrained malice. He held out a folded five-pound note. Instantly, the smile was gone.

"D'you drink much of that?" the proprietor asked, gesturing at the empty cup.

"Gallons."

"That'll cover it, then." The money was pushed away and the man returned to his sandwich-making.

"What'll you do about it?" he queried after a time.

Webb had the binoculars trained on the *piazza*, his hands around them to conceal them from passers-by. He was thinking of Alison. It made it easy, sitting there, his mind on her. It was less of an act, then.

"Knock the hell out of her," he replied.

"That's the way!" The man sliced a tomato and it bled over limp lettuce.

At 9:55 a cab drew up and four men emerged, one carrying a long black tube with folded metal feet. Webb was instantly alert.

"You surely won't need a projection screen," he said to himself. "They'll have thought of that."

He focussed on a short, stocky man in his early forties, getting a good view of the face before he turned away. It was very pink, sharp at the edges against a blur of water from the fountains.

"Marriott!"

The men moved to the building and were soon through the doors and out of sight. Webb signalled the proprietor.

"Do you accept standing orders?"

"How d' you mean?"

"Coffee at twenty-minute intervals until further notice, huh?"

"If you like."

The morning passed slowly. Too slowly. Once, a tall City policeman stood outside the bank headquarters surveying the passing cars and apparently willing them to park where they shouldn't. Webb watched him through the glasses, taking in the details of the great silver helmet badge, noting the straggles of hair behind an ear, residual traces of acne on the cheeks. It felt oddly daring.

Shortly after 12:00 the four men reappeared from the building. They stopped in a huddle on the pavement and the youngest was despatched in the direction of the Mansion House, presumably to find a taxi. Webb swung the glasses onto Marriott, studying his expressions and gestures as he waited impatiently. Soon all talking stopped and the men just stood in a line by the kerb.

"You don't think you're going to win," Webb decided with delight. He stayed for some minutes after the consultants had gone, then carefully folded the binoculars away. The sandwich bar was beginning to fill.

"How much do I owe you?" he asked, rising.

"No luck, then?"

Webb shook his head.

"Coffee okay, was it?"

"I'm developing an immunity," Webb said under his breath.

"It's you, then," the man declared the next morning.

"I'm the determined type," Webb replied, taking the same seat. The place was empty. Perhaps fewer people overslept on Tuesdays.

"Standing order again?" The proprietor was greatly amused.

"Twenty minutes," Webb confirmed. "I don't suppose you could double the dose of Nescafé, though? Flavour the water a bit?"

The man was not sure whether to be annoyed. "It'll cost more."

"Let's live a little," Webb said.

Just before 10:00 a chauffeur-driven Volvo dropped three men outside the Waterman Building. Webb held one of them in closeup, knowing the face but unable at first to put a name to it.

"Ted Gardiner. DSL," he remembered with relief when the men had gone. They had met briefly once at

71

a conference. Gardiner had invited him for a game of golf, instantly losing interest when he learned that Webb did not play.

Webb crouched over the counter. He read his newspaper from cover to cover, then took to watching the street. There was an endless sameness about the passing traffic and businessmen, a sense of constant repetition, like a loop of film played over and over. Alone in the window, as unnoticed as if the glass were opaque, he felt memories stir, of the kind that only a mind emptied by utter boredom can rediscover.

The dark Volvo purred back into view, halting by the kerb just before noon. The men from DSL were out of the building only minutes later. There was a fourth man with them this time, tall and expensively dressed, carrying himself with upright self-assurance. Quickly, Webb had the binoculars on the group to assess their expressions. There was something about the image—the unreal clarity, the way it took him unobserved right up to stare into faces—that banished boredom. It was suddenly all worthwhile.

The newcomer shook hands warmly with Gardiner, holding on as he spoke, then patting his back for good measure.

"Whoever you are," Webb thought, "DSL has just shot into the lead." It did not please him in the least. He had intended to come each morning that week, but it no longer seemed necessary. Anyone but DSL!

He waited until the car left the kerb, then began to scrutinise the figures crossing the *piazza*. A girl walked through the doors with a man at least twice her age. A secretary, he thought, off to an early lunch with her boss, perhaps innocently, more probably not.

"That's her!" he told the man behind the counter, getting up quickly. He dropped some change beside the till.

The man moved to get a better view, squinting with avid interest through the window. The girl was very attractive, walking with long, elegant strides. She placed a hand lightly on her companion's arm, swiftly removing it when she realised it was there.

"I'd bloody thump the both of them," the proprietor

72

exclaimed. He was still bristling with proxy anger when Webb left.

"Was it worth it?" Susan asked.

"I think so," Webb replied, not wishing to elaborate. But she took the chair by his desk and he saw a familiar, determined expression.

"DSL think they will win," he said, giving in. "They have at least one of the Waterman's directors thinking so, too."

"Can you be sure?"

"No, but it's my only clue to how things are likely to go."

"And?"

"They are what I call formidable competition. If I try to meet them head on I don't stand an earthly. Somehow, I have to outflank them."

"I spent days typing that proposal, Chris. Great fat thing. Wasn't that supposed to swing it for you?"

Webb gave a resigned shrug. "It's not enough, Sue. Security is one of DSL's specialisations. Not just the computer side but guard procedures, hidden CCTV, time locks and all the rest—the whole paraphernalia of physical security. I know damnall about that. Until today I'd hoped they would screw it up somehow. Now I have to find a way to persuade Waterman's that none of the physical security bit matters as far as this audit is concerned. It won't be easy. I have to frighten them . . . just a little and very, very carefully."

"Saying boo to a big bank?" She sounded unconvinced.

"If it had been Marriott's things would have been different," Webb added regretfully.

"What was it like, Chris?" She crossed her legs and her pencil tapped perfect teeth. "In the middle of the City, in broad daylight . . . spying on a bank like that?"

"Surveillance," Webb insisted with a smile. "That's what DSL would call it."

"Whatever. I couldn't do it." Her manner said she wanted to know more.

"My background is working class," Webb said.

73

"So you've told me." Instantly, her accent was sub-consciously crisper, he noticed.

"Not any old working class. A rather special kind that you used to find in isolated pockets around the middle of London. Genteel, industrious, law-abiding. People aren't like that any more."

"Slander!" she said, laughing.

Gravely he shook his head. "A different kind of genteel and law-abiding, Sue. The aftermath of the servant class, extinct now, I suppose. They all either went up like me, or down."

"Clever you!"

"Now people try to hide, not wanting to know or be known. But then . . ." His hands fluttered reminiscence. "Their hobby was watching one another, it was all there was to do. And they were bloody good at it! They used the observation techniques you only find now in small villages. It's ingrained in me, I guess."

"I think you enjoyed it today," Susan suggested, part reproachful, part envious. "A brand new toy, watching people come and go."

"To be honest, I haven't felt like that since I was . . . thirteen," Webb admitted. "A strange kind of excitement, alternating with total boredom. The kind of boredom you only feel as a child." For a moment his eyes closed as he remembered. "We used to watch the ghastly family across the street while they watched us back. We lost out, I reckon. We were far more interesting than they were."

When she realised he was not going to continue, Susan leaned forward, speaking very low. "I'm still a fan of yours, Chris." Then, after a considered pause, "I'd love a lift home tonight."

He took an age to decide.

"All right."

Her legs seemed suddenly very long, that was what made his mind up.

"I'll get you some coffee," she said, preparing to go. "To bring you back to the present."

"God, no," he said. "I couldn't."

74

Chapter Seven

Monday, 6th December.

"Leadenhall Street," Webb told the cab driver.

They moved out of Fitzroy Square. Kennedy was balanced awkwardly on a jump seat, his back to the partition and having to grip with both hands as they lurched round the corner.

"What are the slides?" he asked, nodding at the small plastic case Webb was carrying.

"Thirty-five mil."

"I know *that*!"

"You've heard of anti-matter? I call these anti-jargon. If that's what Harrington wants, that's what he'll get. Large quantities of it."

"I sneaked a look before we left," Shulton announced disdainfully after some time had elapsed. "Anti-contract, more like."

"God, you're quick today," Webb said. He skimmed through his notes for the presentation one more time, debugging the sentences yet again, playing over in his mind what he would do and making ready for the unexpected. Especially the unexpected. He closed his eyes, trying to predict what the bankers might say, what could go wrong. But it was impossible. He was too aware of the untidy swaying of the cab and the intrusive noises—the squeaks and rattles that London taxis always make as they move, the characteristic squeal of brakes as they stop. And they were constantly stopping.

"Exchange rates are doing funny things again," Kennedy said to break the silence. The other men stared. "I've been reading up," he explained. "Getting ready."

Webb was suddenly worried. "Say absolutely nothing unless I ask you to," he ordered. "Understand? You're here solely as ballast. Visible ballast."

He noticed Kennedy's clothes for the first time. The leather and denim were gone, replaced by a sober suit of magnificent cut. He leaned over to finger a lapel.

"Glad to see you take this so seriously, Jake."

"Great schmutter," Shulton endorsed, respectfully touching the other lapel.

"I was going to buy it anyway," Kennedy mumbled, feeling hemmed in. "I just did it five years sooner."

Webb began staring out of the window. Anything to stop the others seeing how nervous he was. The buildings drifted by, all looking the same. The people on the pavements moved briskly, their eyes open but turned off, steering by radar.

The meeting room was huge, in a commanding position on the twenty-third floor of the Waterman Building. They entered exactly at 10:00 A.M. Harrington introduced Waterman, Susskind and Clement, who sat in a group at one end of the big central table, each with a copy of the SysTech proposal prominently in front of him. In turn, Webb made his introductions, delighting Kennedy with a temporary promotion to "One of our senior technical people."

"So you're the consultant," Clement said, looking at Webb.

He was a man who had been outside the building the previous week and showed none of the friendliness evident then.

"That's right." Webb was unpacking his 35mm slides.

"You seem to know a great deal about us." Clement chose his words with care, managing to convey disapproval. He flicked the pages of the proposal, his eyes moving very deliberately to Harrington.

"Research," Webb answered evenly. "The thoroughness you'll see if I get the chance to work for you."

"Perhaps you'd confirm that you got none of that information from me?" Harrington requested, slightly flustered.

"Not a word," Webb replied, intrigued by the tension he sensed between the two men.

"Personally, I felt your submission demonstrated a certain amount of initiative," Harrington said. "But it's only fair to tell you that is not the general reaction around this table."

Before Webb could make further comment he pressed a button on an inset panel. The ceiling lights slowly brightened and the curtains were drawn silently together to hide the distracting view. The synchronisation was perfect, the intensity of light in the room barely changing.

"We'd like this to be as informal as possible," Harrington explained, his finger hovering over another button. "There's only one ground rule as such. This session will end no later than noon, whether you're through or not. We've done that with all the others."

Webb finished loading the slides into the Kodak Carousel projector that sat at his end of the table. He walked to the front of the room, carrying the hand control.

"It's your meeting, Mr. Webb." Harrington's finger came down and the room lights dimmed. A screen was powered down from the ceiling and the projector hummed into life, throwing a bright square of light into it.

"They certainly do things in style," Shulton whispered enviously to Kennedy. He was sitting to one side, with a poor, distorted view of the screen, but he was more interested in watching Webb's audience than the slides.

"I sometimes think of consultancy as a form of marriage," Webb said in opening. "The consultant must crawl all over his client, probing, exploring intimately. If there isn't the necessary compatibility between the two of them there's no chance of success. And if the consultant fails to perform there's no satisfaction."

"Are you here to woo us, Mr. Webb?" Susskind asked, equally tongue in cheek.

"I see it more as a shotgun wedding, actually," Webb replied. "I'd like to believe you have no alternative but to settle for me."

The bankers laughed. Webb touched the hand control and there was a gentle click from the projector. The familiar admiral's barge sailed onto the screen, seeming to come closer, as if out of a mist, as he sharpened the focus.

"Waterman's has been around for two hundred years." Webb waved a hand at the picture. "Mature and rich and wearing well, so I understand. A very desirable partner. By contrast, SysTech is only five.

Despite the intimidating age difference I believe we'd work out very well together. My intention today is to persuade you of that."

Susskind rubbed his chin. "Your analogy would suggest that Waterman's is long past performing and that you're too young to be able to yet!" His colleagues laughed again, more loudly this time.

"We mature early in the computer business," Webb declared. "I'm perfectly capable of performing when I'm required to. Very effectively, too, so my other clients tell me."

His suit was dark blue, lost in the dim light. His face, illuminated from the side by the screen, seemed suspended in the air. It was serious, with the mouth set in a determined line. He would look confident to the bankers. Shulton thought, almost agressive. You had to know Webb to see that he wasn't.

The barge was swept away. The new picture showed two men in a wood, one with a dog tugging at a leash, the other carrying a narrow, pointed shovel.

"Does anyone know what is happening here!" Webb asked.

"Guessing games . . .?" Harrington mused aloud.

"Two men and a dog!" Clement stated brusquely. "Now what?"

Waterman was altogether happier. "I suggest that they are likely to be searching for truffles." Despite the choice of words his manner proclaimed him to be certain. "I would guess your photo was taken in Perigord, but it might be Burgundy, at a pinch.

"Normandy, as a matter of fact," Webb told him, pleasantly surprised.

"Trust you to know, Meyer," Susskind said.

"I always understood they used pigs to sniff the things out." Clement was plainly ruffled at not having guessed.

"Most people think that," Waterman remarked. "But dogs can be every bit as good." He looked to Webb for an explanation.

"I'm like that," Webb said, touching his nose. "I can sniff out fraud. Wherever it is, I seem to be able to home in on it. I've done it before, as Mr. Harrington knows. I'll find every problem you have with BANK-NET, if you'll let me."

He stood, silently surveying the men at the other end of the room before continuing. "My dictionary defines an audit as an official scrutiny of accounts. I don't think that's anywhere near adequate as far as Waterman's is concerned. It's too passive, too much after the event. Let's be blunt. What we really ought to be talking about is *crime detection*."

"I know what you mean," one of the directors said. "But I hope not."

"I try to think ahead of the criminal," Webb stated, "to put myself in his shoes and imagine what he will do. So what I propose this morning is to plan a crime with you. To show you how easy BANKNET has made it."

The blank screen was filled again. Big black letters on a red background said, "How to Rob A Bank." The bankers obviously found it funny. Seconds later Webb changed slides again, to a grainy print of the Keystone Cops running from a clapboard Western bank, falling over themselves in disarray. Susskind and Waterman gave unconscious smiles of nostalgia.

"Please interrupt if you see any flaw in the scheme," Webb said. "I'd like us to be in this together. I suggest that we call ourselves the Leadenhall Street Mob, if that's all right with you?"

In quick succession he summoned up another slide—white letters on a black background framed with a scalloped line in the style of a silent movie subtitle. It said, "Or, The Perfect Crime."

"It has to be perfect," he ventured. "Nothing but the best for Waterman's. Are you game?"

The bankers nodded in concert, intrigued by the approach. They had just spent a week hearing serious, almost identical presentations, as Webb was well aware.

Now he's confident, Shulton decided.

"Let's start with fundamentals," Webb said. "What are we going to steal? I don't know about you but I would like this to be an extremely profitable enterprise."

The Carousel notched round and his new picture was of an impressive stack of gold bullion.

"This is an obvious first thought since it represents such a huge amount of money. Unfortunately, it's very heavy and tricky to transport. We can't get rid of it as it stands. If we did we would get a poor price and at the same time advertise to the entire criminal world that it was our Mob who carried out what was undoubtedly a well-publicised robbery. No thanks! Melt it down and we still have the same volume of gold and the same problem of disposal. So I vote against bullion.

"Currency notes, then? Well, since the Great Train Robbery the banks no longer move used money in large amounts. High-valued shipments are always of new paper, with the numbers carefully recorded. So what can we do? We might dribble the money out in small quantities and with a constant risk of detection, but I'd rather not. Or we could sell the haul for untraceable cash, but we'll be paid only a fraction of face value. That doesn't attract me at all."

"Can I suggest forgery, perhaps?" Waterman said, entering into the spirit of things.

"That's percisely what I had in mind," Webb replied approvingly. "But not in the way you might think."

He used his hand control again, sweeping the gold bullion aside to reveal an enlargement of a punched computer card.

"We are modern criminals, gentlemen, thinking modern in a technological world. We decide to steal *data*. It's not kept in a guarded vault. It's everywhere in a computerised bank—inside the machines, moving all the time down the communications links between the computer centres and the branches. Most of that data flow represents money, huge amounts of it. What is the daily cash flow at Waterman's, for example?"

"That's classified information!" Clement retorted.

"Besides, it varies," Harrington added.

"Order of magnitude will do," Webb said, undeterred.

Clement sighed. "It isn't giving much away to say that there are few days when it dips below fifty million in total. And it can go up to several hundred million."

Webb spread his hands wide. "Where else can we find shipments of that size every day of the week! So we'll take data, agreed? The bank itself will convert it for us into legal currency, all conveniently laundered so that the numbers on our notes are irrelevant. That appeals to me greatly, using the victim bank to fence the stolen goods for us."

"You said a moment ago that we were going in for forgery," Waterman pointed out.

Webb leaned against the screen and the image of the punched card undulated over his shoulder and sleeve.

"We don't have to steal actual cash, Mr. Waterman. Or perhaps I should say data representing actual cash. We can create our own. The number one thousand in the system says there is a thousand pounds in an account. Add a few noughts and we have a hundred thousand pounds there, in an instant. It's the ultimate forgery. No special papers or inks, just numbers in a computer."

"We'd get caught straightaway," Waterman interjected. "Indulging in a crude number juggling like that!"

Shulton caught a twinkle in his eye, as if at the thought of danger. Perhaps it was just the reflected light again.

"I don't doubt it," Webb answered. "So we'll use sophisticated number juggling instead. The point is this—we don't need to steal from a real account where the shortfall will be noticed. This is the perfect crime, remember? One of our prime objectives is that no one must ever know it has happened, even well after the event. I believe that to be possible . . . provided we select the right victim."

His new slide was a sepia print of a very old woman, shawled and in a rocking chair, her yellowed skin drawn tight over a bony frame.

"What could be better! Someone old and rich and nervous. Someone who won't put up much of a fight. An old lady who keeps her money under the mattress and so afraid of the neighbours thinking her stupid that she'll never report the crime." Webb glanced down the table, singling out one of the directors in particular. "I hope you recognise the description, Mr. Waterman? I'm talking about your bank." There was an edge to his voice.

The atmosphere changed instantly. Shulton saw the

stonefaced responses. Nought out of four on that, he decided.

"If you really believe we would do nothing . . ." Waterman said.

Webb confined himself to a questioning look. He came forward to sit on the table, one leg over the edge.

"Next, I'd like to select our equipment." He changed slides again, surprising the bankers with an apparently irrelevant picture of a large paperback textbook on computing.

"Personally, I'm against the use of firearms, and I'd suggest that the perfect crime should manage without them. I'm also unhappy about carrying anything that might cause suspicion were we to be stopped and searched inside the bank. So explosives, jemmies and all the usual electrical and mechanical gear are out. This is all we are likely to need."

He gestured at the screen. The book was titled, "IBM Systems Programming Manual."

"No self-respecting modern criminal should be without one," he told the bankers with a grin. "If ever they start giving rehabilitation classes in programming in Her Majesty's prisons I suggest you all run for cover. It's a very potent skill."

He sat properly on the table, making himself at ease.

"So far so good. We need only one thing more. We can't quite do the job ourselves. No disrespect, gentlemen, but we must have an accomplice, someone to provide the crucial criminal cunning we lack as a group."

He produced his next slide. There was a clump of eucalyptus trees against a clear and unusually blue sky. The solitary man in the foreground wore rough clothes and a crude metal helmet with only a narrow slit to permit vision.

"I put out the word on the underworld grapevine," he said, very straightfaced. "Unfortunately, this was the only candidate."

"Ned Kelly . . .?" Susskind remarked in astonishment.

"What I call a traditional criminal. Put a stocking over his head instead of that thing, it makes no difference. Your bank has had two hundred years to perfect defences against his style of robbery. I don't fancy those odds. So you'll be pleased to hear I've turned him down. My choice of ideal accomplice looks like this."

With a flourish Webb brought up a slide of an IBM 370/165 computer. It was a stock photograph from an archive but to the bankers it might have passed for their own London machine.

"BANKNET itself," he announced. "It knows its job thoroughly. It's perfectly obedient, provided you talk to it the right way. And it's in a unique position of trust, handling every penny that passes through the bank. Most important of all, it's grassproof."

He was obviously delighted by the puzzled expressions.

"I mean it will never *tell*. That's probably the single most desirable characteristic in a partner in crime—total loyalty after the event. When we've finished, our programs will self-destruct and the computer will retain no memory of the assistance it has provided."

He moved in front of the screen. The console display flowed, distorted, across his face, and his eyes narrowed against the powerful light of the projector.

"And that, gentlemen, is our crime. It's an extremely elegant and safe form of robbery. It's shatteringly difficult to prevent or to track down. I'm confident it will work."

Susskind was lighting a cigar, deep in thought. After a time he said, "That's only the outline of a crime, Mr. Webb. You haven't actually told us *how*."

"I only wanted to demonstrate the essentials. Be honest, until you let me loose inside your Data Centres I can hardly be expected to know exactly how. Now can I?"

"Probably true," Susskind nodded slowly, feeling let down.

"Which conveniently brings me to my role as your consultant," Webb said then. "Now, I'll freely admit I know almost nothing about locks and bullet-proof glass and so on. If you want advice along those lines go to Chubb or Banham, or to computer companies like DSL who make it their business to know all about physical security. I feel bound to say, though, that you ought to be worried sick if they can teach you anything you don't know already."

"Are you suggesting that physical security isn't important!" Susskind made his disagreement very apparent.

"Have you ever had a computer robbery at Waterman's?" Webb countered.

"No. Not to my knowledge, anyway."

"That's my very point! We're talking about a type of crime against which your established defences are totally untested. From now on, concentrate on what you don't know, not what you do."

"You still haven't indicated how you would help," Clement interjected. "I get the feeling you're avoiding the subject."

"I can tell you all you need to know about illegal programs," Webb replied confidently. "The danger within, I call them. I have more experience in that area than anyone else in the country."

"We already have programming experts of our own," Clement said. "Too many, I sometimes think."

Webb regarded him coldly. "They are *inside*, Mr. Clement. And if I didn't make it plain enough that was an inside job I was just describing."

He moved to one side, pressing the button on his projector control. The outline of a man's head appeared on the screen, featureless and with a large question mark where the nose should be.

"Mr. X," he announced. "He's there at your London Data Centre at this very minute, tampering with your BANKNET programs, getting ready to steal from you in the near future."

Waterman shifted uncomfortably in his chair. "That's pure conjecture."

Webb took his time to reply. "No, he's there all right. I know that as a fact!" His eyes met theirs, confirming how certain he was that he *knew*.

There was a stunned silence. Kennedy's mouth dropped open. Webb had said nothing about Mr. X.

Carefully, Webb scanned the bankers' rapt faces. Then, speaking very quietly, he said, "Actually, I exaggerate a little. I just *think* he's there. I don't know for sure."

84

Waterman was the first to vent his anger. "This really is too much, Alex," he raged, rounding on Harrington. Clement was clearly about to add his vehement protest.

"Please . . ." Webb held up both hands in an appeal for silence. It took a time to come.

"That was just an experiment, gentlemen. I wanted to see how confident you were about the safety of your computer system. You have just confirmed everything I suspected. You could have told me I was wrong. You could have asked me how I could possibly know. You didn't! You were all too scared, too aware of how vulnerable BANKNET really is. That's why you need me for this contract. I told you at the outset, it's a shotgun wedding. You have no alternative." Abruptly, he sat down.

Bemused, Harrington operated buttons on the table panel. The projector was silenced, its bulb dying to an amber glow as the curtain drew back. Eyes straining in the sudden daylight, Shulton saw the bankers with their heads together in urgent, whispered conference.

"Was that a presentation or a confrontation?" he hissed unhappily out of the side of his mouth.

"A calculated tightrope act," Webb replied in his ear. "And you've only got a few lines, Andrew . . . so bloody say them as if you meant them. The fun has hardly begun."

Shulton rose diffidently. "Gentlemen, SysTech claims that Christopher Webb is overwhelmingly the best consultant for your contract. You have his career résumé before you in our written submission. I'm sure you will agree that it substantiates our claim. Now perhaps I can ask for your questions?"

"Thank you," Harrington replied, clearing his throat. "That was most . . . interesting." He paused, glancing at each of the directors in turn. "We have no questions, as it happens. None at all."

Shulton heard Webb mutter under his breath. The bankers must have heard him too, he was sure.

"Oh, my God!"

There was an expensive clock on a side table, baring its parts through sealed glass to prove that no hand ever wound it. It gave the time as just past 10:20.

Chapter Eight

One week stretched into two. It was obvious to Susan that Webb was finding it increasingly difficult to concentrate, to turn his mind to anything but Waterman's.

"Why don't you call them?" she suggested.

He pulled pensively at a lip. "Successful selling requires patience, Sue." The voice took on the monotone of a lecturer. "It's the art of knowing when to show the confidence of doing nothing rather than the uncertainty of action." He had heard that somewhere.

"I still think you should."

He responded irritably. "Look, if I've won they have to call me, anyway. And if I've lost I'm not going to make things easier for that mole Harrington. He can bloody well make the move."

"Andrew asks every day if you've heard yet."

"Vulture!"

"He seems convinced you didn't pull it off."

"He's outnumbered. Jake agrees with me that I probably did."

She was hesitant before confessing, "When I asked him he didn't sound that certain, Chris."

"A floating voter," Webb said scornfully.

"Put it down to inexperience," she proposed out of charity.

At the beginning of the third week she came onto the intercom, very excited.

"It's Mr. Harrington of Waterman's."

"*The* Mr. Harrington? The extinct Mr. Harrington?" He was excited too.

"Good luck, Chris," she found herself saying.

There was a click on the line and then the banker spoke. On the telephone he was different, with a deeper voice and more authority. An altogether bigger man.

"I'm sorry we've taken so long to get back to you,

86

Mr. Webb. But these matters do so often drag on, don't they?"

Webb said it was nothing, really.

"I'd like to be able to tell you now what we have decided, but there are far better ways. And I never regard the telephone as entirely secure. Are you free for lunch today?"

"Yes, luckily I am."

"Then shall we say 12:30? I'll send a car."

"I'll be ready."

The conversation was over almost before Webb realised.

Susan came quickly over. "Does that mean good news, Chris?" She had been listening.

"Frankly, I don't know. But I guess it must. Busy men don't usually buy you lunch just to say no."

"He sounded a nice man, pleasant."

"Hell!" Webb exclaimed in frustration. "He might have bloody said!"

The black Rover turned into Oxford Street. Large traffic signs insisted that only buses and taxis were permitted there. Webb's chauffeur pretended not to see. There were countless other cars whose drivers had done the same.

The crowds were dense. At the junctions uniformed wardens with loudhailers tried to herd them, without much success. The shoppers flowed rather than walked, spilling without looking into the road. Webb noticed the parcels and worried faces, saw a down-at-heel Santa Claus with a sandwich board. Above, on the heavy stone ledges of Selfridges, dark conifers sprouted brightly coloured lights. He had forgotten that Christmas was so near. With Alison gone what was to remind him?

The car made a left turn. They came into a wide cul-de-sac, the entire end of the street blocked by an impressive classical building. It was in pale stone with generous windows. A great arched pediment dominated the front. Above it a pole carried a flag with an emblem that was indistinct at a distance and in the breeze.

Webb had often passed the entrance to the street and half-wondered what the place might be. A stately

87

home in the busy city centre? He had concluded that it had been at one time and was probably a museum now. But he had left it at that, always too busy to find out.

The Rover swept up to the house, and Webb jumped out as it stopped. Denied the ceremony of releasing him, the driver scowled. Looking up, Webb found that the flag bore a green elephant. What had that to do with Waterman's? Examined carefully the building did not seem to be a bank. Certainly he could see nothing that said it was. Before him twin doors wore huge lion's head door knockers. There was a worn brass plate under one of the heads. It said, "Push."

Webb turned to ask the driver what the place was but the car was already accelerating away down the street, trailing a light cloud of exhaust that hung in the chill air. So he obeyed the order on the door and entered. It was the kind of interior that smelled of fresh furniture polish but looked musty. A porter sat stiffly behind a heavy wooden counter. More elephants, in bronze, decorated the dark panelled walls. He vaulted fifty years backwards as he stepped inside.

"Where is this?" he asked.

The porter gave a studied sniff. "Did you say where, sir?"

"I'm meeting Mr. Harrington," Webb explained, changing tack.

"Ah," the man replied. But that was all and he made no move.

At that moment Harrington came from the high hall just visible beyond the lobby.

"How prompt," he said, making no attempt to shake hands. "I suppose you won't have been here before?"

"Never."

"I'm not what you would call a club person. But this one is so handy."

"Which club, exactly?"

"The Oriental. Heard of it?"

Webb shook his head.

"I use it more as a restaurant than anything. This area is the absolute end. Either madly expensive or hamburgers with greasy eggs."

They walked into the main hall. A wide carpeted staircase rose beside them. Mirrored panels lined the upper landing, sending it curving into fading infinity. A small glassed dome let in the pallid midday light of the December sky.

"Oriental?" Webb spun on a heel. "This all looks so English to me. Eighteenth century?"

"English, French, Italian?" Harrington displayed extreme indifference. "I can't tell them apart with these columns and all the marble. They serve an excellent curry here, that's the main thing. That's Oriental enough for me." He led into a corridor with a downward flight of steps. "Not that I eat the stuff myself."

There was a distant clatter of plates. News agency telex listings hung in long curling strips from a notice board, the overseas flashes ringed in red.

"Classy for an Indian restaurant," Webb suggested.

"Never Indian," Harrington declared. "I had a spell in Hong Kong with a bank I once worked for. A number of us in London use the club to keep in contact—nostalgia, I suppose."

They entered a dining room with celadon walls and a high, gently curving ceiling with painted panels. There were the subdued sounds of a superior eating place.

"I thought we'd skip the bar, Mr. Webb. I hope that's all right by you, but I don't myself."

He was obviously well known there. They were instantly seated with elaborate courtesy at a circular table set for two. Chinese waiters presented menus. Webb glanced around, seeing more suburban tweed than city cloth, registering all the thinning hair. He was the youngest diner by a comfortable margin.

"I shouldn't be here according to Rule Ten of the Data Centre," his host said. "It's very close by, you see. But since I drafted the rules myself. . ." He waved the menus away with irritated twitches of the hand. "I've already ordered, Mr. Webb. To save time. I hope you don't mind? I assumed you'd try the curry. It comes with Bombay Duck and all the side-trimmings. Not what I'd call genuine but the kind of thing the English eat out East."

"Curry will be fine," Webb confirmed politely.

"The simple meals are best," Harrington said. "The day you reach forty French cuisine suddenly begins to taste appallingly vulgar. You see if I'm not right." He beckoned the wine waiter. "Perrier water? A large bottle would be good, I think."

"Yes, that will be fine, too." Expense no object, Webb thought with private sarcasm.

"Mineral water, very cold milk and Coca-Cola—the three best drinks in the world as far as I'm concerned." Harrington tucked his napkin over his shirt collar, spreading it wide. "But the Coke only in America, unfortunately. It's so much better there."

"I've found that." Webb shuffled in his chair. When was the bloody man going to say what he had to say?

"Maybe the culture brings out the flavour, eh? Or maybe it's all the crushed ice. I've never worked it out."

The Perrier water came and Harrington sampled it with the expert air of one who could tell precisely when it had been bottled. He looked at Webb over his effervescing glass, noting the signs of impatience.

"I do intend to put you out of your misery, eventually. But I have to get there by stages, as you'll see.

"Your presentation to us was different, Mr. Webb. I'm sure you know that! What you won't know is the effect, the profound effect, you had on my directors." He ran a finger around the inside of his glass, releasing small silver spheres that had clung just below the surface. "You worried Susskind and Waterman, actually worried them. You articulated doubts in their subconscious minds and brought them . . . bubbling out." He smiled at his choice of words. "In doing so, I have to say, you displeased Clement no end. You undid much of the years of hard work he had invested in building confidence. It was a remarkable piece of demolition. I have been trying to do the same thing since I don't know when. Without success."

Webb's curry arrived, and Harrington was presented with a scarcely cooked steak. He prodded it with a knife, giving a satisfied nod when the blood coursed out. A waiter offered him several types of mustard and another gave Webb the choice of six jars of chutney nestling in a woven basket.

"I'm sure you'll enjoy that," the banker predicted, his knife ringing against Webb's plate. "My stomach says no to curry. To mustard, too, but I choose not to hear in that instance. I'll regret it tonight."

Webb discovered raisins in his dish; he hated raisins in curry.

"You scared the hell out of Meyer Waterman," Harrington said. "You convinced him not of the possibility of computer fraud, but of its absolute inevitability. I don't know whether that was your intention but it was certainly the outcome. I don't know, either, whether you believe it yourself?" The banker looked across the table expectantly, pouring more mineral water.

"Yes, I do. That's not a reflection on your bank but a matter of statistics. Simply that. It *has* to happen."

"None of your famous inside knowledge, then?"

Webb had to smile. "No."

Harrington attacked his steak energetically, coating the small cubes he carved with thick crusts of English mustard.

"By the way, did you hire Elliott after all?" he asked suddenly.

"No." Webb made the reply as impassive as he could. It was not easy.

"Very wise. He's nowhere near as good as he likes to make out."

"Pompous," Webb ventured.

"Very."

Something struck Webb as odd. "I don't understand. You said, *did* I hire him . . . ?"

"He's no longer with us. I thought you'd know." Harrington's eyes met the consultant's. "Rule number one of security—stop secrets escaping. Rule number two—if despite your efforts they still do, make sure you know, and how it happened."

"I used those very words in my proposal," Webb countered.

"Why, so you did." The banker turned his attention to his plate. "I digress, I'm afraid. I'm prone to do that if I don't watch myself." Webb did not believe him.

"Your presentation also persuaded my directors of something else. You made a clear distinction between conventional security and the problems we face in protecting our programs. I still can't work out how you did that, Mr. Webb. It's a subtle point. But perhaps showmanship, shall we say, has its place." Harrington cocked his head to one side. "I quite enjoyed your little performance . . . when I got over the initial shock.

"Anyway, Mr. Webb, you highlighted an important issue. That we have concentrated primarily on preventing interference from outside, whereas we have limited protection against certain types of internal fraud. Now, we knew that, of course we did. But you added a sense of urgency. We are, in the expressive word of your proposal, *exposed*. Even Clement concedes that now, albeit reluctantly. As a result, we have considerably altered the original objectives of our audit. You should regard that as entirely your doing."

The steak was vanishing rapidly. He was one of the few men Webb had met who could eat and talk as completely separate actions.

"We will now be awarding a contract for a security audit of the conventional kind. A thorough examination of the Data Centres and selected branches. To be concerned with procedures, our mechanisms for preventing or controlling access—you'll know the type of thing. But not with software. Expressly not." He began watching Webb closely as he spoke. "We will be placing that work with another consultancy. You were refreshingly honest about it not being a particular strength of ours."

Webb nodded unenthusiastic agreement. "Can I ask who?"

"You should know better than that! Next we turned our minds to the possibility of a separate contract to study the internal problem, the risk to our programs. A software audit, in other words. To tell you the truth, that had not occurred to us until you put the idea into our heads."

Harrington gave a smile of encouragement. Normally he had such a tight, small mouth. It was odd to discover how wide he could make it.

"You would put a lot of effort and enthusiasm into such an audit, I expect. You should take some pleasure from the fact that we were all convinced of your ability to do it."

"Even Clement?"

The smile became wider still. "Even Clement." Then it disappeared, to be replaced by a frown. Webb had put down his spoon and fork and was anxiously revolving his glass between his hands.

"However, you also made us aware of a major drawback to that little scheme. The sheer problem, the near impossibility of such an exercise. Computer crime is staggeringly difficult to track down. You own words, Mr. Webb."

"That's no reason not to try!" Webb was becoming alarmed by the warning signs.

"We have decided to award just the one audit contract. The one I've mentioned."

Webb fought to keep his speech low and calm. "And that, you say, is my doing?"

"Yes."

Webb lost the fight. "Then you've bloody used me. Do you realise that!"

A greying head turned at the next table. Webb's voice had been raised above normal club limits.

"Yes, I suppose I have. It was unintentional, I assure you."

"Thanks very much!"

"Which is why I am anxious to suggest something else. We're rather short of effort on several of our projects right now. We could do with some extra help and I'd like you to join us for a while. It's not quite what you originally bid for but it is a . . . consolation prize, eh?"

"Working on what precisely, Mr. Harrington?"

"I'm not really sure yet. Some programming, perhaps. Maybe cleaning up some inefficiencies in the system." An unconcerned wave of a fork. "Does it matter?"

"I'm sure you mean well," Webb retorted angrily. "But do you know what your second prize amounts to? Bloody body shop work!"

"Body shop?"

"Just a phrase we use. It means the cheap end of the programming business."

"Ah."

"I'm too damned good for that."

93

"Mr. Webb, please . . ." Harrington laid a thin hand on the consultant's. "You must see, surely, the problems we face? I would love to go ahead with a proper software audit. The board would, too. But think about it for a moment, please. It would alert my staff to suspicions that are almost certainly unjustified. Worry them."

Webb gave the banker a curious look. "Is alerting them what bothers you!"

"That would be regrettable, wouldn't it. I won't have it."

With effort, Webb kept his eyes narrowed and his hands deadly still on the table. He suddenly wanted to smile.

"Do I assume that this assignment would require me to report direct to you?"

"I think we could arrange that, yes."

"And that I'd be working closely with your programming staff?"

"Like one of them."

"Have the run of the Data Centre?"

"Why not."

Webb was grinning from ear to ear by now. "In that case I could get used to a spot of body shopping. It might be rather interesting."

Harrington remained serious. "Let's be clear on one thing. I won't have a manhunt, Mr. Webb, your normal blunt way of doing things. If you want to follow up any suspicions, that's entirely up to you. But don't get caught doing it, understand? If you are, I won't have put you up to it. I have my staff relations to think about."

"And if I do find something wrong . . .?"

"A fortunate accident, shall we say." Harrington downed the remaining water in his glass as others would a shot of whisky. He used his dessert spoon to scoop the meat juices from his plate. "We'll let Christmas pass, I think. Begin in the New Year. Will that suit you?"

Webb raised his glass to touch it against the other man's. His client's. "Perfectly."

Harrington returned the smile.

"You'll be a spy, in a way. I see you being rather good at that. Enjoying it."

94

Part Two

AUDIT

Part Two

AUDIT

SECURE DATA. Only authorized programs may access the data held on Secure Discs. Any unauthorized attempts—whether in fact, alias, or error—will be inhibited by the Operating System and the console will display a warning message. Hardcopy report ... will be generated on the operator's system log.

—BANKNET Operator's Guide

Chapter Nine

Monday, 3rd January. Exactly at 10:00 A.M. a horn sounded from the square. Webb did not need to look out to know that Harrington had arrived. But he moved to the window anyway to show the man he was coming. Below, a face peered back at him from a big Jaguar saloon and they exchanged polite waves. The square was very still, like an unfocussed photograph composed in greys. Cold drizzle slanted onto the bare trees, washing away what little colour they had and dissolving their outlines. The facing houses might have been flat cardboard. Behind them the Tower pushed against the sky, its top erased by low cloud.

Webb pulled on his dark overcoat and headed for the door. He wore a navy-blue suit, almost black, with a plain blue shirt. His tie was dark blue, too, with an overall pattern of small red spots.

"Sober-looking man," Susan said. "Enjoy the funeral."

The engine idled quietly, hissing to itself as it breathed. The fan wafted warm air at Webb, onto his face and round his feet. After even the short dash from the office door it felt good.

"Is this an XJ12?" he asked.

"Five-point-three litres," Harrington said in confirmation and with evident pride. "You need all the power you can get for city driving these days. You know, to exploit the gaps. Too damned full of cars, that's the trouble with London."

He thrust the gear selector into drive and they left the kerb, accelerating fast. Harrington checked his fascia clock. "Just after ten. That's an hour already gone at your hundred and fifty a day! Still, you'll make up for it, you'll see."

Webb flinched as they merged dangerously with the traffic flowing from the Euston Road underpass. His foot pressed in reflex action against the floor. If anything it made the car go faster.

97

"I've budgetted eight thou for this exercise," Harrington said. "That gives you about three months. I hope it's enough?"

"It should be."

"We're going to the London Data Centre. LDC for short. You know that already. But do you know what an unmarked building is?"

"I think so."

"Tell me."

"One that carries no identification of the company."

"And the reason?"

"Security, of course. Pursuit of anonymity."

"I prefer to call it first-level security, Mr. Webb. Protection against casual interference. Someone who really wants to know, a determined person, can always find out the location. But it keeps away the cranks, the bomb hoaxers."

Harrington tried to race a red light, then changed his mind. His foot hit the brake pedal in the instant that Webb's was pushed hard down on the carpet. Webb was relieved to find that his reflexes sometimes worked.

"The Centre is just off Wigmore Street," the banker told him. "Not actually at Christopher Place, but that is the nearest you will ever direct a taxi. And no mention of Waterman's to the drivers, if you don't mind. I'll also show you the car park in Marylebone Lane, and that is the closest your car is ever to be left to our building. You will also, like my staff, completely avoid all public houses and restaurants within a quarter-mile radius of the Centre. We have a map there, showing the area you must regard as off limits."

"Including the Oriental Club?" Webb asked cheekily.

Harrington was not in a frivolous mood. "As I recall telling you, Mr. Webb, I wrote the rules. Also, I keep my mouth tightly buttoned there. I don't trust others to do the same."

Webb remembered their lunch but thought it best to make no comment.

"You may give the LDC telephone number to your office, to be used with discretion. Our switchboard never identifies the Centre. And they will connect callers only to people who are on the list of authorised occupants of the building. As of today, you sit on that list."

Soon they were travelling south on Baker Street, with Harrington weaving constantly from lane to lane. He moved faster than seemed possible, given the density of traffic. It was far from comfortable.

"You'll sign a confidentiality agreement, of course. I trust you'll take its restrictions very seriously."

The car screeched to a halt at a junction, and Harrington peered wistfully into the damp street with its roof of sombre, scudding clouds.

"It may not look much," he said, pointing up, "but savour it while you can. LDC has no windows, not even one. Once in there you'll have no idea of the outside climate. We have our own and it never varies, twenty-four hours a day, seven days a week. We might as well be moles in there."

He turned into Wigmore Street and a minute later took a right turn, then hurled the big car into the entrance to a multilevel car park. He surged up the ramp, hands snatching at the wheel, rising several floors. Then he threaded between the columns to a corner bay, stopping only inches from the wall. When Webb got out he saw the word "RESERVED" painted in faded yellow at the front of the bay, but no mention of Waterman's.

"Will you be driving here?" Harrington queried, making briskly for the stairs.

"If that's all right?"

"Come far, do you?"

"Chelsea. Near World's End."

"Far enough. I'll get a space allocated." Then, "Not one of those houseboats on the river there?"

"Hardly."

"What do you drive, by the way?"

"Nothing as big as a Jaguar," Webb replied diplomatically.

Disappointed, Harrington gave up the probing. He strode on, ducking between the cars in Wigmore Street before stopping on the far pavement. They were outside the Cock and Lion.

"Know it?" Harrington pointed up to the Grill Room.

"Moderately well."

"Forget it while you're with us! It's way off limits."

The banker turned without warning under the pub and into a narrow mews that punctuated its façade. It was a cul-de-sac lined by tall, grimy warehouses that almost hid the sky, creating a reservoir of gloom. It was a place few would think to go.

"LDC," Harrington announced at the end of the mews, with the air of one who had conjured an entire computer centre out of the air. They entered what seemed to be an untidy garage area fringed with empty wooden crates and rusting metal frames, pushed through massive double doors that opened at the lightest touch, and they were inside the bright, air-conditioned BANKNET building.

Webb had claimed that he knew what an unmarked building was. Yet he had imagined the phrase to describe an ordinary office block with the nameplate conveniently forgotten. LDC was not like that at all. Within the thick outer walls the warehouse had been gutted and expensively reconstructed. The exterior shell, the important disguise of the Centre, had been propped in position while excavation created vast basement areas. People who woked close by or who passed daily never suspected its presence or its purpose. It went beyond anonymity to the point of virtual non-existence.

They came into a lobby, to be faced by three security men in a big glass booth. In front of one was a bank of controls and a row of TV monitors, angled into the desk top. More monitors on the wall behind showed Webb that they had been under observation from the moment they left Wigmore Street. One screen displayed the mews, with the occasional passerby framed in the entrance arch. Another showed the garage they had just come through. There was something about the glass enclosing the men, something thick and refractive, that suggested high resistance to bullets.

They went into a smaller lobby, a kind of pen flanking the glass booth. As the door closed on them there was a delayed *thunk* from the latch that told Webb they were locked in. Harrington spoke into a complex louvre, designed to allow a voice to reach the guards but nothing else. One of the men pulled a lever and a metal tray opened in front of Webb. Inside were two plastic tags a little larger than credit cards. Harrington clipped one to Webb's breast pocket, keeping his own in his hand.

"Your case, Mr. Webb?"

He took the briefcase and pushed it through a hatch. The guard went carefully over every item.

"Don't ever try bringing anything naughty in," Harrington ordered. "And don't try taking anything of ours out, not even a pencil. We search at entry and exit, every time."

"What about homework?"

A firm shake of the head. "Do what you have to here. As the saying goes, we never close."

The case was returned, and there was a click from the door ahead. They entered a third lobby, this one lined by a series of coloured doors. Some were lift doors, others presumably led to stairs or further lobbies and had massive locks with card reader mechanisms. Half the doors were bright red, the others blue.

"Alice in Wonderland!" Webb exclaimed.

Harrington made no comment but beamed as he pressed a button to summon a blue lift. He was softening before Webb's eyes. This was *his* Centre, his manner said.

Webb could just see that the banker's tag carried a small photograph and a signature, spidery and cramped. Across the top was a broad red band. Squinting down he found that his top stripe was blue and that the tag bore the word "VISITOR" in bold letters.

Harrington saw him looking. "Don't lose that ID or you'll have problems. Do it after six P.M. and you're here for the night. The card reader back there will allow you into the exit pen when you want to leave. It retains the tag, it's impossible to leave the Centre with one."

When the lift came he pressed the red edge of his ID into a slot on the inside control panel and a display light glowed its acceptance.

"We use the American notation here, Mr. Webb. The ground floor is Level One. So much more logical, don't you agree?" He selected the button for the

101

highest floor, Level 4. Webb noticed that there were no buttons for Levels 2 and 3.

"When you're on your own," Harrington said, "use the blue edge of your ID to drive the lift. And please don't try a red lift! You'll cause one hell of a noise. Bells and things."

They emerged into a broad corridor, the walls and ceilings stark white, with a slight gloss to the vertical surfaces so that they seemed to shimmer in the colourless light. Brown, hairy squares of Heuga carpet gave the area its only semblance of texture. Webb found it unpleasant to look at and walk on. It was like treading over some dead, coarse-skinned animal.

Down the corridor they came to a meeting room, sparsely furnished with a table and a few chairs. The walls were bare except for a whiteboard that was almost invisible. The light caught alternate squares of the carpet, turning the floor into a chessboard of browns.

For the first time Webb became fully aware of the absence of natural light. The room was big, but with no windows to break the surfaces it was boxlike, claustrophobic. Webb felt packaged.

"And how do you like my fortress, Mr. Webb?"

"It's most impressive. You seem better protected than many military installations."

"They're only defending national pride," the banker replied with a smile. "What little there is left of it. We are guarding money."

He leaned back contentedly in his chair. "This is not only an operational computer centre. It is also the administrative HQ for BANKNET. And our systems development is done here, too, the constant improvements to BANKNET. Bringing all that together in a single building in the heart of London is inevitably complex. I plumped for the suburbs but lost. According to Clement, we would have been too conspicuous there."

"I'm baffled by your security coding," Webb told him. "Which is highest, red or bue?"

"Red, naturally."

"And I have only blue clearance?" Webb patted his ID.

"The same as my software staff. They work just along this corridor. You'll be in there with them."

"And the computer . . . ?"

"Blue as well. You'll have full access to the computer room, of course. Walk in any time you want." Harrington smiled at some secret joke. "Provided the natives are friendly."

"Meaning?"

"That some of the operators are a bit funny, possessive. Exert your rights, Mr. Webb."

"Can I ask what is in the red areas?"

"Zones, Mr. Webb. That's what we call them."

"Zones, then?"

"Mainly data," Harrington said, taking pleasure in the reply.

"Data?"

"As you once graphically pointed out to us, data is money in a bank. I've done my damndest to protect it." Touché, his expression said. "Perhaps I should explain."

He walked to the whiteboard, a bishop's move diagonally across the chequered floor. Taking up a chunky felt pen he sketched what Webb eventually worked out to be a cross section of the building. It was a childlike picture, sparingly done in a bottom corner of the board. Webb counted six floors, two below ground level.

"We are at present on Level Four. This is where my software staff live. Below, on Level Three, we have the computers, two big IBM 370/165s." The pen dipped. "And down on Level One, the entrance area. One does need to get in and out! That is the entire blue zone. As far as you are concerned, the rest of the building is out of bounds."

"I'd like to see it, all the same."

Harrington shook his head vigorously. "We're playing this by the book, Mr. Webb. If any of my people get to hear you've been there, they'll know something is up. We can't have that, can we?"

"Some idea, then?"

The banker did not seem to need much persuading. "You'll be used to the normal arrangement where all computer output is printed in the computer room. An essential part of my security, my distrust of people if you like, is that we don't do things that way in this Centre. The Printing Section is down on Level One, behind one of those red doors you saw on the way in."

"But that means . . ." Webb began.

". . . That the software staff never see the BANK-NET data," Harrington said for him. "And I do mean never. We have a single printer in the computer room, solely for the purposes of program testing. To check out programs I provide dummy numbers, never real ones. Even my most senior system designers are forbidden access to actual customer accounts, to every bit of the money data. So will you be."

"Clever," Webb observed ruefully.

"It makes it difficult to steal when you can't see what you're trying to take, eh?"

"More difficult. Not impossible."

"If you say so."

"What happens underground?"

"On Levels B-one and B-two? Mainly storage. We keep paper listings, mag tape and disc packs in vast amounts. I have data libraries and archives down there. Fireproof, floodproof, bombproof . . . you name it. There is also a games room for the operators. I'm told the snooker table gets unconventional use when we have girls on the night shift."

Webb laughed. "There has to be a joke there."

"Several, Mr. Webb. I've heard them all."

"Your office is in the red zone, I presume?"

Harrington touched his ID, nodding. It was now clipped to his jacket, like Webb's. "It's cosier there. I get left alone."

"Won't we have problems communicating?"

"I'd rather we didn't meet much, frankly. We can talk by phone or get together privately in here. If we have to, we can meet outside. But I hope it doesn't come to that. It seems so melodramatic, doesn't it? Anything else?"

"No, not for the moment." Webb wanted time to digest it all. Nothing Elliott had told him had prepared him for such elaborate precautions. Perhaps it was different up at Manchester.

"Fine. You remembered the CV, I trust?"

104

"Sure."

"And you've changed it, as I asked?"

In reply Webb slid his curriculum vitae across the table. The details of his past career had been altered slightly. All references to work on computer security had been removed and several invented projects appeared to have involved Webb in the study of system efficiency.

Harrington nodded his approval as he finished reading.

"Now we come to the difficult part. I do so hate deception, don't you? Your cover here—I believe that's the correct term—is this." He tapped the CV. "You as you really are but with a little surgery and grafting on your experience. You're here because I'm becoming concerned that BANKNET might be getting a bit flabby, a bit slow and cumbersome with all the additions we've made since it first went on the air."

Webb smiled. "So I crawl all over it, looking everywhere. Into every dark corner. It's a clever idea."

"You might have a bit of trouble with my Systems Manager, Martin Alloway," Harrington warned. "He doesn't like the idea much. I think he sees it as implying criticism of his work."

"Well, in his shoes . . ." Webb began.

"I'll leave you to sort that one out. As it happens, Alloway is up in Manchester until tomorrow. So I've arranged for his Chief Programmer to look after you for the day."

"Name of . . . ?"

"Owen." Harrington's hands were clasped in anticipation. "If you're ready?"

Webb took a deep breath and said that he was.

Harrington moved to the door. "It will be interesting, won't it, seeing how your cover bears up?" He slipped out with odd, repressed eagerness.

Left alone, Webb surveyed the bare room, hearing the hum of treated air. He walked over to Harrington's untidy diagram and smiled as his finger traced the outer line—the windowless walls. He was inside them at last. Inside the money machine.

Chapter Ten

"Jennifer Owen," Harrington announced, producing the Chief Programmer with a minor flourish. The girl inclined her head in welcome. Then she stood in the doorway for a moment, appraising Webb with dark eyes set in a small, serious face.

It was, he decided, Harrington's day for tricks. First the Data Centre and now this. She was very attractive, immaculate in severe, expensive clothes. When she came into the room it was with an easy, flowing stride.

"And this is Mr. Webb, Jennifer," Harrington told her, pointing not at the consultant but at his career résumé on the table. He seated her with fussy attention.

The girl put down an Italian handbag and lifted the résumé. A silk scarf was tied around the handle of the bag, apparently casually, more likely with the dedication of a Japanese arranging a single flower. She took her time reading.

"I don't know Systems Technology," she said to Webb eventually. "What are they like?" There was something about her eyes. Webb found himself trying to see deeply into them but getting no further than the brown surfaces.

"Small but growing."

"How many staff?"

"Just under forty at the last count."

"And when you get to two hundred you'll sell out, I suppose? Buy a big place in the country? Isn't that what the bosses of successful software companies all end up doing?"

"I don't see that happening somehow," Webb said.

If only you knew, he thought. Shulton bloody will one day. But not me. Not on my share.

He saw Harrington pursing his lips, telegraphing for more.

"I'm a dedicated professional," he said, smiling. "The easy life doesn't appeal."

The banker seemed satisfied.

"Fine," she said to Harrington, pushing the CV towards him.

"I thought it was good experience," the banker remarked, probably trying to draw more comment. "Very suitable."

"It seems to be," she agreed. "Time will tell." She gestured studied indifference. Her hand was very tanned, perhaps from recent winter sun somewhere. There were no rings. Webb always looked for that.

"You haven't really explained why you want this exercise carried out, Alex," she said.

"Not me, Jennifer. The board. You know how these things happen."

"I could have done it. Or one of my analysts." Webb detected a trace of irritation in the voice.

"You're all too busy," Harrington said smoothly. "It's better this way."

"It will be very tough on someone who doesn't already know BANKNET." The girl caught Webb's eye. "It's a very big system. Far bigger than anything mentioned here." A finger reached out to brush the CV lightly.

"Let's see, shall we?" Harrington suggested.

"But I'll give what help I can.".

"Splendid, splendid." Harrington eased out of his chair. As he passed behind her he surprised Webb with a conspiratorial wink. It seemed wrong on him, like an affectation improperly mastered.

"Tell me what you find, Mr. Webb. Any flabbiness, eh?"

When he had gone, Webb felt able to look at the girl properly. Even since he had first seen her time had eroded the beauty he had imagined then. She was older than she had seemed on entering the room—thirty-two or thirty-three, he guessed. And analysed quite coldly, each part looked at in isolation—she was actually quite ordinary. She should have been plain, he thought, yet she wasn't. When she moved she was lithe, almost tantalising. Sitting, she was unusually still, perfectly balanced. She *was* beautiful, he judged on reflection. In her own kind of way.

"What do I call you?" she asked, unworried by the scrutiny. "Not Mr. Webb, I hope?"

"Christopher. My friends call me Chris."

"I'll settle for Christopher."

She turned to the résumé again, glancing up at intervals to match him against the words. He found it disconcerting.

"If I'd seen this first I'd never have imagined you as you are."

"Why?"

"You're younger," she stated bluntly. "Cofounder and director of the company. And this is an impressive list of projects."

"Even if they are all smaller than BANKNET?"

Fleetingly, the eyes showed what might have been amusement. Then the shutters closed down again and he could not be sure.

"And how about you?" he said. "You haven't done so badly, either."

"So I'm told."

"Harrington's job someday, I'll bet?"

She smiled at the idea. "Alex is an administrator. That wouldn't be my thing."

"Come on!"

"Sure, I could do it if I had to. But I wouldn't want to. All the battles, the in-fighting . . . you don't know banks."

"You prefer to stick with the nice polite computers?" He said it partly in jest but she took it seriously.

"Definitely. Don't you?"

"Alloway's job, then? You're after that instead?" It was always the way Webb began this kind of assignment, probing for weakness. Money was not always the motive for computer fraud. Sometimes it was frustration, or spite. But this time he found himself uneasy at his own line of questioning.

"Martin and I do quite different jobs. I prefer mine." She answered quickly, looking away.

"How different?"

"He decides what needs to be done. I actually do it. When you've been here for a while you can tell me which is hardest." He had obviously touched a nerve.

"How many staff have you got, Jennifer?"

"Reporting directly? Fourteen. On top of that, most of the others in Martin's department come to me for guidance at some time or another."

"And how many does he have?"

"Thirty, including me."

That makes thirty-two if we add Alloway and Harrington, Webb thought. A hell of a lot of people with opportunity.

She rose, straightening her skirt with care. "I'll give you the Grand Tour, shall I?"

"Please . . ."

In the corridor he asked, "Is Harrington a computer man?"

"A proper one? Hands on the machine and all the rest of it?"

"Yes."

She smiled, with a toss of the head. "He's a banker, drafted in to oversee the computer operations. I get the impression it wasn't what he wanted . . . something of a sideways shunt. He's become quite good at it but there's still a lot he doesn't know."

"Can he program if he has to?"

"Gosh, no."

Back to thirty-one then, Webb said to himself. Not that the man would have brought in a consultant if he was up to something. The Chief Programmer would have to be high on the list, though. Only a few minutes after meeting her he did not much like that idea.

They took a blue lift down to Level 3. The lobby there was identical to the one upstairs except that the carpet was dark blue instead of brown.

"The decorators went a bit wild here," Webb said.

Turning along a corridor, they passed a long counter where a girl sat arranging punched cards in thin boxes of grey metal. Behind her was a wall of large pigeon-holes with some of the spaces occupied by more card boxes and rolled computer output.

"Run Control," Jennifer Owen explained. "When you're ready, your computer runs will be logged in here. I presume you will be making some?"

"A few, I should think. To see how the system responds."

"The output turns up here, too."

The counter ended by a door and she hesitated, the merest change in pace, to let him know he was expected to push it open.

"Thank you, sir," she said when he did.

Now they were in a gallery. One wall was entirely of glass panels stretching from floor to ceiling.

"What do you think?" she asked.

The floor beyond the glass was in the same blue, but tiled. On it was row after row of computer modules in black and a lighter shade of blue. A very carefully judged IBM blue—not dark enough to be sombre but not so bright that it might be considered frivolous decoration for such costly equipment. Two operators moved between the cabinets, a third sat watching the console display screen. No sound penetrated the glass. The reinforcement of fine wires in the panels made the machines seem somehow protected and fragile.

She was waiting for his response.

"When you've seen one . . ." Webb said with a shrug.

"Okay, so you've been around." She moved along, casting a practiced eye on the precise activity. "But there aren't many places where you'll find twin IBM 370s. And this big." She was very proud of the computers, he could tell. Attached to them, even.

"Why two?" he asked.

"We have a horror of machine failure, for obvious reasons. You can't stop banking operations just because a computer has gone phutt. So everything is duplicated. If one 370 goes down the other takes over. There are twin computers up at Manchester as well. If either Centre was to fail totally for a time the other could take on our full computing load for the country."

The machines showed little signs of life beyond the occasional twitch from the tape drives. The operators moved with deliberation, obeying the requests made via the display screen. One passed close to the glass carrying a disc pack with a red handle.

"That's obviously a colour code," Webb guessed.

"Secure data. Customer account files, probably."

"Tempting, all that money in there," he said provocatively.

She stared ahead. "I never think of that side of it. It's better not to."

"Just another computer, full of numbers?"

"If you put it that way, yes."

His eyes raked the lines of cabinets, moving on past the console to the end of the room. He saw a big lineprinter. The paper came out in great concertina folds, every now and then thrown out at high speed. He remembered what Harrington had said about the printer being used only for testing and wondered if there was any way to get it to print real numbers.

Back on the upper floor, Jennifer chose to open a door for herself.

"This is where we live," she said, stepping through.

Following, Webb came into an enormous open plan office. The ceiling was unusually high, with lights in bright clusters. The brown floor made a desert on which were set oases of desks and screens fringed by tropical-looking plants in great round pots. She took a route between the groups of furniture. At first, the room seemed nearly empty, but as they passed through Webb discovered more and more people working in seclusion behind screens and storage units. They were mostly very young, their heads down, intent on the papers piled in front of them.

Jennifer stopped by a desk on the far side of the big room.

"Try it for size, Christopher."

He sat, judging the chair to be comfortable, but only just. The desk was considerably smaller than his own at Fitzroy Square, its top completely clear. The shelves of the open cupboard behind him were quite empty. He opened the desk drawers one by one and found them empty, too. There was nothing in any corner, not even a paper clip. There was the uncanny bareness of a recently vacated house.

"They don't lock," Jennifer explained, pointing to the drawers. "It's a house rule, I'm afraid."

"Why?"

"Security. Think about it."

"I see. You can't bring anything in. You can't take

111

anything out. And for good measure, you can't hide anything when you're in here."

"That seems to be the general idea."

"To cap it all, you never see what you've programmed BANKNET to do!"

"One gets used to it, Christopher. It's actually a very exciting system. That makes up for it."

She began looking around, becoming puzzled. "There was supposed to be some documentation here for you. Some background reading on BANKNET. Perhaps . . . ?" She disappeared behind a nearby screen. When she came back she was not carrying a few reports, as he had expected, but pushing a trolley laden with manuals and large bound folders of computer output. His surprise delighted her.

"I've got you a complete set of the basic system guides," she said, trying to suppress a smile.

"It'll do for a start," Webb remarked drily, surveying the mountain of paper.

"BANKNET *is* a very big system. I did say." She touched a slim manual. "Cut your teeth on this. It's the best introduction to our computer operations."

"Your child's guide?"

"A briefing document for senior management."

"Same thing," Webb said.

"If you need any more documentation the Program Library is down there." She pointed across the room to where a young Indian sat surrounded by high shelves of paper and reference books.

"No thanks. I'm trying to give it up."

She laughed. "Seriously, though. He'll get whatever you need. His name is Sondhi. We call him P.D."

"Which stands for what?"

"Nobody seems to know. Now before I go, is there anything else I can get you?"

"If it's not too much trouble . . ." Webb had to tread with care.

"Try me."

"I'd like a list of all the staff in here. Names and titles, descriptions of what their responsibilities are."

She was intrigued, as he had guessed she would be. "Can I ask why?"

"I'm going to be with you for some time," Webb replied disingenuously. "I wouldn't want to ruffle any feathers unintentionally."

"Can do. You'll have it later today."

"And if possible a seating plan of this office."

Her curious expression returned.

"So I can put names to faces," he explained. "That's all."

"If you want." She said it reluctantly this time, not entirely satisfied.

Soon he was alone at his empty desk. Ahead he could see some half-dozen young programmers, and they could see him. His privacy was minimal. He stared at the thousands upon thousands of pages stacked on the overloaded trolley. The smallest manual was on the very top, the one Jennifer Owen had indicated. He reached first for that.

Chapter Eleven

Tuesday. They started early at LDC. Webb arrived before 9:00 to find most of the others already at their desks in the top floor office.

He finished moving the manuals and binders from the trolley to the shelves behind his chair. He put his *Times* in a corner of the desk in an attempt to cover the bareness. Sitting there was like wearing a suit for the first time, acutely self-conscious of the unfamiliar feel, the small ways in which it did not yet mould itself to the body, the crisp newness.

Precisely at 9:30 his telephone rang, a soft burr inaudible at a distance of more than a few feet from the receiver.

"Is that Mr. Webb?" the voice enquired. "Martin Alloway here. I'm in charge of systems development. We ought to meet, I think. Do you know how to find me?"

Webb said he didn't.

"Then head for the lifts and I'll guide you in," Alloway proposed. Funny, that, Webb thought. Using the phone to make contact within the same room. Why didn't he just walk over, as I would have done?

He set off and immediately located Alloway. A figure appeared and beckoned from about halfway down the office, standing in a gap that Webb had not noticed before. Two lines of storage units ran at right angles to the wall of the building. The entrance was guarded by a luxuriant clump of greenery lit from an overhead light track. Alloway's area was well camouflaged—a generously sized office lacking only a door and windows.

"Alex Harrington tells me you're a good man," Alloway said, his hand wriggling limply in Webb's. "Do grab a pew, won't you." He indicated a chair.

"Thanks."

Alloway lounged in his own far bigger chair, his head against its high back. "And what did you think of our Jennifer?"

"Very lovely," Webb said.

"Not bad, is she," Alloway agreed. "Bloody bright, too. She can program the pants off most men and knows it. Likes to show her superiority."

There was a notable precision about the shelves enclosing the area. The files all stood exactly vertical, with careful writing down the spines. The books were fastidiously arranged in ascending order of height. The desk was neat, too, with small stacks of paper and folders symmetrically placed on it. On a wall a framed notice praised the virtues of, "SPEED, ACCURACY, DEDICATION." Beside it, hanging on a hook, was a creased and decidedly grubby raincoat.

Seeing Webb glance at the notice, Alloway asked, "Does that describe you, would you say?"

"Well, two out of three." Webb thought a display of modesty was in order.

"Far too few people are prepared to work really hard these days," Alloway declared seriously.

He was just under six feet tall, slightly built and with prematurely thinning hair. Webb guessed he was about thirty-two but he seemed to have adopted the mannerisms of a much older man and it was difficult to tell. His suit looked as if it came from a high street tailor, from an off-the-peg range aimed at aspiring junior managers who did not wish to spend too much. The label probably carried the word "Executive." The tie was unfashionably thin, worn over a cream nylon shirt. Heavy hornrimmed spectacles bore traces of white discolouration just in front of the ears and the lenses showed slight smears when the light caught them.

"How do you find it out there, adrift in that sea of desks?"

"I'm getting used to it," Webb replied.

"Which suggests you don't like it?"

"Not much."

"It's all the rage, open plan," Alloway said. "A great idea, according to all the top managers. Efficient and democratic . . . isn't that what they claim? I've noticed that most of them say so from the seclusion of a private office."

"You don't like it either?"

"You can say that again! One of Alex Harrington's bright ideas that didn't work out." Alloway tapped his teeth with a pencil. "One of many."

On a shelf there was a big plastic model of a jet fighter, beautifully painted. He must have made that, Webb thought. He would be the kind of man who did his own car maintenance—by choice, not because he had to. There had been an MGB soft-top in the car park that morning, aging but lovingly preserved. Alloway's, for certain.

Webb's CV had appeared on the desk.

"You once worked for IBM, I see."

"Some years ago, yes."

"I was there, too. I don't think we ever met?"

"I'm sure I'd remember if we ever had," Webb said, sure that he would not. There had been a number like Alloway at IBM, backroom boys mostly. It was always the smarter dressed men who got on.

"I was based at Havant," Alloway volunteered. "You know, down in Hampshire."

"That must be why our paths never crossed. I worked up here in London."

"You know the old saying?" A smile threatened Alloway's seriousness for the first time. "Only the very good and the mediocre escape from IBM. The rest are there for life."

Webb grinned. "I've heard it often."

"Which were you?" Alloway pushed the glasses further up his nose with a finger against a lens. The eyes were alert.

"Let's put it this way—they tried hard to dissuade me from leaving."

"Me, too, actually. I was packed on the first plane to Poughkeepsie for the full errant employee treatment. That happen to you?"

Webb shook his head.

"I left all the same," Alloway said, looking superior. "Waterman's held out more promise."

Webb regarded him with newfound respect. He might make kid's models but a man had to be good for IBM to jet him across the Atlantic to try to stop him resigning. Bloody good.

"Well, you've been here a day," Alloway said, obviously getting down to business. "You've met Jennifer, had a bit of a read. I think you should have a good basic understanding of BANKNET by now."

"Oh, sure," Webb said.

"Ready to plunge in now, are you? Ready to search out all the imagined failings in my system?" The voice had hardened.

"That's not the way I see it . . ." Webb started to say.

Alloway silenced him with an exasperated sigh. "Do you know what bottlenecks are? By any chance, I mean?"

"Of course. Programs that turn out to be very inefficient."

"Programs that slow up the rest of the system, right?"

"Right."

"Does BANKNET look slow to you?"

"I can't say yet. But I'll be most surprised if I find that it is."

Alloway's hands spread wide. "Suddenly Alex wants an efficiency study done on BANKNET! Overnight he's obsessed with the horrors of bottlenecks. Last week, I swear, he had hardly heard of the word. And now . . ." The hands signalled disgust. "He brings in an outsider to search my system. He only wants you to

116

look for bloody bottlenecks!" He removed the heavy spectacles and became surprisingly young. He was pale and plain, his face instantly bare as if he had taken most of it off.

"A month ago I told Alex we could improve KEY-NOTE, know that? Not that you'll have heard of KEYNOTE."

"It's your credit card system," Webb told him soberly.

Alloway acted as though he had not heard the remark. "I could speed up the response when retailers phone in for a check on card holders. And I mean really speed it up . . . I've already worked out how. But bloody Alex didn't want to know. He wasn't giving a stuff for efficiency then." He leaned forward, eyes glinting. "So what's this about, all of a sudden? Has Alex taken you into his confidence?"

Webb tried to give an even reply. "It's something the board asked for, so he said."

"Managers!" Alloway retorted, shaking his head furiously. He began to clean his glasses with the end of his tie. "I don't blame you, don't think that. You're just a pawn. We're all just pawns when managers play whatever games they indulge in to pass the daylight hours."

There was an awkward silence. Webb watched as he held the glasses up to the light for examination, then used a thumbnail to scratch a source of irritation from one of the lenses.

"But pawn or not," Alloway said, jabbing at his desk, "I'm here and you're going to be out there, across the room. So let's keep it that way. I'm buggered if I'm going to raise so much as a finger to help. Why should I help someone to find bottlenecks in my system!"

"Chasing shadows," Webb remarked quietly. "I guarantee not to get in your way."

"On the other hand . . . if you do happen to come across anything that's not as it should be . . ." Alloway was suddenly thoughtful. "By any remote chance, I mean . . . you ought to tell me first. It's only fair. I carry the can round here." He gestured that the meeting was over.

Webb got up slowly but made no move towards the outer office.

"I admire what I've seen here so far," he said. "I'd appreciate the opportunity to learn more about your methods. How about over a spot of lunch?" It had occurred to him that Alloway was likely to be a very awkward enemy. Obstructive, if he felt like it. Worse than that, almost certain to keep a close eye on Webb's every move.

"I usually have sandwiches." The reply was dismissive.

"Can't I twist your arm?"

"Lunch on you, you mean?" There was a sign of interest.

"Sure. Well, on SysTech."

"We can't eat close to the Centre, you do know that?" Alloway rose with deliberation from his big chair. "It would have to be somewhere pretty good to make the walk worthwhile."

Crafty bugger, Webb thought. But he smiled and said, "Wherever you want. SysTech looks after its clients."

"I'll see how I feel. Maybe next week sometime." Alloway came round the desk. His shoes were rather pointed and the leather was like cardboard from lack of polish. "I'll call you to fix up a date."

Chapter Twelve

Saturday, 8th January. The Data Centre was open twenty-four hours a day, seven days a week, Harrington had said. Webb decided to put the claim to the test. He had a definite aim in mind.

He arrived at 11:00. He noticed immediately that LDC had the same unwritten rule about weekend dress as every other office he had known. A studied, casual look was not only tolerated, it seemed imperative. Webb counted seven others working in the room on Level 4, all in polo-neck sweaters. He wore one, too, under a soft leather jacket. The pace of work was more leisurely than he had seen it during the week, with more breaks for conversation. But it was all as serious as ever.

Just before noon Jennifer Owen came into the office. Seeing him, she walked over.

"Hi, slave."

"Lunch?" Webb asked.

"Sorry, but I'm meeting my sister." She carried two plump green plastic bags from Harrod's and gave the impression that a short session of program checking would come as a welcome rest from the rigours of shopping.

"Tonight, then? Dinner somewhere?"

"I really can't, Christopher," she said, conveying what he hoped was honest regret. "I'm tied up, booked up to here." She submerged beneath a raised hand.

She wore a white cashmere sweater. Her tight trousers were in an expensive material posing as denim and printed with a convincing imitation of paint splashes. An hour later she was gone.

Unlike the others, Webb was not there to work. After a solid week of reading program guides and listings he had had enough. More than enough. It was time to try a different approach.

To pass the time he had brought along some magazines: *Fortune, The Economist* and *Penthouse.* He concealed them inside a big systems manual and read as if absorbed in the mysteries of BANKNET. A girl from Sydney sprawled across the *Penthouse* centrefold, thrusting great breasts through a brass bedstead. Inspired by the financial report he had just finished, Webb wrote, "The Gross National Product of Australia" over her. Later, he laughed out loud on realising that the most blatantly suggestive photo he could find was of a chemical plant in New Jersey. Someone looked up, wondering.

Around 3:00 P.M., totally bored, he walked slowly through the office to discover only one other person still there. They exchanged nods but not words, sharing the loss of a Saturday. At 4:00 the programmer was still at his desk.

"Come on, you stupid bugger," Webb muttered.

119

"Don't be so bloody conscientious." But it was another thirty minutes before the man finally left.

Webb waited a long, painfully slow hour to be quite sure no one would return. Then he made one more careful circuit, checking that the floor was really deserted.

The big room was different when only he stood in it. Its emptiness seemed tangible and pervasive, as if circulating with the treated air—blown in or sucked out at the low grilles where the office wind hissed softly over steel louvres. Did the security men tour the building regularly? he wondered. He was a visitor, his ID said so. Would they come to see what he was doing, up there by himself?

He went first to Alloway's area and was struck again by the neatness. He opened the top drawer of the desk and found the man's diary. As he took it out he uncovered an expensive Hewlett-Packard pocket calculator and was intrigued to see that it was not a scientific version like his own but a business model with buttons for compound interest and depreciation. Beside it was a thin book of random numbers, packed with tables of digits guaranteed to have no order, no meaning. Webb had never found any use for random numbers.

The diary showed Alloway's schedule of regular project meetings stretching well into the future. He had noted the precise finishing times of his recent meetings. Curious, pedantic precision, like 17:04 on one occasion and 18:33 on another. There was no hint of how the man spent his evenings. But two weekends were crossed through boldly and the word "Alton" was written in the space for the preceding Friday evenings.

Alloway clearly planned a long way ahead. In July he would be going to Copenhagen for a conference on Computers in Banking. The man would probably go wild over there, Webb thought. In and out of the sex shops in that short grubby raincoat. Well, why not?

The other drawers held nothing of interest. Turning, Webb selected some files at random from a shelf. They were tidy, obviously thorough and also told him nothing. There were dozens of files on the shelves. The rows of bound computer listings would take days to search, he was sure. And looking for what?

To one side of the office there was a tall cabinet with sliding doors. He pushed and found it was locked. There were no locks on that floor, Jennifer Owen had told him, but perhaps Martin Alloway was a reasonable exception to the rule. There would be management records inside, and private personnel files. Webb searched the drawers again, this time for a key, but there wasn't one. He slid his plastic ID tag between the doors and against the catch. Once, he had been shown how to force locks that way. But the catch was square and he could not get the tag under it. He gave up. He had not been told what you did when that happened.

Crossing the room with what was probably unnecessary stealth, he consulted the floor plan Jennifer Owen had given him. He had circled five names apart from those of Jennifer herself and Alloway. All were senior people running small teams. People with what Webb called opportunity.

There was a remarkable sameness about four of the areas. Cleared and clean desk tops, precise filing, diaries that implied no existence outside of LDC. Webb spent ten minutes exploring each area, coming across nothing of relevance, nothing he could call a clue.

The fifth desk belonged to a young analyst called Huxley. His place was a world apart. He must be good, Webb thought, for Alloway to put up with it. It was untidy in a way that suggested untidiness as part of Huxley's style, an important element of his character. There was paper everywhere, unstable looking stacks of output were placed on the floor, the edges curled and often torn. Two photographs were pinned to a cupboard door, one of a singularly plain girl holding a very red baby, the other of Huxley with his arm round the girl, his elbow poking through a hole in his sweater and the inevitable cigarette in his mouth. During the week a permanent haze hung over that part of the office.

Webb sat, and a smell of stale tobacco floated up from the fabric of the chair. He moved a file from the top of the desk to find a distorted Olympic symbol underneath, printed in long dried coffee by the bottoms of plastic cups. He reached for the top drawer, trying to guess what disarray he would discover.

There was a faint noise from the direction of the outside lobby, sounding like a lift door opening. Webb could trace every minute, irregular path taken by the signals that jolted through his brain, and he leapt from the chair, breathing heavily. The aftermath of the shock rolled, echoing, through his body like thunder after lightning, striking at hands and knees and the back of his neck. He sank back into the chair, ears straining. There was the smell of tobacco again and for a moment he was a child again, back at home, creeping into a room he had believed to be empty, searching a lodger's jacket for money, then hearing the man turn in the bed beside him. Webb took deep gulps of air and felt the tingle in his nervous system subside, then die.

But nobody came and when, after a while, he went out to the lobby the indicators showed both lifts to be starionary on Level 1. The relief was intense, almost exhilarating. But he had learned a lesson, and he left his briefcase as if casually forgotten, just ahead of the door where it would fall if anyone came in. Now he became more aware of the sounds in the room and from other parts of the Centre. The hum of the air-conditioning hung disturbingly around him. Occasionally, mechanical knocks or whines echoed through the carcass of the building from somewhere below.

At last, Webb found himself in Jennifer Owen's area. He realised then that it had always been his main objective. The other searches had been . . . well, a kind of tuition. Do-it-yourself detective work.

It was a small area enclosed by a brown screen and two low walls of shelves. There were no plants there, no pictures or personal possessions in view. The desk top and the shelves overflowed with computer printout, but in a well-organised way. A black leather diary lay on the desk and Webb looked through it, finding the expected series of internal meetings, a conference in Brighton in some months' time, a love of opera revealed by several planned visits to Covent Garden. There were no other references to evening activities. The weekend spaces were always blank.

Webb was puzzled by a large red star occurring at intervals through the coming year. Then he noticed the regular frequency and smiled. Periodic Tables, his roommate at Oxford had called that kind of thing. "It's not their past diaries you should read," Edward had said, "it's the current one—the most useful personal intelligence on any bird you're after." But the smile soon faded. Webb dropped the diary back where he had found it. Her private rhythms were hardly . . . relevant. Above him, the building complained at the intrusion. Somewhere, metal had creaked against metal and the sound was carried, vibrating, along the red sprinkler system that patterned the ceiling. Webb became acutely aware of his own breath again, drawn noisily and rapidly.

He turned to the desk drawers. The lower, deeper one contained only project files and yet more program listings. A file chosen at random held only the inevitable notes to her staff and to Alloway. Webb swivelled in her chair, registering the sheer amount of paper surrounding him, just like everywhere else in the room. Who needed locks? The details of an illegal program patch could be anywhere—inserted between valid sheets of printout and looking exactly like them.

The top drawer held miscellaneous small items of stationery, a mirror and several lipsticks. There was a box of paper tissues, and when he moved it Webb discovered a plastic wallet of coloured snapshots. They showed Jennifer Owen on holiday and from the *taverna* in the background of one of them he guessed the place to be a Greek island, most likely Crete. There was Jennifer by herself. Jennifer with another girl. Jennifer in a tiny yellow bikini, looking brown and desirable. Touching her private snapshots, his fingers pressing against her image, Webb felt suddenly ill at ease, and he thrust them back in the drawer.

He left her area and stood for a short time in the middle of the big room, taking in the sounds of the building that never slept as it breathed and fidgeted. It had been a totally wasted day. He had learned nothing useful about his suspects, just a little about himself. He had felt the half-fear, half-elation of a thief at work. But what excitement there had been was gone and only an undertone of cheapness remained. And that was ridiculous, Webb told himself. How are you a thief if you steal nothing? How can you possibly consider yourself one when you have no idea what you are after?

He emerged from the building into evening. The cold city air brushed his face and he stood to breathe it in, tasting the cars, the people, the dirt. "Savour it while you can," Harrington had said at the beginning of the week, and that was exactly what Webb did. He found he forgot time at LDC, forgot the world outside. He got jet-lag just sitting at a stationary desk.

Suddenly, he remembered the hidden cameras and, shoulders well back, he walked boldly away down the centre of the narrow mews.

Chapter Thirteen

Monday, 17th January. Susan Faulkner called Webb at the Data Centre.

"Accounts," she began, assuming he would recognise her voice. "Sales, recruitment, payroll, meetings with the Inland Revenue . . ."

"Hold it, Sue! What the hell is this?"

"A memo to you from Andrew Shulton."

"And that's what it says? Just that?"

She nodded down the line. "I think it's supposed to be a list of all the things he's having to do himself with you away."

"Tell him balls."

"If that's what you want."

"You know what I mean. Write one of those tactful memos you're so good at doing for me. Tell him I'm working my guts out earning revenue. Sign it with my name."

"There's a new tower going up in the square," she told him. "It's called your in-tray."

Webb groaned and said he would be in the office for a few hours that evening. He promised to leave the cassettes from his Pocket Memo on her desk.

For perhaps ten minutes he worked on the bulky

program listing he had been reading when she called. Then he pushed it decisively to one side. It was time to meet Harrington again.

"Five minutes," the banker stated firmly. "That's all I can spare. I'm expected by the Almighty in Leadenhall Street." He declined to sit, to emphasise that he meant it.

"Two weeks and I'm getting nowhere," Webb confessed. "This system of yours just has to be the world's biggest haystack."

Harrington laughed. "And is there a needle?"

"How would I know," Webb retorted irritably. He took one of the meeting room chairs. If the banker wanted to stand that was his business. "I do know this—reading through endless reams of program listings is a complete waste of time. Even if there is a problem with BANKNET I'll never find it that way."

"If you say so. You're the expert on these things." Harrington made no attempt to conceal his amusement.

"So that's it," Webb said. "Progress to date, nil."

"Then what do you propose to do next? Have you any idea?"

"I have a suggestion, yes. But I need your approval because it's . . ." Webb fixed the older man with a resolute gaze. "It's a little irregular. I want to find out where your security is weak, to discover what your staff could get away with if they really tried. So I'd like to test your precautions against interference with the system. The idea is that I try to make an unauthorised program change myself, to see if I can do it undetected."

Harrington said nothing.

"I also want to see who I flush out . . . who I worry and why."

"No," the banker said. "That would be foolish. Totally irresponsible." And despite Webb's reasoned arguments he refused to consent.

"Then what do you suggest?" Webb demanded, as a final resort.

"What do *I* suggest? *You* damned well think of something, Mr. Webb. Earn that hundred and fifty a day! All I want is that you come to me with a clear message at the end of this project. Just let me know my system is clean if it is, or what has been done to it if it's been buggered. How you go about that is your problem. But make sure you play it by the book, understand?" Harrington walked to the door, then turned, wearing an unexpected half-smile.

"Tell me something. Do you like computers much?"

"They're my business, Mr. Harrington."

"Yes, yes, but do you actually *like* them?"

"Right now, not particularly. By Friday, who can say."

"You're being evasive."

"Perhaps."

"I don't like them," Harrington admitted. "Not one bit."

Webb showed his surprise.

"You must know what I mean?" the banker said. "Everything made more trouble, to make it more efficient. Things you need to know become impossible to get at and things you don't want at all are there in microseconds."

"You've just described this assignment perfectly," Webb retorted.

"Why, so I have," Harrington murmured as he left.

Webb stayed in the meeting room, deep in thought. Harrington's attitude, his seeming lack of concern, baffled him. But he was more immediately bothered about what his next move should be.

"Sod playing it by the book!" he resolved at last. And he made up his mind to ignore Harrington's refusal to approve his idea, and go ahead regardless. It would have been better if the man had agreed. Safer. But what the hell.

He decided he would write a program to read private customer information from the secure discs. Strictly, if BANKNET worked as the manuals said it did, the plan would prove to be impossible. But Webb believed he could see a way to carry it off. It could turn out to be a very profitable exercise.

The plan proved to be even more straightforward than he had expected. In only two days he had designed and coded his program and had it keypunched by Data Preparation. The program was christened

"SNOOPY." He was sure Harvey would appreciate that when he told him. On Wednesday, he entered the program at Run Control and checked the time it would be run on the computer.

Webb walked through the computer room to the lineprinter. He looked for a time at the output streaming from it. At first sight the printer appeared to be producing real bank statements, but when he looked more closely he saw that all the customers were Smiths and Browns, and that all their standing orders were to Jones & Company or XYZ Limited. Computer tests were the same the world over, he thought. No imagination.

The run ended and the computer halted, its console lights frozen. The operator came to change the continuous stationery, loading blank paper in place of the preprinted statement forms.

"Cheers," he said sarcastically as Webb moved out of his way.

He was in his twenties, long-haired and with many bracelets on both wrists. Webb was not welcome there, he made that plain without actually saying so.

The computer was restarted and paper began to fly through the printer again. Each new page appeared with the date and a page number, and the lines that followed rattled onto the paper faster than Webb could see. Occasionally, a page command from the computer flipped the paper at even higher speed to a new position. Sometimes the computer had nothing to say and the paper was still.

Four blank pages were ejected as a sign that a job had finished. The next job began and the system gave the programmer's name at the top of Page 1. It was still not Webb's run and he paced idly around the printer. The operator sat across the room at the console, staring disapproval.

Four blank pages were thrown in quick succession at Webb's feet. He moved to the front of the printer and saw, under the perspex cover, the system announcing the start of his program. But the job ran for no more than ten seconds before it terminated abruptly. He caught sight of a line that said simply, before the paper blurred upwards.

Webb tugged the pages away from the continuous strip at the back of the terminal. There were only five sheets, four of them blank. His program had a bug! Swearing, he pushed the listing into a large wastebin.

He was halfway to the lift before realising that he had probably acted too hastily, that he had barely read the computer analysis of his error. He thought he knew what the problem was, but it was as well to be sure. Turning, he went back to the computer room.

In his annoyance he had thrust the paper deep into the bin and the first batch of printout he removed was someone else's. He tried again and the second handful of creased paper was not his either. A glance told him that.

He never knew why one small group of numbers at the top of the page caught his eye but he did know in an instant that something was very wrong. Taking the entire contents of the bin he walked away like a foraging tramp who had struck lucky. As the door closed behind him he heard a shouted, "Oy!" from the operator. Webb piled the crumpled computer paper on his desk and dialled the Data Centre manager.

"Thadeus," the man said.

"My name is Webb. I'm here doing some work for Mr. Harrington."

"I've heard. What can I do for you, Mr. Webb?"

"I'm afraid I've been rather stupid. I dumped some output in the computer room last night and now I find I need it. When are the wastebins cleared in there?"

Thadeus took a moment to think. "Hard luck," he remarked. "We have a break in operations for a while around one in the morning and the cleaners go in then. Sorry, Mr. Webb, but your listing has already been shredded and incinerated."

"Is that certain?" Webb asked. "Absolutely certain?"

"I'm sorry, but it is."

Webb looked again at what he had found. It was a single sheet among the many pulled from the bin. There was no programmer's name on it. But the date at the top of the page was the 17th of January—two days earlier—and according to Thadeus that was impossible. Webb could imagine that paper might be left behind for one day. But for two?

He sat for a time, smiling. Now he knew! Someone really was playing games with BANKNET. He made a call to Susan, then walked to his car, the page concealed in a pocket.

Chapter Fourteen

It was a basement flat in a very ordinary suburb of Bristol. The bell did not work, and when Webb rattled the letterbox the flap stuck, making a timid sound. After some time a light came on in the hall. He could see the bare bulb through a glass panel. The girl who opened the door looked enquiringly at him as he stood in half darkness. She wore a tight sweater over very large breasts, no bra. Exactly Harvey's type.

"Is Mike in?" Webb asked.

Without a word she led him into a cluttered living room. In brighter light she was even bigger, with broad hips under a skirt that dropped to bare feet. Harvey was reclining on a couch, a can of beer in his hand, watching television.

"Jesus Christ!" he exclaimed, jumping up and slopping beer on the cushions in his surprise.

"Just passing," Webb said with a grin.

"Jesus bloody Christ," Harvey muttered, his head shaking in continued disbelief. "You should have called, Chris. Let me know."

"Sue didn't have your number. We have a rule about that, Mike. Always leave a phone number when you're away on site, you know that."

"Mea culpa," Harvey said without seeming especially bothered.

Webb looked from him to the girl and back, raising eyebrows, and Harvey introduced her simply as "Angela." Then he told her, "This is Chris Webb. One of my bosses."

"Oh." She pulled on her shoes, embarrassed.

Webb took a chair next to the paraffin heater. It produced its own kind of heat, vaguely damp and with a warmth Webb could taste. The room was stuffy from it.

"Coffee?" Angela volunteered.

"Please."

"It's only instant," she said apologetically.

"That's okay."

"Mild instant," Harvey said. "Coffee for people who don't like coffee."

The girl went to the kitchen and they heard the tap running and the clatter of cups. Harvey moved to the television and turned off the sound but left the picture on.

"Have you come to Bristol just to see me?"

"That's right."

"It's a bloody long way."

"It's fast, the M4 practically all the way. I find motorways very relaxing, actually."

"Cruising at a hundred and twenty!"

"You should try it," Webb said, smiling.

"No thanks." Harvey returned to the couch and stretched out, his eyes straying when they felt like it to the television.

"What do you think of Angie?"

"Big girl," Webb said, pursing his lips. "A cosy arrangement by the look of it."

"She's an operator. You know, on the client's computer."

"Is it true what they say about operators?"

"You bet!" Harvey's hands fondled compliant mounds of air. "Two months of passion in a far-off town."

"Get rid of her," Webb said. "For an hour or so."

"It's her flat, Chris!"

"Do it."

"Like that, is it?" Harvey said.

"Like that."

When Angela came back carrying a tin tray, Harvey winked at Webb and asked him if he had eaten.

"I didn't have the time," Webb said, taking the hint.

"Be a pet," Harvey said to the girl, "get us some food from the take-away."

"If you want." She was not especially eager.

"Fried chicken, I think. A barrel of the Colonel's best."

"That's bloody miles," she protested.

Harvey's eyes flickered towards Webb and she remembered who he was and shrugged agreement. Harvey produced a fiver from his hip pocket, waving Webb's money away.

"See you," Angela said, pulling on an amazingly tattered fur coat that had probably been quite valuable several owners earlier. Red fox, Webb thought, although he was not an expert. Alison had been the specialist on fur coats, the collector.

Harvey noticed the way Webb stared at it. "She cleans it in a machine at the launderette," he explained when she had gone.

"It's Waterman's," Webb said.

"I guessed as much."

"I'm after two things, Mike. We'll begin with this." Webb handed over the page of computer output. "I need a second opinion."

"What's there to say?" Harvey remarked after some minutes of silent examination, and obviously unsure of what was expected of him.

"See the date at the top?"

"Yes . . . ?"

"I found that today."

Harvey checked the date on his watch. "So?"

"What I mean is, it came off the computer today."

Harvey lay back, contemplating the ceiling. "Did it!" he exclaimed with dawning comprehension.

"So I want your opinion."

"Is there a simple explanation? Special tests being run on the machine or anything like that?"

"No."

"Then someone is frigging the system. What else could it be."

"Go on," Webb said.

"The date cell is in one of the most highly protected areas of computer memory. It's changed automatically

131

by the system at midnight. If the Waterman's procedures are as strict as I'd expect them to be it will be impossible to make a change at any other time. Except, of course, when the computer goes down for a while and gets out of sync with Greenwich."

"It didn't in the last two days," Webb said. "I checked."

"A system handling massive amounts of money," Harvey said with evident delight. "And money transactions have dates. Someone there is backdating . . ." he tried to think of what. "Something," he added with a helpless smile.

"But what?"

"Who knows, Chris. You can't tell from this. It's just a sheet of numbers. No programmer name, no program name, no titles to any of the numeric fields. Not a bloody clue."

"Keep going on the second opinion," Webb requested. "What part of the BANKNET system will he be using to make that change?"

"The Operating System, almost certainly."

"I think so, too."

"And you want to search for the patch? All the way through the OS?"

"What do you think!"

"Then you've got problems. The Operating System will be the most complex single program in BANKNET, I should think."

"Correct."

"How big is it, do you know?"

"Eighty-eight K. I checked that, too."

"Have you got a complete listing?"

"No, but I know how to get one."

Harvey laughed. "The very best of luck," he said. "Searching through eighty-eight thousand program instructions for . . . for what? Have you any idea?"

"Not an inkling," Webb admitted.

"Then you're going to have fun," Harvey suggested with friendly malice.

"Not me, Mike. *You* are."

Harvey's hands shot up to ward off the proposal. "Oh no. Not me. Oh no."

"It's a money machine, Mike. For God's sake, it's the biggest thing either of us will ever see."

"It's a bloody bank," Harvey said. "You must be barmy."

Webb got up with great deliberation. It was not a high room, and he thought standing might intimidate the younger man. The paraffin heater warmed his backside energetically.

"We've done it before," he pointed out quietly.

"Not to a bank!" Harvey retorted. "London Alliance was fun, Chris. Something new, a turn-on. But Kestrel scared the shit out of me. I didn't sleep for a week after you had to erase that program. Never again! And not a bloody bank. Jesus!"

Webb managed to stay remarkably calm. "You and me," he said, "have come up with something unique. *We steal crime.* Other people's. We let them do the planning and the hard work, let them prove it can be done undetected . . . except by us. Then we steal it. It's genius, Mike."

"That's as may be," Harvey said, his mind made up.

"Waterman's is the jackpot."

"All yours, Chris. I won't touch it. You can have this one all to yourself."

Webb crossed the room to sit beside him and a loose spring bit into his thigh. "Look, Mike, I can't search through that bloody OS. That's a young man's game. It needs you, your experience, your patience."

"Not me," Harvey repeated. "Sorry and all that."

Webb rested his head in his hands. Harvey thought at first it was mock despair, maybe even real despair. Then he saw that Webb was grappling with a decision. His mind finally made up, the consultant produced a letter from an inside pocket.

"I got this on Saturday. Read it."

Harvey skimmed through it. "Christ!" he said.

"Not the friendliest of bank managers, is he?"

"If all else fails," Harvey read aloud, "may I suggest with due respect that you consider realising the value of your car, settling for a more modest vehicle until your present financial problems are resolved." He looked up sympathetically. "What a bastard!" he declared. He knew how Webb felt about the car.

133

"You should meet him," Webb said with obvious distaste.

"Financial problems," Harvey repeated. "Mess would seem to be a better word."

"Probably."

"But you earn enough! Hell, if I had your salary . . ."

"I have the expense of a wife with none of the benefits. It goes."

"And there are those late nights and baize tables," Harvey ventured cautiously. He remembered one jaunt to Mayfair with Webb that had cost him too much to count as pleasure.

"That, too."

"And now you want me to help bail you out? Put myself at risk? Why should I?"

"God knows," Webb conceded.

Harvey sat in gloomy silence. Webb saw a box of Long Life beer cans under the sideboard and helped himself. The news had started on the television and without the sound it was impossible to tell what was happening, or where.

"Sorry," Harvey said at last.

"That's final?"

"Not a bank, Chris."

"Then stuff you!" Webb told him and stalked furiously to the door. Harvey followed and caught his arm.

"Chris . . ." he said.

"Okay, so I do it alone."

"I still work for you . . . for SysTech," Harvey reminded him, concerned.

"It won't make a difference. Why should it."

"You're sure?"

Webb managed a playful punch. "You'll be all right, honestly." Then he said, "Forget the letter. You never saw it, okay?"

"The chicken," Harvey said. "You'll stay for the chicken?"

But Webb walked on towards the front door. "A flying visit, you might say," he threw back over a shoulder.

Harvey stopped in the hall, his eyes dark hollows from the overhead bulb. "Jake Kennedy," he murmured. "You won't bring him into this?"

134

Webb gave a scornful laugh. "It hadn't crossed my mind."

"I know you, Chris. Leave him be. He's only a kid."

"He's almost your age!"

"He's a kid," Harvey insisted.

"You don't have much to go on, do you?" he called a moment later as Webb was climbing the stairs from the basement area. Webb could not be certain whether the comment was intended as helpful or disparaging.

He sat outside in the Porsche for a long time before moving off. He saw Angela come back with a plastic tub, a great bedraggled fox with captured fried chicken. She seemed not to see him parked across the street.

Jake Kennedy, Webb thought, and his anger at Harvey evaporated. It was a very good idea.

Chapter Fifteen

P.D. Sondhi was always the last to arrive each day, invariably the first to leave. The following morning, Webb waited for him with growing impatience.

As far as Webb could tell, the Program Librarian was little more than a clerk, keeping guard over the computer listings and IBM manuals held for central reference. It was a near impossible job, everyone agreed on that. Programmers helped themselves when he wasn't there, rarely bothering to log their loans in his record book and creating mild chaos when, weeks later, somebody else requested the same material. He was easygoing, seeming quite prepared to take the blame when that happened, going from desk to desk to track down the lost output. He had a fringe position on the BANKNET project, seeing some of what went on, doing none of it. To Sondhi, one young analyst told Webb with a knowing grin, computing was a spectator sport.

He came unusually late that day, making a public fuss about delays on the underground. He had on a fur hat that made him look vaguely Mongolian, great suede mitts, and a scarf that went three times round his neck, covering the lower part of his face. He took off an overcoat, several sizes too big, to reveal a heavy sweater under the kind of thick tweed suit favoured by retired colonels. He stamped his feet, then sat warming his hands on a cup of coffee. It wasn't *that* cold, Webb thought as he walked over, not for January.

"I need a program listing," he told the young Indian.

Sondhi, beaming, invited him to take a seat. There were several chairs scattered around, all piled high with computer output, and Webb had to clear one first.

"Just chuck it on the floor," Sondhi said. "I'll sort it out later, you know."

To come into his area was to enter a veritable cave of program listings. They surrounded Sondhi on three sides in shelves that reached towards the high ceiling. They covered most of the desk, and some binders had toppled over in a corner, probably weeks ago.

"It's a blinking cold morning," Sondhi said brightly. "Perishing."

Webb nodded noncommittally. Sondhi talked in Peter Sellers Indian, and it was difficult to keep a straight face.

"I'm doing a special project for Mr. Harrington," Webb explained.

"I've heard, we all have. Bottlenecks." Sondhi obviously found the word funny.

"It means I'm going to be looking in detail at the BANKNET listings."

"All of them?"

"Well, most of them by the time I finish. Certainly those most frequently used by the system."

"Martin Alloway says there aren't any bottlenecks," Sondhi said with borrowed confidence. "He's a genius, that man. If he says there aren't any . . ."

"I need the documentation, all the same," Webb told him. "And I expect to take rather a long time over it. So I'd like a copy I can hang onto without being a nuisance to anyone."

"Whatever you want," Sondhi said. "It's what I'm here for."

"I need a copy of the Operating System listing, for a start."

"All of it?" The hands fluttered in surprise.

"That's right."

"Do you know how many pages you're talking about, Mr. Webb?"

"Rather a lot, I imagine."

"That much," Sondhi said, sweeping an excited hand along several bulky volumes on a side shelf. "You can't need all that. Months it would take, reading that, you know."

"It's Harrington's idea, not mine," Webb said. "Can I have it or not?"

"You can borrow it if you want," Sondhi said reluctantly. "But if anybody else comes along who needs to refer to it . . ."

"That's no good, P.D. I did tell you, I must have uninterrupted use."

"Miss Owen has a complete set. She refers to it pretty damned often, I must say, but you could ask."

"No," Webb said. "I'd rather not."

"Martin Alloway, then. He also keeps a copy."

"Sorry."

"You'd rather not," Sondhi guessed.

"Telepathy," Webb said with the trace of a smile. Then he asked, "Now what, P.D.?"

"I'm here to solve such problems," Sondhi said. "To see you get what you need."

"Good," Webb said.

"I'll send down to the Archives for you, get a copy brought up."

"Normally, archived materials are out of date," Webb said, unsure of the idea. "Discarded to gather dust."

"They are. But the changes might be small, I think. You might not mind."

"Sorry again," Webb said. "But I have to study *exactly* what's running on the computers at this very minute. Do you see that?"

"I did have another set here, you know," Sondhi said. "Someone's whipped it, I don't know who. People do that when your back's turned."

"I only want some computer output," Webb remind-

137

ed him, becoming annoyed. "That shouldn't be impossible in this place!"

"There's so much blinking paper," Sondhi complained. "That's the trouble. And half of what I've got walks."

He fell silent, his eyes searching the disorder of his shelves for inspiration. He would have made a good shoe salesman, Webb thought. However often you refused his suggestions he still came back patiently with more.

"Manchester," the Indian said at last. "How does that sound?"

"Manchester?"

"Yes, we can raid MDC. What do you think?"

"That depends," Webb said.

"They keep two sets of the BANKNET listings up there. I'm sure they never use them. They don't need to understand anything, really. It's just a question of running the computers. Routine work, you know."

"It's a different centre," Webb said. "They'll have different programs, surely?"

"No, Mr. Webb, exactly the same programs. They have different branches on-line, different customers, but the programs are identical to those used here in London."

"Are you certain about that?" Webb asked. Now that Sondhi mentioned it, he seemed to remember reading that somewhere.

"Page one of the Introduction To BANKNET," Sondhi said.

"Of course!"

"MDC isn't a development centre like this, you know. They don't really need to understand a blinking thing. It's all routine up there. We even install the programs for them."

"Who does that, P.D.? Just out of interest."

"Paul Huxley."

"Bearded man? Smokes nonstop?"

"That's the one. And if it's a big change, a major modification, Martin Alloway goes along to see to it personally."

"Manchester," Webb said. "You're a smart man, P.D. What do I do, go up there?"

138

"No need for that. I can call the manager at MDC right now, you know, to arrange for a copy to be delivered by our Transit Service. It's what . . . Thursday today? It should be on your desk when you arrive on Monday."

"Can I borrow your set until then?"

"Most certainly. Help yourself."

"Do you keep records of who originally worked on the various BANKNET programs, by the way?" Webb's question came as a casual aside.

"Of course. These people record everything, never throw anything away." Sondhi gave a helpless gesture. "It's so much easier to keep stuff than decide to get rid of it, you know."

"Who worked on the Operating System? Just in case I need part of it explained."

Sondhi tugged a thick ledger from a pile on his desk, sending a number of books crashing to the floor. He took no notice, as though it was a regular occurrence.

"Six people in all," he said after a search. "Owen, Penfold, Huxley, Kovak, Ellison, Andrews."

Webb noted the names. "And Alloway, I suppose?"

"It doesn't say so here. But he gets involved in most things."

Webb moved to the shelves to take the binders. They seemed to grow in size as he gathered them in his arms.

"I'll give you a hand," Sondhi said, and they shared the load.

"Do you know Wembley?" he asked Webb on the way across the room.

"Only to pass through."

"That's where I live, you know. A flat with two friends. I'd like a house there one day. It's a nice area, so convenient. But prices . . ."

"One day," Webb said, his mind elsewhere. The weight of the volumes he carried was intimidating, and Sondhi had still more. Poor old Jake!

They heaped the binders on Webb's desk.

"Not exactly bedtime reading, is it?" Webb said.

Kennedy would need a complete copy of the listing. That wouldn't be easy to arrange. The copy from Manchester had to remain at the center because Sondhi had recorded the loan. But Webb was confident Sondhi's own version would never be missed. And if it was, so what? Output walked. It happened all the time.

At lunchtime, the office became emptier. A group of programmers stayed but moved to a far corner with sandwiches and played bridge. Making sure he was unobserved, Webb removed the listing from the binders and replaced it with an equal quantity of output taken at random from the material Jennifer Owen had given him on his first day at LDC. Then he hid the stolen listings on his shelves for when he could think of a safe way to get it past the security checks.

Later, he called SysTech. Susan wanted to gossip but he told her crisply, "Get Jake to stay late tonight, will you? Say I'll buy him dinner."

"You might have a problem there," she said, "but I'll see."

There was a *thud* from the phone as it was put down and he could hear distant voices and the sound of a typewriter.

"I thought so," Susan said when she returned. "He's in Austria, skiing."

"He's doing bloody *what*?"

"Holiday, Chris. You know."

"Till when?"

"Another two weeks. He's only just gone. Yesterday, I think."

"Hell!" Webb said. "Nobody's ever there when you want them, these days."

He took the listing down again and began working laboriously through it. He stayed until nearly midnight. He did the same the following day. On Saturday, he was at the Centre all day, alone from late afternoon. On Sunday, he had the office completely to himself. When he finally left at eight in the evening he was barely a tenth of the way into the seemingly endless list of instructions. He had discovered nothing.

Chapter Sixteen

Tuesday. Jennifer Owen kept Webb under close surveillance for most of the day, moving her chair a little for better line of sight to his desk. Early on, he went to collect the results of an overnight computer run. The program had obviously failed, and he spent an hour checking the output for the likely bug. There was a keypunch machine in an isolated corner of the office, shielded by padded screens to reduce the clatter, and he used it for a short time—just long enough to change three or four cards, she guessed. Later, she saw him leave carrying the card tray and with a run request form half-tucked into a pocket.

Mostly, he studied a massive program listing, moving a ruler down the page to mark his slow progress. He made copious notes, referred frequently to BANK-NET manuals for guidance, occasionally used his calculator to verify some arithmetic. He drank coffee almost nonstop. He spoke to no one. He rarely looked up, never suspected she was watching.

Late in the afternoon, on an impulse, she left the Centre briefly. There was a small grocers nearby, up a side street. There were mottled marble counters and slatted wood shelves sparsely stocked with tins that had faded labels and had lost their shine. There was a pervasive smell of bread and cheeses, not exactly stale, but not refrigerated as in the supermarkets. She bought some bacon and the man turned the handle on a big, old machine that *swished* through the side of smoked meat, peeling off paper-thin slices. She hadn't seen a machine like it for years.

A little after 7:30 P.M. she judged that Webb was on the point of leaving. Like a sleeper about to wake, his patterns of movement changed and he became distinctly restive. She decided it was time to make her approach.

"You're a chain drinker," she told him. Empty plastic cups lined the front of the desk.

He looked up and smiled, but in a distracted way, his thoughts still elsewhere.

"I was wondering," she said, "if you were thinking of going soon, and without any immediate plans . . . ?"

He stood up, intrigued. "I was, and I haven't."

"A quick drink maybe, Christopher? Somewhere nearby?"

"What a great idea," Webb said, closing the cover on the program listing. His watch surprised him and he asked, "Where did the day go?"

"Time flies when you're having fun." Without moving her head too obviously she could just make out the words, "Disc Subsystem," upside down on the front of the binder. Not exactly pleasure, she thought, if you were new to it.

"Doesn't it just," he said, pulling a face. He put on his overcoat, then searched his briefcase. He did it twice, the second time with great deliberation. He began pulling out drawers, going through pockets.

"Lost something?" she asked.

"Just a letter. I thought I had it with me, but perhaps . . ."

"Someone special?" The thoroughness of the search suggested it might be.

"Sort of. Fevered words from a man in Chelsea."

"Fascinating," she said, raising eyebrows.

"My bank manager, Jennifer," he said, to put her right.

"Oh."

He gave up the search. As he came round the desk the back of her hand brushed his coat to be sure it was cashmere.

"Now I come to think of it," she said, "you do rather look like a man with an overdraft. It's always the smart ones who have them."

He was dubious about the sex appeal of overdrafts. He patted his pockets to remind her the letter was mislaid.

"We'll never know," he told her with exaggerated innocence.

She led the way through quiet, empty streets, taking a route unfamiliar to him that, tacking first in one direction, then another, carried them north towards Baker Street.

"We could have used my car," Webb said.

"I like walking," she replied. A moment later she added, "Besides, I was warned about men with expensive foreign cars."

"And . . . ?" Webb asked. She must have seen it in the car park. The number plate was a giveaway.

But all she said was a knowing, "Ah."

A short distance from the Data Centre they passed along a particularly narrow and ill-lit street. On one side there was a building site protected by hoardings that partly obstructed an already slender pavement. There was a viewhole, a Public Supervision Post, according to the sign beside it, and Webb stopped to peer through. He saw a vast pit extending well below street level, dark and deserted and littered with bright yellow earthmovers, some at crazy angles like forgotten Tonka toys. The façade of the original building had been left standing, kept together by an intricate lattice of weathered steel tubes. It stretched upwards into the black sky, looking unreal in the half-light of a solitary streetlamp.

"It doesn't seem worth all this trouble to preserve," Webb said, pointing up. "It's hardly beautiful." He brushed against the scaffolding and dark rust flaked onto his shoulder.

"I think it's rather touching," she said. "Why should buildings die just because they're old?"

Across the pavement a trail of broken slabs and drying mud marked an entrance for site vehicles. She slipped and had to catch his arm for support. Then as they walked on she tucked her hand further in and left it there.

They came to a small and uncrowded pub just off Marylebone High Street and sat with their drinks in a great curve of buttoned brown leather, worn in places to the colour of parchment. The patterned ceiling was yellowed with years of smoke. It was a very plain, unpretentious place. She liked them like that, she explained. The serious drinkers were too busy complaining about what the brewers were doing to beer to notice what they were doing to the pubs.

"I had a motive in suggesting this," she confessed at last.

"I rather hoped so."

"Seriously, Christopher . . ."

"Look," he said, "my most serious face," and he set his mouth in a firm line to prove it.

"You're making it more difficult for me," she told him. So he kept quiet for a time only to find that she did, too.

"I can be very thick-skinned when I want," he volunteered. "If that helps?"

"It's just that I know what you're doing." The remark was blurted out and she sipped hard at her drink the moment it was said.

"And what *am* I doing?"

"Trying to break the system. I want to ask you . . . please don't."

"My program . . . ?"

"Yes, of course."

"You're a very smart lady," he said, "discovering the crime like that."

"It was pure accident. An operator dropped your card tray last night and shuffled your program deck. I happened to be there. I only wanted to help, but I saw what you were up to."

"It's always an accident, Jennifer. Did you know ninety-five percent of computer crime is discovered by chance?" It sounded more flippant than he intended.

"It's not bloody funny," she said.

But it was, really, Webb was thinking. He had never been caught before. And to be caught by her, of all people . . .

"It had to happen," she said with a shrug. "It's a very clumsy program, Christopher. The others will find out if you go on, they're bound to."

"Have you told anyone?" he asked anxiously.

"Not yet. But if I have to . . ."

"Would you believe me if I said my sole aim was to test the effectiveness of your security?"

She played with her glass before looking up. "I'd like to. But no, I wouldn't." She submerged a piece of dying ice with an impeccably trimmed and polished nail. "You realise it occurs to all of us at first? Fiddling, I mean. There's that big system, those enormous amounts of money. You think how marvellous it would be just to have point nought nought one percent of a single day's cash flow. I mean, it seems so easy. We're all such highly intelligent people at LDC, resourceful."

"I go for the modesty," he said with a laugh.

"We *are*, Christopher." She placed a hand on his arm. "Hell, I'm an elitist and I don't care who knows it. There's the sheer challenge . . . the idea of that great protected computer bust open and robbed like a piggy bank. But it's a silly thought, don't you see? Get caught and you won't have a profession any more. I don't know about you but I couldn't stand that."

"What's a profession," Webb said. "Just a pompous way of making a bit more money than average."

"Hmmph to that," she snorted. She finished her drink and said, "I cancelled your run this afternoon. I told them you'd found another error in your program."

"That was a nice thought. Thanks."

"Your cards are still at Run Control. But don't use them again, please. Promise to do it for me, if not for yourself."

Webb crunched on some ice fished from the bottom of his glass.

"You know, you're quite right, Jennifer. It isn't a very clever program. If I was starting again now . . ."

But she refused to be distracted, insisting, "I want your promise . . ."

"You have it, my word on that," he said, without having to give it much thought. The attempt on the secure data had been little more than a stopgap measure while he considered what else to do. And now he knew about the patch in the Operating System . . .

She smiled and said, "Frankly, it's a bloody awful program. That's entirely the wrong way to do it."

"*Now* you tell me!" he said with a wry grin.

"Well, honestly . . ." She laughed, holding out her glass for a refill.

Looking back at her from the bar, Webb wondered what she was really up to. She might be genuine, he thought, acting out of concern for him. It was possible.

Or she might simply be removing an awkward attempt on BANKNET—one that could attract attention and put at risk some more ambitious plan of her own. Right now it didn't seem to matter. She was very attractive, framed in the sweep of padded leather.

When he went back, he took the opportunity to sit very close, his arm reaching behind her to the top of the bench.

"It's somehow reassuring, knowing you considered fiddling the system, too," he said.

"Not for long, and not seriously." She leaned into his arm.

"And what did you decide? Could you get away with it if you wanted?"

"That's a very sly question."

"It is, rather," he admitted.

"No, I don't think I could."

"Which is why you gave up the idea?"

"Maybe. Then again, maybe I'm just honest."

"Middle-class virtue rearing its head?"

"It's the way I was brought up," she retorted. "A barrister for a father and a solicitor for a mother, alright?" She searched her bag, aimlessly lifting papers and cosmetics, but taking out nothing. Webb was glad she couldn't see his smile. He found it funny that she felt the need to be so defensive about honesty.

"I'd like to hear why you thought you wouldn't get away with it," he said.

"Mainly because a very shrewd man watches everything I and my team do."

"Alloway?"

"Martin, yes."

"So, who watches him?"

"No one, as far as I can tell. At least, no one with the technical background to understand BANKNET properly."

"That's what I thought," Webb said quietly.

"Oh, no," she exclaimed, reading his mind. "No way. Not Martin."

"Woman's intuition?"

"Yes, I suppose it is. Or a woman's eye for detail, which probably comes to the same thing." She moved away slightly, turning to face him. "I knew you'd have

146

a crack at BANKNET the moment I saw you. There's something about you, the way you dress, that flashy car. It wouldn't matter how much money you got away with, you'd still manage to spend it."

"I'd certainly try." Webb's manner was breezy, but he found the insight disconcerting.

"Not Martin, though," she said. "Do you know, he's got only two suits and they're exactly the same? I thought he had just the one, but he came back one afternoon carrying the other under a dry-cleaners' wrap. Can you imagine, Christopher? Only two suits and exactly the same, exactly. I've never seen you wear the same thing twice. Never the same tie, or shirt, or jacket."

"You've been looking," Webb said in a tone of friendly accusation.

"When I thought about it, yes." Her eyes were bothered by the admission and for an instant they clouded over, just as he'd seen before.

She drained the last milky traces of her Ricard and stood, smoothing her coat back to its required perfection.

"I'd like a lift if you feel like it?"

"Delighted."

"My flat's not far. Putney."

"I might have guessed," Webb said. "Just the right kind of neighbourhood. Quite close to the centre of town, thoroughly middle class." He felt like getting at her, for some reason.

"Bastard," she said.

She moved against him, then swung over him. She peered down, unable to see clearly in the darkness of the bedroom. Her hair brushed his forehead and swept across closed eyes. That, or the slow movement of her hand, caused him to stir and return the gaze. She gripped a thigh tightly between her knees.

He looked up, trying to adjust to an almost total lack of light. Her head hung in the air above him, the features shadowed and indistinct. He could just, but only just, make out her eyes and in the blackness they might have been glass. His hand moved off by itself, exploring like hers. She was wet and yielding.

147

"I wasn't very good, was I, Christopher? Too nervous."

"I hadn't noticed." He had but it had seemed not to matter. His hand moved up to trace slow, sticky patterns across a breast.

"I'm not exactly stacked, am I?"

"I hadn't noticed that, either."

"Men always prefer birds with big boobs, admit it."

"I go for faces," Webb said. "Especially eyes."

She sat up abruptly. "I need a drink. Do you need a drink?"

"More energy," he said. "If you've got any of that."

She moved across the room. Silhouetted in the door, she seemed small and very slender, like a much younger girl. Her body wasn't exciting, but it was good to look at, all the same. He lay back, closing his eyes to keep it in his mind.

She came back with two tumblers of scotch and sat on the edge of the bed. Her glass was surprisingly full.

"It's a lonely place, LDC," she said, so quietly he could barely hear. "You wouldn't think so, with all those desks so close together. But that makes it worse, if anything."

"I had noticed," he said, his fingers roaming across her back.

"You're an outsider, Christopher. Imagine what it's like working there all the time. And for a woman . . ." She broke off, raising the tumbler to her lips.

"You seem to manage pretty well."

"I have to, don't I? I have a position, second only to Martin. But I can't be seen to be too involved with the others, too interested in anyone. They'd forgive it in a man, but not with me."

A car moved off down the street, brightening the room as it passed. He saw her eyes, very wide, like those of an animal caught in headlights. He noticed the thin circular rim where the opaque brown met an annulus of clearer, speckled colour. At the edges the surfaces were moister, softer than he had seen them before. Contact lenses! he realised with a start. Plastic! Eyes that had that effect on him and all the time they were only bloody plastic. Strangely, as he got over it, it

148

made her seem more vulnerable, instantly more attractive. He didn't quite know why.

Seeing the way he stared, she leaned close, misunderstanding.

"I'm not a conquest, Christopher, don't ever think that. If anything, it's the other way round. I invited you, remember?"

"Let's call it fifty-fifty, shall we?"

She got back into the bed. "I'll settle for that."

Webb rubbed his nose firmly against hers, a slow circular movement paralleled by his tongue against her cheek.

"You'll stay the night?" she asked.

"I haven't got a wife to get back to, if that's what you mean?"

"To get back to . . . ?"

"I'm not sure where she is. Alison, her name is. She's a bitch."

"They always are," Jennifer said in a matter-of-fact way. Then she moved above him again and asked, "What do you have for breakfast, Christopher. Lots of stuff, or juice, or what?"

"Breakfast?" He laughed. He didn't know for sure what time it was, but it couldn't be midnight yet.

"I don't know why I thought of it," she said. "But I just remembered—I've got some bacon in the freezer, and I never eat it myself."

Chapter Seventeen

Friday. Webb reached the twenty-five-thousandth instruction in the Operating System. He double-checked, rapidly counting pages to be sure. *The twenty-five-thousandth!* Nearly a third of the way through and still nothing, still no trace of the patch.

Kestrel hadn't been like this, he thought with regret, or London Alliance. They had been far simpler systems, sure. But more important, he'd had Harvey around. Harvey ate program listings for the fun of it, read them the way others would read a book. He needed him now, that was the trouble. Or failing him, Kennedy. And where was bloody Jake? Skiing! Arsing around on some Austrian *piste* when there was work to be done.

Webb sat back and closed his eyes, thinking of London Alliance, reliving the pleasure of that moment in the basement tape store when he and Harvey had caught a man in the act. In teletype delicto, as Harvey had called it later. What was the security man's name? Webb could not remember. It would all have looked so easy to him.

Slowly, something began to bother him, pricking uncomfortably at his subconscious. It was to do with London Alliance and it was important. At least, he *thought* it was important. But what? He delved into his memory but could not quite locate it. He probed deeper but the recollection refused to take shape, always moving tantalisingly away just out of reach, always hidden around a corner with only a shadow to hint that it was there. A computer would not have that problem, Webb thought. Computers might be dumb but at least they never forget.

He tried yet again. In his mind he replayed the scene in the data library under Lombard Street. He found he could recall some details with a clarity that surprised him—a tear in Harvey's jacket where it hung over his chair, a scratch on the teletype that he had hardly noticed at the time. But there were obstinate gaps, too. Periods of minutes when the picture went completely blank.

Chambers! That was the man's name, Chambers. And he was after something Chambers had said. No, something he had asked as they tried to explain what was happening on the computer. Of course! Now he remembered. It was about the program patch. That was it. Webb was telling him what a patch was.

"What in hell's name is that?" Chambers had asked.

"A change added after the program had been prepared and tested," Webb had said. "Someone else reading the program listings will see no sign that it's there."

And then Chambers had started to say, "But doesn't that mean . . ."

Yes, Webb thought, that means . . . Amazed at his own stupidity, he stared blankly at the binders on his desk. *Someone else reading the program listings will see no sign that it's there.* In a ritual gesture of disgust he pushed them aside. Very slowly, he stood up, then he marched towards the far door. Acutely aware of the others in the room, he somehow remained impassive as he left. Not until the lift door closed behind him did he allow any outward sign of what he felt. He punched the lift wall viciously, just once, so that it hurt, which was the whole idea.

"Shit!" he told himself. "You stupid shit. Call yourself a professional!"

He walked briskly to the car park to collect the Porsche from a concrete bay on an upper floor. He pressed a button on his door, to send the window sliding silently down so he could hear the high, tearing shriek of the air-cooled engine echoing in the gloomy spaces as he descended the ramp. On the short drive to Fitzroy Square he kept in first or second gear, accelerating hard when he could despite the press of traffic. He eased his fury by throwing sharp sheets of sound at the people and vehicles around him.

Susan Faulkner must have heard him park across the road, the car straddling a yellow line, with two wheels on the pavement. When he arrived at his desk she was sitting there waiting, and faint trails of steam rose from a fresh coffee placed on the blotter just in front of his leather chair.

"There are times . . ." he began, but changed his mind and said instead, "I'm a bloody fool."

"Is it Waterman's?" she asked sympathetically. "Is something wrong?"

"I don't want to hear about Waterman's," he told her savagely. Then he said, "A bloody fool," again, shaking his head.

"Waterman's?" she said, wide-eyed. "Never heard of them."

Webb tried to show a semblance of calm and asked her, "When did you say Jake is due back, again?"

"Monday week."

"I'll wait until then. I've already wasted a bloody week. Another bloody week won't hurt now."

"Andrew Shulton has got him working on a project, Chris."

"We'll see," he retorted. He turned to stare out of the window, apparently forgetting she was there.

"I've got a huge pile of messages and actions for you," she said cautiously.

"Good," he snapped over a shoulder. "Anything to take my mind off BANKNET."

On her desk a tray spilled a mountain of notes and memoranda, topped by a piece of card carrying the word "URGENT" in great red felt-tip letters. She could not have found a better way of advertising to the others at SysTech how behind he was with his work. She dropped the tray in front of him and stood waiting as he thumbed through the papers. Near the top he uncovered a short message in her tidy handwriting. It said:

Mike Harvey called. He hasn't changed his mind but have you remembered that looking at the listing will probably do no good? Have you thought of taking a memory dump instead? That's the only way to find it. (He did that at London Alliance, remember?) He says the best of British luck and would you like Angela when he's finished!!!

"When did he phone?" Webb demanded, waving the note under her nose.

"Several days ago. Monday, I think."

"Thank you very much, Susan," Webb said with heavy sarcasm.

"He didn't tell me it was urgent URGENT," she protested.

"Forget it," he said in a softer tone. What did it matter now, anyway?

She began to walk away but he called, "There's a job you can be getting on with."

She came back and sat down, pencil and notebook at the ready.

"Type me some envelopes addressed to some potential clients, Sue. I'll need twenty, I think. You'll find the names and addresses in the central marketing index. Brown A-three envelopes with 'PRIVATE' marked boldly at the top. And thirty-pence stamps, I guess."

"Will do. But there must be hundreds of names in that index, Chris. Which twenty did you have in mind?"

"Any twenty." Webb gave a weary smile. "You choose."

He worked for several hours, catching up on correspondence and project reports and countless internal memoranda. There were far too many memos for such a small company. Coming back after some weeks away, he could see that. It was like returning home after a long holiday with eyes newly readjusted to the truth and discovering how small all the rooms really were. He came across notes claiming credit for what had gone well, others subtly laying the blame elsewhere for what had not, yet others preparing defences in advance for what, the writers obviously suspected, could very likely go wrong in the near future. Whoever said the age of writing was dead? Here were all these young men writing to one another. All in the same compact building, in adjacent offices even, yet having to exchange notes littered with phrases only a few months old and excuses as old as time. All with nothing to say, when you came down to it. And everyone copying in everyone else who might be remotely interested, or who they thought should be. The Carbon Corporation had plenty to answer for, Webb decided.

Susan interrupted with a curt buzz on the intercom.

"It's Mr. Curtis."

"Curtis . . . ?" Webb knew the name but could not place it for a moment.

"Your bank manager."

"Hell! How does he sound?"

"I can't really say. Like a bank manager, I suppose."

"You might as well put him through," Webb told her in a resigned voice.

"And how do I find you today?" Curtis began. The joviality seemed even more forced than usual.

He was fine, Webb replied, and enquired about Curtis, who said he mustn't grumble, not really. He was nervous, actually nervous. Webb could hear it in the voice.

"Look, Mr. Webb, I don't know whether the Post Office have performed with their usual abysmal efficiency. But did you get my letter yet?"

"Yes," Webb answered hesitantly. "I was going to . . ."

"This morning, it would have been."

"No, not that one."

Another one! Webb thought. Jesus bloody Christ!

"Ah," Curtis said with evident relief. "Look, do me a favour, would you? Ignore it when it comes. It's a rather . . . er, direct communication, that's the problem. When I wrote it yesterday . . . Well, that's all water under the bridge now. Look, it's not the bank's interests that matter most in these cases, do you follow? We try to act in the best interests of the customer, too. I hope you see that."

"Of course," Webb said, just to fill a silence.

"It's most embarrassing," Curtis said.

"You want me to take no notice of your latest letter, is that correct?"

"I really am *most* sorry, Mr. Webb. Of course, if you had thought to advise us of your expectations I would never have acted like that. That goes without saying. But to find myself writing with such . . . finality the very day before a major improvement in your affairs . . . I can only apologise. What else can I say?"

"Indeed," Webb muttered mechanically.

"If you would like me to write formally? Put the record straight, so to speak?"

Webb heard himself say how unnecessary that was.

"Mr. Curtis," he said then, "I'm sure it will be all right but can I check the amount? Just to be certain."

"Nine thousand pounds precisely."

"Did you say nine *thousand?*"

"That's right."

For the briefest moment Webb considered admitting that it had to be a mistake. But then he said, "That's fine. As it should be."

Let them find out themselves, he decided. There was always a remote chance they might not.

"The residue is just over six thousand after the overdraft is wiped out," Curtis said happily. "If you have no immediate plans perhaps I could suggest transfer of the bulk of that amount to a new deposit account? Make sure it stays put for a while, if you follow? How does that sound?"

Webb replied that it sounded just fine and agreed to call in to arrange it. He sat staring at the telephone when he rang off.

Susan came over to ask, "Is anything wrong?"

"Do you believe in miracles, Sue?"

"Not usually."

"Nor me," Webb said.

He went to the basement, to the terminal room. He wanted to be alone, to think. Working out problems was often easier sitting at a terminal and chatting idly to the machine. Computers were undemanding in conversation, answering only when you wanted them to, never changing the subject. Sometimes, Webb felt a computer was the best company you could find.

He locked the door and started the teletype. He dialled the time-sharing service SysTech used and logged in his personal code number.

"PROGRAM?" the terminal asked.

"21," Webb replied, using the keyboard.

The computer, several miles away, spent a few seconds searching its files. Then it confirmed.

"TWENTYONE," and after the briefest pause added,

"GAME NUMBER 7033"

"Is it really?" Webb murmured.

"INPUT MAX AND MIN STAKES," the terminal asked. Webb keyed in £1 and £50.

"NEW DECK," the terminal announced,

"DEALING FOR GAME 1 OF SESSION"

"STAKE?"

Webb used the keyboard to bet £5.

"DEALER UP CARD= ACE," the terminal told him,

"YOUR HAND= 4 AND 8"

155

"CARD," Webb demanded without hesitation, and the computer dealt him a six. In a few moments more he had a total of twenty-one and had won the game.

They started a new hand and his mind wandered. *Where had the money in his account come from?* It was no mistake, he was becoming sure of that. Mistakes of that kind never happen, not when you need them to and certainly never with banks. The distant computer was patient, prepared to wait all day if he wanted. He remembered the game and bet heavily on what looked to be a good hand. The computer won.

"DEALING FOR GAME 3 OF SESSION," it said immediately, eager for more.

"STAKE?"

Webb dropped his bet to £5, forcing caution.

"DEALER UP CARD = 10"

"YOUR HAND = 7 AND 7"

"SPLIT," Webb said. This time he won.

"DEALING FOR GAME 4 OF SESSION," the computer said, without a pause. It would go on indefinitely until he called a halt. Win or lose, its appetite was insatiable.

Webb kept it waiting again. *Where did the money come from?* He did not bank with Waterman's, but he was developing a very uncomfortable feeling that it was connected in some way with BANKNET. It was an obvious thought now, but it simply had not occurred to him when he was talking to Curtis. *Who or what was giving him money? And why?*

On an impulse he asked the computer,

"WHERE DID THE £9K COME FROM?" as if it ought to understand these things.

"ILLEGAL DATA," it said, giving the only reply it could.

"That's what I think, too," Webb said quietly.

There was an urgent knocking on the door and he unlocked it, to find Susan standing there, breathless from running down the stairs.

"I tried to call," she said, "but the extension is engaged."

"I'm on-line to the computer," he explained. Behind him the receiver was off the hook and lying on a table.

156

Carefully, he stood so that she could not see the teletype printout.

"I've Waterman's for you, the London Data Centre. It's the Chief Operator. He's holding on."

"Did he say why?"

"It's about your program."

"What program?"

"The one you're running at the Data Centre. I didn't follow it all, quite honestly." She produced a quizzical expression and said provocatively, "He sounds pretty wild for some reason."

"You can go straight back and tell him I'm not running any program today."

"But he said . . ."

"Just do it, Sue! Okay?"

When she had gone, he remembered that he had not bothered to collect his program cards from Run Control. They might have been sent to the computer room by mistake. But he became distinctly uneasy. Two mistakes in one day and both to do with banks. It didn't feel right.

Susan was back quickly, breathing heavily and looking cross.

"Will you talk to the man *please*, Chris? He makes no sense to me but it sounds serious."

"You told him I'm not making any runs today?"

"He says you are, says your name is as clear as daylight on the display screen. He says you damned near wrecked the system before he realised and killed the run. Is that the phrase? Killed?"

"He said *what*, Sue?"

"That you've erased half the BANKNET programs. You really ought to talk to him."

"Yes," Webb said. "I think I better had."

Chapter Eighteen

Martin Alloway found the Chief Operator's report already on his desk when he arrived on Monday. One of Mr. Webb's tests had run wild, it said, and

157

destroyed a significant number of the BANKNET programs. The duty operator had quickly closed down the LDC computers. She had then arranged for a master copy of the BANKNET system to be sent up from the Program Library and had brought the computers back on stream. The London Centre had been out of action for thirty-six minutes and Manchester had automatically assumed control of the national BANKNET service during that time. That was all there was to it. It had been outside banking hours and the effect on system operations had been minimal. The emergency procedures had worked perfectly. No data had been lost. However, the report pointed out, the accidental destruction of vital programs had serious implications. It was assumed that Mr. Alloway would take whatever action was necessary?

Alloway considered the situation carefully. Of course, the matter would have to be referred to Alex Harrington. But perhaps not just yet. There were one or two questions he wanted answered first. He lifted his receiver and dialled.

Somehow, the moment Webb's telephone rang he knew who it was.

"You have some explaining to do," Alloway began, without any preliminaries. "I believe you know what I mean."

"I can guess," Webb said. It seemed the wrong time to make his protest of innocence.

"I don't think we should get together here, though. Open plan, walls have ears and all that. How about over lunch?"

"Why not."

"It's crazy, really," Alloway said. "I mean, we've got this guarded building, every device you can think of, and yet we've got to escape to some restaurant for a serious talk about security. Still, that's what Alex seems to do, so why not us?"

"There's always the meeting room down the corridor," Webb suggested, thinking that perhaps that way they would get it over rather quicker.

"No, we'll follow the boss man's admirable exam-

158

ple," Alloway insisted. "I fancy a spot of fish myself. That okay with you?"

"Perfectly."

"The Pescatori in Charlotte Street, I think. It's incredibly busy and noisy at lunchtimes. I mean, what could be more private!"

Webb said he knew the Trattoria well. It was a favourite place to take SysTech clients, just five minutes walk from the square.

"One o'clock, then," Alloway said. "There. The table will be in my name."

He sounded remarkably friendly, all things considered.

Webb arrived at the Italian restaurant exactly on time and was shown to a small corner table for two. The sounds hung thick in the air, earnest talk and bursts of laughter and the clatter of cutlery. Webb could never work out how people could make so much din as they ate, how a small number in a restaurant could comfortably rival a football crowd. Overhead, a full-sized rowing boat was anchored in a dusty swathe of real fishing net.

Fifteen minutes later there was still no sign of Alloway. He didn't seem the type to be late unless it was deliberate, a tactic to make Webb more ill at ease than he already was. It would work, too, Webb realised. He ordered a drink and waited, picking at the rush table mat with his fork. Between plaster pillars he saw a large slab ornately covered with raw seafood and the centre-piece of red mullet turned a score of sad, misted eyes in his direction.

Alloway eventually appeared at one-thirty and took the facing chair, rubbing his hands. He made no apology.

"Optimistic fellow," he said breezily, pointing to Webb's Campari. "Looking at the world through a rose-coloured glass, eh?" He sniggered at his own joke. "Have you ordered, by the way?"

"No. I was waiting for you."

"We were going to have a bite together, anyway. I remembered that on the way here."

"I called several times last week, but you were always out."

"Manchester," Alloway said. "You've got to hold their hands up there. Can't do a bloody thing for themselves." He studied his menu, puckering his lips thoughtfully. "D'you like food, Webb?"

"Good food, yes."

"I love it," the other man said with animation, "absolutely love a good meal. But as for choosing it . . . where's the pleasure in that! I mean, for a proper lunch, you have to come up with a combination of three dishes, right? Each to be selected from a list of ten or more. That's a bloody mathematical problem, not fun. Back at the office I don't mind the odd bit of mathematics. But at lunchtime, when a wrong answer hits you here, in the gut . . ." He patted his stomach vigorously, then resumed his desultory examination of the menu.

"Alex Harrington has got an ulcer, poor sod," he said. "He doesn't let on, but you can tell. He finds eating absolute agony. On the other hand, choosing what he'll have is dead easy. I mean, he's *got* no real choice, has he? It's an ill wind and all that."

He lowered the menu to reveal steady, confident eyes. "Know what you'll have yet, Webb?" His lenses were spotted with what looked like dried rain drops. It hadn't rained since yesterday morning, Webb remembered.

"I thought the Mullet Livornese," Webb replied. It meant one less pair of dead eyes watching him from across the room. It seemed as good a way of choosing as any.

Alloway screwed up his nose to show what he thought of the choice. "You know, I have this thing about pleasure, Webb. Doing it is fine. Thinking about it before or after can be even better. But *planning* it . . . that's a frightful bore. I mean, half the people in this country spend two weeks a year on holiday, four weeks talking about how great it was, and the rest of the bloody year thinking about what they'll do next time. That's crazy, I reckon. Are you like that, by any chance?"

Webb shook his head, but the other man had already glanced back to his menu. "I don't know," he was muttering, "I really don't. It all looks so good, except for the mullet."

"You said you wanted to talk about security," Webb said, making his impatience as plain as he could. The late arrival and the idle conversation—it was all too obvious, too lacking in subtlety. Webb liked adult games to have style.

But Alloway ignored his remark. "The answer's simple, when you come to think about it," he said, laying the menu down at last. "A computer terminal in every good restaurant. Great idea, eh? You enter. You tell them how hungry you are on a scale from one to ten, whether you fancy fish or meat, whether you can take rich food. You say whether you want wine. They hit the keys and there you are—your order done for you. The most difficult decision of the day made automatically."

"Whatever turns you on," Webb said.

"We could have an Ulcer Option for people like Alex," Alloway said with a sly smile. "A special key. Boiled fish and cold milk, see."

A plump waitress came for their orders. After more dithering Alloway decided to have Parma ham and Sole Meunière. He asked whether the most expensive Chianti they had was served very cold. The waitress kissed her fingertips and promised it would be chilled to perfection.

"Computers are used for all the wrong things, I reckon," Alloway said seriously, leaning half across the table. "I mean, who applies them properly to leisure activities? That's where the real potential is. For instance, when I want to screw I want it guaranteed. No preliminaries, no embarrassment—just a bird I like and one who'll like me. A bird guaranteed to be randy. You'd think someone would have cottoned onto that by now and offer an on-line service, wouldn't you? I mean, have you ever tried what passes for computer dating?"

"Just once," Webb admitted, with a smile he couldn't help. "She had bifocals and was determined to stay a virgin. I asked for my money back."

"Exactly. They've got no idea how to exploit the

161

huge possibilities of computers. Done properly, the social implications could be fantastic. Satisfaction guaranteed. I mean, that's what we're all after, right?"

"Why did you want to see me?" Webb demanded. "Not just to talk about computers as electronic pimps, surely?"

"That's very good," Alloway said with a loud guffaw and he sat well back, turning his face up to the rowing boat as he considered the idea further. "I like it, Webb. Pimps."

"You remind me of Harrington," Webb told him. "He seems equally incapable of coming straight to the point."

The comparison had the desired effect. Alloway was instantly serious. "Alex is a nice guy who knows buggerall about computers. Maybe that's why he needs you around, to search BANKNET for him. Is that direct enough for you?"

"Go on . . ." Webb said noncommittally.

"There's a company called DSL who've been going round the Centre checking the effectiveness of the security. When I was up in Manchester last week I came across another of their guys there, doing the same thing. They're a very similar company to yours, know what I mean?"

"They're rather bigger, actually. And we don't specialise in security problems."

Alloway shook his head and said, "Come on! You appear at the Centre the same time they do. They report direct to Alex Harrington. So do you. One can make a fair guess at what you're actually up to. Anyway, Sondhi has been filling me in on your choice of reading material."

"Harrington will tell you that . . ."

"I prefer to believe this," Alloway snapped, tapping his forehead with his fork. "When is your report due in? I presume there's going to be one."

"You'd better take that up with Harrington."

"Was wiping out BANKNET programs part of your brief from Alex?" Alloway asked. But before Webb had a chance to reply he sneered, "Bet it bloody wasn't! Private enterprise, that's how I see it."

162

The waitress brought Alloway's ham and placed a bowl of thick, steaming fish soup in front of Webb.

"Care to tell me about Friday?" Alloway asked quietly, spearing a slice of melon. A hint of reassurance, almost of sympathy, had come into the voice.

"What I can. I went back to the Centre after your operator called me in a huff. I found that someone had changed my program deck—two cards pulled out and ten new ones put in. It was *changed* on me, Alloway. Turned into a destructive program, just like that."

The other man was very thoughtful. "Suppose I believe you, Webb. And I said suppose, mind. Do you reckon Alex will buy a story like that?"

"Maybe," Webb said doubtfully. "Maybe not. It was very cleverly done. I'll show you when we get back."

"Why, do you think? What was the idea?"

"God knows. You tell me."

"Who then? Any thoughts on that?"

"I've had a weekend to think about it. I've got a pretty good idea, actually."

"So, who?" Alloway leaned forward, intensely interested.

Webb hesitated, clearly unsure whether to say.

"Who?" Alloway demanded again.

"Sorry. I'd rather not tell you."

"I know . . . one of my staff and all that?"

"Quite."

"How very noble," Alloway observed. Then he gave a knowing wink and said, "Or is *gallant* a better word?"

He grinned broadly when he saw Webb's reaction. Just the barest flicker of the eyelids, but it was enough. He gave a long-drawn out "Aaah," to show he knew. He watched Webb closely for a while from behind his grubby glasses, running the back of a thumbnail between a gap in his front teeth.

"Shall we get down to business," he said suddenly. "A certain degree of mutual co-operation is called for, I think."

"I'm listening."

Alloway glanced cautiously around the restaurant. The noise surrounded them, pressing in, insulating them to his satisfaction.

"I wonder if you've had a personal bank statement lately?" he asked with delight, and his eyes were transformed, glinting with a sharpness he'd kept hidden until then.

"Do you enjoy playing games, or something?" Webb said angrily. "Playing cat and mouse when it's you all the time!"

"I prefer to see the other man's hand before I show mine, that's all. I wasn't sure quite how much you'd found out, see?" He leaned across and said in a slow, taunting whisper, "You know fuckall. Absolutely sweet F.A."

Webb said nothing for a long time. Occasionally their eyes met. Mostly they ate as if strangers forced to share a table.

"Nine thousand pounds is a fair amount of money," Webb remarked eventually, more to break the deadlock than anything. "An unexpected gift."

"Dear me, no." Alloway feigned surprise. "It's *never* a gift, Webb. Not nine K. That would be far too generous. It's a consultancy fee, got it? I expect you to earn it."

"How, exactly?"

Alloway chewed a large slice of Parma ham. He poked his fork close to Webb's nose.

"You will stop investigating," he said, with his mouth still full, "stop searching. You will report to Alex Harrington that there's nothing amiss with BANKNET. In short, Webb, you will stop crowding me, okay?"

"You raise a number of interesting questions," Webb said, taken aback by the offer. It took him a moment to realise it, but that's what it was. An offer.

"Try me," Alloway said. But the waitress appeared with the wine and he stopped to taste it, slowly and affectedly. "It's certainly nice and cold," he told her. Then, when she left, he raised his glass to Webb. "To be perfectly frank, I've got absolutely no sense of taste. What's it called . . . bouquet is lost on me. But years of trying have made me a remarkably good judge of temperature." He sipped at the coldness with relish.

"Nine thousand pounds," said Webb. "Just to do *nothing?*"

The other man nodded energetically.

"Which means you will make considerably more than that yourself? Will . . . or already have."

"Good thinking. But no comment, as they say."

"A lot of time and effort invested in it, too?"

"Over a year. That's why I'm not having it screwed up now."

"Suppose I refuse to play ball? Suppose I see Harrington and blow the whistle on you, tell him what I know. What then, Alloway?"

"Go ahead," the other man said, with no trace of concern. "Let's meet him this afternoon, if you like. But remember, *I'm* not the one with nine K of Waterman's money sitting in my bank account."

"Clever," Webb said. "Very clever."

"It goes something like this, as I see it. Me . . . you . . . Alex." Alloway moved the salt and pepper pots to the dead centre of the table and marched a small bottle of salad oil towards them with a slow rocking motion. "Well, *I* call him Alex," he said, stroking the bottle affectionately on the stopper. "You're still at the Mr. Harrington stage, I imagine. Pity that. You start things off, if you like. Martin Alloway is planning to defraud the bank, you say. Or maybe already has, who can tell. How? asks Alex. Ah, that's the problem, you say. But if you and I were to spend a few months searching the system together, instruction by instruction . . ." The bottle hopped about in annoyance.

"Martin, old chap, what's your version of all this? Alex says to me, giving you up as hopeless. Alex, I tell him, there's this small matter of a cheeky program that I've stumbled across. It breaks some of your security rules and wipes out half the system. Why? he asks, dumbfounded. Ah, I say, it's only a guess but it must be to obliterate all trace of another naughty Webb program. Another! he says. That's right, I say, the one that transferred nine thousand quid to Webb's account. But that means the swine has destroyed all the evidence, he says angrily. Not so, Alex, I say. There's still the *money*. Webb banks with NatWest. He's obviously forgotten that their computer system will have a full record of the transfer even if it's been erased from BANKNET. Alex scowls at you, feeling betrayed. By

165

the way, I add, since BANKNET keeps details of every transaction, the fact of a missing record is incriminating in itself. *Isn't it, Alex?*"

Alloway flicked the salt cellar over and it rolled towards Webb, then lay quite still in a pool of spreading white.

"Clever," Webb said again.

"Very," Alloway agreed.

"You ought to be in the Guinness Book of Records," Webb said. "Using a computer to frame a man and to buy his silence at one and the same time. It has to be a first. Computerised blackmail!"

"Blackmail isn't a word I like much," Alloway said sharply.

"I might decide to chance it and see Harrington all the same."

"Be my guest. The clincher is, you were flat broke this time last week. Over three K in the red, and Nat-West screaming for your blood."

"My briefcase," Webb said furiously. "You went through my bloody briefcase!"

Grinning, Alloway reached into a pocket and produced the missing letter from Curtis. He held his hand high above the table and let it flutter slowly down.

Webb grabbed for it. It was all there—the size of his overdraft, his account number, what Curtis was planning to do about it. It was a very complete story.

"You're very good," Webb conceded. "You really are."

"Ta very much."

"But suppose I say nine thousand isn't enough?"

"Then you can get bloody stuffed. That's all you're getting. Keep quiet and that money is yours, your fee. Make waves and it becomes a trap. Think about it."

Webb obviously was thinking about it. After a time he said, "No more tricks, right?"

"Tricks?" Alloway seemed almost offended. "A guy who pays in advance and you ask about tricks?"

"You've got a deal, then."

Alloway nodded approval. "Realists I like," he said.

The chubby waitress was back, to whisk their plates away, sliding oval platters of fish in their place with quick, practiced movements.

166

"Is good," she told Webb, indicating his mullet. "Delicious."

"You know, I almost wish I could tell Curtis about all this," Webb said. "If he hadn't written he would never have solved my problem for me. That's what I call good financial management."

Alloway showed mild surprise, then suspicion. "You're too unruffled for my liking. I'm not sure I like that."

"No tricks from me, either," Webb promised with an air of innocence, hands raised submissively. "How could I?"

"You just bloody try," Alloway said sharply. "I don't see you liking jail somehow. Not jail. Me, I don't think I'd mind if it came to it. I'd manage to keep myself occupied." He tapped his head. "But you'd go bonkers after a few weeks. No German sports car. No smooth clothes. No getting your end away with my staff." The voice had turned to a threatening sneer.

"Jail!" Webb said dismissively. "Come off it."

"You don't believe me?"

Webb made no reply.

Alloway picked up some French bread and buttered it liberally. He tasted the butter with the end of his tongue. "Most people can't tell fraud from embezzlement," he said. "Can you?"

"I know the legal definitions, yes."

"In my case it would be embezzlement, if they ever got me. I mean, the BANKNET money is entrusted to me, isn't it? But in your case . . ." Alloway peeled the white flesh of his sole from the backbone. "Fraud is a nasty business, as the judge said to the defendant. Sordid. Society has to be protected." He watched Webb for a time, then leaned forward and said, "I fucking mean it. Don't think I don't fucking mean it."

"No tricks," Webb told him again, in a quite different tone to the one he had used before. There was no mistaking that the man meant what he said.

Alloway sliced off another large piece of fish. "This is superb, thanks," he mumbled through a full mouth.

"Thanks . . . ?"

"You're paying. After all, you can afford it now."

"Why not," Webb said. He forced a smile. "I've never entertained a big league bank robber before."

His eyes were on the man across the table, taking in the crumpled clothes, the tousled hair. Even as he spoke, he thought how ridiculous it sounded.

Chapter Nineteen

Later that day Webb remembered something Andrew Shulton had once said. They had been in a pub and Andrew was as drunk as he ever got, which meant he'd had two lemonade shandies and switched to tomato juice. Still, it was enough to make him solemn and philosophical.

"Correct answers," Shulton had said, "never go away. That's how you can be sure they're correct. It's the persistence that lets you know."

He had started out as a mathematician, he reminded Webb. And mathematicians have this funny habit when the answer doesn't come out the way they want. They simply do the calculation all over again. And if it still doesn't come out as they want they do it again, and again. And they go on until eventually the answer wins by sheer obstinacy, by refusing to go away. The right answer, Shulton had said, wears you down until *you* give in. That was what he had liked most about mathematics. It was the most persistent, most pigheaded subject he could think of.

It was late in the evening when Webb remembered him saying that. He had spent hours doing the same piece of analysis time and time again, always coming up with the same solution. The fact that he didn't like it made no difference. The answer refused to go away.

He and Alloway had said what to all appearances was a friendly goodbye outside the Trattoria. The other man had headed south and Webb had stood watching him go until he turned the corner towards the Data Centre. Then Webb had gone in the opposite direction to Fitzroy Square. He went straight down to the basement room without telling Susan he was there, and locked the door behind him. He used the small whiteboard next to the terminal to evaluate his options. He was as systematic as Alloway seemed to have been.

Webb listed all of Alloway's likely next moves. What he might do if his plan succeeded. His defensive tactics if he were to be caught. His possible actions should he suspect that someone at Waterman's suspected him. Then Webb wrote down his own countermoves. And however much he tried he always arrived at the same conclusion. And always he didn't like it one bit. Alloway should never have described it as a *trap*, that was the trouble.

Finally, he thought it best to let the computer decide for him. Alloway had used a computer against him, why shouldn't he do the same? He started the terminal and dialled a connection to the time-sharing service. He wrote a short program and had it ready in under an hour. He only wanted the computer to choose one of several possible actions, each with different odds against selection. It was the simplest program he had ever written.

Webb fed the first three options into the machine and asked it to read them back.

"1. GO ALONG WITH IT," the terminal said,

"2. TELL HARRINGTON"

"3. DEMAND A HALF SHARE"

Satisfied, Webb gave the computer several more alternatives. He sat for a time staring into space, wondering what to do if it didn't agree with him. And what to do if it did. Then he acted.

"CHOOSE," he ordered.

Instead of the immediate response he expected, the terminal took its time. So he waited. It was late, nearly midnight, and the computer should have been lightly loaded, but perhaps it wasn't. Perhaps other users at other terminals spread around London were simultaneously demanding its attention to their problems. Perhaps the computer was as unhappy as he was at having to decide. But in the end it did and the print-head shot across the paper as if trying to make up for lost time. Somehow, the letters seemed much larger than usual.

"KILL ALLOWAY," the computer said.

Webb sat back, curiously relieved that the machine agreed with him. He had set the odds at five to one against that choice and still it had come to the same conclusion he had. Shulton was quite right, he thought. You can't escape a correct answer. Carefully, he erased the program from computer memory.

Webb slipped out into the square. His car was still in Marylebone Lane, and he assumed the car park would be closed for the night. He walked past the Post Office Tower and reached the BBC before finding a taxi to take him home to Chelsea. The city was busier than it had any right to be at that hour.

Death was supposed to be a lonely business, he reflected. Planning death was equally lonely. There was no one you could safely go to for advice, no textbook you could read to tell you how. He had missed army conscription by months and regretted it now, for the first and only time. He had no experience of killing to draw on, no training. He would have just one chance, and getting it wrong would mean disaster.

He had handled a gun in earnest only once. Shortly before they started SysTech, when he and Andrew were still close friends, he had been invited for a long weekend at the Shulton family estate in Norfolk. Andrew had gone out with his own precious Purdey side-by-side. Webb had been loaned one of old man Shulton's reserve guns, a battered single-barrel Webley. It was good enough for a beginner, Andrew had said haughtily. Just point and pull and the spread of shot would do the rest. He had then proceeded to bring down six grouse and Webb had failed to bag a single one. The noise had been terrific and the jolt against his shoulder became more and more painful at every attempt because, he found out later, he had failed to hold the gun properly as he swung it up. It had been a glorious autumn morning, with a clearing mist and pale sunshine that made the coarse ferns on the moor seem as soft as purple suede. The shooting had spoiled it. It was, Webb thought at the time, a stupid way to try to kill something. Noisy and uncertain. Nasty.

The following day he watched Alloway as well as he could. He saw him come and go from his office but was unable to see him at his desk except by walking past, and he kept that to a safe minimum. Alloway stayed at the Centre for lunch and Webb guessed he took sandwiches from his briefcase, washed down with a plastic cup of milk that he saw him fetch from the coffee room. Not once did he notice Alloway look in his direction.

The man went quite early that evening, still tugging his coat on as he emerged from his area, and slinging his briefcase under his arm because the handle had broken off at one end. Webb followed at an interval of half a minute, when he was out of sight. In the outside corridor the indicator showed Alloway's lift arriving at Level 1 just as the second lift door slid open. When Webb got to the downstairs lobby, Alloway was already in the exit pen and a guard was searching his case. The stitching was badly adrift at one corner, with several inches of thread hanging free.

Alloway left the building without looking back and Webb pushed his ID into the reader and entered the pen. The guard began examining his case. On the rear wall one of the monitors showed Alloway walking with his distinctive hunched action along the darkened mews. The picture was fuzzy and the synchronisation was poor. Once, the image jerked suddenly down, cutting the man in half before slipping lazily back to join him together again.

Webb's case was pushed back through the hatch, but he stood where he was, staring at the screen. Alloway was now nearly at the arch to the street and almost lost in the night. In front of the guard was the bank of controls with, by his hand, a large red emergency button. If only, Webb found himself thinking, he could reach through the glass screen to press it, and somehow wipe Alloway off the face of the earth. That was what he needed. Something silent and foolproof and anonymous. Something that saved you having to look into the other man's face as he died. Some means of pressing a button and having it happen. A program to execute for him. It was only then that he realised what

171

had been bothering him for the past twenty-four hours. It wasn't *whether* to kill Alloway. It was *how to*.

Webb walked out into the mews and through the arch to Wigmore Street. He looked in both directions, but Alloway had already disappeared from view.

Chapter Twenty

Webb met Jennifer Owen briefly in the coffee room, later that week.

"You're a bloody fool," she told him. "And after all I said to you. After you promised."

As far as she was concerned Webb had broken a solemn agreement not to use his program again. It was all over, she said, looking more sad than angry. To her, honesty was an essential part of any relationship. What little there had been between them was finished. It hadn't been much, but she would remember it all the same. Perhaps they could remain friends? she suggested, but nothing more. Distant friends, she added, having second thoughts.

"If that's what you want," Webb said.

He suspected she was laying it on rather, overdoing the regret and the love of honesty. Women never liked being badly wronged, who did? But he often felt they positively revelled in being *slightly* wronged.

He followed her back along the corridor, his eyes on the slow sway of her hips. It could have been good, he told himself, given half a chance. It had felt right. But that was all the thought he gave her at the time. His mind was on Alloway.

How do you kill a man you hardly know? How can you learn more about him without raising suspicions? How do you kill a man and get away with it?

Is Alloway married? Webb tried to guess. Does he live alone or with someone? In a neat semidet with a bay window, in an avenue of prim identical houses? Or in a single room, shabby like him? What does a man like that want with so much money?

Webb knew only that Alloway worked at the Data Centre. That he travelled there each morning, spent the day in that big open plan room surrounded by some thirty others, left there at night. Webb walked every inch of the blue zone. He went between the Centre and the car park, to every nearby underground station and taxi rank, to every restaurant he thought the man might visit.

Suddenly, he found he knew enough. He had known enough for weeks. Killing someone nervous might be tricky. Dealing with a confident bugger like Alloway had to be easy.

He used his pocket calculator to check that what he wanted to do was possible—a simple series of computations on traction and friction and acceleration. When he finished, the glowing red figures on the tiny LED display confirmed the idea as sound. It wasn't quite the plan he had hoped for since he would have to be there when it happened. But it was good enough. He wouldn't see the other man's eyes, that was the important thing.

The next morning he left home in a weekend anorak. He went to a part of London where he knew no one, south of the Thames to a shop in Brixton chosen from the Yellow Pages. When he spotted it he drove past and picked a side street a quarter of a mile further on. He parked with great care, well away from the corner, well past the point where the yellow lines ran out. He paced slowly around the Porsche to be certain that the chance of being struck accidentally by another car was remote. Then he walked to the shop for an inexpensive item bought with cash. It was a commonplace, innocent thing and his precautions were probably unnecessary. But at this stage he wanted to take as few risks as possible. The actual killing was not going to be as foolproof as he'd have liked. Far from it.

With almost fanatical discretion he began watching Alloway for most of the working day, waiting. The other man took absolutely no notice of him, even when they met in the corridor or shared a lift. No word passed between them. It was as if Alloway wished it to be seen that he had no connection with Webb, not the slightest interest in him. He showed no sign of concern, gave no hint he might have considered the possibility that Webb would strike back.

Day by day Webb continued to watch and wait. Every morning he checked the programmer's log at Run Control. Every evening he walked north from the Data Centre for several minutes before turning back to collect his car. Once, late at night, he drove to the area with a small can of white paint and a brush. He made sure he wasn't seen.

Monday, 7th February. At last, Webb saw from the programmer's log that Alloway was making the only program test that evening, with his run scheduled for just before eight. If he stayed on to read his computer output he would be at the Centre, probably alone, until eight-thirty at least. If not, well, Webb had lost another day, that was all.

He went back to his desk and prepared to go, placing his briefcase, apparently carelessly, on the very edge of his chair. Pulling on his overcoat he fell clumsily against the chair and the case crashed to the floor. All around faces looked up, and as he left everyone saw him go.

Webb wanted a suitable place to let time pass while he thought of nothing. He drove to Hyde Park and chose the car park on the north side of the Serpentine, slipping the Porsche into a space beside Rotten Row, with the bonnet towards the lake. He eased the seat back into a half-reclining position and picked a cassette of gentle, unhurried piano music. He ran the engine at intervals to keep the car warm.

Few people walked in the park that afternoon. A well-wrapped Japanese photographed a friend sitting stiffly on a bench as a stranger blurred across the foreground, then they scuttled back to the shelter of their car. A single rider passed, kicking up sand that hung for an instant before being blown over the path and into the lake. The water was fringed with a thin crust of broken ice, and the wheeling seagulls fought the wind.

The music was suddenly wrong, wavering and off-key. Webb came to with a start, realising he was draining the battery. Quickly he ejected the cassette. The car had become very cold.

It was nearly dark outside, and he hardly knew where the hours had gone. Lights were coming on across the Serpentine, their reflections shivering in a rising mist. It was impossible to tell where the water ended and the mist began. The stationary ducks seemed to float in the air.

He had scarcely thought of Alloway. With the coming of night, as the time drew near, doubt set in. He left the car for a moment to open the front luggage compartment and the light came on automatically, shining on his weapon where it lay coiled on the carpet. As he looked he became certain again.

Webb dialled the Data Centre from a call box and asked the night operator for Martin Alloway. He heard the faint, repeated buzz of the extension and could picture the phone ringing endlessly in an empty room. He was on the point of giving up when the sound stopped.

"Alloway," a voice said.

"I'm glad you're still there," Webb told him. He had planned to say it but the relief he projected was real.

"Hold on a minute." There was a muffled thud as the receiver was put down and a long silence. Then a series of clicks and Alloway said, "Yes . . . ?"

"It's Christopher Webb."

"I know. I recognized your voice."

"We have to meet," Webb said in a low, urgent tone.

"It's bloody late, you know that?" Alloway sounded irritable.

"I've had a nasty shock, Alloway. We're in trouble, I'm sure of it."

There was the long pause Webb had expected. He could hear the other man breathing.

"Can you come here? The others have all cleared off if that's what you're worried about."

"NO!" Webb almost shouted. "I told you, it's trouble. Real trouble."

"Where, then?"

"Do you know Tilers Place? It's very near."

Another pause before Alloway said he did.

"I'll wait for you in my car. It's a silver Porsche."

"I've seen it in the car park," Alloway said sourly.

"We can go on somewhere private. Wherever suits you."

"When?"

"Now. As soon as you can make it."

"Ten minutes?"

"Fine," Webb said. "Don't be longer, Alloway. I'm bloody worried."

Alloway put the phone down and moved back to his desk. Tilers Place was to the back of the Data Centre, where not many bank people went. It seemed a sensible choice, just far enough to be a safe rendezvous, yet close enough to emphasise urgency. Nothing about the place caused him any concern. But the call itself did. Webb had sounded very anxious, almost hoarse at one point with the tension. *We* are in trouble . . . The words chipped at Alloway's confidence. He was at a crucial stage in his plan and had already had one setback earlier that day. The more he thought about it the more alarmed he became. What had the fool said or done?

He took a scribbled note from a drawer and locked it in his cupboard. He tore a sheet from the fresh output on his desk and got rid of it, not in his own wastebin but in another at the far end of the room. He bound the remainder well into the centre of one of the many thick folders on his shelves. The pages were most unlikely to reveal a thing to anyone else, but Alloway liked to think he never took chances.

He picked up his raincoat and grabbed his briefcase. When he had some free time, he thought, he ought to get the handle seen to.

Alloway turned the corner into Tilers Place. He saw the Porsche gleam in the dim light on the other side of the street and crossed towards it. The pavement was uneven and he stubbed a toe on a broken slab.

Webb obviously saw him coming. As he approached, the starter motor cut into the silence. The engine idled with a powerful, metallic rasp and white wisps trailed from the exhaust. The car moved forward and stopped again, bathing the road behind it with the lurid glow of its brake lights. Thinking Webb was leaving, Alloway quickened his pace. He was several minutes later than he had promised. As he drew level, the engine gave a deafening howl and he smelt the burning rubber from wildly spinning tyres. The car crouched as if ready to spring, then shot from the kerb. Alloway shouted, throwing up an arm in useless protest. For some reason his only immediate thought was that Webb had forgotten to turn on his lights.

If the Porsche had driven at him he would have taken fright and run, perhaps clambering desperately through the hoarding and onto the building site. But he just froze and watched. For the car was moving away.

The audible hand brake warning ticked away the seconds. Webb had never known time pass so slowly. He sat staring anxiously into the driving mirror, imagining figures in the gloomy street. When Alloway first appeared he looked like just another fleeting shadow. Then he moved into a pool of light and Webb saw the briefcase humped under an arm. He couldn't make out the face.

The man stopped by the kerb, exactly where Webb had expected he would. He looked towards the car and began to cross, right where Webb had guessed he must. Webb snatched at the ignition key and the engine spluttered briefly before roaring into life. Suppose it hadn't fired. He pressed the clutch down and pushed the gear lever, feeling the teeth grate as first was engaged. He edged forward for a few feet until the car was level with the mark he had painted on the hoarding, then he depressed the clutch again. He revved the engine to the limit and its bellow bounced back at him in the narrow street. His foot jerked off the clutch, and the car shook as the plates banged together.

177

For a second the Porsche strained but hardly moved. The engine note dropped ominously. Then the tyres gripped and he got the traction he wanted. The seat pushed hard into the small of his back. He thought he heard Alloway cry out.

Three steel columns were torn from the scaffolding and followed the car, crashing together, clattering along the road. The rest of the framework held, as if nothing had happened. It stayed where it was for longer than seemed possible and Webb felt a sickening sensation in the pit of his stomach. *It wasn't going to come down!* Then the scaffolding collapsed, outwards and downwards, terrifyingly fast once it started. And all the time Alloway stood below, not moving.

Alloway was unaware of the danger, to begin with. His attention was on the fast-disappearing car and something dark that dragged behind. The first warning creaks from high above him were drowned by the harsh near-scream of the air-cooled engine.

Then he realised. All around him the rusting steel was caving in. He panicked and ran out into the road. From four storeys above came a long metal tube, like a spear, hitting other parts of the falling frame, bouncing and slithering, forcing its way through. It penetrated Alloway's skull and he was dead as he fell. More metal hit him, viciously grinding dark red surfaces against his skin, tearing down to broken bone. As the tons of steel piled up, his body flowed like thick paste between the tubes.

Accelerating away, Webb saw the scaffolding crash down. It was all right, he had decided, to watch a man die in a driving mirror. All right, somehow, to see an indistinct image wiped out. But he didn't see. He lost the running shape in shadow as it bolted from the pavement. When the car skidded round the corner the steel was still tumbling down into the road.

He slowed, pressing the button to lower the window and he could hear no clatter directly behind. The tubes he had dragged away had already shaken free of the loops in the cable and whatever faint *swish* the trailing wire made was masked by the engine. He passed

178

several pedestrians but none of them looked his way. They were standing quite still, heads turned to the seemingly endless, frightening noise from somewhere close by.

He turned two more corners, then stopped and got out. He unclipped the tow hook from the back of the car and threw it, with the cable still attached, into the front boot. There was a different, deeper rumble and the ground shook beneath his feet.

The façade of the old building had given up its doomed attempt to stay standing. The scaffolding had failed in its job of holding it up. Now, in its dying moments, the building took its revenge, beating savagely down, crushing and bending the great tangle of steel. Burying Alloway deeper.

The street became silent again and very still. A cloud of dust filled the air, slowly settling like snow on the new mountain that straddled Tilers Place. The gusts chased particles across the freshly covered slopes.

Webb drove to the Thames, a quiet spot near Petersham where he could park within feet of the water. He sat waiting for a couple with a dog to move on into the night.

Somehow, Alloway had rigged BANKNET, to steal a fortune from Waterman's. At least, Webb assumed and hoped it was a fortune. The plan was finished . . . or nearly finished. He didn't know and now there was no one to tell him. But it was *his* plan now. Alloway was dead. He had to be. And he had died intestate, with Webb as the only beneficiary, the natural inheritor.

It suddenly came to him that he had had done it. Actually done it. It was all over. Profoundly relieved, he laughed in the darkness, and a single tear coursed of its own accord down a cheek. He tasted the salt.

He threw the coiled wire into the Thames, and it dropped silently under the black water. It would never be found. But if it was, it would mean nothing. No connection with Christopher Webb or Martin Alloway. Just a cable lost from a passing barge.

Part Three

INHERITANCE

CUSTOMER CONFIDENTIALITY. Under no circumstances is customer account status to be divulged to other than the authorised account holder(s). Persons attempting access to information they are not entitled to know are to be reported without delay to the Branch Manager. Staff in breach of this regulation are liable to summary dismissal.

—Waterman and Company
Branch Office Procedures Manual

Chapter Twenty-One

Jake Kennedy had a small, battered desk on the over-crowded fourth floor at Fitzroy Square. His corner got less than the regulation amount of light, but that didn't bother him particularly, and he had never found quite the right moment to complain. In the few months he had been with SysTech he had made his area habitable, as much like his bed-sitter as he could, with far too much crammed untidily into too little space. The others joked about the perpetual mess, but he said simply that he preferred it that way. Neatness, he maintained, was bourgeois. Untidiness was a clear indication of efficiency, a sign that you were too busy being productive to file reports or throw away papers you no longer needed. On the wall behind him he had stuck a large picture of Jane Fonda, produced late one night on the lineprinter of a client's computer. Close to, there was just a jumble of letters—the eyes were a scattering of O's and the nose a wedge of X's—but as you walked away she was suddenly there with her serious, concerned half-smile. It was a pretty good likeness, quite alluring in the right light. It was almost art, Kennedy claimed, the Mona Lisa brought up to date. Not bad for a single evening's work.

He was busy chasing a bug that kept slipping away from him to evade capture. At least that was how it seemed after several long days of pursuit. He would work out where it had to be and move in on it, only to find it wasn't there. You sod! he told it, wherever it was. He searched the computer listing, tirelessly reading and rereading the same short piece of program. He scratched his head, or his chest through his open-fronted shirt, or a leg just above a crumpled sock. He chewed the rims of his plastic coffee cups to shreds. He paced the floor constantly, quietly cursing. He was enjoying himself enormously. It was good to be back.

"You're a masochist," someone said, and he looked up to find Webb standing there.

He gave a cheerful, "Hi, Chris." Then, rubbing his chin thoughtfully, he said. "I guess I am, really," and the idea seemed to please him. He glanced around, to discover that it was later than he had realised. The rest of the floor was deserted.

"A tough problem?" Webb asked.

"You bet."

"I've got a tougher one. I think you'd like it. Interested?"

"Not if it's Waterman's again!"

"Right first time."

As politely as he could, Kennedy said, "It was fun before but I'm not a money man. I told you that at the time, Chris. Right now I prefer what I'm doing."

"Mail order!" Webb remarked scornfully. "It's only a bloody mail order system."

"It's my very own project. That matters a lot."

Webb dragged a spare chair around the desk to sit beside him. He was carrying a small bundle of folded computer output.

"This time it's nothing to do with banking, Jake. I want you for a tricky technical problem. A big programming riddle in a bloody great computer system. It's right up your street."

"I can't, honestly. I have to finish this project first. I'll be another two months at least."

"I need a really bright young mind," Webb said. "I need you, it's as simple as that."

Kennedy sighed and shuffled awkwardly with indecision. His project was not actually that interesting, now he thought about it. But it was *his*, the very first assignment he had ever been asked to handle completely by himself.

"Know what you're turning down?" Webb asked. "Only the most difficult problem you'll ever see."

"Oh, yeah?"

"I mean it. It's beaten me. But I have a feeling you'd lick it, Jake. Sharp young brain, plenty of persistence . . ."

"You're a jammy bastard," Kennedy said, clearly

184

weakening. "Like Andrew Shulton says, you could sell Johnnies in a geriatric ward."

"Does he!"

Kennedy assumed a blank expression, as if to say, "You know Shulton."

"Well?" Webb asked. "What do you say?"

"I can't, Chris, even if I wanted to. This job is for Andrew's latest pet client—some friend of a friend of his father's. He'd never agree."

"Listen," Webb said. "Tomorrow, the day after, maybe next week, you finally find your bug, okay! Big deal! A very ordinary little computer somewhere begins posting plastic buckets to housewives in Doncaster. Where's the challenge in that? Where's the sense of achievement?"

Kennedy looked away to his listing, idly thumbing through the pages and obviously very tempted.

"It's a damned hard bug, though," he muttered. "The hardest I've ever had."

Webb started to get up. "Harvey, then," he said softly, as if to himself.

"*What* was that?"

"Mike Harvey. I'll get him on it. If you don't want the job that's your loss."

"Wait!" Kennedy caught his arm. As Webb sat down again, he pushed his listing decisively to one side. "You're a poacher," he said with a grin, "and on Andrew Shulton's territory." But he held out a hand and Webb clasped it warmly.

"Welcome to my select little team, Jake."

"What about Andrew?"

"Leave that one to me, huh."

"So, give," Kennedy said eagerly. "What's so difficult about this job of yours?"

"I want you to become an expert on BANKNET. To know parts of the system better than anyone at Waterman's. The catch is, I can tell you virtually nothing about it."

The programmer's eyes narrowed.

"Waterman's insist," Webb said quickly. "You know what they're like about security, Jake. I'm forced to operate on a very strict need-to-know basis." He unfolded the listing he was holding and spread it out on

185

the desk. "This is a sample of what you'll be working from. You'll get nothing else except what I'm able to tell you, and that won't be much."

"But this is just a heap of numbers," Kennedy exclaimed after cursory examination. "No explanation of what it's supposed to be. No comments of any kind."

"That's right. It's a core dump."

"I can see that."

"I've got more of it downstairs, Jake." Webb delivered a disarming smile. "A bloody great stack. You should see it."

"Come off it! This is absolutely useless if you don't already know the system like the back of your hand. I'd need to have been involved with BANKNET from the design stage to make any sense of this."

"On the contrary," Webb said with a quick shake of the head. "It's the best possible way of finding what I want. This dump tells you precisely what is happening inside the Waterman's computer at this very minute. It's an exact record of the programs they're using. Not what the bank *thinks* is there but what is *actually* there."

"I do know what a dump is," Kennedy protested. "Okay, so it's accurate. Some use if I can't understand the bloody thing. I bet you've never had to interpret a dump of a totally unfamiliar program!"

"No and I wouldn't want to try. That's why I need you." Webb reclined lazily, his head against the wall, his feet on the desk. "What do you think?"

"I'd say it can't be done."

"Very probably." Webb grinned wickedly. "I'm so glad you like my little problem."

"Nuts!" Kennedy said.

"Where's your sense of humour, Jake?"

Kennedy snorted and waved a hand at the listing. "Just pages of densely packed numbers. I've got to have more than this, Chris. Some proper program listings at least. And some of the system manuals."

"Nothing doing. It was bad enough getting the bank's agreement to bring a core dump out of the Data Centre. I only managed it because, as you've pointed out, a dump gives almost nothing away. But full program listings . . . ? No way."

"Well, it's original, I'll say that." Kennedy slumped in his chair, pensively sucking his knuckles.

"Aren't you going to ask what you're supposed to be looking for?" Webb said with a suitable show of surprise.

"By the way," Kennedy said, "you haven't told me what I'm supposed to be looking for."

"I want you to track down something that has eluded me for weeks."

"And that is . . . ?"

Webb looked heavenwards. "That's the problem, the big challenge. I don't know. I haven't the faintest idea."

"Look, if this is some kind of silly joke . . ."

"I've never been more serious. I wish I knew, but I don't."

"You've been looking for weeks," Kennedy said incredulously, "and you don't know what for?"

"I guess it does sound a bit funny," Webb agreed.

"Humour me some more, Chris. In that case, how would you know when you'd found it?"

"Oh, I'd *recognise* it if ever I get to see it. Just as you will."

"But that's crazy," Kennedy said.

"Not really. You see, you're going to be searching for a Weevil."

"I follow. A Weevil. I should have guessed."

"They're dead secretive, Jake. Far worse than bugs."

"A Weevil, you say?"

Webb gave a tantalising nod. He laughed at the younger man's puzzled face.

"And what the hell is that?"

"The exact opposite of a bug, of course," Webb said. "A bug is an error in a program that should be in the system. right? A Weevil is a correctly working program that most definitely *shouldn't* be there, a secret insertion burrowing deep into BANKNET. It hides from view and gobbles money. You'll certainly know when you've found it. All you have to do is look for something that has no business being there. Got it?"

Kennedy's manner changed instantly. He looked delighted.

"A fiddle!" he yelled. "You've discovered some big

fiddle going on at Waterman's, exactly as you predicted at the presentation. And I thought that was just a smart sales pitch."

Webb frowned. "Think that if you like. But you haven't heard it from me." Fiercely, his hand grasped the programmer's arm. "I don't want a word said about this to a soul. Is that clear?"

"Sure."

"Not so much as a whisper. Not to Shulton, or Harvey, or anyone."

"Sure," Kennedy said again. "I said sure." Only then was the grip released.

"A Weevil," he said, ruefully rubbing his arm. "That's a new one."

"I made it up. Rather descriptive, I thought."

"And this one at Waterman's . . . ?"

"I think it's in the Operating System, but I've got no idea where."

"How big, then?"

"I haven't a clue."

"Complex, or simple, or what?"

"I would imagine quite complex, but I couldn't swear to it."

Kennedy forced a laugh. "That's really all you know? You tell me that and you expect me to find it? Using only the core dump of a system I don't understand?"

"That's right."

Kennedy laid his head back against the top of his chair, turning his eyes to the ceiling, then covering them with his hands. His mouth pulled like rubber into pleased, excited shapes that flickered across what Webb could see of his face.

"Delicious," he murmured. "Fucking gorgeous."

"I knew you'd like it." Webb said.

"Beats plastic buckets any day."

"I don't have all of the dump here yet. I should have the rest in two or three days. I want you to start then, okay?"

The hands dropped away and Kennedy rolled his head in Webb's direction. "The sooner the better. But there's still Andrew, remember?"

"That's no problem," Webb said. "I'll just use money."

"We normally charge fifty pounds a day for Kennedy," Susan said after some quick digging in a file.

Webb dictated a short memorandum to Shulton. He explained that he needed Kennedy for special temporary assignment to the Waterman's project. It would take at least two weeks and could well be longer. Webb left it to Shulton to sort out any problems with the mail order client. If it was any consolation, the bank would be paying £90 a day. But Kennedy had to start almost immediately, that was the condition.

"I've heard that Jake is good," Susan remarked. "But he's still very inexperienced, surely? How did you pull off a deal like that?"

Webb tapped his nose and gave a knowing, "Aaah." He could hardly tell her he intended to pay the fee himself, using some of the money Alloway had transferred to his bank account. He quite liked the idea of putting it back into BANKNET. It seemed a good investment.

Chapter Twenty-Two

Wednesday, 16th February. *The Guardian* carried a small back page item about the inquest on Martin Alloway. The headline said, "Contractor Criticised for Building Collapse." The coroner had made passing reference to the high winds that swept the South East on the day in question, lifting roof tiles all over London and bowling dustbin lids along the pavements. But he had said sternly that the building contractor could not escape some measure of blame for the accident. The scaffolding had stood for too long without attention. The sample produced in court was scandalously rusty and the structure had obviously become unsafe. It was a miracle only the unfortunate computer expert had died. The verdict was death by misadventure.

Webb wished he had gone to see who else was there, but he hadn't dared.

The inquest continued for a time at the Data Centre, with everyone repeating what they had said the day after the accident. A programmer said how terrible it was, another how pointless and what a waste. Several commented on how badly Martin would be missed. P.D. Sondhi said he had always known the building to be unsafe, you only had to look to see. He was sure he had said so before, a number of times. A girl vowed she would never walk under scaffolding again, rusty or not. By midmorning things were back to normal.

But there was a residual effect, a subconscious sign of mourning. For some weeks staff went home much earlier than usual and the office was always empty by six. It may have been a coincidence, a temporary drop in work pressure that would have happened anyway. Webb preferred to put it down to a primitive fear of ghosts—no one wanted to be last, to be left alone in the room where the dead man had been not so long before. They would never have admitted it, he was sure, but that's what it was. They were all so young and intelligent and unsuperstitious, too. Webb found it rather amusing.

He stayed behind that evening and by a quarter to six had the office to himself. As soon as the last man left, he was out of his chair. He was certain no one would come back.

He walked quickly to Alloway's area and stood briefly in the entrance, staring in. He had expected it to be different, to be more . . . perhaps *dead* was the word. Instead, it looked exactly the same. Just empty, as if Alloway might return at any minute. He remembered how often he had seen it empty like that when he had passed. Alloway had been away so frequently, now he came to think about it—perhaps as much as two or three full days every week. On legitimate business, Webb wondered, or to work on some part of his plan? *Doing what?*

He tried the cupboard first but it was locked, as it had been before. He swore and left it alone. He opened the top drawer of the desk and, lifting a pink-covered book of random numbers, found Alloway's diary, precisely where he had last seen it. His fingers snatched at the pages, turning to Wednesday the seventh. The space was completely blank and he breathed more freely to find no hasty last note of the meeting in Tilers Place.

He sat in the dead man's chair and went carefully through every entry from the day he had arrived at the Centre, nearly eight weeks earlier. His name was mentioned only once. On the day he had first met Alloway he read, "Brief C. Webb (SysTech Consultant)." There were the regular staff meetings and the sessions with Harrington he had seen before, and a few more recent engagements that seemed of no interest. He found the two weekends he had noticed on his previous search, with the cryptic entry, "Alton." And that was all. Everybody scribbles in diaries, he thought. Odd phone numbers, useful addresses, actions that must not be forgotten, silly doodles. But not Alloway. Somewhere there had to be another, proper diary. Maybe he had always carried it with him and now it was beaten to pulp. Like him.

Webb took a final look at the office. It wasn't much for a man to leave behind. Precisely stacked, systematic files. In a slim, leather-covered book in a desk drawer the briefest possible record of his last weeks, lived out in a bright, windowless building. Confined to only two floors and never even seeing the information his BANKNET system was created to handle. A lonely wasted life . . . except for the Weevil. Did *it* know he was dead? Or was it still working for him, stealing money once a day or once a week, and hiding it safely away? Patiently waiting for someone to collect its hoard.

Alton. That was all he had. Was it a person or a place? He crossed the office to a corner table where they kept a small selection of general reference books. He took the A-D volume of the London Telephone Directory and found twelve Altons. At a guess, there might be another hundred in the rest of the country. How would he know which one it was?

He pulled out an Atlas of the British Isles and

191

turned to the index. There were three Altons—one in Derbyshire, one in Hampshire and one in Shropshire. He had no idea which one it might be or what to look for if he went.

He returned to his desk and put the final section of the core dump listing in his case. Then he left the Centre and drove to Fitzroy Square. Flakes of snow drifted lazily down onto the windscreen and the fan blew too cold to melt them.

Chapter Twenty-Three

Jake Kennedy surveyed what he had. It wasn't much.

"I'm underwhelmed," he told Webb just before he was left alone with his new project.

He had completely cleared his desk for the first time in weeks, stuffing the accumulated papers into drawers or heaping them on the floor around his chair. He gave the desk top a quick polish with his handkerchief before placing the listings Webb had given him in two separate piles. Each was marked on the top sheet in Webb's bold handwriting—one called "ARCHIVE" and the other "CURRENT." He went to the small company library on the ground floor for an IBM reference manual on 370/165 computers. On the way back he stopped on a landing where a stationery cupboard protruded from a shallow alcove, and helped himself to a virginal notepad and a set of coloured felt-tips.

For the first hour he did little more than fidget with the listings, opening them at random to see what he could find. He became fascinated by the regular breaks in the paper and spent some time simply counting pages. He was used to dealing with listings just as they came off the computer—often as much as several hundred pages in a single, unbroken run of concertina-folded paper. But the BANKNET output was in small sections, each of exactly fifty pages. Why was that? Had Webb done it?

Kennedy's notepad remained untouched. He told himself he was deliberately taking his time, working his way into the project like a careful driver assessing the controls of a strange car before moving off. In fact, with Webb gone, he was suddenly intimidated by the prospect of having to find the Weevil. Webb's Weevil, he called it.

"This is the Operating System the bank was using six months ago," the consultant had said, pointing to the ARCHIVE listing. "And this is what they're using now." He touched the stack labelled "CURRENT." "Simply find where the two differ. Then examine the differences to see whether they are legitimate improvements or whether you've unearthed the Wevil. You'll know it when you see it, believe me."

Well, Kennedy decided, Webb was making three rather important assumptions. First, that the Weevil was actually in the Operating System. There were a great many other programs in BANKNET, perhaps as many as two or three hundred thousand more instructions. The Weevil could be anywhere. Second, that the secret program had been planted in the system in the last six months. If not, looking for differences was a complete waste of time. Challenged on that, Webb had admitted he was guessing. He had mumbled something about the change *having* to be recent. But he had looked very uncertain. Third, Kennedy thought philosophically, it wasn't simple!

He closed his eyes, wondering about the man who had created the Weevil. Webb had referred to him as Mr. X once. Was he good? Suppose he was exceptionally good, better than Webb, better than anyone Kennedy had met in his career in computing. A master analyst turned to crime. That would make finding his buried program very difficult indeed. The more he thought about it the harder Kennedy found it to start.

Susan Faulkner was consumed with interest about Webb's activities at Waterman's, and his constant silence served only to fuel her curiosity. She waited until he left the office to return to LDC, then she went up to the fourth floor.

"How's it going?" she asked Kennedy in a way intended to imply she knew what it was all about.

He held a hand across his mouth, miming a gag.

"You can tell me, Jake."

"Sorry, Sue. Chris Webb says no."

"I *am* his confidential secretary," she protested, looking hurt.

"True," Kennedy said.

"Well?" She took a seat, anchoring herself in front of him.

Kennedy was grateful for the interruption. Talking to her might help him to work out the best approach. That made it seem all right. So he told her about the Weevil.

"Suppose the only difference between these two sets of output is an area of program code in one particular place," he said. "Webb's Weevil, in other words. To find it I track through the lot, comparing instruction by instruction between the two listings. It's tedious but straightforward. It's made a bit messier by this . . . you see? The pages don't match exactly. The printer has spewed out new pages at different points in the two listings, so if I'm not careful I'll lose my place."

"Tick as you go," she suggested.

"Of course. But now it starts to get complicated. Computer programs modify themselves all the time as they run—rather like people changing clothes to suit the weather. Since these two versions were made at different times, parts of the program that are really the same will look different. So when I find a place where the code doesn't match it might be the Weevil or it might simply be a perfectly normal change the program has made on itself. Off I have to go on a time-consuming analysis to decide which it is. Mostly it won't be the Weevil. Still with me?"

"Hmmm," she said.

"But it gets worse still."

"I had a feeling it might," she said, and Kennedy grinned to see her face growing blank.

"You see," he told her, "the whole Operating System has been rearranged between these two versions. Think of it as having been shuffled."

"For what reason?"

194

"Who can say? Sometimes for improved performance, I suppose. Sometimes just for the hell of it. For
all I know it was done by whoever buried the Weevil,
to make detection that much harder. But it means that
whenever I find a section of program that really *is* different it might just be the result of shuffling—a valid
piece of code brought forward or pushed back in the
overall sequence. So I have to track through the entire
bloody Archive listing to find whether it was there before but in a different place."

Susan shook her head. "Could you repeat that,
Jake? Like, from the beginning!"

"And I thought all the secretaries in this company
were brilliant system designers," he said, teasing. "Shall
I try another way of putting it?"

"Why not. I've got an hour or two to spare. My boss
is out rather frequently these days. You may have
heard."

Kennedy was quiet for a while, pensively tapping
one of the stacks of paper for inspiration.

"Do you like analogies, Sue?"

"Addicted, Jake."

"Well, imagine that I'm a detective. No, make that a
great detective."

"It's your story," she said.

"I'm hunting for a man and my only clues are two
group photographs. Each shows a hundred men and
they were taken . . . let's say five years apart. The
men are standing in identical positions—all except one
who has been replaced in the latest picture by the man
I'm after. I've never seen him and I've got no description."

"Code name Weevil?"

"Right. They've all grown older, changed clothes,
lengthened or shortened hair, cut off or sprouted
beards."

"So you compare them face by face," Susan said,
"trying to see which one can't possibly match. Not too
difficult, surely?"

"Quite simple, in fact. But I have to be systematic,
remember. Suppose my crook turns out to be the hun-
dredth man? I'll have spent hours searching and on the
way I'll have had a number of false alarms."

"Boring, yes. But not impossible, Jake."

"No, it isn't. Except that I now introduce my musical chairs variation, my shuffle. Between the two photos some of the men change places. And I don't know which or how many."

Susan considered the new problem. "I see what you mean. That could be nasty."

"Now let's make it even more fun," Kennedy said. "Not just a hundred people but photos of the entire crowd at Wembley Stadium on Cup Final day. Nearly ninety thousand people, Sue." He pointed at the output on his desk. "There are eighty-eight thousand instructions in each of those piles."

"You win," she said. She laughed, and he had never before realised how attractive she was. Webb was a lucky guy if it was true what they said.

"If I manage it . . ." he started to say. Then he stopped.

"Go on. If you manage it . . . ?"

"How about coming out one evening?"

"A sort of reward, you mean?"

"Nobel Prize for Persistence."

She laughed again, slowly appraising him.

"But will you?" he demanded.

"Probably, Jake. Try me even if you don't. A man who brings in ninety quid a day has to have something." And she left, with a toss of her long dark hair, to go back to her typewriter.

Kennedy pondered his analogy and liked it. He pictured himself, square-shouldered in a bulky trenchcoat, wandering through the vast crowd, searching. It was an eerie scene. They stood silent and still, quite frozen as he examined faces and peered into unseeing eyes, trying to peel away the changes of time.

"You'd sure better be right, Chris," he muttered. "Your bloody Weevil had better be in the Operating System. We'll look rather foolish if I'm at Wembley when the man we're after is up at Hampden Park. Or worse still at the Oval, watching a totally different game!"

He forced himself to get down to work. He took the ARCHIVE listing and turned to Page 1. He set the

CURRENT listing beside it, also opened at the first page. He picked up a red Pentel to mark his trail through the output. Then he started. It was going to be a long search.

Chapter Twenty-Four

Webb telephoned Harrington to ask for a meeting.

"I'll come to you this time," the banker said. "I'll visit your office, if you like. It'll get me out of here. I feel like a change of scene."

That night Webb slept badly. It was dawn before his brain gave up its restless struggle, and then he fell into a slumber so deep that he failed to hear the alarm. He arrived late at the office to find Harrington already there, next to his desk and staring out of the window, across the square.

"Poor Alloway," Webb heard him say quietly. "Poor bloody man."

He did not turn, apparently seeing the consultant's faint reflection in the glass as he came hurrying in.

"I'm sorry I'm late," Webb said. "Traffic in Kensington. You can never predict how bad it will be."

Harrington fluttered a hand indifferently. "What a waste," he said with a deep sigh. "Working after hours on the bank's behalf and a terrible thing like that has to happen."

"It was awful," Webb agreed. "What can one say?"

He joined the banker at the window. Below, a traffic warden stalked the Jaguar, her eyes raking the square for the errant owner. Harrington ignored her, his face turned up to the scudding clouds. After a moment he moved away and took a chair, not waiting to be asked. His eyes were lined and sunk deeper into the face than Webb remembered. The skin was very pale, almost transparent, drawn so tightly over the angular cheekbones that the merest touch might break it. He looked fleetingly at Webb, then down to his hands, which moved constantly. His gaze, meeting Webb's, showed no suspicion, no trace of accusation. Webb relaxed, one of the purposes of the meeting accomplished.

"It was good of you to come," he said, settling into his chair. "All things considered, I mean. You must be very busy right now."

The shoulders twitched in reply. "You said it was important, Mr. Webb?"

"I wanted to discuss how we stand now. I hope nothing will change? I wouldn't want you to think I'm indifferent about Alloway . . . but I still have a job to do."

"Please . . ." Harrington raised a hand. "I've had all of Martin's people ask me the same about their work. They had to, and so must you. Yes, of course life must go on as before."

"I'm pleased to hear it."

"With me, things are different. After all, the man reported to me, built BANKNET the way I asked. I'm allowing myself the luxury of a few days' misery. But a few days only, and I don't expect others to react the same way."

The words struck Webb as odd in some way. Perhaps they had been said so often recently that they were beginning to emerge without thought or feeling.

Susan came across with a tray. She held out a glass of milk to Harrington, saying, "It's very cold. That's right, isn't it?"

He took it with a grunt of approval. "You have sharp eyes and a good memory, Christopher." It appeared to cheer him up a little.

"How do you want me to proceed?" Webb asked.

"It's high time I had a formal report from you, don't you agree? Let's say a week from today. Just a concise statement on what you have or haven't discovered."

"Haven't," Webb said quickly. He hoped the banker did not see the startled look Susan gave him from across the room.

"Haven't, then. I ought to have some form of report for my files." He fixed Webb with an enquiring stare. "You're not going to find anything, are you? That's becoming clearer by the day."

"One never knows."

"We'll finish the whole thing when I have your note,

I think. Suddenly I have a fresh raft of problems. A backlog of work and no Systems Manager."

"Let's do it properly!" Webb sat bolt upright. "Let's wind the project down in an orderly fashion at least. A week is nowhere near enough."

Harrington sipped his drink. "If it's your fee you're worried about? I'd be happy to make some arrangement, some fair termination." His lips became white with the milk, making him more pallid still.

"Stuff the fee!" Webb retorted. "It's a matter of professional pride. I like to do a job properly, Mr. Harrington. I like to finish what I start."

"If you insist." The banker seemed not to care one way or the other. "One more month then—but no more. That should be quite enough to tie up any loose ends, surely?"

"I'll do my best," Webb said. Kennedy had better be quick, he was thinking. Damned quick.

Harrington drained his glass. "It's odd, you know. I never wanted to believe there could be anything wrong with my system. Yet the closer you get to proving I'm right the more pointless the whole exercise seems. I told the board that at the start."

He placed the glass on the desk, perilously near the edge.

"I know we've discussed it before, but I do need access to actual bank data," Webb said. "Details of customer accounts, especially. Otherwise there's no way I can do a thorough audit."

"No!" Harrington said abruptly, showing irritation. "That is just not possible. Why must you keep on so?"

Webb could see that argument was useless. So he gave a suitably edited commentary on his recent activities at the Data Centre. The banker appeared happy enough, but he was evidently preoccupied and he asked few questions. Suddenly, with Webb in midsentence, he jumped up and went to the window.

"Is it always this quiet?"

"It's not exactly Piccadilly Circus," Webb said

"Fancy never seeing a tree again," Harrington muttered. "That's what death means, being cut off from the simplest things we take for granted. It's not sleeping, as they try to tell us. It's imprisonment, never-ending imprisonment." He gave an involuntary shudder. Again, his manner struck Webb as strange. Was it possible that he was pleased by Alloway's death and was trying hard to hide it? That made no sense.

Webb swivelled round to face him and asked sympathetically, "Did Martin have anyone? Any relatives? Any close friends that you know of?"

"I can't say. To tell you the truth he was really David Clement's man, not mine. I even resented him at first. Clement hired him against my wishes, do you see. I had another person in mind for the job. It took me a while to get over it, to learn to respect Martin's ability. He was very clever, you know, very determined."

"Then there was no one? I find that rather sad."

"Parents, yes. But I don't know of anybody else. It's amazing how you can work with people for so long and know so little about them, isn't it? I knew his face, the quality of his work, his salary. But I had to go to his personnel file to discover where he lived."

"Where was that?" Webb asked.

But Harrington, his eyes on the sky, said only, "That was all I knew of the man. Can you imagine?"

Webb walked with the banker down to the street and over to the car. An official seal of disapproval decorated the windscreen, taped in a polythene wrapper. Harrington peeled it off.

"I met Martin's father just the once," he said. "I came across them by chance one evening, together in a restaurant. I remember I quite took to Alloway Senior. He and I are both occasional anglers, as it happened, so we talked for a while. I envied him, I remember that now. I manage to get out fishing far too infrequently, you see. I have to plan my trips well ahead, get the licence arranged each time. I've never bothered to sort myself out and join a club. Alloway's father is luckier. He lives in some of the best fishing country there is."

"Where, by the way?" Webb's question was a throwaway comment, a mere courtesy.

"I don't recall exactly," Harrington said as he got into the Jaguar. "But close to the River Itchen, that sticks in my mind. Somewhere in Hampshire."

Chapter Twenty-Five

Saturday. Jake Kennedy worked at Fitzroy Square from early morning, alone in the building. After several hours he thought of a simple trick to increase the speed of his search. He took two large pieces of card and cut rectangular holes, just big enough to reveal a single computer instruction, in the centres. Then he placed the cards over his listings to make a kind of peepshow. His hands would slide the holes to the next position. His eyes would dart between the framed numbers and, if they matched, the hands would move again, just a flick of the fingers to bring the next pair of instructions into view. When he found a discrepancy he switched to pen and paper to work out why. Once, stretching for the pen, he knocked one of the cards and failed to notice. It was twenty minutes before he realised why the numbers were suddenly making no sense. He was careful not to do it again.

He began to feel like a machine, hands and eyes moving precisely in sequence, his brain doing little more than the most elementary comparison. The eyes started to ache. He became acutely aware of their softness, of the tiny muscles that twitched them from side to side, of the tender inner surfaces complaining at the unaccustomed effort. He imagined he could actually feel the light boring its way through delicate pupils to batter against myriad minute nerve ends. Every so often the eyes would demand a break and he had to stop, dropping his face onto his hands and shutting them. The numbers persisted in his head, overlapping and comparing themselves as they drifted in a red-speckled void. Soon he could start again, refreshed as if by sleep, but the breaks became ever more frequent. There had to be a better way, he told himself. There just had to be. Playing about with your eyes like that could send a young man blind.

He developed techniques for comparing the numbers he trapped in his cardboard holes, learning to recognise almost instantly when the differences he found meant nothing. They always did, in the end. His progress was desperately slow. Time ceased to have meaning, and he discovered no trace of the Weevil.

Just after seven in the evening his vision finally gave up and he saw double. Two fourth floors floated before him, transparent and oscillating. Dizzily, he strained to bring the images back together. Resisting at first, they slowly merged and he could see properly again. He stared ahead and his mouth dropped open.

"Eureka!" he yelled, the shout echoing around the room. His eyes had told him what to do. He had stumbled on his better method.

Kennedy paced the floor, pondering the idea and becoming still more delighted—he was convinced it would work. The problem was that he needed help from Eleonore Price and he had called her only hours before to cancel their date that evening. Her reply had been to slam the phone down. He wondered whether Webb would ever know how seriously he was taking the assignment.

He tried to call Ellie again, letting the dialling tone ring in his ear for several minutes before hanging up.

"All right," he said, "so she's getting her own back. I should care."

Normally, he would have been angry, even a little jealous. This time he was grateful to find her out. It meant he could stop at last and forget the Weevil until morning.

He flicked an ancient switch to plunge the building into darkness and slammed the front door behind him. The square was deserted, silent except for the distant rumble of traffic on Euston Road. He blinked at the streetlights, noticing their harsh, shimmering halos. His only thought was of bed, and the relief of shuttering his eyes against the light.

Chapter Twenty-Six

Sunday. Susan Faulkner opened her door to find Webb standing there in faded jeans and a black polo-neck.

"Well, well," she said, taken aback. She had expected the milkman, and a hand demurely secured the top of her dressing-gown.

"Just passing by, Sue." He gave her a peck on the cheek, much too platonic for her liking.

"I believe you," she said.

He invited himself in and settled into a great old chair with worn arms and sweeping walnut sides that made it look like a dodgem car.

"Where are Josie and Whatshername?"

"Still in bed, of course."

"I'd love some coffee if there's some on."

"You got me up, Chris. But I'll see what I can do."

She was back in a few minutes with two steaming mugs.

"It's been too long since you were here, know that?" She sat on an arm of the chair and ruffled his hair.

"I wanted a favour," he said. "I hope you don't mind."

"Surprise, surprise."

"I'd like to borrow your car, just for the day."

"My *what*?"

"Your Volkswagen, assuming it still moves."

"Is yours broken or something?"

He shook his head. "I just felt like yours. An uncontrollable urge."

"That doesn't make sense."

"All right, so I need something a bit less conspicuous. How does that sound?"

"But you're not going to say why?"

"Clever lady."

"Do I get to come?"

"Nope."

"Suppose I want to go out myself later?"

He reached into a pocket and tossed his car keys onto a low table. "Then you take my Porsche. It's a swap, Sue. Okay?"

"Really?"

"That's what I said."

"You actually trust me with it?"

Webb laughed. "No. But it seems a fair exchange." His hand had moved under her dressing gown and was caressing a rapidly erect nipple.

"Don't I get even a teeny word of explanation?" she asked, moving closer.

"Nope."

"You'll stay awhile, though? The natives are very friendly."

"With Whatshername two feet away in the next bed!"

"There's here. They'll be asleep till midday."

"Sorry, Sue." He jumped up, gesturing apologetically. "Sure as hell today's the day they decide on the healthier life. And surprise entrances are bad for my system."

Scowling, she went to get her car keys and when he took them he gave her another perfunctory kiss, the back of a hand brushing across her breasts.

"I'll be back," he promised. "You're all so helpful here at Swap-A-Car."

"We try harder," she said.

"Pig!" she snapped at the door a moment later as it closed behind him. She moved to the window to watch him drive away. The front of her old VW was badly dented and the exhaust pipe drooped dangerously close to the ground. The whole business struck her as crazy.

She found Kennedy's telephone number and called to see if he felt like a ride, but a sleepy voice said there was no reply from his room. She looked at her watch and it was just past nine.

"Naughty old Jake," she said gloomily.

She dressed in her most expensive clothes, rarely touched on Sundays except for the family teas she detested, and took a long time making up. A nice leisurely cruise around town, she told her reflection. Along the Kings Road once or twice, around Sloane

Square . . . up to Hampstead would be a good idea, driving very slowly and publicly into the car parks of a a man for her nothing could.

Kennedy climbed the stairs to Eleonore Price's flat carrying his listings in two cardboard boxes. He leaned on the bell push with an elbow. Nothing happened, so he did it again, keeping the elbow there until the door finally opened. She was in an elegant bathrobe, her hair tousled, eyes lidded. The early morning face dissolved into a smile when she saw him.

"I dig the classy brown luggage, Jake," she said with a yawn. "You certainly travel in style."

couple of the smarter pubs. If Webb's car couldn't pull

Her years in London had worked interesting changes on an accent nurtured in Maine. Kennedy liked the result. It was, he sometimes teased her, like Cockney with the edges knocked off. She could, he told friends, turn him on from across the room with his eyes closed.

"I didn't know you were planning to move in at last," she said as he pushed by.

"Just your visiting listomaniac," he replied breezily. He hurried down the narrow corridor and into her crowded studio. She followed, to find him sitting at the wide bench where she worked on her interior designs. He was eagerly examining the light box she used for tracing.

"Bloody man. So that's what you're after."

"I had this great idea, Ellie. I just have to find out if it works."

"Had breakfast?"

"I didn't stop to think about it."

"I'll fix something. Eggs okay?"

"Sunny side up," he drawled in what he fondly believed was accurate New England Irish.

"God, that's awful," she said.

He heard the door close. His hands ran over the light box like those of a child with a new toy, alternately pressing hard, then hardly daring to touch.

Kennedy pressed the switch at the side of the box and the frosted glass top was illuminated with a restful, even light. He placed the first sheet of the ARCHIVE listing on the glass then slid the first page of the CUR-RENT version over it, carefully aligning the edges. Everywhere on the paper the groups of figures merged in the light. He moved on to the next pair of pages. This time a small area of totally different numbers showed clearly as a dark patch halfway down the listings. The locations were already circled in red from his search the previous day. His new method worked! Yesterday, finding those first discrepancies had taken over ten minutes. He bent over the light box to kiss it gratefully.

"I love you," he told it. "You're gorgeous."

"And you're mad," came a voice. "Utterly kinky."

Kennedy spun on the stool to find Ellie still there, leaning languidly against the door.

"Hell," he said.

Laughing at his embarrassment, she came over to put her arms around his neck. The bathrobe dropped open.

"Not now," he said without conviction.

"Prefer your little box, Jake?"

"You wouldn't understand."

"You're damned right I wouldn't."

"It's work, Ellie. Somthing urgent."

"Uhuh."

"I want to do well. I want to get on."

She licked his ear and whispered, "That sounds more like it."

"Hell," Kennedy said again. But he gripped her tightly, his hands feeling a soft body that still felt very warm from bed. What did an hour or two matter? he thought. The Weevil would still be there.

Webb arrived at Alton just after midday and was surprised at the size of the place. Harrington's remarks had led him to expect a village clustered around a clear trout stream. He found a country town with occasional old houses to hint at a pleasant past. But there was a modern central shopping street looking the same as a hundred others and a proliferation of yellow no-parking lines. The town was dominated by a great, factory-like brewery, its giant harp symbol constantly appearing between the houses as he drove.

He went first to the railway station, leaving the car

in an almost deserted compound. The telephone box he wanted was just in front of the station building. Standing in a puddle, he leafed through a tattered directory and found a P.L. Alloway, shown as living at 61 Alresford Road, Alton. There were no other Alloways listed in the town. The booking office clerk directed him to the other side of the old market place.

It was a street of superior semi-detached houses, set well back behind neat lawns bordered with carefully manicured hedges. The driveways were of random paving edged with thick, dark concrete and there was wrought iron everywhere—used for lavish garden gates, supporting lamps in the porches, pressing against the opaque glass panes that let light into the halls. Newly cleaned Fords and Austin Allegros stood on display on damp patches in front of the garages. There were a few Rovers and Volvos, apparently new but with five- and six-year-old registration letters that gave the game away. It could have been Golders Green, Webb thought, but for the elderly cars.

Some of the houses had names, some numbers, and some had neither. He saw no sign of Number 61 at first and had to count from a numbered house further along the street to locate it. The house was little different from the others, with lilac curtains framing the back of a dressing table in an upstairs window, and a maroon Triumph 1500 in the driveway. Driving slowly by, Webb caught sight of a man behind the car, crouching to polish a bumper. He drew up twenty yards further on, across the road. Reaching into the glove compartment he took out his miniature Zeiss binoculars and unzipped them from the case. He saw a curtain move at a window, then another several houses along.

"Sod!" he said, getting out with an anxious face to kick each of the tyres in turn. The Volkswagen had been resprayed in places, with no attempt to match the colour, and each door was decorated with a large multicoloured flower. Back behind the wheel he reluctantly packed the binoculars away. Changing cars had been a mistake. He could hardly have chosen a more conspicuous vehicle.

In the driving mirror he saw an elderly man come

from the garage at Number 61 to inspect the garden, peering at flowerbeds and picking at imperfections on the close-cropped grass, rubbing his back each time he unbent. At a distance Webb was unable to see any resemblance to Martin Alloway, but before he could leave the car, to stroll past the garden for a closer look, the man went into the house. Webb continued to watch the mirror, uncomfortably aware of being under close observation himself. He had no plan and liked none of the ideas that came to him.

For nearly an hour there was no movement from the house. Then the door opened and the man re-emerged, wearing a black homburg and a dark overcoat. He was followed by a woman of about the same age, late fifties, Webb guessed, and also soberly dressed. She moved slowly, almost wearily, leaning on the man's arm as she climbed into the Triumph. Webb heard the engine start and watched the car back gingerly into the road. Then it passed, with the elderly driver crouching stiffly over the wheel. He waited for several minutes before following, but he took a left turn where it had gone straight ahead. He stopped to scribble an address on a scrap of paper, then left the car to walk back into Alresford Road.

Chimes, not a bell, he predicted as he pushed through the iron gate to Number 59, and when he touched the button the chimes rang out like a summons from an ice cream van. Soon a portly man was at the door, wearing slippers and still holding his Sunday paper. Webb gave a friendly smile and thrust a hand at him.

"Mr. Alloway? I'm Peter. You know, Peter Matthews."

The man looked surprised. "You've got the wrong house, young man. You want next door . . . Number 61."

Webb pulled his piece of paper from a pocket to read it, wrinkling his brow.

"I was definitely told fifty-nine," he said. "Mr. Alloway . . . works up in London?"

The guess was correct and the neighbour nodded.

"Civil servant, if I remember?" Webb suggested.

That's what the man had looked like. That, or a bank manager.

"Accountant," the man in the doorway said, beginning to eye Webb with suspicion.

"It's not really him I've come to see," Webb explained. "It's his son. Martin and I are old friends, you see. I don't suppose you have any idea where I can find him these days?"

Distress showed on the man's face. He put out a hand but stopped it awkwardly in midair.

"He was killed . . . a couple of weeks back." The words were rushed out, as if to minimise their impact. "Some terrible accident. I'm sorry you didn't know."

"Jesus Christ!" Webb said.

The neighbour stood looking at him, shifting uncomfortably.

"How has he taken it?" Webb gestured to the adjoining house.

"Not at all well."

"But still going to work, I hope? To help him forget, I mean."

"He is now. But he was off for over a week. Took him very badly, it did."

"Look," Webb said, "if that's the case I don't feel I should see him. It wouldn't be right." He walked a short distance down the path, then turned. "I'd rather you didn't upset them unnecessarily. Please don't mention I called."

Webb drove back to the railway station to discover the times of the morning trains to Waterloo. An elderly accountant, he thought, would be the type to get to town early, promptly returning in the evening with the first wave of the rush hour. The train at 7:29 seemed the most likely but the 6:52 was also a possibility. Webb was not looking forward one bit to rising that early.

He went for a roast beef lunch at the Swan Hotel, along the main road and not far from the station. Then he took a room for the night, borrowing a paperback from the girl at the reception desk to help pass the time. It was evening, too late to do anything about it, before he realised he had only the clothes he stood in. He sat on the bed, surrounded by empty drawers and

209

facing a wardrobe bare except for its wire hangers. No change of shirt or underwear, no toilet gear. His spare cordless razor was still in the door pocket of the Porsche.

In the flat at Belsize Park, Kennedy worked through the computer output, his eyes grateful for the gentle light of his newfound aid. At times the listings diverged completely and he had either found the Weevil at last or just another place where the program had been shuffled. Then he had to slide line after line, page after page over his reference ARCHIVE output until he reached a place where they matched again. His record for the day was a displacement of over ten thousand locations. It took over an hour to find and he had no idea why it had been done.

At eight in the evening, tracking what he assumed was merely another relocated section, he eventually reached the very end of the output without discovering a match. So he began again at Page 1 and finally returned to his starting point. He had come across some new code! But he restrained his excitement. It had happened several times already and always when he had analysed the insertion it had proved to be an innocent improvement—nothing that could conceivably threaten BANKNET.

This time, Kennedy tried to translate the numbers into computer instructions and failed. They were definitely not part of a program. Nor on careful study of the figures could he make any sense of them. They couldn't possibly be meaningful data, he concluded. Baffled, he spun on the stool, scratching his head. He had discovered an area of exactly two hundred computer locations. They weren't blank. They didn't contain a program. They didn't hold data. And he knew of nothing else one could find in the memory of a computer system.

At eleven Ellie brought him a mug of hot chocolate and announced an early night. He blew her a preoccupied kiss and continued to work. He had just uncovered another meaningless area, not far from the first. An hour later he found a third. From then on the comparison went quickly and there were no more peculiarities.

Taking a pencil, he realised he had detected a total of five hundred locations—a precise, round number, too exact to be a coincidence. A space large enough to contain a very powerful program, except that there was no sign of one.

"Ridiculous," he murmured. "Bloody crazy."

He pored over the numbers, trying to read some sense into them. Whatever he did—rearranging, reversing, regrouping—made no difference. In the end it was the sheer lack of sense, the apparent randomness of the figures, that struck him most forcefully. Suddenly he had a theory. There was one way he might be able to check it—only *might*, he repeated to himself—but it would have to be done in the morning at Fitzroy Square. Kennedy knew he still hadn't found the elusive Weevil. But he was almost certain he had discovered its hole.

"You cunning bastard," he said respectfully, as he packed the listings away.

He slid into bed beside Ellie. She moved slightly as his arms went around her. The lines of numbers began to drift away from his mind. Then she stirred and turned and he forgot all thoughts of Weevils.

Chapter Twenty-Seven

Monday. Webb left the Volkswagen in the station car park. Without a topcoat he became very cold on the short dash to the booking office. It was one of those mornings, he decided, when there is nowhere as desolate as a railway station. The overcast sky reached down close to the tracks, threatening to stay for the day. The bird song had died away. Only the dripping leaves disturbed the sullen silence of the countryside. He hurried to the waiting room and stood close to the stove.

The early commuters were arriving to line the platform at careful intervals, each taking what Webb assumed to be a regular personal place. There were a few workmen who retreated to the far end of the platform. Most of the others looked like small businessmen—the kind who had little to say at the best of times and nothing at all at 6:45 on a bleak February morning. Webb saw no sign of Alloway's father and wondered whether he would know him anyway from those brief distant glimpses the previous day. He began to pace the room, less because of the cold than at the prospect of waiting for the next train. The old Philishave borrowed from the hotel porter had done a mediocre job, and his hand tested the roughness. His clothes felt of yesterday.

There was a whisper from the tracks, a faint mechanical hiss that grew to a rumble. The passengers edged forward, folding their newspapers. Then a stocky man bustled onto the platform. He held a half-finished sandwich, devoured in hasty gulps as he passed the waiting room window. He was instantly recognisable, uncannily like Martin Alloway, although much older and with thinning silver hair. The build was heavier but the stooping walk exactly the same. As the train screeched to a halt Webb moved out behind him.

The man chose an empty compartment, taking a corner seat. Webb followed and chose the facing corner. The carriage might have been refrigerated.

"Cold day," Webb volunteered with a shiver.

The man gave only an uncommunicative grunt. He frowned at Webb's closeness and raised his *Telegraph* as a barrier. Somewhere ahead the diesel engine throbbed and the train juddered into motion with a chorus of complaints from the couplings. Webb brushed sticky yellowish mist from the window with the back of his hand. The station slid away and the houses of Alton thinned into country. The cows in the fields were all lying down. Webb tried again.

"I missed my gardening yesterday. We had the wife's family around, that's what did it. I depend on the exercise. I find I'm in poor shape for the week otherwise."

"Important, gardening," Alloway muttered, his gaze not straying from the austere type of his *Telegraph*.

"I work all day in an office," Webb said. "Like a lot

212

of people, all day, all week. Life wouldn't be bearable without the weekend. You know—gardening, fishing, that kind of thing."

Alloway peered briefly over his paper fence, eyes narrowing at the younger man's sweater and jeans.

"Can't say I mind the office myself," he replied gruffly. The paper was raised again with an air of finality.

"Of course, there are offices and offices." Webb leaned closer. "Mine is better than most, I suppose. I'm in computers, actually."

He saw the other man stiffen. Slowly, the newspaper came down.

"My son was in computers," Alloway said quietly. He was staring not at Webb but out of the window. It was opaque with condensation and he could have seen nothing.

"Really? Which firm?"

"One of the big banks."

"Very nice, too."

"He was one of their top technicians. An analyst."

"Did you say *was*?"

Alloway gave a laboured nod and touched a black fabric band on his left arm

"I'm sorry," Webb said. He decided to bide his time. The man gave no sign of wanting to continue the conversation.

Minutes later they jerked into the next station. A face stared in through the grimy far window, then disappeared. The door slammed loudly on the adjoining compartment. Soon a shudder ran along the train and they were moving again, gathering speed.

"It's an exciting business these days," Webb said. "Very well paid if you're good."

"I'm sorry, what was that?"

"You were telling me about your son. You know, computers."

"I don't think you'd be very interested."

It sounded to Webb more like a hopeful question than a statement.

"It's a long journey," he said. He held out his hands to show he had no paper then folded his arms purposefully.

213

"You're in the business yourself, you say?" Alloway settled back in his corner, studying him with new interest.

"That's right."

"Small world."

"I'm a consultant, actually." Webb excused his sweater with a tug. "I've got a free day today. Normally you'd see me in my pinstripes, the full rig."

"I was wondering."

"And your son . . . ?"

"Martin, his name was."

"He worked for a bank, I think you said? They're very choosy."

"So I'm told. I didn't want him to move into computers, to be perfectly honest. But he liked it well enough." Alloway dropped his newspaper onto the seat beside him. He delved for a pipe.

"Do you mind?" he asked, pointing hesitantly with the stem to a No Smoking sign.

"Go ahead," Webb said, and Alloway took his time, carefully shredding the tobacco, stuffing the bowl and getting the pipe burning to his satisfaction.

"Aircraft were his first love," he said, wreathed in smoke. "The computers came much later. When he was a boy it was aircraft, morning, noon, and night. It was all he could talk about—how he was going to design the fastest and the best."

"I was like that, absolutely crazy about racing cars. Things never seem to work out the way you plan."

"He was all aircraft and textbooks. You couldn't get him onto a sportsfield. Not that I minded." Alloway puffed contentedly. "Ever been to the Farnborough display, by any chance?"

"Once, as a kid."

"We always went on the final Sunday. To Martin it was more important than Christmas or birthdays. It was still a big thing then, of course. Every year for a whole week it was the only thing that seemed to be happening in England. I never knew a Farnborough when the weather was anything but perfect. Not a cloud in the sky, just the planes tracing their patterns. Brilliant, fast, British planes. Some moved so quickly you hardly saw them come till they were over you,

214

climbing straight up. You could see clear into the red-hot jets."

"I remember," Webb said, producing an enthusiastic nod of nostalgia.

"Funny, isn't it," Alloway said. "We'd get complaints now about the noise. Then the pilots made sonic booms just for the fun of it, diving down to bounce the sound off the crowds."

"I bet they loved it, too?"

"Noise never hurt anyone." The man's eyes were on Webb, but looking through him and straining to see back into the past. A time when the son was young, and alive.

"All week we had the planes from Farnborough roaring over us at Alton. Martin knew them all—Swifts, Lightnings, Gannets, Victors . . ."

"And Hunters," Webb added. "Always in bright red and in close formation. They were the best." Spreading his fingers wide, he flew a hand over his head.

"Those were the days," Alloway agreed with a sigh. "There was a navy fighter—the Buccaneer, I think it was. Well, one year a Buccaneer turned low over our garden, every day for a week at the same time and the same exact height. You could set your watch by it and Martin would be out there, waiting for it by the hedge. Aircraft were the only thing in his life. The only thing he wanted to do as a career, or so we thought. He took a degree in aeronautical engineering, you know. First in his year, he was."

"All that and he ended up in the computer business?"

"When he left the university he found the aircraft industry dying on its feet. At least that's what he told me. I said he was wrong . . . I still think so. People need to fly and someone's got to build the planes. Well, it's obvious. There was Martin and his splendid degree, his room full of model aircraft . . . and turning his back on it all. I told him he was mad but he wouldn't listen. When he went around the aircraft companies for his interviews he said he sensed the end. He was too late for aircraft, he said, he'd missed the best times. There was all that money pouring into the industry in the fifties, all that achievement. A few years later the Government pulled the plug out and it was as good as over. It was becoming just a spare parts industry, Martin said, building engines and wings but not the whole things, not real aircraft. He got out without ever being in."

"And into computers . . . ?"

"He looked around to see what else there was. Computers were the latest thing, he decided, coming in as the planes went out. Lots of opportunity and a chance of making good money. You know how it happens at that age. Suddenly money was more important than job satisfaction."

"Sounds a smart move, all the same," Webb suggested.

"Turning your back on what you really want to do!" Alloway snorted indignantly. "*I* couldn't have, not after all that study! But Martin was like that. He was going to get out of computers next and into God knows what. That's what he told me over Christmas. A year off work, just travelling round the world. That was his latest notion."

"Very nice if you can afford it," Webb said, leaning closer.

"Oh, I dare say he would have managed it if he wanted. He would have gone somehow. He was like that, our Martin. Very stubborn, a mind of his own. I told him what I . . ." Alloway stopped himself, glancing down to his black armband. He wriggled awkwardly in his seat and reached for his paper, cheeks reddening.

"You never hear of Farnborough these days," he said, clearing his throat. "Have you noticed?"

"Now you come to mention it . . ."

"Nothing on the television, not a word in the papers. I don't even know when it's on any more." He turned his attention to his *Telegraph* and was soon hidden behind it.

They completed the journey in silence. The compartment gradually filled, and Alloway put out his pipe, opening the window to clear the fumes. Webb soon gave up watching the endless, uniform clutter of outer London, the same narrow backyards with their lean-to sheds and upturned tricycles and washing lines.

Half-dozing, he listened to the train rattling over the points and found he missed the regular click the wheels had once made over the gaps in the rails. All the fun had gone out of trains when the welded track came in.

At Waterloo, the carriages disgorged a horde of hurrying passengers and all the doors were left open. Webb walked along the platform with Alloway. He was struck by a sudden thought.

"Your son . . . did he mean it about going round the world?"

"I think so."

"Would he have gone with anyone?"

"Why do you ask?" Alloway demanded tetchily. He stopped abruptly and the press of commuters streamed around them, shoving towards the barrier.

"No particular reason. I'm sorry if . . ."

Alloway strode on, and Webb had to elbow his way through the crowds to draw level.

"There was someone," Alloway mumbled, looking resolutely ahead. "At least he tried to tell me so."

"That's good."

Alloway grunted disagreement.

"Well, isn't it?" Webb asked.

The other man made no reply. A brisk march came from the public address system, echoing tinnily under the arched roof.

"I wouldn't fancy a year of travel all by myself," Webb said. "I'd want a friend along with me."

"He used to joke about it, pull my leg. Just me and Smith, he used to say, seeing the world in luxury. I never knew if he meant it or not."

"Smith?"

Alloway said nothing.

"A close friend?" Webb asked.

"Someone from the bank."

Webb stopped dead in his tracks. *Someone else at Waterman's?* he thought frantically. What the hell . . . ? He battled to catch up again, succeeding only as they reached the ticket barrier.

"A girl, I presume?"

"What was that?"

"This person Smith. Was it a girl?"

Alloway gave him an odd, sad stare. "I have no idea. But one would very much like to believe it was."

The face was suddenly tired and very old. He walked away towards the underground without a word of goodbye.

Chapter Twenty-Eight

Webb took a taxi home to Chelsea, where he shaved, luxuriated in a hot shower and had a huge breakfast, grilling almost everything he could find in the refrigerator. It was nearly ten when he arrived at the office.

"How was the car?" he asked Susan.

"Out of this world," she said rapturously. "So fast I scared myself silly."

He went to his desk to sort idly through the morning mail. She walked over, searching her handbag for his car keys.

"There is one small thing I should mention," he said. "I had a spot of trouble with your Volkswagen."

She raised her eyebrows enquiringly.

"It refused to start this morning. I had to abandon it in Hampshire."

"*What*!"

"It's nothing to worry about. I'll explain where it is and you can arrange to have it brought back. Charge it as a company expense."

"*I've* never had that happen!"

"Perhaps it just didn't like me."

"Well, don't ask me again, swap or no swap."

"Don't worry, I won't," he said, addressing her receding back.

She called him on the intercom almost immediately, assuming the aloof, formal manner usually reserved for unwelcome visitors.

"I forgot to say—Jake is dying to see you. He insists it's terribly urgent."

"Is the meeting room free?"

"This time on Monday? Should be."

218

"Tell him I'm already there." Webb was up and moving away as the phone dropped into the cradle.

Kennedy charged into the room, his arms full of computer output.

"I found it, Chris," he yelled. "I found a hole."

"A what?"

"A hole in the operating system."

"I haven't the faintest idea what you're talking about."

Kennedy hopped from one foot to the other, wondering what to say next.

"Just calm down," Webb told him. "Take a seat, take a deep breath, then talk me through what you've been up to."

So Kennedy sat next to him and explained about his search over the weekend—how he had hit on the idea of using the lightbox, how he had discovered the baffling areas in the CURRENT listing.

"Here they are," he said, opening the output where a piece of card marked his place. "Three separate areas, a total of exactly five hundred locations. Not four hundred and ninety something, but an unmistakably round number. Plenty of room for a program designed to spirit loot away from BANKNET. But it isn't a program, that's the twist."

"It certainly doesn't seem to be," Webb agreed.

"It isn't, take my word. And those numbers aren't ordinary data, either. I'll prove it to you, if you like."

"I believe you."

"So I had found three areas of very random-looking numbers. That's as far as I had got last night."

"There's more to come," Webb said, scanning his mobile face. "I can tell."

"You bet. I got here early this morning for a bit of research. I never dreamed it would actually pay off, but it did." Kennedy lifted some of his output to extract a slender pink book. "It was only a wild hunch but..."

To his astonishment Webb snatched the book from his hand.

"Where the fuck did you get that!"

219

Kennedy flinched. "The library here, of course. What's up, Chris?"

Webb breathed out heavily, passing a hand over his eyes. "Of course," he said with a nervous laugh. He threw the book on the table.

"It's just a standard book of random numbers," Kennedy said defensively. "Every technical library has one."

"I know."

"So what's up?"

"Nothing, Jake. It's just that our man had one of these. I caught sight of it once in his desk drawer. Absolutely identical, down to the slightly tattered cover. It gave me quite a shock for a minute seeing it, that's all." He patted Kennedy on the back. "A hunch, you said? You're bloody amazing."

The young man beamed. "It only took me a few minutes this morning. It turns out that those five hundred locations precisely match a sequence near the start of the book. Incredible luck, really."

"More like brilliant thinking," Webb suggested.

"No, it really was luck. I mean, your crook and I might have used completely different books—there are several on the market. But I *was* lucky, so here we are. It definitely is a hole, as I suspected. He's left a space to pop the Weevil into when he wants it to do its dirty work."

"Hold it!" Webb said. "I'm not with this business of the random numbers, yet. What's the point?"

"Disguise. It's a clever way of covering up the hole. Put in a string of zeroes and it would stick out a mile. Put in the actual Weevil and there's a risk one of the Waterman's programmers might chance across it and realise what is going on. The random numbers are to make the hole merge, Chris. Camouflage."

"But *you* found it!"

"Yes, but I was looking, remember. And I suspect I have the same kind of quirky mind as your crook."

"Could be," Webb said, with private satisfaction. "Just could be."

"He really is bloody clever, you know. It's not easy to explain, but in nearly ninety thousand instructions I

220

can't believe there can be three better places to hide something. He must know BANKNET inside out."

"Oh, he's cunning, all right."

"Well, that's it. What do you think?"

"I can hardly believe it, actually finding it at last. What goes in the hole, Jake?"

"Search me."

"Eh!" Webb said, his face darkening.

"I mean, I don't know."

"You don't bloody know!"

"No. I'm sorry."

"But you must, Jake. You must have some idea?"

"Honestly, Chris. I don't."

"Hell!" Webb exclaimed, striking the table with a fist.

"It's not my fault," Kennedy said anxiously. "Look at it this way. If the Weevil is going to be loaded into the hole there has to be another simple program to do it. All it needs is a few instructions."

"Well, naturally."

"But I've found no sign of one in that lot. It I had, it would have been dead easy to follow the trail back to the Weevil. But there's nothing. Your Weevil is somewhere else and so is the program that pops it into its hole. I haven't the remotest idea how to track them down."

"Do you know how many programs there are in BANKNET?" Webb demanded.

"I can imagine."

"Can you guess how much disc storage there is on those computers?"

"I know, I know. Literally billions of places to hide a program away."

"Then we've got nowhere, Jake," Webb said wearily. "You realise that? You've proved our man was preparing some cunning assault on the system. Well, I knew that already. You tell me he's very clever . . . technically shit-hot. I found that out weeks ago. We haven't moved a bloody inch."

Turning slightly, Kennedy could see the dead look in his eyes, the dejected expression. Webb seemed utterly beaten.

"I hoped that at least you'd be pleased about the hole," Kennedy ventured cautiously.

Webb raised an index finger slowly into the air.

"That to the hole!" he said angrily.

Chapter Twenty-Nine

Jennifer Owen had been managing the BANKNET project since the accident, acting informally as Alloway's successor. Harrington obviously decided a decent interval had elapsed and he issued a note confirming her appointment. It came as no surprise at the Centre and excited little comment. Webb only learned the news from a copy of the memorandum pinned to the noticeboard in the coffee room.

She wasted no time in assuming command. Two men in brown coats came to help her move the forty feet or so to Alloway's old office. They began by walking back and forth a number of times to assess the scale of the problem. A protracted tea break followed, while they talked about it further. Only then was she able to get them to pack her various papers into tea chests. As the chests were trundled towards the office, Webb ambled over to see Sondhi. He requested loan of the first BANKNET manual that came to mind.

"Sure thing," the Indian said, rummaging for it.

"Would you mind if I read it here? I won't be a nuisance."

"Be my guest," Sondhi said.

Webb moved his chair slightly and had a perfect view across the room and into the office, with the locked cupboard directly facing him.

Jennifer made the workmen sit while she walked around sizing up her new territory. Then she ordered some changes—an alteration in the angle between the desk and a wall, a minor realignment of a screen, some of the shelves raised or lowered a few inches. The idea did not seem to be to improve the appearance of the area, as far as Webb could tell. It was more like an attempt to exorcise all trace of the previous occupant.

When it was finished the office looked hardly any different, but she seemed pleased enough, sitting in her grand new chair for a time to get the feel of it and nodding her satisfaction.

At last, Webb saw her discover the locked cupboard. She searched the desk thoroughly for the key before sending one of the men off. Meanwhile, she persuaded the other man to begin unpacking. Kicking off her shoes, she perched on her new desk, clearly enjoying the activity as he bundled books and files roughly onto the shelves.

Harrington dropped by to inspect the changes. He fussed around the office even more than she had done and she backed down diplomatically when he insisted that the screen looked far better in its original position. He ordered the workman to take more care with her books. Then he sat chatting with her, his head turning this way and that and a rare smile showing his pleasure at his contribution. The sense of occasion spread like a ripple through the big outer room. Work came to a virtual standstill and staff trooped past on a variety of excuses, glancing in to see what was going on.

It was twenty minutes before the man who had gone for the key came back. He was empty-handed. The problem was explained to Harrington, who led the others across to watch him put a shoulder to the door, as if that was all it needed. It refused to budge. Soon afterwards he left, deep in thought.

The workmen followed his example, attacking the door in every way they could think of. Jennifer kept intervening to prevent actual damage. Finally, she lost her temper and ordered one of them away again. When Webb saw him returning with a bag of tools he decided it was time to take a closer look. Thanking Sondhi, he went to the entrance of the office, making no attempt to hide his interest.

"Trouble?" he asked.

Jennifer looked up with a friendly smile, the first she had given him in weeks.

"We can't seem to find the key anywhere. It looks as if brute force is the only answer."

"How fascinating," Webb said, moving in.

The workman took a hacksaw to the lock, scraping

223

slowly through the bolt while his assistant paced about complaining at the bother.

"My personnel notes are in there," Jennifer explained. "I'm dying to see what Martin thought of me."

Webb sat on the edge of her desk. "I've been meaning to ask, do you have any Smiths on your staff?"

"Locksmiths," she replied with a toss of the head.

"I'm serious, Jennifer."

"None. One Jones and a Brown, but no Smith. Why?"

"What about in other departments in the bank?"

"The *whole* bank?"

"Yes."

She laughed. "I should think there are plenty."

"But can you think of one who has any kind of connection with BANKNET?"

"No one who comes to mind."

"Even the slightest connection? A man who gets regular management printout from the system, say?"

"I said no."

She was obviously about to ask again why he wanted to know when the workman interrupted.

"There you are, miss."

Proudly, he slid the door open just enough to prove the job was done. Then the two of them went off, still grumbling loudly.

Jennifer went to the cupboard and opened it wide. Webb saw her stoop and stretch out a hand. What looked like a stack of systems manuals toppled over and spilled out onto the floor.

"Wow!" she exclaimed. She rose, steadying herself against the door.

Webb jumped up and peered over her shoulder.

"How about that?" he said with a whistle of astonishment.

At her feet lay a collection of glossy magazines. There were fifty or more and a bundle of photographs had scattered with them. He saw a score of naked bodies, suntanned and glistening with oil—seemingly the entire stock of a Piccadilly Circus paper seller. Bending to sift through them, he realised that all the pictures were of men. The magazines had titles like "Adonis" and "Muscle" and "Splendour of Boyhood."

224

He straightened, holding one open at a massive bronzed specimen of body building.

"At least Alloway's skeletons were well covered," he said, with a click of the tongue.

"We all need a hobby," she commented. He thought at first she was shocked but when he looked closely she appeared to be trying not to smile.

"You knew, of course?" she said.

"I should have realised. I just didn't read the clues."

"You *really* didn't know?" She sounded surprised.

Webb was thinking about the dead man's father, standing at the ticket barrier with that strange expression. "With hindsight, perhaps I did."

"I guessed the first week I was here. He was the only boss who never made a pass at me." She crouched again to look through the magazines. "I was quite put out until I worked out why."

Webb kept his head inclined as if looking down, but his eyes were raking the upper shelves. There were two rows of suspended files, the pockets filled with bound or loose papers and each tagged with a label in Alloway's neat handwriting. He began reading the labels and they all seemed innocuous, relating only to everyday Waterman's business. He withdrew a few of the files. They were exactly what the labels said they should be. Jennifer was too preoccupied to notice what he was doing.

"My God, look at this one," she muttered, standing to show him a picture of an amazingly well-endowed teenager.

"Trick photography," Webb said brusquely.

"I do believe you're jealous, Christopher." She prodded his arm cheekily with a finger.

"No. I just hope that Martin behaved himself in here with this lot." Her lack of embarrassment disturbed him, just a little.

"That's plain nasty," she said. But she dropped the magazine as if scalded, saying, "It's not really very funny, is it?"

"Not much."

Subdued, she turned her attention to the files, trying them at random as he had done.

The highest shelf had an assortment of computer

output and manuals, with an unmistakeable air of being discarded. Webb spotted a folded piece of paper protruding from a narrow gap between two books. It caught his eye as the only thing in the office not perfectly in place—it had the look of being hastily pushed there. His hand went up to rest casually on the edge of the shelf, inches from it.

"Ah ha!" Jennifer said triumphantly, tugging out a folder.

"Mine," she explained, showing him her name on the cover. As she went to her desk to browse through it, Webb's hand closed over the note. He turned his back squarely to her before unfolding it. It was short, written in an untidy scrawl that was difficult to decpher in places. The paper was cream-colored, heavy and expensive. Printed importantly across the top were the words, "From the desk of David Clement." Webb read,

7th February
Dear Marty,
Quite by chance, I learn from the Security Division that Alex is monitoring your extension. What the Dickens is going on that I ought to know about?? Can't phone you for obvious reasons!!! Am at a meeting out of town till morning. Please give me a ring then. Use an outside phone, for heaven's sake.
Fondest regards,
David

Webb caught his breath. The seventh, as he could hardly forget, had been the day of the accident. He remembered his call to the Centre that evening, every word he had said, almost everything Alloway had said in reply. Suddenly, he had a recollection about the line—a series of clicks, he thought, at the start of the conversation. Nothing to worry about at the time, but now . . .

"Fucking hell!" he said out loud.

Jennifer looked up. "Oh, do give over, Christopher, or I'll begin to suspect your habits, too."

With difficulty he forced a smile before turning.

"You should know better," he said.

"True," she murmured, her eyes boldly meeting his.

He edged towards the outer office. What the hell, he was thinking, was Harrington up to! What had he known or suspected about Alloway, for all his repeated insistence that nothing was amiss at LDC?

Jennifer flapped her file in the air to stop him. "I'm outstandingly good, know that? The all-round professional, it says here."

"How nice for you."

"Well, I had to find out while I could. Alex wants all this moved down to his office later today." She indicated the cupboard.

"I bet he does," Webb said quietly.

"I'll dispose of the art collection first, though. I wouldn't want to shatter any illusions." She held a finger across her lips. "Not a word, Christopher. Right?"

"How very respectful," Webb said, inclining his head minimally in reply.

"Sleeping dogs," she said.

"Since you mention it, where is Harrington's office? I've never seen it."

"Me neither. On Level One, I believe. But I've no idea where, exactly."

Her eyes were back on her file as she spoke. She glanced up to ask why he was interested, but he had already gone.

Chapter Thirty

Webb had learned what little he knew of burglary in two short private lessons from Henry Larcomb. Larcomb was not a burglar, nor did he catch them. But he understood them perfectly, or so he claimed. He was an insurance loss assessor, a man who came after they had gone, to see what they had taken and how. The first time they met, the little man wore a permanent frown and his manner was that of a headmaster with a none too bright child.

"You deserved to get done, know that?" he had said. "You're damned lucky you haven't had the lot nicked, every last stick of furniture. The protection on this place is laughable, Mr. Webb. Get better locks, eh? I'll tell you a good outfit to go to. And how about a nice burglar alarm while you're at it? I'm going to insist on that. With stuff like this around, my company has a right to demand an alarm."

"Stuff like what!" Webb had said, gesturing at the denuded living room.

They met again a year later, almost twelve months to the day. Webb was shattered by his latest losses. Larcomb proved to be friendlier than before, even managing a frosty smile once or twice.

"They've taken even more this time," Webb had complained bitterly.

"So it would seem," Larcomb had said.

"Bloody everything."

"Well, of course," Larcomb had remarked blandly. "I mean, that alarm outside . . . great red thing stuck on the wall right where everybody can see it. That's an advertisement of affluence, that is. You always get a better class of burglar with an alarm. It's a known fact."

He had prowled around, moving silently on crepe-soled suede shoes. He had refused to take off his stained fawn raincoat, and his spectacles had enormously thick lenses that might have been magnifying glasses. He examined the back door, then the upper hall window.

"This where he got in?"

"Yes, we found it wide open."

"Amazing," Larcomb had said, looking at Webb sadly. "All so horribly predictable." He had taken Webb's arm in a reassuring way. "People think a key is a small metal thing that fits in a lock, you know. Well, it needn't by. Dear me, no. Knowledge is the best key, Mr. Webb. Knowledge of weakness."

He had padded along to the study.

"This was locked, I suppose?" The door was swung to and fro as he searched for evidence.

"Naturally. All my cine equipment, my spare cash . . ."

"Hmmm." Larcomb had given an irreverent sniff.

228

Out came an ancient wallet from which was taken a credit card.

"Lock it, please."

"Now?"

"Well, of course now."

Webb had locked the study. Then Larcomb had slipped his plastic card between the door and the jamb. A quick jiggle against the catch and the door was open.

"Try it yourself." The card was handed over.

Webb had attempted to repeat the trick, only to find it far harder than it looked.

"No, no, no." Larcomb's hand pressed over his to guide it through the correct actions. Within minutes Webb was an expert, or so the insurance man proudly informed him.

"You're lucky, really," he sad said then. "It was a careful bloke who did this, a pro. Considerate. Some I know would have taken a whopping great screwdriver to the door. Bust it open, see."

They had retired to the living room to sit sipping Scotch while Larcomb filled in his report. Light patches on the walls showed where pictures had been.

"Know my ambition, Mr. Webb?" Larcomb had said as an aside. "And I'm only kidding, mind. I'd like to do a branch of Barclays. You know, using only a credit card, some pliers and a few feet of flex. I've seen the very place, a small country branch near where I keep my caravan. It's quite possible, I reckon. I'd use a Barclaycard on the window catches. That strikes me as ironical."

Thinking back on it, Webb could imagine what Larcomb might say about Harrington's security study at the Data Centre—the one Alloway had confirmed was being done by DSL.

"A commendable aim," he would judge. "Identifying weakness in pursuit of greater strength. The objective is fine. But your consultant's report is a nasty risk, you know. By spelling out your weaknesses it becomes the weakest link itself. Guard it well, Mr. Harrington. It's a key to LDC."

229

Webb asked Susan to get DSL on the telephone.

"Hand over as soon as they answer," he told her. "And don't say who we are."

He watched her thumbing through the directory, then dialling.

"Data Studies," the operator said, a moment later.

"Waterman's Bank here," Webb said. "Accounts Department. Look, I've got a query on your latest invoice and they haven't given me the name of your contact man there. Who's running the job?"

"Waterman's, you said?"

"Correct." Webb gave an edge to his voice, talking from the back of his mouth as accountants always seem to do. Just as Alloway's father did.

There was a long delay before the girl was back saying, "I'm putting you through now."

The line crackled, then a different voice said, "This is Mr. Fuchs' secretary. Is that Waterman's?"

"That's right, love. How do you spell that? F-O-U-...?"

"F-U-C-H-S."

"And he is what ... the senior man on our project?" Webb was jotting the name on his blotter.

"Yes. He's in conference right now, but if it's important ..."

"No problem," Webb said affably. "I'll call him back later." And he hung up before she could make any reply. He buzzed Susan.

"Give it an hour or so, then call DSL again. Get the extension number of a Mr. Fuchs, would you. And Sue ... I'm sure you won't, but don't give them any cause for suspicion. And don't tell them the company name."

"You're doing it to me again," she remarked sourly.

"I sure am," Webb said.

He doodled circles around the name on the blotter. Handy that, he mused. Very handy, him having a secretary.

Two floors above, Kennedy sat with his feet lodged on a part-opened drawer, staring into space. He was still brooding about the Weevil, wondering where it might be hiding. Webb had taken him off the Waterman's project temporarily—off the case, as he pre-

230

ferred to call it. But he couldn't stop thinking about it, and why should he? He felt starved of information on BANKNET. Webb had refused to provide him with listings of any of the other programs, saying that the bank was very cautious about letting material like that out of their sight. And he had refused to say a word on what he knew about Mr. X. It was, it seemed to Kennedy, a crazy way to carry on.

Behind his chair a large open cabinet filled the corner. A disorganised mass of paper, books and files overflowed down it, spilling like a frozen torrent from shelf to shelf. It was rumoured by Kennedy's colleagues on the fourth floor that a forgotten umbrella lay fully open under all that paper.

"How can you be so systematic up top?" Andrew Shulton had once said, tapping his temple, "and yet so bloody untidy."

But the mess was rational as far as Kennedy was concerned, quite workable when you knew how. The deeper he dug in it, the earlier the items had been put there. It was the simplest filing system he could think of.

Looking at it all, he suddenly remembered his early efforts on the Waterman's job, when he had worked briefly for Webb during the proposal stage. He delved to a depth of three months, then deeper still. Soon he retrieved a grubby buff folder labelled "Waterman's." The titles of four previous projects littered the cover, all roughly crossed through. He didn't believe in waste.

The folder was almost empty, with little more than his scanty notes on his initial research into Waterman's. Reading through them, he found a sheet with just the date and a few short sentences. He recalled writing it on his knee as he had sat talking to Webb.

Meeting: Chris re Waterman's.
Chris very flattering about report I got from Levene's. Headhunter phoned. Chris planning to interview guy from bank. Cheeky!

A slow smile appeared as he thought back on it. Chris Webb on the phone, taking some pricey headhunter for a ride. Taking some poor sod from Waterman's for a ride, too, bringing him all the way down to London just to pump him dry. The smile froze. His eyes opened wide.

"That's bloody it!" he shouted. He kicked the drawer shut and ran from the room.

When Kennedy dashed in, Webb was on the telephone to a security firm, trying to arrange a demonstration of their latest devices. The man at the other end was doubtful whether a visit was possible for some weeks. Kennedy put his face close to Webb's, mouthing words.

"Everyone's gone so security conscious, all of a sudden," the man was saying. "That's the trouble. But . . ."

Kennedy pushed the phone away, whispering loudly, "I've got it, Chris. I know where it is."

"The Weevil?"

"Yes, the Weevil. What else!"

"I'll have to call you back," Webb said into the receiver, then banged it down.

Kennedy dropped into a chair as if he had run miles. "You should have reminded me there were two," he said. "I completely forgot till just now. We'd have saved days if you'd said."

"Two? What are you on about?"

"Data Centres, of course. Don't you see, that's where your Weevil has to be." Smugly, Kennedy folded his arms. "It's up at the other one. It's bloody hiding in Manchester."

"Hang on," Webb said, his face transfixed. Briefly, he considered the suggestion, then shook his head, saying, "It can't be. Surely not."

"Bet it bloody is. It's so obvious I could kick myself. I mean, it's exactly what I would do if I were him."

"But the programs up there are the same!"

"Oh yeah?"

"Well, so the bank people seem to think." Webb was starting to smile, too.

"Do they have any programmers based up there?" Kennedy demanded, the words coming out with a rush.

"Not a one."

"I knew it! Just operations staff, I bet."

"Spot on," Webb said in admiration.

"I'll make a further guess. The programs *will* be the same, right down to the same three holes in the operating system. Except that the Weevil will be in them ... hiding where it was never supposed to be found."

"Could very well be," Webb said. Then he struck his forehead, shouting, "Christ!"

"What?"

"It's just that I have a copy of the Manchester listing already! I have it on my desk at the Centre at this very minute."

"But if it's a normal program listing, the Weevil still won't show up. It has been patched in, remember."

"Sure. But it so happens that they issued me with a Manchester core dump at the same time. I didn't specifically ask for it, but I chanced across it, stuck in the back of one of the binders. I haven't given it a second glance since." Penitently, Webb struck his head again several times. "Hell! I go to the trouble of getting a copy of the London version for you and all the time the Weevil was under my very nose."

"That's life."

"It's been staring me in the face for weeks. Fucking thing."

Kennedy couldn't help a chuckle at Webb's annoyance. Then, intoxicated by his success, he began predicting with great confidence how he believed the Weevil took the money. But Webb half turned to gaze out of the window and obviously was not listening. He began to count days on his fingers.

"Is something wrong, Chris?"

"Be quiet a minute, will you. I'm trying to think."

Webb screwed up his eyes and deep lines radiated from them, creasing his skin. Kennedy felt he was definitely looking older just lately.

Webb was pursuing a different line of thought on the Manchester theory. It had been a constant mystery to him why Alloway had suddenly acted as he had, paying over the £9K "fee" long before he was in any real danger of discovery. He had not seemed the type to take panic action irrationally. Now at last Webb understood. He remembered how he had gone to Sondhi to ask for a copy of the Operating System listing and how the Indian, in all innocence, had suggested getting one sent down from Manchester. Within days Alloway had made his move. No wonder, Webb said to himself. The poor bastard believed I was onto him. Totally certain now, he spun back to face Kennedy.

"You're absolutely right, Jake. That's where it is."

"Didn't you believe me?"

"I don't make a habit of jumping to conclusions." Impulsively, Webb leapt to his feet. The tense facial lines had softened again. "You're quite sure it will be in the same three places?"

"Well, as sure as I can be."

"Doing anything tonight?"

"I was thinking of . . ."

"Cancel it! I'll have that listing back here in a couple of hours. By midafternoon."

"Smashing," Kennedy said, rubbing his hands.

At the Data Centre, Webb tore twelve pages from the Manchester listing, double-checking the positions of the three areas against numbers Kennedy had written in the back of his diary. He folded the output and slipped it into a stamped brown envelope bearing the address of a company in Glasgow. His finger pressed firmly on the self-sealing flap.

In the exit pen, a guard lifted the envelope out of the briefcase to see what else he could find. As always, Webb's heart missed a beat. But, as always, the envelope was returned with barely a second glance. It was the "PRIVATE" typed across the top, Webb thought, that was what did it. It worked like a charm on men trained in security.

Chapter Thirty-One

Fifteen minutes after leaving the listing with Kennedy, Webb was outside the DSL building in Mortimer Street. It was on a very narrow frontage, fairly new, and severe in red engineering brick and black-framed windows. The glass was bronzed, more for show than as protection against sunlight. Three bricked steps led to glass doors painted with the DSL trademark in great gold letters. Peering in from the pavement, Webb saw an entrance hall empty of furniture. No desk or chairs, no receptionist. It was a cheerless space clad in shiny marble which reflected cold light from fluorescent ceiling panels. A sign said, "RECEPTION—FIRST FLOOR," and an arrow pointed to stairs that clearly led down to a basement level as well as up. A single lift door in drab blue completed the picture. The indicator showed no sign of movement. The showroom next door sold denim.

Webb crossed to the other side of the street for a better look. He could see a few heads and a man standing, telephone in hand, gazing absently down. Lights blazed to a height of five storeys and he got the impression that there was one more level set well back behind a parapet. There could not be much space up there, with most of it taken up by water tanks and lift machinery. But he guessed there would be sliding doors onto a small paved terrace and they would probably refer to it as the Penthouse.

Satisfied, he walked in the direction of Oxford Street, stopping to buy an evening paper. He found an Italian restaurant open for coffee, and the *capuccino* was good enough to order another.

Susan had established Fuchs' extension number to be 38. And the man had a personal secretary. That should help considerably. Amongst the expected forest of desks he would only be interested in those with typewriters. Scooping a spoon through thick froth, he tried to visualise the plan of the building.

He knew DSL to be a very different company to Sys Tech. There would be no computers in the office, no junior staff working late on program debugging in the way they did at Fitzroy Square. DSL was older by five years, which might as well have been a lifetime. Computer Establishment, Shulton called them in a voice tinged with envy. They were rather arrogant people, in Webb's opinion, somewhat stuffy, striving hard to emulate the IBM style and mostly succeeding. They claimed to work chiefly at the highest management level for big companies and government agencies. They produced reports, not systems, one of their top consultants had once told Webb at a conference banquet. Their main concern was with business strategy, what he called "The sharp end of corporate decision making." Writing software, he had declared, was best left to lesser outfits. He had then pounced on the cherry Webb discarded from a dried half grapefruit and they had found no more to say to each other.

Webb was back in Mortimer Street at 5:15. The entrance hall was still deserted and the indicator showed the lift moving up to the fourth floor. Do it! he told himself, taking a deep breath. A moment's hesitation, then he was pushing through the doors, moving to the stairs, bounding down two and three steps at a time. On the landing he found a men's lavatory. He ducked in and chose the end cubicle, pulling down the pan cover to sit and wait. It was Friday. With luck, most of the DSL staff would leave promptly—within the next half hour or so, he hoped. There was little news in his paper so he began the crossword, but soon gave it up. Crosswords, he decided, were like physical exercises, agonising if you didn't do them regularly.

It was quiet outside for a time. Then, at 5:30, there was a sudden flurry of activity. He heard doors slam, taps running, the grate of the towel as it was jerked down from the dispenser. The catch on his door was rattled and there came a gruff, "Sorry." The room was small and airless and the atmosphere was fetid for some minutes after the last footsteps clattered away over the ceramic floor.

After 6:20 there was no further movement outside, but he waited until 7:00 before venturing out. He stretched to chase away the stiffness and stirred dulled senses by dashing cold water on his face. The newspaper was dropped into a bin and he draped his jacket over a hook by the door. As an afterthought, he removed his wallet to his hip pocket. Then he emerged onto the landing in rolled-up sleeves, a tie slipped several inches below an open collar, and carrying a notepad and pencil.

He started up the stairs, pausing just out of sight of the hall to listen. Then up the next flight, moving rap-

idly so as to be visible from the street for as short a
time as possible. But not too quickly. Not surreptitiously. His rubber soles made little sound, just the occasional squeak on the steps.

Double doors decorated with a huge yellow "1" led
from the next landing. He held one ajar to assess the
layout. Beyond a small reception area the floor was di-
vided into what looked to be very constricted rooms. A
corridor stretched to the far end of the building, bare
except for doors to either side. The first three were
closed and there was no way of knowing whether they
were occupied. Webb passed, not daring to try. The
fourth door was wide open and he entered a bleak box
with little more that a table and some chairs. The telephone number was 65. As quickly as he had come
onto that floor he left it.

He ascended to the next level, beginning to breathe
harder and with an artery throbbing at the side of his
neck. It was the effort of climbing the stairs, he told
himself. Reaching the landing doors, he glanced
through a glass porthole, pushing at the same time. But
he snatched the hand away and froze, leaving the door
rocking gently to and fro. In the centre of an open plan
room two men sat at a table, talking over some papers.
Pausing only long enough to establish that there were
no typewriters in sight, Webb turned and sprinted up
to the third floor.

He came to what was obviously a senior management area. A deep piled mushroom carpet flowed
across the landing and a lithograph in a heavy gold
frame hung on the lobby wall. It was the first picture
he had seen in the building—the Arc de Triomphe
shrouded in mist, or perhaps it was Marble Arch, there
was no way of knowing. A quick look through the
porthole to see that all was clear and he was striding
boldly in.

Only one of the ceiling light panels was on and the
floor seemed deserted. The offices were clearly
spacious, with the partitions and doors in dark veneer.
Each had its own outside secretarial area—big rosewood desks bearing black typewriters. Each was tucked
into a private alcove but had a strategic view to the lift.
No lights showed under the office doors.

The number of the telephone on the nearest desk was 36. "Ah," Webb said, darting to the next. It was numbered 38 and he smiled with relief as he saw it. But the door to the adjacent office was locked and when he returned to the secretary's desk he discovered that the drawers there were also locked. "Bugger," he muttered, rattling them furiously. He began lifting loose papers, the ashtray, the blotter. He looked under the typewriter. A slim white stationery cabinet stood by the desk and he searched the drawers, snatching them out in turn to poke under envelopes and sticky labels and boxes of paper clips. As he pulled out the bottom drawer, a key lay in full view. It looked far too small for the door so he tried it on the desk lock. It fitted and he tugged at the top drawer. There, half under a pair of scissors, was a more promising-looking key. Seconds later he was enteing the office. He switched on the light and closed the door behind him. He took a deep gulp of air and rubbed his forehead without thinking, to find it wet with perspiration.

First, he checked the telephone to be quite sure it was Fuchs' office. The number was 38. Only then did he begin to look properly around the room. It was expensively furnished and dull. A huge plant grew in a corner, stretching spiky green fingers to the window. The leather-topped desk was vast and almost completely clear of papers, with a silver-framed family snapshot propped dutifully to one side. A hefty executive toy lay readily to hand, a tangle of chrome tubes to stroke or dismantle in times of stress. An onyx slab held pens poised like missiles. There was a single picture, almost identical to the one on the landing—mist swirling about a suspension bridge that could easily have been Hammersmith as the Golden Gate.

Webb went to a big glass-fronted cabinet packed with books and reports. The books all seemed to have "Management" in the titles and the unblemished dustcovers looked never to have been touched by hand. Scanning the documents row by row, he listened intently, his nerves at full stretch, straining for the slightest sound outside. He could hear his own breath, so loud it threatened to drown any warning of danger.

238

A pulse beat relentlessly across the very top of his scalp, making the hair stand on end.

Then he saw it. In clear view on a middle shelf a thick file had the word "Waterman's" typed across the spine. Instinctively, he pushed on the sliding glass door to take it. The door refused to move. His eyes dropped to where it stuck and only then did he notice the catch securing the bottom of the glass. He gave an angry, "Damn," and turned to search the single shallow drawer of the desk, but it held only a diary and a cigarette box. Spinning back, he shook the lock in frustration. It was a small, flimsy, thing—a cylinder on one door that gripped a serrated metal tongue attached to the other. Breaking it would be easy. But broken, it would be noticed. He leaned against the desk, wondering what to do, wondering if the risk was worth it.

It was then that a folder caught his eye, lying face up on a lower shelf. He bent, pressing against the glass to read the title. "Thank you very much, Mr. Fuchs," he breathed gratefully. Then he went out to the secretary's desk to pick up the scissors in his handkerchief. He prised off the lock, leaving it where it fell, among slivers of glass on the carpet. He withdrew the Waterman's file, again using the handkerchief. Under a sprung flap inside was a report entitled, "LDC Security Audit—DRAFT."

The list of contents directed him to the very back of the report where, in an appendix, plans were given for each of the six levels at the Centre. Harrington's office was clearly marked on one of them, a big room off the main corridor on Level 1. Webb made a quick sketch of the plan on his notepad. Then he went back to the contents page, to find reference to a chapter on "Conclusions and Recommendations." He turned to it in a flurry of pages. His watch told him he had been on the third floor for just over five minutes. Ten was the maximum he wanted to be there. Henry Larcomb had said to him that the best intruders try not to stay around for more than ten minutes. Not if they can help it. Webb's eyes devoured the words.

The DSL consultants, he found, had high praise for the security procedures at the Centre. In their opinion unauthorised entry from the street was impossible under any conceivable circumstances. Webb skipped several paragraphs, searching for a single word. And there it was! Internal security, the report said, was also outstanding—well planned and scrupulously executed in the main. But . . .

"Ah," Webb said in triumph. "There just had to be a but."

"But all rules are subject to the vagaries of human frailty," he read. "Tiredness, resentment of the inconvenience caused by regulations, even the deliberate flouting of rules for what seem to the employee to be the best of motives—these are often the greatest dangers faced by high-security systems."

The report went on to discuss three areas of concern, cases where the consultants had encountered inadequate controls or lax practice. There was no serious problem, it was emphasised, but some changes should be made.

Any chink in the armour, however small, is always a cause for nagging doubt. We would therefore recommend that the appropriate remedial action is put promptly in hand. A slight tightening of existing (and generally satisfactory) regulations is all that is required. These matters are little more than a question of discipline.

It was the last of the three problems that particularly interested Webb, the most frequent malpractice, according to the report. He thumbed forward again to the plans, to compare the layout of Level 1 with that of the top floor, where he had his desk. Then, with a contented smile, he dusted the report with his handkerchief and returned it to its original place.

Now he took the other folder he had seen, not bothering with the handkerchief. The buff cover carried a small black crown and the lettering was in a distinctive, rather old-fashioned typeface. Under the words "Ministry of Defence (Procurement Executive)" came the title "Feasibility Study for Project Mondrian." Across the top, stamped in red, was the word that had attracted his attention. It said, "SECRET."

"Tu tut," Webb murmured as he took the file.

"This is hardly a secure cabinet, Mr. Fuchs. And this is definitely not a secure office."

He dusted the glass, the drawers and the door handle. He left the door open and went to the outside desk. A few quick rubs with the handkerchief, then he reopened some of the drawers he had previously closed so carefully, tipping one onto the floor. Stopping by the swing doors, he switched on all the lights. The lift took him to the lower ground level, where his jacket was still where he had left it.

He stopped at the bottom of the stairs. There was no sound from the hall. He moved swiftly, up the stairs and across the marble floor, to shove at the glass doors. They were firmly secured. "Hell," he said. But even as he cursed, he saw the key just above his head, protruding from the upper door frame. He turned it and withdrew it, leaving the door unlocked behind him. From across the road, he looked up to the bright third floor windows. The rest of the building was quite dark now, with few lights burning. A glow against the sky indicated someone still at work in the Penthouse.

My, my, he told himself, there will be a fuss tomorrow.

He dropped the door key down a drain and walked back to Fitzroy Square, where he put the defence file through Shulton's paper-shredder without reading so much as a word. Then he went up to see how Jake was getting on, but there was no sign of him.

At his flat in Chalk Farm, Kennedy pored over the printout for much of the night. First, he decoded the numbers in the dump, writing the computer instructions they represented in correct sequence on a notepad. It was a largely mechanical task requiring little thought. But even as he was doing it, it became clear that the Weevil was not a single program but three, one in each of the three areas. When he finished transcribing he tried to work out what the programs were intended to do. He managed to make partial sense of them. But he was unable to understand them completely because the programs made a number of operations on data stored on discs. He had no idea what the various disc items were and Webb had not provided the BANKNET reference manual that would tell him. Some of the items, he was sure, were amounts of money. That came as no surprise. But the others baffled him.

By the time he finally gave up he had positively identified two of the items as representing cash—he assumed they were in sterling. One of the programs was easy to follow and was obviously designed to transfer exactly nine thousand pounds from one account to another. It's stealing, he thought. Great! A second program caused him problems. It appeared to make tests on an account holding the fixed sum of £1252·47. Why? he wondered. And why such a strange amount. Still, Chris Webb would probably know what it all meant.

The time was 04:27, according to his much-prized new Japanese digital watch. He slumped on the bed in the tiny room, feeling very tired. His earlier excitement at the chase had gone and he was left with a feeling of acute anticlimax. At the start of the assignment he had been convinced that he and Webb were on the track of something really big, a fraud involving hundreds of thousands of pounds, maybe even millions. Why else go to all that trouble? But now all he could think of was those two sums of money and how greatly they disappointed him. They were so much smaller than he had expected.

Chapter Thirty-Two

Saturday, 26th February. Webb was waiting impatiently in his office when Kennedy arrived, late and bleary-eyed.

"A night on the tiles, Jake?"

"Oh, sure," Kennedy said.

He spread his notes out on the desk and explained what he had deduced, making his feelings about the likely size of the theft very apparent. Webb grew progressively more stony-faced as the tale unfolded.

"And that's as much as you know?" he asked, finally.

"It's the best I can do."

"Okay, leave things with me. I need time to think it over."

"Can I help?" Kennedy stifled a yawn.

"Thanks, but no. Let's meet back here at . . . shall we say three this afternoon?"

"I was going to the match. Arsenal."

"They'll have to manage without you," Webb said.

Kennedy returned promptly at the agreed time. As he entered the room the close, smoke-laden atmosphere snatched at his throat and he coughed. Beside Webb's elbow an ashtray was filled with the butts of small cigars. Numbers and unintelligible diagrams covered the whiteboard on the wall.

"Phew," Kennedy said, fanning the air.

Webb looked up. "Open the window if you have to."

"No, I'll survive. It probably kills all known germs, anyway."

Kennedy went to take the facing chair but was signalled around the desk to sit beside Webb. Close to, he could sense the consultant's satisfaction. Suppressed excitement shone in the depths of the eyes.

"Well, Chris?" he asked eagerly. "Have you solved it all yet?"

"Not quite. The general scheme of things is clear. But I still need your help on a number of outstanding problems. And I'm going to have to do some more digging at the bank. I don't quite know how, yet."

"What I really want to know is . . ."

Webb silenced him by rapping his pen sharply on the desk.

"First things first. This is my show." He glanced at a sheet of paper on which he had noted the questions that still bothered him. "Let's begin with the Weevil's journey, shall we? I want you to go over it with me again—how he comes out of hiding and down to London."

"I thought I did that pretty thoroughly this morning."

"So do it again!"

Kennedy showed his irritation by speaking in a rapid monotone.

"As I see it, the Weevil comes down the communications line from Manchester in the form of a routine transmission to the London Centre. It seems to work as a direct computer-to-computer process and there will be nothing to suggest to the duty operators that anything out of the ordinary is going on. It happens every twenty-four hours, on the dot at midnight."

"I know now why that is," Webb cut in. "I paid a quick visit to the Centre to check their computer schedules. The main daily update on the customer account files begins promptly at a quarter past midnight. Are you with me?"

"Ah. And the Weevil is always there first, waiting to get its greedy mitts on the money!" The irritation melted.

"Quite."

"He's a very punctual creature, our Weevil," Kennedy said. "Punctual to ten-thousandth of a second—I think that's the accuracy of an IBM crystal clock. Bang on twelve he comes scampering down that line."

"A provincial Weevil after City money," Webb said.

"Hence the hurry," Kennedy agreed, grinning broadly. "He gets loaded into his London hole to do his thieving. Later, when he has finished, he calls down the set of random numbers from a permanent file on disc storage. *Splat!* The Weevil is overwritten and the London computer is back to its normal state of apparent innocence. It's bloody ingenious."

"Not bad, is it," Webb said. He leaned intently towards the younger man. "Think very carefully about this next point, Jake. It's vitally important. You told me this morning that all this is happening now, that it's already ticking away day after day. Are you still convinced of that?"

"Absolutely," Kennedy said with a laugh. "He's a very busy Weevil. I doubt if he's missed a day's work in his life."

"How about that," Webb breathed. He turned his eyes upwards, trying not to show his feelings. God Almighty! he thought, it's posthumous robbery. Another entry for Alloway in the Guinness Book of Records. And it's my inheritance.

"How much has he collected so far?" he heard Kennedy saying, as if from a distance. "Do you have any idea?"

"Not an inkling. I'll explain why in a minute."

"All the same, you must have been able to work out what the programs are doing. I get that feeling."

"More or less, yes." With a wry smile, Webb tore a page from his notepad and slid it, face down, along the desk. He kept a finger on a corner, warning Kennedy off.

"You were quite right about there being three programs. It's a gang, Jake, that's what it is. Our crook isn't just a clever computer man, he's a totally dedicated and informed bank robber. He knows that an effective raid needs a group, each applying specialised skills to a particular task. Someone to carry out the actual theft, someone to drive the getaway car, and—very important, this—a fence, someone who can convert hot cash into safe spending money. So he's produced a gang of computer programs to do all of those things."

The finger was lifted with ceremony, and Kennedy snatched at the paper.

"What the hell is this? Not the gang, surely?"

"Those are their names. Or, to be more precise, their aliases. We may never find out what he called . . . calls them."

Kennedy was too surprised by what he read to notice the slight slip of the tongue. "Robin Hood? Wheels? Carbon? Are you pulling my leg?"

"Never. They're damned good aliases. I took almost as long thinking them up as I did studying your notes and the listing. They're very apt names, actually."

"But what do they mean?"

"It should be obvious. Robin Hood steals. Wheels is in charge of the transport. Removals, got it? And Carbon copies, although I still find him a bit of a mystery."

"The Weevil Gang," Kennedy said, thoughtfully scratching behind an ear. "They don't exactly sound the sort to strike fear into a big bank."

"That's the secret of their success. Surprise attack."
Webb was clearly enjoying himself immensely.

"Can we start with the theft, Chris? I couldn't grasp
that at all last night."

"That's done by Robin Hood. He steals from the
rich to give to our man. Not from Waterman's themselves, by the way, and not from any old customer.
Just from the rich, and he's very selective. He does it
by imposing a kind of tax on the biggest accounts,
choosing those where the bank charges exceed a certain amount, and increasing the charges. My guess is
that if any sharp-eyed customer should happen to notice, Waterman's would fall back on the corny old ex-
cuse of 'computer error' and probably believe it
themselves. Anyway, the bank gets its normal rake-off,
Robin Hood gets his slice off the top, and the customers are unlikely to be any the wiser. Do a trick like
that often enough and a small amount of money each
time soon adds up."

"It could hardly be simpler," Kennedy remarked. "I
find it a bit of a letdown, to be honest. Technically
speaking, I mean."

"Stay with it a minute. It happens to be a very old
dodge, Jake. And that was the big problem our man
faced. How does he get the money out without being
caught? You see, if the books are to balance, which
they must, and if he is to take advantage of the normal
BANKNET facilities . . ."

". . . Which he has to," Kennedy chipped in. "Otherwise the Weevil programs would have to be too huge
to conceal."

"Right. Well, if he is to do all that, the account the
stolen money accumulates in has to be *real*, apparently
no different to any other at the bank. So it is there for
all to see. Open, in fact, to discovery and audit by
whatever inspection team Waterman's use under their
secret security procedures."

"And what kind of things do they look for?"

"As I said, that's secret—Waterman's are hardly going to tell me. But I'm pretty confident our man knew
what he was doing, so I would expect the account to
be very unlikely to arouse suspicion. It will simply look
like any other with a rather healthy balance. Neverthe-

less, there has to be some risk it will be spotted and it's for that reason Robin Hood is forced to work in a gang. Our man never intended to draw money direct from the Robin Hood account. He uses it merely as an intermediate hiding place . . . a left luggage locker, you might say."

"Do you know which account it is? Whose name it is in, for instance?"

"All I have is the account number. There's no way we're going to find out from these listings how much money has been salted away so far."

Kennedy's face fell.

"Luckily," Webb continued, "that doesn't matter too much. The other account—the one our crook actually draws cash from—is far more interesting. And it is friend Wheels who moves the money there."

"Ah," Kennedy murmured. "I begin to see."

"Usually, every BANKNET transaction is recorded in detail. The file for an account making a payment records the number of the destination account, and vice versa. But Wheels doesn't play by the rules. He removes some of the cash from the left luggage locker and places it in a second account, right? But he leaves no record in the left luggage file of where the money has gone, so there is no trail for the investigators to follow. Meanwhile, in the new account the money is shown as having come from somewhere quite different—anywhere other than from Robin Hood."

"Like a football pools company? A lucky win?"

"Yes, that would do very nicely. And now our man is safe. He can walk into his branch at any time and withdraw his money. His account looks absolutely normal and there is no obvious link back to Robin Hood. I mean, you and I have pored over these programs for hours and *we* still have no idea exactly how they have been used up to now."

"But how does Wheels know where to move the loot?" Kennedy asked. "If the details are built into the program there's a trail, a giveaway."

"He picks up his instructions from a disc. Just a few numbers that our man can leave there at any time during the preceding day. I presume he uses a simple and

247

very ordinary-looking test run. No one at the Centre would think twice about it."

"It's a post box," Kennedy said with enthusiasm. "Exactly like a dead letter drop in espionage."

"A nice analogy," Webb agreed. "You see, having created the Weevil, our man can't risk being caught communicating directly with it. Yet he has to make contact. This seems a pretty safe way. Anyhow, if there's no message waiting, Wheels simply packs up for the night. If there is, the numbers tell him what to do—the sum of money to be moved, the account it is to go to, and so on." Webb reached for the Manchester listing, pointing to a number he had circled in red. "This figure here—nine thousand. That appears to have been left there from the last time Wheels did a job. As I interpret it, he slipped nine thousand pounds into another account. That was some weeks ago."

"I spotted that, too," Kennedy said. "I realised it had to stand for a sum of money, although I couldn't see how it was used."

"Well, I'll tell you one especially naughty use. If required, Wheels can extend his activities outside of Waterman's. He can pay cash into any of the other main clearing banks."

"Honestly?" Kennedy sounded surprised.

"Really. Provided he initiates a transaction to a valid existing account, the clearing house's central computer system will do the rest. Nice, eh? There might be a very slightly increased risk but I'm certain it can be done, and has."

"And the other bank wouldn't even suspect?" Kennedy said incredulously.

"No, how could they? The money will be real enough, so why should they have any doubts?"

"What puzzles me, though, is why he should ever bother with amounts as low as nine thousand pounds. That gave me a sleepless night."

"Low? For heaven's sake, it's well over twice what you earn in a year!"

"You know what I mean. Obviously I wouldn't turn it away if it was offered me. But given this elaborate setup, it sounds a relatively small sum. So why?"

248

Tantalisingly, Webb confined himself to a smug smile.

"Why, Chris?" Kennedy demanded again.

Webb shook his head. "Sorry. Let's say it's *sub jud-ice.*"

"Oh, come on . . ."

But Webb looked away and said, "Shall we deal with Carbon now?"

"The final member of the gang," Kennedy noted sullenly. "I think you said he was a bit of a mystery?"

"Ah yes, dear old Carbon. Money copied while you wait."

"Very droll," Kennedy said.

"But that's virtually all he does—copy. Now, I really don't understand it, I can't work Carbon out at all. It's almost as if he isn't pulling his weight on the gang, and that makes no sense." Webb turned the listing to a page liberally sprinkled with heavy red lines and margin notes.

"Here we have that post box trick again. Carbon picks up a single number left for him on a disc. That signifies a branch of the bank so he breezily opens an account there! Then he simply copies another file into it, exactly as it stands. See here, Jake, always from this one—account number 734282 at branch 10053."

"It has to be a way of *creating* money," Kennedy suggested. "A more sophisticated form of robbery."

"I thought of that but it can't possibly be. There's far too little money involved, not even nine thousand pounds this time. Carbon checks the amount as a routine precaution and account number 734282 has a fixed balance of only twelve hundred and fifty-two pounds."

"And forty-seven pence, Chris. Don't forget that."

"You saw it, too?"

"Yes, and it certainly is strange. Are you sure your man isn't just a twisted genius?"

"He's definitely a queer bird," Webb conceded with a loud laugh.

"But a guy with modest needs, that's what I mean. A man who loves writing difficult, illegal programs but doesn't really want much money."

"I bloody hope not!" Webb exploded.

"I only asked," Kennedy said, mistaking the cause of the anger.

Webb gave him a desultory pat on the arm, and his light-hearted mood had evaporated. "I've got better ways of spending my time than chasing petty thieves."

"Still . . . if the guy is this clever . . ."

"Balls to cleverness," Webb retorted. He jabbed furiously at the listing. "I checked the codes at the Data Centre. 10053 is the Knightsbridge branch. One of the biggest in London."

"So you'll be finding out all about it?" Kennedy rubbed his hands in glee.

"No, I bloody won't," Webb said angrily. "Believe it or not, the bank won't let me within a mile of the customer files. Privacy considerations, they say. Damn it, Jake, Waterman's will end up with their customers all blissfully private and robbed blind. Sod them, I can't look up so much as the name on that account. All I have is the alias."

"And you can hardly walk in and announce yourself as Mr. Carbon!" Kennedy remarked with a grin.

"Hardly." Webb was not at all amused.

"Interesting little problem, that," Kennedy said, and he bent low over the listing, re-examining the programs and making frequent comparisons with his original notes. Webb watched him in silence, still simmering.

"Strange," Kennedy said at length. "Have you noticed how much of this is concerned solely with moving money from account to account? Just moving, nothing else?"

"I already pointed that out to you!"

"Yes, but to make this all worthwhile our crook must have more than the single withdrawal account you've talked of so far. It's the only possible explanation. And if you look at it that way, Carbon suddenly becomes a very valuable member of the gang."

"Go on." Webb's expression was transformed to one of rapt attention.

"Well, I think it goes like this. Robin Hood steals, we agree on that. Then Carbon creates the new accounts, probably a number over a period of time. Finally, Wheels moves the money into them. And bingo!"

"I like it," Webb said. "Our man would then be withdrawing somewhat smaller sums from a number of separate accounts. It would attract even less attention, lower the risk of detection."

"And on that hypothesis," Kennedy suggested, "the twelve hundred and fifty-two quid begins to make sense. It's just an initial dummy amount to get the account rolling, don't you see? Not too much, nothing too precise, just an ordinary, lowish sum that will scarcely be noticed by the branch staff when the account shows up. What do you think?"

"It's certainly plausible. Frankly, that idea didn't occur to me, but I have a feeling you're right again. Smart man, Jake."

"All part of the service," Kennedy said brightly. "Ninety pounds a day and all that."

"We make a good team, you and I," Webb observed. Then he caught his breath audibly at a sudden thought. "Team," he repeated slowly, his fingers rapping a tattoo on the desktop.

"Are you thinking what I think you are?" Kennedy asked.

"Our man doesn't have to take the final risk himself, does he?" Webb said, trancelike. "He can send someone else into those branches."

"Cool," Kennedy murmured. "Just like his programs."

Webb retrieved the sheet of paper on which the program names were written and began to scribble on it. Kennedy looked, to find he had added the single word "SMITH" in large block letters.

"The gang grows," Webb said very quietly. "I wonder who? I wonder where he is?"

"Well, he's doing very nicely, that's for sure." Kennedy was suddenly excited. "I've just been doing a mental sum. How many accounts do you suppose they have?"

"Lord knows, Jake."

"I reckon ten at least. I mean, why not? With nine thousand pounds in each that comes to a hefty ninety thousand pounds."

"Yes, but we've agreed that nine thousand pounds is

251

almost certainly too little. Not the usual amount by any means." Webb's voice had caught the excitement.

"Okay, so we have to guess again. Let's assume Wheels usually shifts money in batches of . . . what, fifty thousand pounds? Just imagine . . . fifty thousand pounds in each of those ten accounts. That would add up to half a million, Chris. Half a bloody million!"

Webb cupped hands behind his head. "It's a damned interesting theory," he said softly, eyes closed.

"I'll say."

"Half a million," Webb echoed, relishing the words. "Think of it. Half a million."

"They almost deserve to get away with it, don't they? All that clever planning. I feel a bit bad about it, actually, helping to screw things up for them. I mean, without me . . ."

"My, my," Webb remarked, "you are a surprise."

"Well, really. What harm has been done?"

"Tut tut," Webb said smiling.

"All those grabbing capitalists being taken for a ride. A touch of their own medicine, that's how I see it."

"Typical of your generation," Webb observed. "You'll be off occupying computer rooms next for political ends. Squatting on the console."

"Don't take the piss. I was serious." Kennedy tucked his chin firmly into his chest.

Webb placed a paternal hand on his shoulder. "Then how about one final bit of serious thinking for me? Why on earth does he change the date? I can't figure that out at all."

"Date?" Kennedy said blankly.

"Yes, Jake, the bloody date. He changes the standard system date. He puts it back two days sometimes. Why?"

"Date?" Kennedy looked more puzzled than ever. "Are you quite sure about that?"

"Of course I am."

"Bet you he doesn't! I'd have come across the bit of program that does it, wouldn't I? Besides, he has absolutely no need to play around with the date. That's obvious from what we've just been saying.'

Webb's mouth went quite dry.

"You might at least explain, Chris . . ."

"What was that?" Webb was miles away.

"This date thing? Are you going to tell me about it or not?"

Webb hesitated before committing himself with an exasperated, "Oh, why the hell not." He recounted the story of the single sheet of output he had found weeks before in the computer room wastebin. As he finished, Kennedy roared with laughter.

"Lateral thinking, Chris!" he spluttered, tapping his head.

"What's so damned funny!"

"Well, honestly. Who ever heard of office cleaners who do a thorough job! They run a mile from my corner. You missed the obvious explanation."

"You could just be right," Webb admitted.

"I bet I am."

"Except that was the clue that put me onto the Weevil in the first place. That was how I came to be searching the Operating System."

Kennedy let loose another roar. "In that case your crook was bloody unlucky, that's all I can say."

"Yes, I guess he was," Webb said soberly. He glanced at his watch and got up. "It's the weekend," he said, as if he had just realised it. "let's call it a day."

A solemn wave of farewell and he was gone. Kennedy stayed put, wondering why he had not seen the funny side of it.

Chapter Thirty-Three

Monday, 28th February. Late in the evening, Webb parked the Porsche a few streets away from the Data Centre. From the glove compartment he took a slender torch which he clipped out of sight like a pen, a tube of quick-drying epoxy glue which went into a trouser pocket, and a wooden object rather like a large hinged flap, which was slipped inside his overcoat. Stopping along the street, he examined his reflection in an unlit shop window, his hand smoothing the coat down over the hinge and feeling the slight bulge. Because he knew it was there it seemed to grow as he touched it to a great lump on his side, and as he strode towards the Centre he became very apprehensive. But there was a sense of excitement, too—submerged yet trying to break to the surface.

The guard at the entrance squinted at a wallclock. It was 10:15 P.M.

"Working late, then?"

"Don't bloody rub it in," Webb said, sourfaced.

"Like that, is it?"

"Anyone still up on the top floor? Any company for me?"

The man ran a finger down his log. "Not as I can see."

"Just my luck," Webb complained as he was waved through.

The top floor office was in total darkness. He tried the switches until he found the one that operated the panel over his desk. The rest he left off. A thorough search of the entire floor, then down to Level 3 where a girl sat reading listlessly at Run Control. She gave him a cursory nod of recognition and they exchanged a few polite words. She found nothing strange in his request to see the evening's computer schedule, and he soon established that none of the late runs were likely to bring any of the programmers back to the building.

"Nice body, that," he said as he left, pointing to the lurid cover of her paperback.

"Oh, I look after myself," she replied archly.

Returning upstairs, Webb took the hinged flap from his coat. He bent it at an angle, then released one of the arms and a spring snapped it back into position. He unclipped his ID tag with its conspicuous visitor's colour code and placed it in a pocket, then went to a corner of the room. Part-shielded by a row of cupboards, a pair of firedoors opened onto a concrete staircase running down to the street. A firm push on the handbar and a door swung open, to close again with a well damped but positive action. Webb did it again a number of times, studying the way it always secured itself shut however hard or softly he pushed.

Over the weekend he had experimented with it in exactly the same way, and had also explored the firestairs to ensure that they corresponded to the sketch plan he had taken from the DSL report. They served every floor in the building, leading right down to B2, the lowest basement level. On Level 1 a pair of firedoors opened out from the main corridor and close by were located the escape doors into the mews. The exit, he had discovered, was covered from outside by a TV camera. In addition, he guessed that anyone leaving that way would trigger an alarm at the central security console. As the DSL report had emphasised, there was no means of opening any of the internal doors from the staircase side.

It was 10:37. Webb jammed the doors ajar with his briefcase and walked down the stairs, his footsteps echoing harshly in the bare spaces. Reaching the landing on Level 1, he glued the wooden flap to one of the internal firedoors, attaching it well above head height and leaving some six inches of the hinged arm protruding across the companion door. He counted to thirty before testing with a firm tug. The glue had set fast and the gadget held. Returning to the top landing, he sat on a cold step to wait.

In the computer room a routine update session came to an end. The duty operator entered a string of instructions on the keyboard and a line of tape drives began a high-speed rewind. The console audible alarm sounded and he looked up at the display screen. The message said,

1. DISMOUNT DISC PACK SYSO11
2. PACK IS SECURE. REPEAT SECURE
3. ATTACH LABEL L8
4. DIPATCH PACK ASAP TO SECURE
   DATA LIBRARY

A sheet of preprinted adhesive labels lay on the console desktop and the operator peeled one off, sticking it to a perspex disc-pack cover. He went over to a disc drive and pressed a control button to bring the rapidly spinning metal discs to a standstill. A touch on the

255

OPEN button and a deep drawer was powered out in front of him, with the discs inside and ready for removal from the spindle. He dropped the cover over them, securing it with a flick of the wrist before lifting.

There was a metal hatch in a nearby wall and he slid it open to place the disc pack in a small goods lift. Then the door was slammed shut and he listened to the lift dropping away.

The computer display lights were quite still. He cast a practiced eye around the big room to satisfy himself that the machine could be left unattended for a while. A digital wallclock gave the time as 22:58. Punctiliously, he waited until the precise moment it clicked over to 23:00 before going out for his rest break. After locking the computer room he went into a men's lavatory, where he pulled a tattered toothbrush from a jacket pocket for a perfunctory scrub. Wet hands brushed his hair to settle loose strands behind the ears. His moustache underwent close scrutiny, with an index finger stroking softly where it drooped past the mouth. He was still fondling the moustache as he waited, whistling, for the lift down to the underground rest room.

Below on Level 1, the girl whose duties on that shift included a spell in the Secure Data Library was tidying up for the night. She finished logging the tapes and disc packs sent down from the computer room over the past two hours. Rooting in a handbag, she found her comb and ran it through long, silky blond hair. Then she dug again for a mirror and recoated her lips, giving a final lick to make them glisten. She walked out and the library door snapped shut behind her. At the far end of the corridor a handwritten sign faced her, stuck across the firedoors:

IMPORTANT
ALWAYS use the lifts
The "short cut" to the rest room
is now explicitly PROHIBITED

The girl stuck her tongue out at the notice and pushed defiantly through.

It was 11:06 when Webb heard the noise from below. First there was the metallic rattle that he took to be the door mechanism, the sound becoming muffled and diffused as it rose in the bare stairwell. He jumped up and leaned cautiously over the handrail. A single light burned on each landing and the stairs twisted away below him into near darkness. Next he heard the clatter of heels, fading as the girl descended to the lower basement. The echoes fought, mixing into a confusion of sharp, repeated taps. He saw only a hand on the rail and even that was soon lost in the gloom of the bottom levels. The footsteps halted far below and he could just discern what he assumed was a knock. Then a wait before the doors on B2 were opened, followed by an unexpectedly loud crash as they slammed shut. It took an age for the noise to die and silence never quite returned, the echoes seeming to persist as a low and hollow roar. When Webb started down the stairs the noise began anew, his every step magnified and channelled through the building however carefully he trod.

On Level 1 he almost cried out with delight. The hinge had worked! The arm had been pushed aside as the girl emerged and had then sprung silently back. Now one of the firedoors was resting against it, just clear of the lock. Webb kicked off a shoe and wedged it into the gap while he ripped the flap away with a hard downward jerk. It left a small patch of glue near the upper frame, invisible in the poor light on the landing. Holding a door open, he slipped the shoe back on. Then he entered the red zone.

His sketch plan had shown a similar arrangement of corridors to that on the top level. Even so, he was surprised to find how closely the floors resembled each other, with the same whites and browns, the same carpet and potted plants. He let the door close quietly against a hand, waiting for only a moment before walking briskly in the direction of Harrington's office. There was no one in sight, no sign nor sound of activity.

Off the main corridor he came to the open recess where Harrington's secretary sat. A pause to look both ways down the passage, then he went to the office door. As he had fully expected, it was locked. Bending to examine the keyplate, he found it precisely the same type as that on the top floor meeting room, which he had studied at length on Saturday evening and practiced on. He extracted the plastic ID and slipped it against the catch. The door was open almost immediately.

"What was that word of yours, Henry Larcomb?" he said in a hushed tone. "Ironical?" And he grinned at the plastic card.

He did not touch the light switch, keeping the door open only long enough to orientate himself in the light from outside. Then it was closed securely, again using the ID.

The pale, narrow beam of the pocket torch picked out the desk, moved past a teletype and found a tall cupboard. The doors swung open at a touch to reveal rows of suspended files, each with a typed number as the only identification. The spot of light explored the darkness and discovered an index on the inside of a door, fixed with autumnal Sellotape, yellowed and brittle at the edges. The light moved slowly down the list, settling on, "W/8351: SECURITY DIVISION REPORTS/10." There were other references to the Security Division but the entry looked to be the most recent, added by hand under the many typed lines.

Webb located the folder and took it to the desk, where he found that he could lodge the torch on top of a tablelamp to give an acceptable pool of light. He sat, crouching forward on the very edge of Harrington's modest armchair. The file fell open at a page saying,

MEMORANDUM   Addressee only
FROM: T J Batchelor
TO: A Harrington   28 January
SUBJECT: Internal Telephone Monitor
This is to confirm that, in accordance with your instruction of 26 January, a 24-hour tap has been placed on LDC Extension No. 125. All outgoing and incoming calls are being recorded. Transcripts will be forwarded daily as requested.

"Now that was never a routine piece of security, Alex," Webb murmured. "What the devil set you thinking?"

He turned back to the top sheet of the file, to find,

258

MEMORANDUM   Addressee Only
FROM: T J Batchelor
TO: A Harrington   11 February
SUBJECT: Internal Telephone Monitor
This is to advise the discontinuance of the tap
on LDC Extension No. 125, as requested. No
calls have been received or made on this number
since the evening of 7 February.

The very sight of the date made Webb's heart beat
faster. He thumbed forward with an urgency bordering
on panic until he came to the final report.

STRICTLY CONFIDENTIAL
FROM: T J Batchelor
TO: A Harrington
SUBJECT: EXT 125 Transcript for Monday 7
February.
Total calls monitored: 5
1. Timed at 10:47. Incoming
LDC: Alloway.
CALLER: Ted Anderson here, Martin. Man-
chester Data Centre.
LDC: How are you?
CALLER: Fine and you?

It was a routine conversation about trouble with one
of the communications links. Webb skipped the rest of
it. He passed quickly over more incoming calls at
11:18 and 11:34, both on the same subject, and an
outgoing call at 16:40. Eventually he came to,

5. Timed at 20:16. Incoming
LDC: Alloway.
CALLER: I'm glad you're still there.
LDC: Hold on a minute.

And that was all! No mention of Tilers Place. Nothing by which the caller could be identified. Nothing to
show that Alloway's last telephone call might have
been connected in any way with his death so soon afterwards. Quickly, Webb turned the page, to find the
start of an earlier report. Then back to his conversation

259

with Alloway, to notice that it ended well up the sheet. Someone, presumably Harrington, had pencilled a large question mark in the space below.

Webb sat absolutely rigid, trying to comprehend. He read the brief transcript again, matching it in his mind with what he recollected of the call—the long, almost endless ringing, the receiver being lifted, those few words, those clicks on the line. Then he remembered the note from Clement. Alloway *must* have seen it earlier that day.

"You crafty bugger!" Webb said in an excited whisper. "You switched the call to another extension! You only bloody fooled them!" He was so relieved he almost laughed. His outstretched hand was suddenly steady and his breath became even and calm. He might have been sitting in his own study at home.

He sat there for a time just staring ahead into the darkness of the room. Then he worked systematically through the entire file, searching for some clue to what might have first alerted Harrington. But the conversations were all brief and unrevealing, all on routine bank business except for one chatty call to Alton, apparently to the mother.

The hands of Webb's watch warned that he had been on Level 1 for over fifteen minutes. The folder was replaced in its pocket and the cupboard closed. He swung the torch beam around the room for a final look, to be sure everything was back in place. Against the far wall it picked out several tea chests that he had not noticed before and he moved across. They were packed with binders of program listings, a thick layer of dust covering those at the top. He peered closer. They were BANKNET listings and after a moment he deduced that they were the contents of Alloway's cupboard upstairs, removed on Harrington's orders some weeks before. He ran a finger across a cover, cutting a groove into the dust.

Without conscious thought he glanced again at his watch. Then, creeping across the office, he held an ear to the door before sliding the plastic tag against the lock. Moments later he was through the firedoors and climbing the stairs.

Back home in Chelsea, Webb filled a large tumbler with malt whisky and relaxed with it in a steaming bath. Harrington knew nothing about that final call to the Centre after all. No one did. At least no one alive. He raised the glass in a toast to Alloway.

"You were a great guy, Martin," he said respectfully. "A trick a minute."

And yet . . . He eased back, letting the water rise to his chin. And yet . . . Harrington must still have had some reason to suspect the man, for all his cunning. Suspected him seriously enough to involve the security people. Seriously enough to hire SysTech, perhaps? Could that have been what the computer audit was really about all the time? Suspected him of *what*?

"What the hell did he do that I mustn't?" Webb said aloud.

He took a deep sip, swilling the pale liquid round to taste it with every part of his mouth and tongue. It was smooth, sweet rather than potent . . . until he swallowed. Then it nagged at a spot on his stomach wall, etching like acid.

Chapter Thirty-Four

The recollection came to Webb in a flash the following morning. He was in a slow crawl of traffic on Chelsea Embankment. The clutch grew progressively heavier under repeated use as the car edged forward, making little headway. For many people it would have been a time of acute frustration, a time for the radio, turned well up to drown the complaints of impotently idling engines. For Webb it acted as a stimulant. Maybe the adrenaline produced to feed anger worked instead in subtler ways. Or maybe the constant starting and stopping induced deep thought by a form of hypnosis. He was never sure. All he knew was that he tried to avoid traffic jams, yet often got his best ideas in them. And, suddenly, he remembered the dust on the program listings.

261

He moved forward only to stop a few yards further on at a red light.

"Christ!" he said aloud, as he realised what it might mean. No, not might. What it *had* to mean.

"If I'm right, Alex," he murmured with a dawning smile, "that makes it open season from now on."

At the Data Centre he telephoned Harrington to ask for an immediate meeting. The banker pleaded an already crowded day of engagements but Webb persisted.

"Very well then," Harrington agreed with bad grace. "The meeting room on your floor. Let's say in fifteen minutes."

Webb went straight there and passed the time with his morning paper.

"This had better be urgent," the banker declared from the door as he entered.

"I think you'll find it is."

Harrington sat facing him, hands as restless as ever.

"Well, then?"

"It's extremely awkward," Webb said. "Here I am, close to the end of my work for you, just beginning my final report. About to give your system a clean bill of health, too."

"Do get to the point, Mr. Webb."

"Someone is tampering with BANKNET, Mr. Harrington."

"Someone . . . ?" The banker was instantly attentive.

"I know it sounds crazy but it rather seems to be Alloway." Embarrassed, Webb averted his eyes. "It's all very strange."

"*What* did you say?"

Webb could sense the banker stiffening. He glanced back to see the hands now quite still on the table. The eyes were steady, too. Determinedly steady. Not with surprise, Webb was sure, but because that was how Harrington felt they should be.

"Alloway," Webb said, "That's the only person it could be. He was up to something fishy. I first caught a

262

hint of it over the weekend. Last night I came back in to..."

"Do I have to remind you, the man is dead," Harrington interrupted brusquely.

"But his program isn't, that's what I'm saying. It's still in the system, still busily working. He may be dead, Mr. Harrington, but he's robbing you all the same."

The eyes opened fractionally wider but otherwise did not move.

"Would you mind saying that again?"

"As far as I can tell he patched a program into BANKNET. It's still..."

"I heard you the first time," Harrington snapped. He leapt up and paced the room moodily.

"This is quite absurd," he said at length. "Your previous reports to me have said nothing of this. No suggestion, no hint."

"I told you, I only discovered it in the last couple of days."

The banker came back to the table, choosing a chair beside Webb and putting his face close, his thin nose inches from Webb's.

"I don't like it, not one bit. This is not what I expected from you at all." Anxiety swam in the eyes.

"It's what you hired me to do," Webb said in mild protest. He turned away, unsure of what his own eyes might show.

There was a long silence, which Harrington broke with an impatient, "Well...?"

"I'm sorry? What do you expect me to say?"

Harrington gave an agonised sigh. "I want to know what in hell's name is going on in my system. What do you think!"

"I don't know about that," Webb said quietly. "I don't think I ought to say."

"You bloody *what?*"

Now it was Webb's turn to walk pensively away. When he turned back he was apparently wrestling with a problem of conscience.

"The man is dead, Mr. Harrington, as you just pointed out. I wouldn't want to accuse someone who can't..."

"For God's sake!"

"I'm not sure yet, don't you bloody understand!" Webb exclaimed with a show of anger. "How can I possible black his character when I'm still not sure."

"Heaven help us," Harrington uttered, his head shaking in frustration.

"I think he was robbing you. I'm almost certain. But I'm not yet absolutely certain."

"Oh, do sit down," the banker said. "All this walking up and down won't get us anywhere."

Webb obligingly returned to his chair. "Someone is taking money, that's a fact. I've discovered the program that does it. In my opinion Alloway was the person most likely to have put it there."

"Damnit, Webb, he was one of my best men."

"I know. How do you think I feel?"

Harrington was broodily quiet for a time, then he asked somewhat lamely, "What do you suggest we do?"

"We have to be sure of our facts," Webb said. "I want your full support while I find out more."

"Go on . . ."

"First, I am under strict instructions from you to wind up the project and give you my final report. That was on the assumption, of course, that BANKNET was . . ."

"Forget it," Harrington asserted with a peremptory wave of the hand. "As of now your deadline is scrapped."

"Second, I must have access to the customer files. There's no other way I can track that program back to its source."

"You already know my position on that."

Webb's eyes flashed. "If rules are more important than clearing up embezzlement, Mr. Harrington, you can have my resignation from this job right now."

The banker rubbed his brow. "But I must have more details, some hard facts to go on. This is all so irregular."

"I only have my nose," Webb said. "This whole business smells of Alloway, but that's all I can say. Trust me and we can have it settled in a matter of days." He paused. "The customer files, Mr. Harrington? What do you say?"

"It might just be possible," the banker replied almost inaudibly. He got up, muttering, "Alloway . . . who would ever have thought it," and shaking his head sadly. Then he strode decisively to the door.

"Don't go," he commanded, adding emphasis with an outstretched finger. He left with an uncharacteristic slam of the door.

It was a long twenty minutes before he returned, holding two sheets of paper, one of which he slapped down on the table.

"Sign that."

Webb saw a memorandum from himself to Harrington with that day's date. It was an undertaking that he would not copy any of the private computer records which Waterman's might, at their discretion, make available to him. It also guaranteed that all such information would be held in the strictest confidence. Webb signed on the dotted line.

"This situation may be serious," Harrington told him, "but I am still not prepared to set a precedent by giving you clearance to the red zone here. I have arranged for you to have access to the records we keep in the archives at Leadenhall Street. They are in every way identical to those maintained here."

"That sounds fine," Webb said evenly.

Harrington then handed him the second note, which said simply that his contact at Head Office would be a Mr. Tuckman, and gave a telephone number.

"When will I be hearing from you, Mr. Webb?"

"Soon. As soon as I know more."

Harrington opened the door and went ahead into the corridor.

"I'm sorry if I seemed a trifle touchy earlier," he said. "Quite honestly, it's refreshing to find someone with proper respect for the dead." He was notably controlled now, his handshake relaxed as they parted.

What have you got up your sleeve, Alex? Webb wondered as he walked on to the far office. That was a bit too quick. A bit too damned easy.

Most visitors to the Waterman Building went up, few had cause to venture down. Above the street there was the surface gloss expected of a leading bank—deep carpets, hide furniture, exotic woods, subdued hues. Below ground the building was naked. There was an air of workmanlike purpose, a feeling akin to being in a refinery or a power station. Unconcealed service trunking and pipes in primary colours snaked above bare passageways. Even the pervasive hum of the environmental control system was different—more throaty, with none of the discreet softness heard in the public areas above.

The Central Data Archive was along a corridor floored in vinyl, three levels down. The room was unexpectedly small. Tuckman sat at a cluttered desk just inside the door. He was probably just coming up to thirty, a skeletal, ginger-haired man whose deadly pale face suggested he never went up to the daylight. He wore baggy corduroy trousers and a frayed wool pullover. It was a style of dress Waterman's would almost certainly not have tolerated elsewhere in the building.

Only when he had examined the pass issued to Webb at the reception desk did Tuckman give a toothy smile of greeting.

"You based at LDC, Mr. Webb?"

"Mostly," Webb replied. The pass made no mention of the fact that he was not an employee of the bank.

"I can't remember the last time I had someone here from the Data Centre."

"That would have been Martin Alloway, I suppose?"

"The name doesn't ring a bell. Is he in Security?"

"One of the computer staff."

"Alloway, was it? No, I don't believe he was ever down here."

Tuckman came from behind the desk and beckoned Webb across to a visitor's table. Shelves lined an adjacent wall, packed with meticulously labelled binders of just the right size to hold computer printout. But there was remarkably little there. Sondhi had three times as much paper in his area at LDC.

Webb helped himself to a chair. "Who uses the archive?"

"SD Five, mainly."

"Who are they?"

"Security Division Five. You know, the fraud team. I had a couple of them in only last week, didn't I. Very entertaining it was."

"Did they find what they were after?" Webb asked in a matter-of-fact way.

Tuckerman narrowed pale eyes. "You in SD Five?"

"No." Webb laughed at the very idea.

"You sure?"

"Positive."

"Anything to do with Security?"

"Far from it. I work on the BANKNET programs."

Tuckman turned a chair around to sit astride it, arms folded over the back. "Well, these two SD Five characters come in, don't they. The usual performance—all stiff-lipped and not so much as a good morning. So I ask them what this one's about. They do the big clam-up act, don't they. Not a flipping word. I tell you, those guys think they're *It*."

"I know the type," Webb said.

"Anyway, what's so great about fraud investigation? It's no great shakes, is it? Just a question of looking at numbers. Those guys are only jumped-up bookkeepers as for as I'm concerned."

"Get them in often?"

"Two, three times a month. More at Christmas, usually, what with the extra credit card fiddles and that. Last week it was only some crummy cheque dodge. A couple of grand, that's all. Not that they said, but it was dead easy to work out."

"Can I ask how?"

"You quite sure you're not in Security?" Tuckman said suspiciously.

"Word of honour."

"Well, I just looked at the records they asked for, didn't I." Tuckman picked at a loose strand of wool on his chest. "When they'd cleared off, I mean."

"Ah," Webb exclaimed.

"That one was pretty simple. I can't always figure out the complicated ones."

267

"But you like to try, eh?"

Tuckman gave a self-satisfied smirk. "Well, it passes the time, doesn't it. Bit of excitement now and again." The way he lolled on the chair suggested he would be happy to chat all day.

"I really ought to get started," Webb told him. "Can you explain about the records you keep?"

"Just about everything that comes off the computer. Branch files, customer files, cross-references of every kind you can think of."

Webb glanced at the single wall of shelves. "It doesn't look that much, frankly."

"Oh, that," Tuckman said with a raucous laugh. "That's just the flipping index. The actual record store is through there." He pointed over his shoulder to a closed door.

Webb started to get up. "I'd like to see it now, if that's all right with you?"

"Hang on. The arrangement is you fill in a form and I retrieve the record you want. That's the way we do things." Tuckman indicated a pad of printed slips on the table. "You can miss out the customer name if you like," he said helpfully as Webb took a closer look. "The account and branch numbers will do."

Webb jerked a thumb at the shelves. "Any financial information over there?"

"Course not. It's only an index."

"Then am I allowed the complete set of records for a branch?"

"Sure." Tuckman gave a malicious grin. "Just as long as you fill out a form for each customer."

"Hell!" Webb said through clenched teeth.

"It's the rules," the archivist insisted. "You know how it is."

Webb was silent for a moment, inwardly furious at Harrington. He should have known from that confident manner when they parted at the lift. He could guess the rest of it, too.

"Tell me," he said, "did Mr. Harrington call you this morning?"

"Just before you did."

"Then he must have explained to you what I'm doing here?"

"Not really. Something to do with a computer error, that was all he said."

Webb was thoughtful again.

"Anything else?" Tuckman asked.

"Not right now."

"Just fill out the forms when you're ready and I'll do the rest." Tuckman turned to walk back to his desk.

"Oh, there is one more thing," Webb called after him. "I was wondering about the copies of these forms for Harrington. Will it help if I take them back to the Centre with me later?"

"No sweat, he said he'd . . ." Tuckman spun round, disconcerted. "I didn't realise you knew about that."

"He and I are working hand in glove on this, what do you bloody think?"

"He told me he'd be here in the morning to pick them up."

"Why, so he did," Webb said softly.

Tuckman cleared a space on his desk and unwrapped a large paper bag of sandwiches. What looked like black coffee was poured from a flask but the room soon filled with the smell of Bovril. He read his *Daily Mirror* as he ate, peering round it constantly to look across the room, although whether from curiosity or because he had been instructed to, Webb could not guess.

Webb took his time examining the index volumes. He discovered that he could refer to any given customer in several ways—directly by name, by account number or by working through the complete customer list for the branch at which he banked. As far as he could tell, the date when each account had been opened was the only potentially useful new piece of information available without recourse to Tuckman's full records.

Well, he concluded, the very least he could do was to find out what the index included on the Knightsbridge account that figured so prominently in Alloway's plan. The number was noted in his pocket diary but he had no need to read it—it was printed indelibly in his mind. Taking down the binder for branch 10053 he quickly searched the customer list.

"You corny bugger, Martin," he breathed as he found the entry. He had to turn his back to Tuckman to hide a spontaneous smile. For the line said,

734282 MR J V SMITH

The account had been in existence for ten months. It must have been opened well before Alloway had finished work on his Weevil programs. That showed a certain confidence. One had to admire the man.

"Corny maybe, but damned sensible," Webb decided on reflection. A name nobody was likely to look at twice among the thousands of others at the branch.

He tried the customer name index, to find only a single reference to Mr. J.V. Smith, shown as banking at Knightsbridge. Then he looked in the account number index, with the same result. It was hardly surprising. Alloway was far too careful to risk accidental discovery as a result of anything as simple as an index. Webb assumed that all index references to the other Smith accounts were probably suppressed by the computer. It would be easy enough to verify that at the Data Centre.

He returned to the table and sat leafing slowly through the Knightsbridge file, not actually reading but trying to think of a way to learn more without giving anything away to Harrington. Suppose there was no way? What then? However close he got, the damned money always seemed to recede. Always just out of reach, as if Alloway had planned it that way.

"How's it going?" Tuckman called over.

"Give me a chance!"

"Any time you're ready." The archivist began munching an apple and there were two bananas beside his elbow. It was hard to see how he stayed so thin.

It was some time before Webb realised what to do next. And the idea was so simple, so glaringly simple, that he was annoyed with himself for not seeing it sooner. The Smith references could not possibly all be suppressed! They had to appear in the individual branch lists or the local managers would guess that something was amiss. So, he would search the entire branch index, all twelve hundred or more binders, to see how many J. V. Smiths he could find. Jake believed the number to be ten, Webb himself was more inclined to think it could be as high as twenty. But those were only wild guesses and the truth should be interesting. It might not help much but it was better than nothing. He took down the binder for branch 10001. That had been Waterman's very first office, he remembered having read in the Annual Report, and still operated from the same Mayfair premises where Samuel Waterman had established his banking business back in 1773. There was no mention of the elusive Mr. Smith. Perhaps Alloway respected tradition.

Webb's procedure was basically straightforward—removal of the next branch index, a rapid hunt through the customer list, recording the details on a notepad whenever he encountered a J. V. Smith. But he varied the routine to make it less obvious to Tuckman what he was doing. Often he would continue to read through an index long after he had found out all he could. And occasionally he would move on to another part of the shelves, always returning later to his original position so as to miss out none of the branches. The search could probably have been completed in two hours. The tactics for Tuckman's benefit stretched it out to well over four.

The list on his pad grew. Webb wanted to stop to total it, to ponder what it all meant, to cry out in astonishment. Instead, he forced himself to work mechanically, trying hard not to wonder at the picture of Alloway's activities that he gradually uncovered. Above all, trying to give no indication to the ever-watchful Tuckman that he had found as much as a single fact of more than passing interest.

When he had finished, he filled out request forms for ten customers, chosen completely at random.

"This all?" Tuckman said.

"It'll do for the time being."

"Not that I'm complaining. I just thought . . . I mean, all that looking . . ."

"It's your stupid rules," Webb asserted. "They've caused me one hell of a lot of bother."

"They're not *my* rules," Tuckman pointed out as he unlocked the record store. Soon he was back with the ten red-herring files. Webb carried them over to the

271

table and sat facing the archivist with his notes concealed in an open file. Only then did he allow himself the outright amazement he had contrived to fight off for the past few hours. He counted, then counted again.

"I just don't believe it," he murmured. He counted one more time. The answer was the same. Out of 1,276 branches operated by Waterman's in the United Kingdom, Mr. J.V. Smith was shown as having two hundred and fifty-six accounts.

"I don't bloody believe it," he observed again. Two hundred and fifty-six accounts! His mind went blank.

A pointed cough from Tuckman brought him back to reality.

"I'm off home now," the young man said. "Afraid I've got to lock up. You know how it is."

Protesting that he had hardly begun, Webb was ushered out into the corridor. He turned, holding a hand against the closing door.

"One more thing. Do you happen to keep the statements for bank employees in there?"

"I've got the lot," Tuckman replied. "Everything that comes off the computer."

"Of course. You said."

"But you'll have to come back in the morning."

"No bother," Webb said. "It can wait."

It was dark outside, the pavements packed with a human tide surging towards bus stops and tube stations. Webb walked to St. Paul's before finding an empty cab. He slumped in the back. Two hundred and fifty-six accounts. Not in his wildest moments would he ever have guessed it. Two hundred and fifty-six accounts! The man was incredible. It was bravado that went beyond mere greed.

It's another world record, Webb thought in awe. Robbing a fifth of the branches of a major bank. Getting away with it, too. And no threats, no violence.

Two hundred and fifty-six accounts! With no way he would ever be able to get at the money in them. He realised that, suddenly. He could see no means of getting a copy of Smith's signature. More to the point, he could not take the chance that the man's face would be

272

remembered from his visits to the local banks. All that money likely to sit there forever. Forever out of reach. Wasted. Not that it mattered much. The Weevil was still at work, arriving from Manchester every midnight to siphon money into the left luggage locker. Webb could easily repeat the trick, opening his own accounts and doing exactly what Alloway had done. But still . . . all that wasted money. It was criminal.

He did a mental sum on the size of Alloway's estate. Each account, he knew, held at least £1252.47. That meant a total of over £320,000 locked away in BANK-NET. But there was more than that, much more. If by any chance Jake was right in his guess of £50,000 . . . It did not bear thinking about. The City, the traffic, the crowds outside, passed in an unnoticed blur.

Not until he reached Fitzroy Square did Webb feel sufficiently calm again to be able to analyse his notes in more detail. The most recent of the accounts had arrived at the Finsbury Park branch, in North London, only a matter of days before Alloway's death. All of them, with the exception of the original one in Knightsbridge, had been opened in the past five months. On one day in October ten had turned up at different branches in the Manchester area. A week later six had appeared in Nottingham. Could one person have handled all those visits unaided? Surely not. Perhaps the counter staff at Finsbury Park might remember something about Smith, provide some clue. It seemed worth the risk to find out.

But that would have to wait until morning. He pushed the notes to one side. On balance it had been a successful day, he decided with satisfaction, played exactly the way Martin would have done it. He swivelled and through the window saw a cat slink between the railings across the road, moving low to the ground, stalking a bird or a mouse invisible in the night. It was a pity about Martin. Together they would have made a damned fine team.

273

Chapter Thirty-Five

Waterman's policy on the appearance of its high street banks dated back to 1973. Until that time it had followed its rivals in striving for immediate identification, achieved through sameness the country over. A branch in Bolton had been identical in all but size to one in London's West End, in much the way that every Marks and Spencer's looks just like the rest. Meyer Waterman had masterminded the change, starting singlehanded and winning the board over by untiring persistence. The existing approach to corporate design, he had said, could satisfy only the designers. It was easy, economical, apparently logical. It was unspeakably boring. All those padded counter fronts in similarly coloured PVC, the heavy, varnished woods to suggest dependability, the parquet floors in rigidly decreed patterns. He argued instead for what he termed local identity. That would involve, he explained, a conscious attempt to reflect the immediate surroundings—the mood and history of the area—in the style of each branch. In a tough business world one had to be seen to be different and that was most effectively done by making each and every branch different. There would have to be limits, of course. There was a degree of grandeur it would be tasteless to exceed, a level of plainness to which no branch should descend. But the concept would express Waterman's to perfection. It would be, he claimed eloquently, a way of reaching out to the customer through an image they could respond to—something banking had always been about. The argument carried weight and the jokes about colour-keyed sawdust on the floors in Glasgow soon died the death. Within three years only the golden barge crest remained as an essential, dominant element wherever the bank operated. That and the toughened glass screens to protect the money.

The Finsbury Park branch was a prime example of the new ideal. Located in a high street that could at best be called unprepossessing, it had the look of belonging that epitomized Waterman's objective. The bank was quite small, with an abundance of Formica and a notional amount of pale wood that might as well have been plastic. The colours were identical to those to be seen in a nearby betting shop. Like the neighbourhood, the bank appeared anything but middle class.

Webb chose a time around midmorning when the place became busy, with short queues forming at each of the counter positions. He joined one line, stayed there briefly, then hopped to another. As an adjacent queue lengthened, he moved there. His efforts seemed badly timed, so that he never quite reached a teller. Cheque book at the ready, a carefully positioned hand concealing the fact that he banked with National Westminster, he scanned the faces of the counter staff. There was a freckled girl wearing an engagement ring, two men in early middle age, and a man of twenty-five or so, tweed jacketed and with longish hair. Webb studied their eyes, their expressions as they dealt with their customers, the way they handled the money. After a time spent watching the girl, he returned to the queue leading to the youngest of the men. A sign in front of the position gave his name as Ronald Gates. Soon Webb spun on his heel and left, muttering a complaint about the time he had wasted in waiting.

At 12:45 Ronald Gates emerged from the bank and headed along the high street. As he stood by the kerb for a gap in the traffic Webb touched his arm

"I'd like a word, Mr. Gates. It won't take a minute."

"What was that?" Gates barely turned. A quick glance told him he did not know Webb. He showed the disdain affected by so many Englishmen when approached by a stranger, putting a foot in the road as if to move off. But the use of his name seemed to bother him and he paused uncomfortably.

"It could be worth your while," Webb told him. "Very well worth it."

"What could be?" Gates decided to cross.

"All in good time," Webb said, matching him stride for stride. "Are you off for lunch?"

275

On the opposite pavement the bank clerk stopped to peruse him more closely. He gave a measured, "Yes," that was as much a question as an answer.

"Where?" Webb asked. "A cafe, a pub or what?"

Gates pointed to a nearby corner pub. "The Blackstock, just there. That's where I usually go."

"How about a beer on me? What have you got to lose?"

"I don't need insurance, if that's your game. If you're trying to sell something . . ."

"Buying, actually," Webb said, effectively silencing the other man for a while.

In the Saloon Bar he bought two beers and a couple of hot meat pies. Meanwhile, Gates commandeered a corner table. The pub was still quite empty.

"I believe you work in the bank just up the road," Webb remarked conversationally as he took a seat.

"Yes."

"Assistant Manager?"

"That'll be the day."

"Do any of your colleagues come in here?" Webb took a slow, careful look around the bar. It was not done surreptitiously but Gates noted the caution with growing curiosity.

"Not at lunchtimes," he replied. "Evenings, now and then."

"Let's not beat about the bush," Webb said, turning to face him. "I want some rather unconventional help."

"To do with the bank?"

"That's it."

Gates gave a long drawn out, "I see," regarding Webb with suspicious, lidded eyes.

"Just some numbers, that's all. Nothing crooked, if that's what you're thinking. I'll pay well."

"What do you mean, numbers?"

"Some details on one of your customers. No one need ever know."

The bank clerk took a deep draught of beer. Wiping his mouth with the back of a hand he asserted, "It's against the rules. Don't try to kid me you don't know that!"

"Rules!" Webb gestured his unconcern. "It's worth fifty quid. What do you say?"

276

Gates indulged in another protracted sip, probably to buy thinking time. "We're always being warned about this kind of thing," he remarked. "The bank takes a dim view of it."

"Just one number, Mr. Gates," Webb said persuasively. "The current balance in an account."

Gates put down his glass and began a searching examination of the faces in the bar, much as Webb had just done. "Who's the customer?" he asked, turning back. The even voice conveyed his decision.

"That's more like it," Webb said. "Do you know a man called McAllister?"

"Elderly chap? Runs the hardware shop the other side of the bridge?"

"Could be."

"He was in only this morning. I handled a deposit for him."

"That's the one. Will you do it?"

"What do you want with him?" Gates demanded in a hushed tone. "What's he been up to, ordinary chap like that?"

"Will you do it, Mr. Gates?"

The bank clerk pursed his lips. "Fifty quid, though. I'd be putting my job on the line."

"Take it or leave it," Webb said in a manner that left no doubt that he meant it.

"It depends," Gates said. "Depends when you want it done."

Webb gave a ready smile. "Now, actually."

"*Now!*"

"This very minute. You are to go straight back to the bank, take a peek at the file, and hot-foot it back here. I'll be waiting with the money."

"Heck, I can't bloody do that," Gates protested loudly, then dropped his voice to a whisper. "It's too obvious. You'll get me bloody shot. What's wrong with this evening?"

"It has to be now or no deal," Webb insisted. "If anybody asks, you forgot something. Your wallet . . . I don't care what."

Gates gave a resigned shrug. "McAllister, you said?"

Webb nodded, touching his wristwatch. "No more than ten minutes, Mr. Gates, or you'll find me gone."

The bank clerk slid along the bench to get up. "Look, if you don't see me again it'll be because I've changed my mind. Okay?"

"You'll be back," Webb said confidently to himself as the man vanished from view. He finished his pie as he waited. It had got very cold.

In scarcely more time than it could have taken to walk briskly to the bank doors and back again, Gates was slipping into the seat beside him. He was flushed and breathing heavily, but not from exertion. Webb found the nervousness reassuring.

"A bit over two thousand," Gates muttered from the side of his mouth and not looking at Webb. "Okay?"

"How much exactly, to the penny?"

"Two thousand and thirty-three pounds eighty-nine pence."

Silently, Webb passed five folded ten-pound notes under the table. The other man's hand felt hot and sticky.

"That's done me for the day, I can tell you," Gates said, still looking fixedly ahead. "Bloody nerve-racking."

"Pity," Webb said. "I'm not through yet."

"You what?" Gates' head shot round.

Webb made no reply. His eyes were on two men who had entered the bar just behind the bank clerk. Attracting the publican's attention, they ordered beer and moved to a table by the far wall. At no time did they as much as glance towards Webb's corner. He touched Gates' arm to tell him to stay where he was and went to the door, looking both ways along the high street. Then he strolled to the corner to peer down the side street. When he returned to his seat he gave a slow nod of approval.

"You're smart," he said. "I like that."

It took Gates a moment or two to catch on. "Christ! Didn't you trust me?"

"I do now," Webb observed evenly.

"Bloody heck."

"One can't be too careful in my business, Mr. Gates," Webb said. "Now, do you want to earn an-

278

other easy fifty quid? Plus the chance of a bonus extra fifty on top of that?"

"I couldn't pull that stunt again, not now. It would have to be this evening."

"I can wait." Webb passed over a slip of paper. "I want all you can find out about this man. How much he has in his account. Whether he has visited the bank recently. Everything your files say about him. That's worth fifty quid."

"And the other fifty?"

"You get that if you can describe him accurately to me."

"I can't say if I know the chap from this," Gates declared, frowning over the account number.

"Then try to find out whether any of the others do. But handle it carefully, understand? I don't want any suspicions aroused."

"Don't worry on that account," Gates replied forcefully. "I bloody don't either."

"When do you finish?" Webb asked.

"Tonight? Should be around five-thirty. Shall I meet you here?"

"Not if any of your work mates are likely to show up. Where else is there?"

"How about the King's Head? It's about five minutes from here."

Webb nodded agreement. "I'll find it."

They left the pub and paused on the corner before going their separate ways.

"Are you an enquiry agent?" Gates asked.

"Sort of." Webb had anticipated the question.

"It's none of my business but I hope this is nothing really bent, nothing that . . ."

"Don't think twice about it," Webb said reassuringly. "The man owes my clients some money. Rather a lot, actually. They're trying to decide whether to sue him for recovery."

"So?"

"Well, there's not much point if he turns out to be broke, is there?"

"I get you."

Webb patted the bank clerk on the shoulder. "You're siding with the good guys, take my word."

"That's all right, then," Gates said.

Webb arrived at the King's Head promptly at 5:30, to find his man already in the Saloon Bar.

Gates asked, "Want one, Mr.—?" indicating an almost empty pint mug on the table. He had obviously left the bank at the earliest possible moment.

"Thanks but no. Have you got what I asked for?"

This time Gates displayed no inhibitions. "Where's the fifty quid, first?"

Webb dropped a tight roll of banknotes into the hand that was held open by his knee.

"The name is Smith, right?" Gates said.

"Full name?"

"James Victor Smith."

"That's the man."

The bank clerk referred to the back of an envelope. "He's in credit to the tune of twelve hundred and fifty-two pounds forty-seven pence. Been with us for just coming up to a month. As far as I can make out he's only been in to see us once. Took nothing out, deposited nothing. He was with another branch before us . . . Knightsbridge."

"Is that all?"

"Were you hoping for more than twelve hundred quid?" Gates gave an enigmatic smile.

"Quite a lot more."

"Then you're in luck. When he came in it was to see the manager. It seems he's in the process of moving into this area. He's selling his present flat and planning to buy a new one around here for quick cash. So if your clients pounce before . . ."

"How much will he get for the flat, did he say?"

"Nine grand, he reckoned. It's a lease in South London."

Webb leaned closer. "Nine thousand *exactly*?"

"That's what he told us, yes. He reckons he can knock the one he's got his eye on down to ten."

"How about that!" Webb exclaimed. "The magic nine thousand."

"Good, eh?" Gates said, sharing the pleasure. He jiggled his glass, now completely empty. "Are you sure you won't . . . ?"

Webb declined again. "Any joy on what he looks like?"

"I was wondering about that," Gates declared with a searching look. "If your clients know this bloke why . . ."

"They might but I don't," Webb injected hastily. "Besides which he's changed address to give us the slip. I want to be certain I've located the right one."

Gates sat in silence, considering whether the explanation made sense.

"I asked you," Webb prompted. "What did you find out?"

"Well, funnily enough I saw him myself the time he came in. He came over to my position to ask for the manager."

"Really . . ."

"Not that I remember much. A thin chap, he was. About your age."

"You'll have to do better than that," Webb said.

"Quite well spoken . . . a London accent, I think. Not from the North, at any rate." Gates shrugged disconsolately. "And that's as much as I can tell you."

"Did he wear glasses?"

"I don't think so." There was uncertainty in the voice.

"Did he or didn't he!"

"No, I'm pretty sure he didn't."

"Could you say whether he *usually* wore glasses? Could he have left them off?"

"What a question! How should I know?"

Webb let out a sigh of frustration. "Anything else?"

"I only saw him for a minute or two. And it was some weeks ago now."

"Did you notice his shoes, by any chance?"

"What about them?"

"Were they scuffed, unpolished?"

"You don't see shoes, not from behind the counter."

"His coat then . . . can you remember that?"

Gates tugged at an ear, thinking back. "A raincoat, I believe. Light coloured, probably. One of those Burberrys with the . . ."

Webb gripped his arm. "Grubby? Was it grubby?"

There was a smile of recollection. "Funny you

281

should mention that. I remember wondering at the time why he didn't spend some of that money on a new one."

Webb closed his eyes. "Incredible," he said, voicing his thoughts. "All by himself. All done bloody single-handed."

"That was him, I assume?"

"No doubt about it." Webb quite openly held out a wad of fivers. It was snatched away and quickly concealed under the table. Gates cast about before slipping it into a trouser pocket. "You look pleased with yourself," he observed then.

"Do I?"

"Do you work on a commission?"

"You might say that, yes." Webb got up, obviously about to leave.

"Aren't you staying for that drink?"

"Some other time. It's been a pleasure doing business with you, Mr. Gates."

Webb stopped at the door to give a wave of farewell. But the bank clerk's eyes were down and he appeared to be checking the money.

The Porsche was parked close by in a street of mean terrace houses, littered with wind-tossed paper. Across the road an old Ford was propped, naked of wheels and doors, on piles of bricks. Webb made his escape, driving up to the high road and turning for home. He adopted an unusually sedate pace as the final pieces of the puzzle came together in his mind.

It was always nine thousand! He couldn't get over it. Why had he ever thought otherwise? Exactly the same technique used to implicate him as to steal from the bank. It was always nine thousand pounds! And that would give a total of £10,252-47 at each branch where there was a Smith account. The rest was obvious. Withdraw precisely ten thousand pounds in cash, as the manager had been primed to expect, leaving a small residue just to keep the account alive. It might be months, even years, before anyone began to wonder what had happened to Mr. Smith, and by then the bank staff would have forgotten what he looked like.

Webb halted at a pedestrian crossing to let home-ward-bound crowds stream across.

And all done singlehanded, he thought. What a virtuoso performance!

He shook his head in admiration as he realised he would have to admit defeat to Alloway on sheer scale of operation. He did not have months in which to work, did not have the relaxed confidence that must have come with believing nobody at Waterman's had any idea. There was going to be no way he could rival that total of two hundred and fifty-six accounts. But maybe fifty, he thought. That sounded more realistic. It could be he might even manage as many as a hundred with luck. It all depended on how long he could stall Harrington. One month more at the Data Centre should see the project through. Two months would be even better.

Yes, a hundred accounts. He liked the sound of that. A nice round million pounds.

"A million," he said aloud, almost tasting the words. Once he and Jake had guessed that the fraud might involve half that amount. Now there was no need to guess any more.

A horn voiced its impatience. Webb looked up to see that the crossing had cleared. He shoved his foot hard down so that the exhaust howled derision at the car to his rear as he left it far behind.

"And I," he said to himself, "rather fancy being Mr. Jones."

Part Four

DEBIT

The Mark IV Automatic Teller is the most impressive of the cash dispensers demonstrated to us. Connected to the BANKNET system it would provide a day and night service at the branches. During banking hours cash withdrawals should be significantly easier, assisting both customer and counter staff.

—Confidential Waterman's Board Minute

Chapter Thirty-Six

Friday, 4th March. Webb waited by the kerb in Marylebone Lane, the thin skin of his umbrella low over his head against heavy rain. After ten minutes he could feel the cold pavement through the soles of his shoes.

The dark green Jaguar appeared from the car park just along the street, swinging sharply towards him. Harrington flashed his headlamps and pulled over, leaning across to release the door.

"Nasty night, Mr. Webb." He frowned as the umbrella was dropped in the back, to drip on his carpet.

"I'm sorry about meeting like this," he said, "but I wanted a word. The Centre didn't seem the best place, all things considered. You know how it is."

"It's no trouble at all." Webb clipped on his seatbelt.

"My wife always expects me home early on Fridays. Dinner with the neighbours and bridge to follow. It's a fixture, unavoidable. But if you don't mind a trip . . ."

They turned the corner and were swallowed by the rush hour traffic in Wigmore Street.

"I live out at Harpenden," Harrington explained. "Just off the M1. We'll be through well before then, of course. I suggest I drop you off at a tube station. How would Hendon suit you?"

"Fine," Webb said. "Anywhere on the way."

It was cold in the car. A white mist grew before their eyes, covering the inside of the glass, and Harrington switched the fan to full volume to clear it.

You can't escape the sound of cool, moving air, Webb thought. First at LDC and now in the Jaguar. He and Harrington in a mobile extension of the Data Centre.

"Music?" Without waiting for a reply Harrington nudged a cartridge into the stereo player. Strings began in mid-movement somewhere behind the seats.

"Prokofiev," he declared. "The Classical Symphony. Like it?"

"So, so." Webb seesawed a hand.

"I wanted to be a musician once."

It was very black outside. There were bright shopwindows and countless car headlamps but the wet streets fragmented the light, then soaked it up. A man stepped in front of them, barely visible through the still obscured wind-screen, merging with the background like a drenched chameleon.

"Damned pedestrians," the banker muttered, making him run.

"Well?" Webb asked. Why was it that Harrington always had to be asked?

"I'm surprised you haven't been back to me, that's what I wanted to say. Very surprised. I was expecting a report on your progress."

"At the Archive, you mean?"

"Yes, of course at the bloody Archive!"

"It was a false alarm," Webb said evenly. "I found nothing. Zilch."

Hartington's eyes met his. *"Nothing?* You barge in, tell me a dead man is playing games with my system and now you expect me to believe it was nothing!"

"I'm sorry, but that's the way it is."

"Now listen here. This program of Alloway's, the one you were telling me about . . . you sounded so certain."

"It was there one minute and gone the rest. Vanished without trace." Webb tried to sound disappointed.

"Ah, now I'm with you," Harrington said with heavy sarcasm. "Suddenly there *was* dirty play after all."

"Sure there was. But when Martin died his program seems to have chucked in the towel. As far as I can tell, it simply wiped itself out a couple of weeks after his death. Anyway, there's no sign of it now."

"Gone? Just like that?"

"These things happen," Webb said. "I've come across similar tricks before. It was probably a defence mechanism, protection against discovery."

They halted at a red light and Harrington turned, anxiously.

"How much did he take? Do you know?"

"Nothing, not a penny. The accident . . ." Webb spread his hands wide.

"Thank heaven for that," the banker breathed in relief.

The signal changed to green and he put his foot hard down. The rear wheels slipped for an instant on the greasy road, then he moved close behind a Mercedes. Too close.

"Come on, come on," he told it.

The rain became heavier and he prodded the wipers to a faster speed, dousing the windscreen with jets of water from the washers. Grime clung obstinately.

"Gone," he said after a time. "Well I'll be damned." His hands relaxed their tight grip on the steering wheel.

"What do you want me to say in my report?" Webb asked almost casually. "Do I give a reconstruction of the crime or forget it ever happened?"

"Both, I think." The instant answer showed that Harrington had already considered the matter carefully. "A full report for me, for my files. I'd like to know all the details."

"Forensic interest?"

"Probably. But let me have a heavily censored version for official consumption, would you! I think that would be best. I'd rather not put the wind up my board, not if the danger's passed. Reassurance is more the order of the day."

"Happiness is a reassured banker," Webb said.

"Quite."

The cartridge player clicked to a new track and a slow march came from the hidden speakers.

"'The Love of Three Oranges,'" the banker declared, his right hand conducting. "Glorious stuff, eh? Stirring."

They reached the Finchley Road, moving in close convoy. Harrington worked his way up to the front, using alternate bursts of speed and heavy braking.

"I'll never understand computers, Mr. Webb," he remarked conversationally. "Never."

Webb smiled. "I'm not sure I ever will."

"It's not so much the computers, it's what they do with them."

"They?"

"Them." Harrington pointed upwards. "The people who buy the blessed things. I mean, look at how the bank has been changed in the past few years, transformed beyond recognition. That's what happens with computers. They're bulldozers, Mr. Webb, ever thought of it that way? The company gets demolished and reorganised around the machine, and the poor sods who work there have nothing to identify with any more, no tradition to cling to. There are the odd few men like you and Alloway who know their way round the system. A few privileged experts. But the rest of us are left thrashing around in the dark." He looked strangely satisfied by the thought. A moment later he hurled the Jaguar across into the empty bus lane to leave the other cars behind.

"Why didn't you tell me you knew about Alloway?" Webb asked suddenly. "You could have told me right at the start."

Harrington glanced at him, seeming about to deny the accusation but then apparently thinking better of it.

"Frankly, it didn't seem that important. Does that surprise you? You're a smart fellow, Mr. Webb. I knew you'd find out for yourself sooner or later."

"And if I hadn't . . . ?"

"It never came to that, did it? Then, when Alloway died what was the point?"

"Requiescat in pace," Webb murmured.

"A reasonable sentiment, wouldn't you say?"

"How very considerate of you, Alex!"

The banker appeared not to notice the familiar use of his first name. "In any case," he said, "a man in my position can't be too careful. Life goes on. It would have reflected badly on me if the story had got out."

"I don't see why. Alloway was Clement's man. I remember you saying so."

"But he reported to *me*. He was my responsibility. Damnit, the whole shooting match is my responsibility, the whole of BANKNET." Harrington flooded the windscreen, using irritated jabs on the washer switch.

Webb waited a minute or so before saying quietly "Do you remember when you had Alloway's files taken down to your office? At the time, I assumed you wanted to search them, to go through them with a fine-tooth comb."

Harrington dismissed the comment with a sweep of the hand, but his expression was fleetingly curious.

"It wasn't until a couple of days ago I realised you had no intention of searching," Webb continued. "Quite the opposite."

"Meaning what, exactly?" Harrington asked haughtily.

"That you had them just to gather dust, Alex. Safely hidden in the red zone where no one else could look at them."

"Like who, for instance?"

"Like me, for instance. Or Jennifer Owen. I bet you never gave those papers so much as a glance."

"Great piles of Program listings," Harrington said. "Clutter."

"But then you always were secretive about the BANKNET files, weren't you," Webb remarked coldly. "Like those accounts in the Archive. God knows why it took me so long to work out why you were keeping me away from there. I could kick myself."

"Privacy considerations, Mr. Webb, I told you that. A simple matter of Data Centre rules."

"Balls!"

"I *beg* your pardon!"

"I went back to the Archive this afternoon. I paid a surprise visit."

"Why? You said you found nothing before."

"This time I asked to see a different set of accounts. A total of fifty files. You'll be hearing what they were on Monday, I expect. Tuckman will be sending you the details."

"Well, well," Harrington murmured. His hands moved from the centre bar of the steering wheel back to the rim and the knuckles showed white.

"Actually, I only wanted one of those files. The rest were camouflage." Webb turned to watch the banker closely. "Your file, Alex. Just so you know."

Harrington stared fixedly at the road ahead.

"I discovered a very interesting transaction among the mortgage payments and the gas bills," Webb went on. "On seventeenth November last year. Does the date ring a bell?"

"It wasn't what you think," Harrington said, subdued.

"Exactly nine K paid into your account and no trace of where it came from. Very awkward that."

"I can explain . . ."

"No need to. I know where the money came from. I know who put it there."

Without warning Harrington cut across the traffic to pull in to the kerb. A chorus of horns sounded as a line of cars formed behind.

"And how much more do you know?" The voice was low and tired.

"Only part of it," Webb said. "I've had to guess at the rest."

Harrington looked away. After a moment's thought he pressed his face against the side glass.

"Hendon," he said, as if to himself. "Good Lord, it's Hendon already."

Impatient flashes of light exploded across the rear window.

"I'll settle for the end of the line," Webb suggested. "I've never seen Harpenden in the rain."

"Just as well," Harrington said. He took advantage of a gap in the traffic to pull away. They swept past a huddled group at a bus stop. Water swished underwheel and the wipers beat a regular rhythm on the windshield. The music faded, giving way to a quieter piece.

"The trains are quite frequent from Harpenden," Harrington remarked almost inaudibly. "Slow, though, I find."

"Tell me about it," Webb said eventually, tiring of their silence.

"What's there to tell? Martin was spending far too much time out of the Centre, going up to Manchester more often than was really necessary. There were parts of the system only he was allowed to touch. I got to thinking about it, put two and two together. I had no

292

idea *what* he was doing. I just had this gut feeling it had to be wrong. Then, when I challenged him . . ."

"Zap!" Webb said. "Suddenly there's nine K in your account. A kind of fee for your silence."

"That's one way of putting it, yes."

"So you did keep quiet. For four months you haven't dared to touch that money, pretending it isn't there. And now Alloway is dead and *still* you've said nothing. Done nothing."

"I wouldn't say that, exactly," Harrington countered without conviction.

"Christ, he must have scared the shit out of you. What was his line, Alex? Did he threaten you with his friend Clement?"

Harrington stared. After a pause he murmured, "You wouldn't understand."

"Try me."

The banker made no reply.

"I can imagine how it must have been," Webb said, trying to sound sympathetic.

"Can you?" Harrington retorted bitterly. "Can you really?"

They turned onto the curving approach road to the M1, passing a sign that ordered a maximum of twenty-five miles an hour at over forty, the tyres snatching precariously at the glistening surface. There was a short right-hand bend and the Jaguar lurched. Then the motorway was stretching ahead into a haze of rain. The car settled onto its haunches and the needle flicked rapidly round to eighty-five.

"It's usually busier than this, Fridays," Harrington observed in a distracted way. He moved over to annex the outside lane. Tail lights, glowing fuzzily, floated swiftly towards them.

"Tell me about Clement and Alloway," Webb prompted.

"A very close relationship, shall we say? Cosy lunches in all the best places. Clement chancing by my office every salary review time to enquire how big a rise I was planning for Martin. Generally, what one might call a fatherly eye on his career."

"*Fatherly?*" Webb laughed at the word.

"That's probably all it was. My God, thinking of Alloway that's about all it could have been." There was no emotion in the voice. Harrington might have been describing strangers, briefly glimpsed.

"He buggered BANKNET, if nothing else." Webb said, managing not to smile.

The banker snatched at his sleeve and the car slowed. "I wouldn't want you to think I did nothing. I didn't sit idly by."

"Come on! Authorising a phone tap on the spur of the moment! That's hardly action, Alex."

"My, you *are* well informed," Harrington said soberly.

"What was the idea? To tip off the security people? Did you seriously think Martin would give himself away over the phone? That he'd say something indiscreet to Clement? Come off it, Alex, the man was no fool."

"There was always the chance. Having it in black and white would have got me off the hook."

"And where did *I* figure in your plan of dynamic action?" Webb demanded. "Were you hoping I'd get it in black and white for you, too?"

"Well, what do you think!" Harrington burned a Capri from his path with flashes of light that seared ahead into the downpour.

"You're a bastard, that's what I think. A frightened bastard. I don't find it funny, being used."

"There was always the chance you would stumble across . . ."

"I'll tell you what I think." Webb had intended a display of anger but it emerged as real. "I think the other three—your directors—wanted DSL to do the audit. So you headed them off. You hired DSL but kept them as far away from Alloway as you could. And you got me in to do the rest. You hoped I'd nose around the Centre for a while, find nothing and clear off. You stacked the cards, making my job as difficult as possible. Hell, I bet you even kept Alloway briefed on what I was doing."

"Think what you bloody well like!" Harrington snapped, meeting anger with anger.

The rain eased a little and the speed of the car gradually crept up until the needle hovered just below the hundred mark. The Radiomobile 8 clicked again and Peter began to hunt his wolf across the back seat. Webb reached over to turn the volume down.

"You've got quite a problem," he said. "You can hardly go to Clement now and explain why you've kept your mouth shut for four months. You can hardly admit you were afraid he was in on the act."

"You appear to have grasped the situation remarkably well," Harrington returned drily.

"I have a proposition for you, Alex." Webb said it quietly.

"I'm listening."

"Alloway's program has done a convenient self-destruct. Only you and I know it was ever there. I could forget what I've seen. I could still do what we were discussing earlier . . . report to your board that BANKNET is clean."

The banker was startled. "Why? Why on earth should you do that?"

"*Requiescat in pace,* remember?" Webb gave a slow smile. "Besides, you're my client and SysTech believes in looking after its clients."

"There's still the money," Harrington pointed out.

"That's your problem. Get rid of it any way you want. Just flush it out of sight."

"That's easy enough to say," the banker protested. "Once I move it I lay myself open to . . ."

"Just bloody do it! Spend the evidence. Give it to Oxfam. I don't care what."

"Maybe. I hardly care any more." Harrington rubbed his eyes.

"There's one condition."

"I had a feeling there might be."

"Business is a bit slack at SysTech. If I finish this assignment now there's no other work in view. Another two months at a hundred and fifty pounds a day comes to a handy six K."

"My God," Harrington said.

"That's less than you've got," Webb retorted. "I'm sure you can dream up some way to keep me at the Centre for a few more weeks."

"Blackmail," Harrington complained. "That's what it is."

"Let's call it a consultancy fee, shall we. For services rendered. I prefer the sound of that."

"You're almost as bad as Alloway." Harrington contrived a smile to show he intended no real offence.

"Thanks!" Webb said.

The Jaguar climbed, leaving the motorway, and soon they were speeding along narrow, winding roads. The headlights went ahead to feel the corners and beyond the beams there was nothing. Webb closed his eyes, half dozing in the warm and soporific cabin air.

What would Kennedy do if he suddenly discovered nine K in his bank account? Webb found himself thinking. Probably, a sum like that would buy all the things he wanted. But what would he do if it came to it? Keep quiet? Or blow the whole thing? No, Webb decided, the risk was too great. A pity, really. It would have been gratifying to see Jake getting something for his trouble. Fair.

There was a lurch and he stirred, to see the forecourt of Harpenden Station over the hunched, spattered bonnet. Silently, he got out, smelling the wet freshness, letting in the cold and rain that dotted the leather and the carpet.

"I've been thinking." Harrington bent low over the wheel to keep him in view. "I wonder if you'd care to do another audit for us? On KEYNOTE, this time. You know, the credit card system?"

"I could probably manage that." Webb reached back in to retrieve his umbrella.

"Only don't look too hard. For God's sake don't find anything."

Webb laughed. "I'll try not to."

The Jaguar moved away, cutting a tunnel into the rain with its headlamps, then vanishing into it. Webb listened until the engine note faded into the distance. He held up his watch to the pale light that came from the station building. It was nearly seven. In just over five hours the Weevil would be travelling down from

Manchester again for its brief few seconds of nightly work.

It was funny, he realised, but since the time he had first called it the Weevil he had come to think of it as almost having an identity, as almost being alive. And it was just a set of numbers in a computer, moving other numbers from one account to another. Not caring who it worked for. He wondered what the safe lifetime of a Weevil might be. Months? Years? He stood, the umbrella at his side, not noticing the downpour.